A LIGHT
BEYOND THE
TRENCHES

Books by Alan Hlad

THE LONG FLIGHT HOME

CHURCHILL'S SECRET MESSENGER

A LIGHT BEYOND THE TRENCHES

Published by Kensington Publishing Corp.

A LIGHT BEYOND THE TRENCHES

ALAN HLAD

JOHN SCOGNAMIGLIO BOOKS
Kensington Publishing Corp.
www.kensingtonbooks.com

JOHN SCOGNAMIGLIO BOOKS are published by

Kensington Publishing Corp.
119 West 40th Street
New York, NY 10018

ISBN: 978-1-4967-2844-9

ISBN: 978-1-4967-2846-3 (ebook)

First Kensington Trade Paperback Edition: April 2022

10 9 8 7 6 5 4 3 2 1

Printed in the United States of America

In honor of guide dogs

PART 1

PRELUDE

CHAPTER 1

YPRES, BELGIUM—APRIL 20, 1915

On the eve of the war crime, Max Benesch was crouched in a trench on the western front. The shelling had paused and the battlefield was calm, except for sporadic barks of machine guns. He joined a small group of his fellow German soldiers who were gathered around a metal container, reminiscent of a tarnished milk can. Taking turns, they scooped tins of watered-down potato soup laced with specks of beef sinew.

Max—a tall, lean man with hair and eyes the color of chestnuts—took a spoonful of soup, bland and cold. He looked at Jakob, a haggard boyish-faced soldier. "The war will soon be over, and you'll be devouring sauerbraten and spätzle."

Jakob, his eyes dark with fatigue, smiled and spooned a bit of soup.

The trench, a three-meter-deep by two-meter-wide excavation, stretched for over twenty kilometers through the Belgian area of Flanders, creating a semicircular front line. The Imperial German Army had acquired higher ground, and they had the Allies—French, British, Canadian, and Belgian troops—partially surrounded. But the transport of soldiers to the eastern front to fight the Russians had depleted German forces. Both sides were dug in. Between them ran two hundred meters of no-man's-land, a barren field scarred with shell holes, barbed wire, and mud. And despite artillery bombardments, ground attacks, and an escalating death toll, the Ypres battlefield remained a stalemate.

Max, a twenty-four-year-old Jewish German soldier, had arrived at the front six months earlier. Prior to entering the military, he had attended the Royal Conservatory of Music of Leipzig. A pianist and aspiring composer, he dreamed of someday performing at the Great Hall of the Musikverein in Vienna. But his ambition was placed on hold when war erupted in Europe. For Max and many other Jews, serving Germany created hope of being treated equal to non-Jewish Germans for the first time. However, Max was discouraged to learn that Jewish soldiers were limited in rank and could only become officers of the reserve, not the regular army. Regardless of his education and combat training performance, he was given the position of a *soldat*, the lowest rank of enlisted men in the army, and he was assigned to the front.

The initial weeks in the trenches were nearly intolerable for Max. The muddy, rat-infested conditions were abhorrent, spawning influenza, typhus, and trench foot. Artillery cannons perpetually boomed. The ground quaked. Shrapnel whistled through the air. He'd witnessed men, some of whom he'd befriended, die in battle. A looming sense of dread, knowing that he could be maimed or killed at any moment, haunted him like a shadow. Under a rain of shellfire, it was luck—not valor or skill—that determined who would live or die.

As weeks had turned to months, Max learned to accept that there was only so much he could do to influence his fate. *Keep my head down*, he'd told himself, crawling under a hail of machine gun fire. He hoped that he could endure six more months. After reaching his one-year anniversary on the front, he would receive a two-week leave, and he'd go home to his fiancée, Wilhelmina. He longed to see her and wrote to her often, but his deep-seated will to survive wasn't solely driven by the hope of reuniting with her. It was fueled by the death of his parents, Franz and Katarina.

Max's parents had perished in the sinking of the *Baron Gautsch*, a passenger ship that sank in the northern Adriatic Sea at the onset of the war, after running into a minefield laid by the Austro-Hungarian Navy. One hundred and twenty-seven passengers and crew members died in the sinking of the ship, and his parents' bodies were never recovered. He prayed that they didn't suffer. Heartbroken, he often viewed a photograph taken of him and his parents at a piano performance in Leipzig, which he kept in his *soldaten* leather wallet, alongside a picture of Wilhelmina. *Do I make you proud?* he would often silently ask. *Will I be forgiven for what I'm required to do?* After closing his wallet, he would return to his duties, resolved to live another day, and another day after that.

Max sipped his soup to the squelching of footsteps approaching in the muddy trench.

"Disinfection Unit," Jakob said, nudging Max.

Max looked up. A mustached *oberleutnant* stopped and directed two soldiers following him. One of the soldiers used a wind gauge, which was attached to a pole and raised high in the air, while the other inspected a grouping of large, metal cylinders, partially buried in the base of the trench. The officer recorded notes on a clipboard. Their unit had routinely traversed the area, but the frequency of their inspections had increased over the past few days.

Max and his comrades lowered their spoons. Their meal conversation faded.

Otto, a stout soldier with a lantern jaw, called to the officer. "Is there anything we can do to help, sir?"

"*Nein*," the officer said in a hoarse, bass voice. He scribbled on his paper.

Otto lowered his head.

Weeks ago, several thousand metal cylinders were installed along the trench lines by a special squad called the "Disinfection Unit." The cylinders were buried—except for their tops—into the base of the trench, like giant iron carrots. Rubber hoses, attached to the cylinder valves, ran up and over the trench. At the end of the hoses were lead nozzles, which faced the enemy line. Although the handling of the cylinders was the responsibility of the Disinfection Unit, Max had come to the aid of a unit member who was struggling to lug a cylinder to a hole. The thigh-high cannister weighed nearly forty kilograms, Max estimated, and it appeared to contain some type of gas. Rumors about the cylinders spread through trenches, especially when a few, privileged officers were speculated to have received some type of breathing apparatus used for miners. But as days and weeks passed, the soldiers—who were toiling to stay alive—paid less and less attention to the idle cylinders.

The mustached officer recorded another wind reading, and then disappeared with his men down the trench.

"They work hard to keep their duties a secret," said Heinrich, a wiry soldier from Cologne who loved to play cards.

"Maybe the cylinders contain disinfectant for lice," Jakob said.

"I don't think so," Max said. "The nozzles are pointed toward the enemy, and they're measuring the speed and direction of the wind."

Jakob shrugged.

"Maybe the French have worse lice than us," Otto said, grinning.

A few of the men chuckled, but the jesting abruptly faded.

Whatever is inside the cylinders cannot be good. Max stirred his soup, and he wished that the heavy spring rains would return, burying the cylinders and the entire western front under a river of mud.

Jakob finished his food and turned to Max. "Do you think the farmhouse that we visited on our leave has been destroyed by shellfire?"

"I don't know," Max said, surprised by his friend's inquiry.

"On our next day off," Otto said, "we need to go there, assuming it's still standing."

"*Ja,*" Heinrich said, wiggling his fingers. "Max plays the piano beautifully."

Max smiled.

Three weeks earlier, Max's unit had been given a twenty-four-hour leave. Heinrich, who had won several bottles of schnapps in a card game with a neighboring trench unit, suggested that they find a secluded spot to drink his winnings. They settled on a vacant farmhouse, which had been partially bombed by Allied infantry. The house was empty, except for a broken sofa and an upright piano, which was likely too heavy for the fleeing family to take with them. After a meal of roasted quail, thanks to Otto's marksmanship, the men urged Max to play the piano. Placing his hands on the ivory keys resurrected fond memories of his parents, who had encouraged his dreams of someday becoming a professional pianist. He began with some of his favorite pieces, Beethoven's *Moonlight Sonata* and Mozart's *Rondo alla Turca*. His friends applauded and urged him to play more songs. Desiring for his comrades to participate, Max turned his selections to German marches and pieces with lyrics, even though he rarely, if ever, performed them. With full bellies and light hearts, the men gathered around the piano. They drank, passing the bottles, which they slid across the top of the piano. Spilled schnapps turned the piano keys sticky. Max played. The men sang. And for the first time in months, they were joyful.

Otto finished his soup and wiped his mouth with his sleeve. "You're a superb pianist."

"*Danke*," Max said, feeling grateful for the compliment.

Otto nudged Max with his elbow. "But I would stick to playing marches. People would pay to hear them."

Max nodded.

The men cleared their tins and gathered their rifles. Otto and Heinrich made their way to a dugout, a protective cave carved into the side of the trench, while Max waited for Jakob, who was on his knees with an ear pressed to a dry section of ground.

"What are you doing?" Max asked.

"Listening for tunnelers," Jakob said.

Max's heart sank. An image of a German-occupied hill—exploding in a mountainous fountain of earth, iron, and bodies—flashed in his head. He shook away his thought and said, "You have little to worry about."

"The thousand men who were blown to pieces on the ridge probably thought the same thing," Jakob said. "If British miners are capable of tunneling into the highest point in German territory and loading an underground chamber with explosives, they can surely reach our location."

For months, we fear death raining down from the sky, Max thought. *Now, we worry about wrath rising from hell.* He approached Jakob and extended his hand. "They won't tunnel under us."

"How do you know?" Jakob asked.

"They want the high ground. Our position is on one of the lowest areas of the line."

"Are you sure?"

"*Ja*," Max lied, hoping to quell his friend's angst.

Jakob clasped Max's hand and stood. The tension in his brows softened.

Max patted him on the shoulder. "Join me. I'm going to write a letter to Wilhelmina. You should write one for your *mutter.*"

"All right," Jakob said.

Reaching the dugout, they found Heinrich standing near the makeshift door, which was constructed from a tattered piece of canvas. Several soldiers, strapping their helmets to their heads, rushed down the trench.

"What's happening?" Jakob asked.

Heinrich removed his helmet and ran a hand through his oily hair. "The infantry has been given orders to conduct a forty-eight-hour bombardment."

Jakob's shoulders slumped. "When?"

"Tonight," Heinrich said.

A prelude to an infantry attack, Max thought. Every soldier on the front knew that a ground attack followed a sustained bombardment. Soon, he and his comrades would be ordered by pistol-wielding officers to climb out of the trenches and run into battle. Burying his apprehension, he opened the canvas door and gestured to Jakob. "Letters."

The men spoke little for the next few hours. They hunkered in their bunks to either rest, read, or write. Under the flickering flame of a *Hindenburglicht*, a flat bowl filled with waxlike fat and a short wick, Max retrieved a paper and pencil. By evening, he finished his letter to Wilhelmina and sealed it in an envelope. Jakob, who appeared to be having difficulty concentrating on anything other than the impending battle, struggled to draft a message to his *mutter.* Seeking a bit of fresh air before having to spend forty-eight hours hunkered in a cramped, timber-lined hole, Max left the dugout. The sky was dark, except for a crescent moon. The scent of burnt tobacco pervaded his nose. Along the trench, helmets shimmered with moonlight. Cigarette embers glowed and faded like fireflies.

As he glanced to his luminous dial watch, German artillery

guns exploded. Within seconds, the boom of guns swelled into a unified, ferocious thunder. Red spheres pierced the sky. French rockets shot up light flares with attached parachutes, which slowly drifted to the ground. The flares burned for a minute, turning night into day. Showers of white and red stars filled the atmosphere. Soon, French artillery guns fired. Above Max, the air was permeated with shrills and whistles. Adrenaline surged through his veins. Explosions behind German lines trembled the ground beneath his feet. The acrid scent of gunpowder grew. Fear rippled through him.

A wave of Allied shells exploded, one after another in close proximity, compelling him to press his body to the side of the trench. As he turned to run for the dugout, a concussive blast detonated, knocking him to the ground. A high-pitched ringing buzzed in his ears. As the fog cleared from his head, a loud hissing, like a ruptured steam radiator, emanated from the vicinity of the dugout. Coughs and screams turned his blood cold. A stench of pineapple and pepper burned his nostrils. An overhead flare illuminated the trench, revealing a ruptured cylinder, spewing a green-yellow vapor.

"Jakob!" Max struggled to stand. "Heinrich! Otto!"

The mist swelled and rolled through the trench. His comrades scrambled from the dugout and were engulfed in thick gas.

Max staggered forward.

Jakob, gasping and choking, collapsed to his belly, as if he were drowning in a green sea. Heinrich and Otto flailed on the ground. Froth spewed from their mouths.

Max, attempting to help his friends, lunged forward. Although he held his breath and covered his nose and mouth with his arm, the gas scorched his lungs. His eyes burned, as if he'd been doused with acid. Tears streamed from beneath his closed eyelids. He retreated, stumbling blindly. His lungs heaved, desperate to expel the poison and refresh his body with oxygen. Unable to outrun the gas, he scrambled to climb out of the trench. Suffocating, he frantically clawed his hands over rock and soil. He gagged and choked. Pressing upward, he prayed for air.

PART 2

GAVOTTE

CHAPTER 2

OLDENBURG, GERMANY—APRIL 17, 1916

Anna Zeller—a twenty-three-year-old Red Cross nurse with blond hair, a dimpled chin, and eyes the hue of cornflower—stuffed a bundle of bandages into her apron and maneuvered her way through the overcrowded hospital ward. Groans, coughs, and rasps permeated the room. She and a team of nurses and doctors, exhausted from working double shifts, labored to keep pace with the growing number of injured soldiers.

"Emmi," Anna said, passing a young nurse with coarse black hair peeking from underneath her headcloth. "Morphia. Bed eleven."

Emmi nodded and darted to a supply station.

The large room was filled with scores of single, metal frame beds, each containing an injured soldier. The beds were spaced an arm-length apart, allowing enough room for the nurses to navigate the ward. Despite an open window, the air reeked of sweat, carbolic, and gangrene. Several nurses, wearing blue-and-white-striped dresses with white aprons, cared for the men, all of whom had come from the western front. The nurses treated a vast scope of battlefield injuries. Bullet and shrapnel wounds. Burns. Missing limbs. Mutilated bodies. Exposure to poison gas. Infections. Fractures. Head injuries. Each day, more injured men were transported to the hospital, where doctors and nurses waged their own battle: repairing the bodies of broken men.

"I'm Anna," she said, reaching the bedside of a trembling soldier with a turban-like field dressing wrapped around his head. *Possible skull fracture.* "Can you tell me your name?"

The soldier cracked open his swollen eyelids. "Johann," he wheezed.

"You're going to be all right, Johann."

Emmi, holding a hypodermic syringe, arrived at the bed.

"My friend Emmi is going to give you an injection of morphia to soothe your pain," Anna said. "A doctor will examine you, and then I'll clean and rebandage your wound."

He groaned and placed his hands to his temples.

Emmi touched his arm.

He flinched.

"It's okay," Anna said, softening her voice. "I'll hold your hands while Emmi administers the medicine." She gently clasped his fingers, lowered his arms to his side, and then nodded to Emmi.

Emmi injected the morphia.

He squeezed Anna's hands. His fingernails, blackened with dirt from the trenches, dug into her palms.

As his breathing slowed and his muscles relaxed, Anna released his hands. She turned to Emmi and whispered, "I couldn't do this without you."

Emmi, her eyes darkened with fatigue, drew a faint smile and left to tend to another patient.

Anna delicately unwrapped the soldier's field dressing, all the while praying that his cranium was intact.

Anna, determined to do her patriotic duty, began working at the hospital when the war erupted. The initial days as a nurse were strenuous for her. The yowls of men, suffering excruciating pain, rattled her nerves. Her hands trembled while dispensing medicine, and the duty of cleaning infected wounds turned her stomach. Also, the technical aspects of nursing had not come easily for Anna, who had needed more practice to master tasks, such as the precise measuring of drugs and the insertion of needles. To compound matters, the hospital was short-staffed, due to a number of doctors and nurses who were transferred to field hospitals. Therefore, the staff in Oldenburg often worked double shifts. When she wasn't laboring in the hospital ward, or taking a brief rest on one of the cots in the basement boiler room, she went home—which she shared with her *vater*, Norbie—and collapsed onto her bed.

As months passed, Anna gradually grew accustomed to the stressful hospital environment, as well as more proficient at her duties. *I need to be strong for them*, she'd told herself while replacing a dressing over a severed leg. Although her father had raised her to be a pacifist, and she deeply loathed the war, Anna believed she was doing something good by serving as a nurse. However, much of her mending of bodies felt provisional, considering the bleak futures of permanently disabled men. *Who will care for them after they leave the hospital?* she often wondered. *How will they survive on their own?* Her heart ached for the soldiers, whose bodies and souls were savaged by war, and she wished that there was more that she could do to improve their quality of life.

After a frenzied morning of caring for patients, Anna joined Emmi for a brief meal break on a bench in the hospital garden. Although the vegetation was dormant, the weather was brisk and a welcome change from the dank hospital air.

"How is our patient in bed eleven?" Emmi asked.

"Surgery won't be needed," Anna said, unwrapping a hunk of bread. She broke it in half and gave a piece to Emmi. "He might make a full recovery."

"It's your bedside manner that makes them well," Emmi said.

"*Danke*," Anna said. "But everyone knows that I'm one of the least technically adept nurses on the floor."

"Doesn't matter," Emmi said. "There's more to medicine than picking shrapnel from wounds. You give them compassion and hope."

Anna smiled, feeling appreciative for her friend's kind words. She took a bite of bread and turned her thoughts to Emmi's husband, who was serving as an army medic at the front. "How's Ewald?"

"I received a letter from him yesterday," Emmi said. "His spirits are good, although I know he would never tell me otherwise."

"I'm sure he's safe and well," Anna said.

Emmi picked at her bread. "I can't stop worrying about him."

"I feel the same way about Bruno." Anna rubbed Emmi's arm. "We must have faith that the war will end, and they'll come home."

"*Ja.*" Emmi blinked her eyes, fending off tears.

Anna met Bruno, an army officer with an arm fracture, soon after she began working at the hospital. He was one of her first patients. Despite the ugly cast she had created for him out of plaster-soaked bandages, he asked to see her after he was released from the hospital. She initially declined, but after his numerous requests, including two that were written in the form of a poorly constructed poem, she agreed. Bruno stayed in an Oldenburg boardinghouse for his entire three-week medical leave, rather than return home to his family in Frankfurt. Although they had different upbringings—Anna's *vater* was a humble clockmaker and Bruno's family owned a large dye manufacturing business—she was smitten by his charm. The day before he returned to the front, he proposed. She accepted, and they planned to marry after the war, which they both suspected would be in a matter of months. But months turned into a year, and now, nearly two years into the war, there appeared to be no end to the conflict in sight.

As Anna and Emmi finished their lunch, a bespectacled doctor with fine, stubbled gray hair entered the garden. In one hand, he held a leash, tethered to a German shepherd. Using his free arm, he guided a battlefield-blinded soldier, who was staring ahead and shuffling his feet.

"It's kind of Dr. Stalling to bring his dog to the hospital," Anna said. "It enlivens the patients."

"*Ja,*" Emmi said. "I wonder how many dogs he has at home."

"Why do you say that?" Anna asked.

"He's a director of the German Red Cross Ambulance Dogs Association."

"Oh," Anna said, feeling a bit embarrassed by her ignorance about Stalling's work.

"Ewald often writes about the ambulance dogs, and how they help medics locate and recover wounded soldiers on the battlefield."

"They must be incredibly brave," Anna said.

"And smart," Emmi added.

"I've always wanted a dog," Anna said, glancing at Stalling's shepherd, wagging its tail.

Emmi nudged Anna with her elbow. "Maybe you and Bruno will get one after the war."

"That would be lovely," she said.

Emmi stood and brushed bread crumbs from her apron. "I should get back to work."

"I'll be there in a moment," Anna said.

Emmi nodded and went inside.

Anna left the bench and stood in the garden, observing the trio maneuver over the grounds. She admired the gentle manner in which Dr. Stalling walked with his patient, and the obedient behavior of the dog, padding alongside him. Most of all, her heart ached for the blinded soldier, who would soon face monumental challenges upon leaving the hospital.

A nurse flung open the door to the garden. "Dr. Stalling! We need you in room twenty-eight!"

Dr. Stalling waved. As he led the patient and his dog to the building, his eyes locked on Anna. "Fräulein Zeller."

Anna straightened her back. "*Ja*, Dr. Stalling."

"Could you take over for me?"

"Of course, sir." Anna darted to him.

Stalling handed her the leash.

She glanced at the dog. Its coat was black, except for wisps of brownish gold on its ears and neck, like it was drizzled with caramel. Her pulse quickened. She inched close, doing her best to pretend that she knew how to handle a canine.

"No need to worry, Fräulein Zeller. She won't bite." Stalling patted the patient on his shoulder. "And neither will Horst."

Horst gave a weak smile.

Anna's shoulder muscles relaxed.

Stalling left and entered the building.

"It's nice to meet you, Horst," she said. "I'm Anna."

"*Hallo*," he said. His eyes were dark and motionless. Deep scars covered his brows and cheeks.

"Would you like to continue walking?"

"*Ja*," he said, extending his elbow.

Anna clasped his arm and looked at the dog. "Does she have a name?"

"I don't know," he said. "Dr. Stalling didn't have much of a chance to introduce us. He saw me in the hallway, and he suggested we go for a walk."

The dog perked its ears, as if she was listening to the conversation.

Anna tugged the leash. "Okay, girl. Come with us."

They walked through the garden. The dog, requiring no prompting, heeled close to Anna's side. Gathering her confidence, she increased the pace and led Horst through a narrow path bordered by evergreens.

"The plants smell good." He inhaled, raising his nose.

"Juniper bushes." She glanced to him. "How were you blinded?"

"Shell shrapnel."

"I'm sorry," she said. "Are there any plans for surgery?"

"There's nothing they can do."

Anna swallowed. "When will you be going home to your family?"

"I only have a brother, and he's at the front."

Her heart sank. She dreaded the thought of his care falling to the government. In the government's view, vision was considered the most important of the senses, and a blind person was deemed one-hundred-percent disabled. She feared that he, as well as countless other maimed men, would become lost in Germany's bureaucratic system. She buried her angst and made another lap through the garden.

Pausing near a barren flower bed, the dog nuzzled her leg. She kneeled and stroked its head, the fur tickling her palm. Her anxiety faded. "Let's trade places."

She took Horst's hand and placed it on the dog's back.

He ran his fingers through its coat.

"Here," she said, giving him the leash.

He hesitated, biting his lower lip.

"It's okay," she said. "I'll walk close behind you."

"All right." He patted the dog, and then shuffled forward.

The dog followed, staying close to his side.

They meandered through the garden. At first, Horst moved cautiously, as if he feared veering from the path and tripping over bushes. Initially, Anna placed her hand on his shoulder to guide him on turns. But when she observed the dog nudging Horst's leg to keep him from straying off the path, she gradually weaned away her assistance. Minutes later, she settled on the bench, while Horst and the dog explored the garden.

The door to the hospital opened, and Dr. Stalling entered the garden. His eyes widened.

Anna shot up from her seat. "I'm sorry—"

Stalling raised a finger to his lips.

She tilted her head.

He stared, observing the manner in which his dog was helping Horst. "How long have they been walking together?" he said, his voice low.

Anna approached him. "Several minutes."

"How far?"

"A couple circles around the garden." She swallowed. "I'm sorry. It was neglectful of me not to accompany them."

"Not at all, Fräulein Zeller."

The dog paused near a tree and licked Horst's hand.

Horst laughed and rubbed the dog's head.

Anna, curiosity swelling within her, looked at Stalling. "How did you teach your dog to guide people?"

"I didn't," Stalling said.

Anna's eyes widened. "She's incredibly intelligent."

He nodded.

An image of sightless soldiers, sitting alone on hospital benches, filled her head. A wave a sadness washed over her. "I wish all blinded veterans could have a dog like yours."

"Me too." Stalling raised his chin and beamed, as if an idea bloomed in his brain. "Maybe we can provide each of them a companion."

"What do you mean?" she asked.

"We already train shepherds to be sentries, scouts, messengers, and ambulance dogs," he said. "I see no reason why we cannot train dogs in great numbers to guide blinded veterans."

Anna's mind raced. "It would enable ex-soldiers to return home, rather than be confined to a hospital. And they'd be given a chance of regaining an independent life."

"Precisely." Stalling grinned. "What do you think about a guide dog school in Oldenburg?"

"It's the most magnificent thing I could imagine, sir."

"I'm glad you think so." Stalling glanced to his dog guiding Horst around a bend in the garden path. "Advanced weaponry is producing some of the most horrific injuries ever seen, and an enormous number of battle-blinded men are returning from the front. We cannot allow these men—who sacrificed their sight in defense of our country—to be beggars, social outcasts, or objects of charity. I want to give them a chance of rebuilding their lives, and I believe that guide dogs can serve as mobility aids for them. They'll no longer be solely reliant upon family and friends to care for them. They'll gain their independence and ability to work. Most importantly, a guide dog can provide veterans with emotional support and help restore their confidence."

"It's quite an admirable endeavor, sir," Anna said.

"Indeed." Stalling looked at Anna. "It will be a challenge to gain financial and government support, but I'll find a way to open a guide dog school. We'll begin with small classes to refine our instruction techniques, but soon we'll expand to train hundreds of shepherds and veterans. The school will grow with locations across Germany. And, someday, the practices we develop will benefit thousands of blind people around the world."

Anna, feeling wonderstruck by Stalling's vision for the school, clasped her hands. "That would be glorious, sir."

Stalling nodded.

Together, they watched Horst and the dog slowly traverse the garden. *I'm witnessing a momentous event*, she thought. A swell of hope rose up inside Anna, and she longed to be part of something bigger than herself.

CHAPTER 3

OLDENBURG, GERMANY—APRIL 17, 1916

Anna, eager to tell her *vater* about the day's events, finished work and left the hospital. In the distance, St. Lambert's Church—its neo-Gothic spires towering above the town's clay tile rooftops—formed a silhouette against a magenta sky. She scurried toward home, disregarding crosswalks and taking shortcuts through backstreets and alleyways. She dodged horse-drawn wagons and bicyclists, as well as a skinny-wheeled motorcar that was transporting a high-ranking military officer. Ten minutes later, she reached her home, a narrow three-story brick building on a cobblestone street. A carved wooden sign above the storefront read *Uhrmacher* (clockmaker).

"Vater!" Anna shouted, stepping inside. She took in gulps of air, attempting to catch her breath. A scent of ancient timber, varnish, and clock oil permeated her nose. Rhythmical timepiece ticking thrummed in her ears.

"I'll be right there," a voice called from a storage room.

The street-level floor of Anna's home served as her father's workshop. The walls, workbenches, and dust-covered glass cases contained numerous timepieces, either functioning or in various stages of repair. Wall clocks. Grandfather clocks. Watches. Alarm clocks. Mantel clocks. Pendulum clocks. Regulator clocks. Carriage clocks. Cuckoo clocks. After the war erupted, most of the residents of Oldenburg refrained from servicing their clocks, and the sale of refurbished pieces dwindled to almost a stop. Norbie Zeller, who had once been charged with caring for the town's most prized timepieces, including the clock towers in Oldenburg Palace and St. Lambert's Church, struggled to earn a living.

Norbie, a fifty-nine-year-old man with salt-and-pepper hair, beard, and mustache, entered the workshop. He adjusted his round, wire-rimmed glasses, which were balanced on the tip of his bulbous nose. "*Hallo*, Anna."

She hugged her *vater*.

He squeezed her. "Is everything okay?"

"*Ja*," Anna said, releasing him. "Something good happened at work. I raced home to tell you about it."

"I'll close the shop and make us a bit of coffee."

She glanced at a wall of clocks, their pendulums swinging out of sync. "But you're open for another hour."

"I'd rather hear about my daughter's day." He locked the door and placed a *Closed* sign in the window.

Anna smiled. A memory of her childhood flashed in her head of when Norbie shooed away customers to create time to listen to her rehearse lines for a school play. *I love that you always drop what you are doing to make time for me.* Feeling grateful for her *vater*'s undivided attention, she followed him up the stairs, leaving the ticktock resonance of the workshop behind.

Minutes later, they sat at the kitchen table. Norbie poured coffee into porcelain cups, hand-painted with white roses and green wreaths, which they typically used for holidays.

"I wish we had cream or sugar," he said, sliding a cup to Anna.

"*Danke*," she said. "But we should be saving the coffee. The rationing is getting worse. It's unlikely we'll find more."

Norbie blew on his coffee. "Good news rarely arises from a military hospital. I see hope and excitement in your eyes, and that makes me want to celebrate."

Anna smiled, and then sipped her coffee. The bitter, acidic taste invigorated her mind, spawning images of her afternoon in the hospital garden. For the next several minutes, she told Norbie about the battle-blinded soldier, who was guided along a garden path by Dr. Stalling's German shepherd.

"It was lovely," Anna said, rubbing a finger over the rim of her cup. "The man followed the dog's lead, routing him around the garden. I wish you could have seen the happiness on the man's face."

"Incredible," Norbie said. "I didn't know that shepherds were trained for the blind."

"They're not," Anna said. "But they've been trained for many roles in the military. Dr. Stalling is a director of the Ambulance Dogs Association. He believes that dogs can be trained in great numbers for the blind, and he plans to request funding from the government to establish a guide dog school in Oldenburg."

"Where?"

"I don't know. But Stalling mentioned that he plans to gain the support of the Grand Duke of Oldenburg to acquire ground for the school."

"That is wonderful news." Norbie sipped his coffee. "Stalling must be quite an influential doctor."

Anna nodded. "We've admitted scores of battle-blinded soldiers at the hospital, and more are coming in each day from the front. With the medical staff occupied with caring for the critically injured, the blinded men are often unaccompanied while they sit on benches or wander the floors of the hospital, gliding their hands over the walls to find their way."

"My goodness," Norbie said.

An uneasiness swirled in her stomach. "Some of the blind have no family to care for them, and they have little chance of living a life outside of a government care facility. Guide dogs might give them hope and independence."

Norbie leaned over the table and looked into her eyes. "I'm proud of you."

Gratitude swelled inside her. "But I didn't do anything. I merely happened to be in the garden to witness the event."

"You work to save lives, each and every day," Norbie said. "And you must have done something special, otherwise Dr. Stalling would not have confided in you."

"*Danke*," Anna said. An image of Stalling's dog, licking the soldier's hand, flashed in her brain. "If the school opens, I would love a chance to observe them train."

"Why don't you volunteer to help?" Norbie asked.

Anna straightened her spine. "The training will likely be carried out by the Ambulance Dogs Association. Besides, I know nothing about working with dogs, and I have little free time away from the hospital."

"I think you'd be good at it," he said, rubbing his beard. "I've always wanted you to have a dog."

"You have?"

"*Ja*," he said.

"Why didn't we have one?"

Norbie clasped his cup. "Your *mutter* and I had planned to get a dog when you were a child, but things changed when she became ill."

She glanced to the living room, where her *mutter*'s piano had remained silent for years. A dull, timeless sorrow rose in her chest.

Anna's *mutter*, Helga, died from cancer when Anna was five years old. Helga had been an affectionate mother and spouse, and a soft-spoken, artistic woman who adored to sing and play the piano, despite having no formal musical instruction. Although Anna was young when her *mutter* died, her memories of Helga were kept alive by Norbie's tales of his beloved wife, which he told often and with copious variations to entertain his daughter. He often spoke of the angelic timbre of Helga's voice, which lifted the spirits of parishioners when she sang solos in the church choir. The time that she'd helped Norbie trim his beard and inadvertently snipped off half of his mustache. The day that she gave birth to Anna, making Norbie and Helga—according to Norbie—the happiest couple in Deutschland. Aside from Norbie's stories, Anna's fondest memory of Mutter was of sitting on her lap while she played the piano. Despite the passing of years, she could still visualize Helga's nimble fingers cascading over the keys. And she could almost feel the warmth of her *mutter*'s kisses, pressing into her hair.

"I was devastated when Helga died," Norbie said. "I was overwhelmed with being both a *mutter* and a *vater*, and I was struggling to earn enough money to keep us fed and a roof over our head. But if I could do it over again, I would have gotten you a dog."

"You were a wonderful parent," Anna said. "I wouldn't have changed a thing."

He patted her hand, and then finished his coffee. "Perhaps it's never too late to get a dog."

It'd be difficult to properly feed a pet, given the rationing. Not wanting to dampen Norbie's optimism, she smiled and nodded.

"I have something for you." He stood, chair legs scraping over the weathered wood floor, and retrieved an envelope from a counter. "A letter arrived from Bruno."

Anna's heart leaped.

He gave her the letter, kissed her on the top of the head, and then made his way to the stairs.

"You don't have to leave," Anna said.

"There's no need for me to infringe upon my daughter's privacy. If you wish, you can tell me about it later." He wiped his eyeglasses with a handkerchief from his trousers and descended the stairs to his workshop.

Anna, anxious to read the letter, retrieved a paring knife from a cabinet and opened the envelope. Her pulse quickened as she unfolded the paper.

Dearest Anna,

I was thankful to receive your letter. I remain in the land of the living and send my deepest apologies for not writing the past several days. I hope that my delayed correspondence did not cause you to worry.

I am rarely in the same place, my darling. Our unit will soon move to a new location, which will serve as a station to provide support to the men at the front. Please know that I am doing everything I can to aid in bringing this war to an end.

Are you still wearing the diamond I gave you?

Anna glanced at her bare finger. Her engagement ring was stored inside a pine keepsake box in her room. Due to her nursing duties, which required sterility, the wearing of jewelry on her hospital ward was prohibited. Although she had a sound reason for not wearing the ring, a twinge of guilt fluttered in her stomach.

I miss you, darling. Words cannot begin to describe the loneliness that burdens me. Thoughts of you soften my torment. In the evenings, I gaze at your photograph, and I see the woman who mended my bones and captured my affection. I long for the day when the war is over, and we begin our journey together.

Affectionately,

Bruno

P.S. Please know that I am safe, and I hold you in my thoughts.

"I miss you," Anna whispered.

She wiped tears from her eyes, and then placed the letter into the envelope. Her heart ached for Bruno, the maimed soldiers at the hospital, and the countless men who would die before the fighting came to an end. *How much longer must we wait until the war is over?* Attempting to dispel the ache in her chest, Anna retrieved a pencil and paper, and she began to write.

CHAPTER 4

HULLUCH, FRANCE—APRIL 28, 1916

Bruno Wahler—a mustached, twenty-six-year-old German *ober-leutnant* with a dense, muscular build, like a Greco-Roman wrestler—was hunkered inside a small dugout, reinforced with rough-cut timber and sandbags. Sporadic shell explosions rumbled the earth, dropping bits of soil into his hair. It was after midnight on the western front, near the village of Hulluch. After two days of vicious battles, the trench attacks had paused. But before the sun would rise, another lethal German offensive—one that would utilize Bruno's unique expertise—would commence.

Bruno approached a soldier in his dugout, who sat at a table made of scrap wood from a demolished wagon. "When was your last wind measurement?"

"An hour ago, sir," the soldier said, a cigarette tucked in the corner of his mouth.

Bruno poked his head out of the dugout and peered to a moonlit sky. Clouds slowly drifted toward the British lines, but an angst remained in his gut. "Do it again."

"*Ja*, sir." The soldier took a drag on his cigarette, and then snubbed it out it in an ashtray made from a brass shell casing. He gathered his wind vane and anemometer, which was used to measure the speed and direction of the wind, and left the dugout.

Alone, Bruno sat at the table. Under the dull glow of a lantern, he took out a letter he received from Anna.

> My darling Bruno,
> I was elated to receive your letter. I'm relieved to know that you are well. I pray each day for your safety, and the end of the war.
> I have the ring you gave me in safekeeping near my bedside. Nurses are not permitted to wear rings due to sterility requirements at the hospital. I hope you understand. When the fighting ends, and there are no longer injured soldiers requiring my care, I promise to place the ring on my finger and never take it off.

Bruno smiled and rubbed stubble on his chin.

> I witnessed an extraordinary event at the hospital. While I was taking a break in the garden, a doctor, who was accompanying a battle-blinded solder, was called away and left his German shepherd. Without any coaxing, the dog guided the patient over a winding garden path. It was a miraculous sight. I wish you could have been with me to see it. When the doctor returned, he was so impressed with his dog's caring behavior that he vowed to establish a guide dog school for blind veterans.

An image of blinded soldiers flashed in Bruno's head. He'd seen many of them—victims of gas, shrapnel, and splinters—shuffling in single file, eyes bandaged and their hands on the shoulders of the sightless soldier in front of them to guide their way.

Did you ever have a dog? I never had one, but Norbie believes it's never too late to acquire a pet. Perhaps when you come home, we can adopt a dog.

You're quite a caring soul, Bruno thought. *It's one of your many adorable qualities.*

I miss you, my darling. Please take care of yourself and write more when you arrive at your new post.
Your fiancée,
Anna
P.S. There is still much that I need to learn about your family. With the war lingering on, I often wonder when I will meet your parents. Do you think they will like me?

They'll adore you. A mixture of longing and chagrin flowed through his veins. *However, it's I who will struggle to gain their affection.*

Bruno had expected for the war to end soon after their engagement, and that they'd now be married and living in Frankfurt. But the conflict had intensified and, despite the enormous death toll, the front was a stalemate. It might be years, Bruno believed, before he'd permanently reunite with Anna. German soldiers had to serve a year at the front before they had the possibility of going home for two weeks, and it would be many months before he'd see her again. The only chance of curtailing the war, Bruno believed, was to surpass Allied forces with military technology.

Bruno's parents, Stefan and Eva, lived in Frankfurt, not far from Bruno's much older half-brother, Julius. Stefan's first wife had tragically died from drowning when she'd fallen through thin pond ice while skating on the family estate. Less than six months after the woman's funeral, Stefan married Eva, who had been his mistress. She was twenty-three years younger than Stefan, and she'd caught his attention, according to rumors amongst Frankfurt socialites, while performing as an exotic dancer. A year after their marriage, Eva gave birth to Bruno.

As a child, Bruno wanted—more than anything—to win the endearment of his parents. However, his *mutter* had little experience, nor the desire, to care for a child. Instead, she dedicated much of her time to social events, trips to purchase fine jewelry and clothing, and frequent getaways to a family chalet in Switzerland. Most, if not all, of the child-rearing duties had been provided by nannies. Meals. Discipline. Bedtime stories. Visits to the park. Help with schoolwork. The bandaging of skinned knees. Even the consoling of hurt feelings was delegated to employees. To Bruno, Eva was more like a distant aunt than a nurturing *mutter*.

While Eva was occupied with spending her newfound wealth, Stefan was consumed with his thriving business, Wahler Farbwerke, a large dye manufacturer which he ran with his son, Julius, who was nearly old enough to be Bruno's *vater*. Striving to fit in with the Wahler men, Bruno studied sciences throughout his school-age years, even though he would have preferred learning about arts and literature. Eventually, he obtained a degree in chemistry from Ludwig-Maximilians-Universität in Munich. His *vater* was pleased, and he gave Bruno an apprenticeship in the family business. Within months of Bruno beginning his career, war erupted and Wahler Farbwerke entered into lucrative supply contracts for the military. "Your brother and I would like for you to meet a friend," his *vater* had said, rolling a cigar between his fingers. "His name is Fritz Haber, head of the Chemistry Section in the Ministry of War. He's recruiting chemists to join a special unit, and I told him he should speak to you."

Eager to please his *vater*, as well as to serve the Fatherland, Bruno joined the military while Julius, who was too old to be mandated to fight, stayed home to help run the family business. Young and naïve, Bruno believed that the war would result in a swift victory for the German Empire, and he'd be welcomed home as a war hero. Most importantly, he'd be given a chance to be viewed—in his father's eyes—as equal to Julius. After all, he would have the distinction of being a protégé to Fritz Haber, a brilliant chemist who invented an artificial nitrogen fixation process which would provide Germany a source of ammonia for the manufacture of explosives. He assumed that he'd be working to develop bigger bombs or more accurate artillery shells. But upon his assignment to mentor with Haber—a bespectacled, bald-headed man with a methodical timbre to his voice—Bruno was shocked to learn that he would be working on a far more nocuous project than he could ever have imagined—chemical warfare.

Fearing retribution with a court martial or a firing line, he followed orders. After his arduous mentorship under Haber, Bruno was assigned to Pioneer Regiment 36, one of two gas regiment units under the command of Colonel Petersen. And for reasons of secrecy, his unit was called "Disinfection Unit."

Bruno folded Anna's letter and slipped it into his jacket pocket. *How does one tell their fiancée about the horrors of war? If she knew what I'm required to do, would her feelings for me change?* He gulped water from a canteen, attempting to drown his trepidation.

"Sir!" the soldier shouted, running inside the dugout.

Bruno put away his canteen and faced him.

"The wind has decelerated," he gasped.

"How much?" Bruno asked.

"Five knots."

Bruno's hair stood up on the back of his neck.

"Did you conduct measurements in multiple locations along the flank?"

"*Ja*," he said. "Precisely like you taught me."

He glanced at his watch. 1:17 a.m. A decision burned beneath Bruno's sternum. His mentor, Fritz Haber, was away, and Colonel Petersen was in the field with his other regiment. He thought about going up the chain of command, but it would take time, which he didn't have. He scribbled a message onto a piece of paper and gave it to the soldier.

"Find a messenger and have him deliver it to Colonel Petersen," Bruno said.

"*Ja*, sir," the soldier said.

"Afterward, conduct another wind measurement and have a messenger deliver the results to General von Stetten's bunker. I'll be there to receive it."

The soldier nodded and fled the dugout.

Bruno ran through the trench, his leather boots sinking into muck. Some of the soldiers, who would soon be going into battle, were writing letters to their loved ones or removing valuables from their pockets. Determined to reach the general before the attack commenced, he lowered his head and forced his legs to move faster.

Twenty minutes later, after winding through an adjoining trench that led away from the battlefield, he arrived at General von Stetten's bunker. He sucked in air, attempting to cool the burning in his lungs. He approached the entrance and was met by a *hauptmann*, who was smoking a cigarette.

"Oberleutnant Wahler, Pioneer Regiment Thirty-six, sir," Bruno said, snapping to attention. "I have urgent information for the general."

"What kind of information?" He took a drag and blew smoke through his nose.

"An unfavorable wind change, sir."

The *hauptmann* frowned and flicked his cigarette. "Follow me."

Inside the bunker, General von Stetten and several officers were gathered around a table, which held a map.

"General," the *hauptmann* said. "This pioneer regiment officer has wind information that he claims is urgent."

General von Stetten, a man in his mid-fifties with a thick, well-groomed mustache, reminiscent of a horse mane, approached them.

"Sir," Bruno said. "The wind has turned unfavorable; it has decelerated to five knots."

"What does your commander have to say about this?" the general asked.

"I sent a messenger to inform Colonel Petersen. With the change in wind, I thought you would want to know immediately."

The general stroked his mustache.

"I recommend that we delay the attack," Bruno said.

The officers, who were examining the map, raised their heads, and then joined the general.

Bruno swallowed. "The wind is showing signs of a stall, and it might change direction."

"Does the wind continue to blow toward the enemy?" the general asked.

"For now," Bruno said.

A few of the officers shook their heads.

"General," the *hauptmann* said. "As long as a breeze travels toward British lines, I see no reason to suspend our plans."

The general's eyes locked on Bruno. "We continue the attack."

"Sir," Bruno persisted. "I've arranged for another wind measurement to be taken and delivered here. May I stay to interpret the message when it arrives?"

"Very well." The general turned and resumed scouring over his map.

Bruno stood near the bunker entrance and waited for the wind measurement, which he hoped would provide clear evidence to stop the attack. *If my message doesn't reach Colonel Petersen in time, I must find a way to convince the general to suspend the offensive.*

Minutes later, a messenger arrived. Gasping for air, he retrieved a slip of paper from his pocket and handed it to Bruno.

Wind at five knots, traveling in direction of enemy line.

Bruno's hopes sank.

The general looked up from his map. "Any change?"

"*Nein*," Bruno said. "But I remain concerned that—"

"Prepare your men for the attack," the general said.

"*Ja*, sir." Dread burned like a hot coal in Bruno's gut. "Sir, as a precaution, I recommend that we order the infantry to carry their respirators."

The general lowered his brows. "That will be all, *oberleutnant*."

Bruno saluted and left.

At 3:45 a.m., Bruno stood at his post on the trench, where his regiment had installed 7,400 gas cylinders along a three-kilometer front. He instructed his men to carry their gas masks, and he wished that he had the authority to command the thousands of infantry soldiers to do the same. The orders to prepare for attack filtered down the lines, and the men of Pioneer Regiment 36 stood ready to open the valves of cylinders containing a highly lethal mixture of chlorine and phosgene gas. Infantry soldiers fixed bayonets to their rifles and gathered near ladders.

Death is death, regardless of how it is inflicted, Fritz Haber's methodical voice crowed in Bruno's head. His stomach turned sour, producing the urge to vomit.

The German infantry sent up a green flare, immediately followed by a red flare. Soldiers, their eyes filled with fear, looked to the sky. Seconds later, German artillery exploded. Shells bombarded the enemy trenches. The British launched rockets with parachute flares, which illuminated the battlefield.

Lord, forgive me for what I must do. Cold sweat dripped down Bruno's forehead. "Release the valves!"

Down the long, winding trench, soldiers of Pioneer Regiment 36 opened cylinder valves. A thick, green gas spewed from nozzles, positioned at ground level, and drifted into no-man's-land.

Compelled by his sense of duty, Bruno scaled a ladder and peeked over the trench. Using field binoculars, he scanned the battlefield. The gas cloud, hanging low to the ground, moved slowly toward British trenches.

Artillery guns exploded. The earth quaked. As the gas cloud reached the British lines, German infantry officers blew their whistles, sending soldiers up and over the trench.

British machine guns barked.

Several German soldiers, their bodies pierced with bullets, tumbled into the trench. But the masses continued their attack. Soldiers, hunched over and pointing their bayonets, scampered over the barren, shell-holed tundra.

Bullets whizzed above Bruno's helmet. He pressed his chin to the ground and adjusted his binoculars. As the battlefield came into focus, he watched the gas cloud stall, and then veer away. *No!* Within seconds, the wind changed, sending the poisonous mist from whence it came—directly toward the German lines.

"Gas! Gas! Gas!" Bruno shouted.

Alarm gongs sounded. Men, who were preparing for the second wave of ground attack, scrambled to find respirators.

Bruno slipped on his gas mask. Breathing hot, recycled air, he felt as if he were suffocating. His lungs heaved, and his pulse pounded in his ears. Through thick lenses, he watched the gas cloud swirl over the battlefield, and then swallow German soldiers. Between explosions, screams filled the air. *Oh, God!*

The poison floated into the trenches. Men choked and vomited. Through the thick green mist, Bruno struggled to aid soldiers find respirators. But they didn't have enough gas masks for everyone.

CHAPTER 5

LEIPZIG, GERMANY—MAY 14, 1916

Max, woken by the clopping of hooves outside his apartment window, rolled over in bed. Being careful not to rouse his fiancée, Wilhelmina, he slid his hand over a bedstand until he located a metal alarm clock. With his fingers, he touched the hour and minute hands. *5:30 a.m.* Unable to go back to sleep, he listened to the cadence of Wilhelmina's breath. He tried to visualize her face—cheekbones, nose curvature, lips, and nut-brown eyes—but her image was faded, like a photograph that had been left out in the rain. Despite being close enough to absorb her warmth, he felt choked in desolation. *I overheard you weeping before you came to bed. I hate being a burden to you.*

Max returned home several weeks ago, following months of hospitalization. Like many other Jews, he'd left to fight for the Fatherland with hope of being treated equal to non-Jewish Germans. But in his quest for egalitarianism and to serve his country, the war had stolen everything—his health, his aspiration to be a composer, and a chance of a joyful life with Wilhelmina.

Poisoned by chlorine gas on the western front, he'd been taken to a field hospital. Wails of men, mixed with a stench of carbolic and gangrene, filled the air. His eyes and trachea burned like they'd been doused with kerosene and set aflame. A medic poured an alkali solution over Max's corneas, but it did nothing to restore his vision, nor relieve him from the searing pain that flared under his eyelids. With each labored breath, his lungs gurgled and wheezed. Gasping, he'd managed to ask the medic what had happened to his friends Jakob, Otto, and Heinrich.

"Dead," the medic had said, dabbing Max's eyes with gauze.

Max was gutted. As he struggled to take in oxygen, he wondered how many hours or days he would be required to suffer until he met the same fate as his comrades. He prayed for quietus. But his diaphragm continued to contract. His heart continued to beat. Eventually, he was given an injection of morphia, which dulled his pain and regulated his respiration. Under a drug-induced haze, he dug his fingernails into his thighs as the medic swabbed his eyes again, and again.

With his eyes tightly bandaged, he spent four days in a field hospital being treated for bronchial pneumonia. Eventually, his breathing stabilized. Too weak to stand, let alone walk, he was carried on a cot to an ambulance, which transported him to a train station. Accompanied by a nurse—whose calm, rhythmic voice reminded Max of his *mutter*—he traveled to a military hospital in Cologne. In a crowded ward filled with maimed soldiers, a doctor listened to his lungs with a stethoscope. And as the doctor began to remove the bandages, Max prayed that the medic had washed away the poison in time to save his sight.

The doctor, his breath smelling of cigarette smoke, leaned in to examine him. "Can you see anything?"

Dread surged through Max's veins. "*Nein.*"

The doctor placed a hand on Max's shoulder. "I'm sorry. Your eyes and lungs are scorched."

"Is there anything that can be done?" Max asked.

"Your blindness is permanent. But with time and treatment, you might regain lung capacity."

Max lowered his head into his palms. He took in jagged breaths and fought back tears. He listened to the doctor step away, his shoes clicking over the tile floor. For the rest of the day, he could not bring himself to eat or drink. His mind and heart reeled with a life that would never be. That evening, he enlisted the help of a nurse to scribe a letter to Wilhelmina, informing her of his condition, and promising that he would do everything within his power to regain his health and return home.

He remained in the Cologne hospital for four months. During this time, he received breathing treatments, most of which entailed draping his head with a towel and inhaling steam over a bowl of hot water laced with medicinal oils. Twice, he endured having a rigid bronchoscope inserted into his airways to break up scar tissue. The worst part of this procedure, for Max, was that it was completed while he was awake, using a topical cocaine as a local anesthetic. His loss of vision never changed, but as months passed, his lungs slowly improved their ability to process oxygen. Fighting to regain his stamina, he shuffled over the floors of the hospital. Often unaccompanied, he ran his hand over the walls to guide his way.

Upon his discharge from the hospital, he was sent to a government rehabilitation center. He was instructed on how to use a walking stick, which he tapped over the ground in front of him to identify obstacles. He, along with sixteen battle-blinded men, a mixture of gassed and shrapnel-injured veterans, were enrolled in a course to learn to read braille. He was anxious to return home to Wilhelmina, and he thought that the worst of his tribulation might be behind him. But Max discovered that he'd lost far more than his sight when a secondhand upright piano was acquired by the rehabilitation center. He took a seat at the piano, eager to play for the first time since he and his comrades had celebrated with music, roasted quail, and schnapps at an abandoned farmhouse. *Even if I'm blind, I can make a living as a pianist.* His fingers glided over the keyboard as he played Mendelssohn's Piano Concerto in A Minor. As his right hand ascended the keys, the musical notes disappeared. At first, he thought the upper registry strings were broken. But when a staff member, as well as an audience of blind veterans, informed him that all of the piano keys were in perfect working order, he realized that his eardrums, damaged from a concussive shell blast, were unable to register high-pitched tones. He was devastated. And his dream of becoming a piano composer, along with his hope of being able to support himself, was shattered.

Wilhelmina rolled out of bed, stirring Max. Her footsteps faded, and the washroom door closed. He placed his hand on the warm spot of her pillow. *The distance between us feels like a chasm.* Burying his thoughts, he got dressed and went to the kitchen.

"We're almost out of food," Wilhelmina said, entering the room. She buttoned the top of her tan coveralls. "But there's enough leftover fried potato to last you a day."

Max, running his hand over the wall, approached her. "I'll pick up our rations."

"*Nein*," Wilhelmina said. "You might get lost."

"I've been practicing the route while you're at work," he said, hoping to impress her. On his trips with Wilhelmina to pick up provisions, he had paid close attention to the path, counting steps and making mental notes of streets, curbs, and intersections. For the past week, while she worked at a munitions factory, he'd rehearsed the route. He started with trips around the block. But each day he traveled farther and farther, until he reached the market.

"It's not safe for you to go by yourself," she said. "I'll go after work."

"I want to do it," he persisted.

She paused, rubbing dark circles under her eyes. At twenty-five, the war had stolen her vigor, her once-black hair prematurely turning gray with the passing of days reunited with Max, as if caring for him had accelerated the aging process. "Okay," she said reluctantly.

Max nodded, wondering if her affection for him, dormant since his return to Leipzig, would rekindle once he became self-reliant.

Wilhelmina ate a slice of black bread and washed it down with a glass of water. She gave him a scant peck on the cheek and left.

Anxious to gain his usefulness, he gathered his identification papers, wallet, walking stick, and a wicker basket with a lid, similar to a fishing creel. Standing outside the apartment, he heard the clamor of horses and wagons in the street. A clacking of shoes on the sidewalk grew, and then faded as a pedestrian passed by him.

I can do this. He tapped his cane over the ground and made his way to the corner. *Turn left, travel two blocks, turn right, travel one block, turn left, travel three blocks, and turn right.*

As he slowly shuffled along the route, his confidence began to build. Other than occasionally jabbing himself in the belly with his walking stick, when the tip caught on cobblestone, his trip was uneventful. Thirty minutes after his departure, he arrived at the market. Locating the entrance, by the jangling cowbells attached to the door, he entered and stood in line. Minutes passed. Step by step, he moved closer to the clerk at the counter.

"What happened?" a young girl's voice asked, standing next to him.

Max turned.

"Hush," a woman's voice said.

"It's okay," Max said to the woman, whom he presumed to be the girl's *mutter*. "I was injured in the war. I'm blind."

The girl stared at Max's milky eyes. "Can you see anything?"

"I'm afraid not." Based on the girl's voice, he estimated her to be between four and five years of age.

"How did you get here?" the girl asked.

"Franziska," the *mutter* said, sternly. "It's not polite to ask questions."

"I don't mind," Max said. He raised his walking stick. "I tap this over the ground in front of me to guide my way." He waited for the girl to respond, but she spoke no further. Disappointed, Max turned and waited for the line to move forward.

Reaching the counter, Max was greeted by the nasally voice of a store clerk named Georg, whom Max knew from years of making trips to the market with his parents. As Georg filled his basket with war bread, bits of preserved meat, and potatoes, Max's mind flashed with memories of his *mutter* and *vater* gathering ingredients to make delectable holiday meals. Schnitzel with savory kugel noodles. Goulash, a spicy paprika meat stew. *Kaiserschmarrn*, sweetened pancakes with plum preserve. Potato latkes drizzled with applesauce. Challah, a braided eggy bread with a poppy seed–studded crust. But by far, Max's favorite was his *mutter*'s *krokerle*, spiced chocolate hazelnut cookies, which she served with mulled wine. They'd only been dead a few years, but for Max, it felt like a lifetime. A melancholic ache filled his chest. *God, I miss them.*

"Will there be anything else, Max?" Georg asked.

"*Nein.*"

Georg marked the ration card, placed it inside the basket, and closed the lid.

Max extended his open wallet. "Do I have enough?"

"*Ja.*" He took out several marks, and then gave Max a bit of change. "It's good to have you home."

"*Danke.*" Max hooked his arm through the basket handle, and then made his way through the crowded market. People stepped away, creating a path, as he tapped his cane over the ground.

Outside, he created his mental map. *Turn left, travel three blocks, turn right, travel one block, turn left, travel two blocks, turn right.* He headed toward home, a sense of accomplishment swelling within him. But halfway into his journey, the sound of footsteps came from behind him. He slowed to allow the pedestrians to pass, but the group stopped. Continuing his trek, the clack of footsteps resumed. Hairs raised on the back of Max's neck. He picked up his pace.

Shoes clattered on cobblestone.

Max's adrenaline surged. He turned. A hand grabbed his jacket and pulled him into an alley.

"Give us your food," a male adolescent voice said.

"*Nein,*" Max said.

"Then we'll take it," another boy said.

"And your money," a guttural voice added.

Three? A cold sweat covered his skin. Despite his battlefield experience, he was no match, he believed, without his sight. Unwilling to give up without a fight, he pressed his back against a brick wall and raised his walking stick like a club.

The boys chuckled.

A concussive blow to the head toppled Max to the ground. In a daze, he struggled to raise his cheek from the cold cobblestone. Touching his forehead, his fingers turned wet. He attempted to stand but lost his balance and fell. As his vertigo waned, he placed his palms on the pavement, shards of a broken wine bottle digging into his skin. His basket and wallet were gone, and his walking stick had been snapped in half.

He stumbled out of the alley. His head throbbed, and his stomach turned sour with humiliation. *Wilhelmina was right. I shouldn't have tried to go by myself.* He couldn't imagine her having to care for him for the rest of his life. But deep down, he feared being alone. Disoriented, Max shuffled his feet over the sidewalk. Rather than wait for someone to come to his aid, he pressed a sleeve to the gash in his scalp and struggled to find his way home.

CHAPTER 6

OLDENBURG, GERMANY—JULY 18, 1916

Anna, her eyes filled with fatigue from working the night shift, entered the kitchen. The pantry was bare, except for bits of wilted potato and carrot. She lit a wood-burning stove, drizzled a miniscule amount of sunflower oil into a pan, and then sautéed a handful of leftover potato peels. *When was the last time I made Vater ham and eggs for breakfast?*

Rationing limited citizens to only one egg per week, which was used in increments to add nutrient to meals. Last year, the German government ordered the *Schweinemord*, the slaughter of over five million swine, which they deemed as competitors for scarce food resources. But the bureaucratic government's endeavor to produce food and preserve grain had not taken into account the use of pig manure on farms, and fear of a disastrous fall harvest was rampant. The shortages were becoming worse. Grain was scarce and bakers resorted to using potato flour to make the black war bread called *kriegsbrot*, which often contained various additives, including corn, lentil, and sawdust. She wondered, although briefly, if Germany would be able to survive the British naval blockade, which forced the country to be self-reliant with producing food.

Anna's stomach grumbled as she prepared a pot of substitute coffee made from tree bark. But the ache in her abdomen was not solely due to hunger. For the past several weeks, the frequency of

Bruno's letters had dwindled. When he did write, his words were sparse, and he provided little detail about what was taking place on the front. *He might be occupied with fighting, or maybe he's trying to protect me.* It saddened her to think that he was carrying his burden alone, and she wished that there was something she could say in her letters to end his solitude.

"Good morning, Anna," Norbie said, entering the kitchen. His clothes sagged on his thin frame, and an extra hole was cut in his leather belt to hold up his trousers.

You've lost weight. Anna scooped sautéed potato peels onto plates, making sure to give Norbie a larger portion. "Did you sleep well?"

"*Ja,*" Norbie said. "How was work?"

"Okay." Anna buried images of a soldier with gangrenous legs who died during her shift. *I'll tell him about it later.*

Norbie poured the bark brew into cups.

"We're out of coffee beans," Anna said.

He took a sip. "It's lovely."

"That's sweet," Anna said. "But we both know that it tastes like ash."

They sat at the table, and Norbie said a prayer, asking for peace and the safe return of soldiers.

"You gave me more," Norbie said, forking a bit of potato onto Anna's plate.

"I sometimes get extra food at the hospital," Anna said.

"But you're off from work today," Norbie said.

"How did you know?" Anna asked. "I didn't have a chance to tell you that Emmi and I traded shifts."

"You're wearing your engagement ring, and your *mutter*'s locket." Norbie, appearing proud of his detective skills, tapped a finger to his temple.

Anna clasped the silver heart-shaped locket, which had been an anniversary gift from Norbie to his wife. Inside was a Lilliputian-size clock, which Norbie had crafted from a tiny, second-hand watch.

"I always wear the locket," Anna said. "I keep it hidden under my uniform."

"I'm glad," Norbie said. "Your *mutter* would have loved seeing you wear it."

Anna nodded.

Norbie ate a forkful of food. "I never knew potato peels could taste so good."

She smiled, feeling thankful for her *vater*'s efforts to lift her spirits.

"What do you plan to do with your free day?" he asked.

"I have clothes to mend, and I need to pick up our rations."

"Nonsense," Norbie said. "You haven't had a day off in weeks. The weather is beautiful. You could take a book and spend the day in the park."

Anna took a bite of potato.

"Or perhaps you could pay a visit to the guide dog school," Norbie said.

"Another time," Anna said, putting down her fork. "I have much to do here."

Weeks ago, Dr. Stalling gained approval from the government to open the world's first guide dog training school. According to the newspaper, the town of Oldenburg was selected because it already housed the headquarters for the German Red Cross Ambulance Dogs Association, but Anna believed it had much to do with Stalling's influence, as well as his desire to help blind veterans. The opening of the school, which was to take place in a few weeks, was often a topic of Anna and Norbie's meal conversations. He'd encouraged her to talk to Dr. Stalling about serving as a volunteer or, even better, getting a job at the school. Although she desired to be part of something that could have a long-lasting impact on a veteran's life, she'd dismissed Norbie's suggestion on the basis that she knew nothing about training canines.

"The mending can wait," Norbie insisted. "I'll pick up the rations."

"The lines are long, and you have clocks to repair," Anna said.

"Fixing timepieces can wait." Norbie pushed away his plate. "I know that you want to be part of what is happening at the school. What's holding you back from talking with Dr. Stalling?"

Anna shifted in her seat. "I'm not qualified, and I'm quite sure that all of the trainers are men. It's unlikely they'd require some-one like me on their staff."

"Maybe a nurse is exactly what they need," Norbie said. "I thought the purpose of a guide dog was to care for the battle-blinded men. In a way, aren't the dogs serving as nurses?"

She hadn't thought of it that way, but Norbie's words resonated with her. "I suppose you're right. But even if I were permitted to volunteer, we can't live without my one-mark-per-day salary, even though I'm only paid every three months."

"We'll find a way to survive," Norbie said. "What harm can come from talking with Stalling?"

Anna wiggled her toes inside her shoes as she attempted to think of a rebuttal. "Most of the hospital staff, including Dr. Stall-ing, must know that I'm one of the least technically competent nurses. When the war is over, I'll likely be let go."

"You're as good as they are." Norbie clasped her hand. "Harbor your heart."

Harbor your heart, Anna thought. It was the affirmation that Norbie seldom spoke, but in times when Anna needed it most. It was his way to symbolize how one can protect their heart in the worst of emotional storms. He'd first spoken the affirmation when he gave Anna her *mutter*'s silver locket, soon after her *mutter*'s death. She'd visualized placing her heart inside the locket to pro-tect it from the wretched sorrow swelling in her chest. And now, when Anna had horrid days at the hospital, he used the phrase to provide comfort. Norbie's affirmation was, and always would be, his mantra to protect and encourage his daughter.

Anna squeezed his fingers. "Okay, I'll talk to Dr. Stalling. But when I come home, I want us to drop the subject of me training dogs."

Norbie grinned. "Of course."

After a thirty-five-minute walk to the outskirts of Oldenburg, Anna arrived at the Schützenhof, a large property with towering pine, poplar, and beech trees. The grounds were recently acquired for the purpose of housing the guide dog school by the Grand

Duke of Oldenburg. In a clearing was a long, barnlike structure with white siding and a wood shingle roof.

Her disquietude mushroomed as she approached the building. She clasped her purse, which contained a lunch of black bread and sliced, raw potato that Norbie had insisted on packing for her. An authoritative, male voice, tending to make one think of a military drill instructor, shouted from behind the building. Her skin prickled. *I came too far to turn around now.* She buried her angst and followed a stone path, which led her to the source of the noise.

Three trainers, wearing light gray uniforms, walked over an obstacle course with German shepherds. Black bandages covered the men's eyes, simulating blindness. In one hand, each trainer held a wooden cane. The opposite hand clasped a rigid handle, which was attached to the harness of a shepherd. Together, the trainer and dog traveled around the course, littered with stationary obstructions: puddles, rocks, felled limbs, wooden barrels, and mock curbs. Walking against the flow of traffic was a supervisor, holding a clipboard, who appeared to be serving as a pedestrian obstruction.

Anna's eyes locked on a shepherd, guiding a blindfolded trainer around a series of logs. She smiled. *Vater is right—a dog can be like a nurse.*

"*Hallo*, Fräulein Zeller," a familiar voice said.

Anna turned. "Dr. Stalling."

He tipped his hat. "To what do I owe the pleasure of your visit?"

"I have the day off from the hospital." Anna, attempting to collect her thoughts, fidgeted with her purse.

"Did you come to watch them train?"

"I came to speak with you," she said.

"Oh," Stalling said, sounding surprised.

"*Halt!*" the supervisor shouted. He pulled down a trainer's blindfold. "Don't rely on your cane. Follow the dog's lead."

The trainer nodded. He fixed his blindfold and resumed his position beside his dog.

"Rolf Fleck is the supervisor," Stalling said, lowering his voice. "He's a bit rough on his trainers, but he has a stellar track record of producing top-notch ambulance dogs. I'm counting on him to do the same with guide dogs."

Anna nodded.

"Why did you want to see me?" Stalling asked.

Her pulse quickened. *Harbor your heart*, she thought. "I'd like to work at the school."

Stalling paused and rubbed his chin.

"I hope you do not view me as presumptuous," Anna said. "If there isn't a vacancy, I'd be honored to serve as a volunteer."

"Are you unhappy at the hospital?" he asked.

"To the contrary, sir. I find it immensely rewarding to care for patients. But ever since that day in the hospital courtyard, when your dog guided the blind soldier around the garden, I can't stop thinking about how grand it would be if every disabled veteran had a dog like yours." She glanced to a shepherd, steering a trainer away from a puddle. "They're like a prosthesis for their eyes and soul."

"Indeed," Stalling said. He removed his hat and held it to his chest. "I never properly thanked you for what you did that day in the garden."

"I was only there to witness the event," she said. "I'm sure you would have gotten the school started, whether I was there that day or not."

"True, Fräulein Zeller," Stalling said. "But you inspired me to expedite my timeline."

Anna smiled.

The sound of clopping hooves compelled them to turn. Two horses, pulling a wagon that contained a driver and two shepherds, their snouts pointed skyward and sniffing the air, stopped at the building. The dogs jumped down from the wagon and wagged their tails, while the driver lifted a third dog, which was lying in the back of the wagon, and placed it on the ground. The dog hobbled, as if thorns were stuck in its paws, and then flopped onto its side.

You poor thing, Anna thought.

"Shepherds are in short supply," Stalling said. "In addition to sourcing them from all over Germany, we'll be attempting to retrain a few ambulance dogs, which are no longer able to perform their duties at the front."

Anna nodded.

"You're fortunate to find me here today," he said. "I came to inform Fleck that the veterinarian, who was supposed to be assigned to the school, was sent to the army."

Anna glanced at the trainer, frowning and scribbling on his clipboard. *If he's ill-tempered now, I wonder what he'll be like when he learns that he's lost a veterinarian.*

"Are you certain you want to work here?" Stalling asked.

"*Ja,*" she said. "I haven't trained dogs, but I think I could be helpful here."

"You're needed at the hospital," Stalling said.

"I'm not as competent as the other nurses," Anna said.

Stalling raised his brows. "Patients are quite fond of you."

"Thank you, Doctor," she said. "But something tells me that I should be here."

"You should know that I will not always be at the school," Stalling said. "Fleck is in charge of daily operations, and he selects the staff. I have other commitments that will occupy my time, such as government funding and working with our board of directors to select veterans who will undergo training with a guide dog." He gestured to the obstacle course. "I have ambitious plans for this school. Soon, we'll be training hundreds of dogs per year."

Anna's eyes widened. She imagined the grounds filled with veterans and their dogs.

"If Fleck permits you to work here," Stalling said, "it will not be easy for you. It will require extensive hours per week, perhaps even more time than the hospital. Also, you'd be making a bit less than your nursing salary."

"May I ask how much?"

"Slightly under a mark per day. Employees are paid monthly."

At least I'd be paid more frequently. "Okay."

"Would you like me to speak to Fleck?"

"Please," Anna said.

"All right." Stalling put on his hat, walked onto the course, and approached Fleck.

Anna took a deep breath and exhaled. While Stalling was speaking with Fleck, her eyes gravitated to the lame dog, lying on its side. *What happened to you?* She approached the trainer, who was attaching harnesses to the other dogs.

"I'm a nurse," Anna said. "May I examine your dog?"

He nodded. "Her name's Nia."

Anna kneeled. "*Hallo*, Nia."

The dog's eyes were red and filled with discharge. Malnourished, her caramel- and charcoal-colored coat clung to her ribs.

Anna extended her hand.

Nia sniffed and lethargically wagged her tail.

"Good girl, Nia," Anna said, stroking the dog's head. She removed a handkerchief from her purse and gently wiped away yellow matter from Nia's eyes. Examining the paws, she discovered the pads to be hot and swollen. She looked at the trainer. "She's come from the trenches, hasn't she?"

He nodded. "I convinced a solider not to euthanize her. I hope she'll live."

"She will," Anna said, attempting to hide the concern in her voice.

Anna had seen what muddy trenches can do to a soldier's feet. The prolonged cold, wet conditions restricted blood flow and damaged skin tissue. In the worst cases, amputation of toes or the foot was required. She hoped that this would not be the case for Nia.

"Fräulein Zeller," Stalling said, approaching with the supervisor. "This is Rolf Fleck."

Anna stroked Nia and stood. "It's a pleasure to meet you, sir."

Fleck, a stout, middle-aged man, folded his arms. His beard was meticulously groomed, and his polished jackboots shined like obsidian. "Normally, I would not permit a nurse to be hired," he said, twisting the end of his mustache. "However, our veterinarian has been reassigned, and I don't know when we'll receive another one."

Anna swallowed.

Fleck looked at Nia, her eyelids partly closed. "Can you make her well?"

"I will try," Anna said. "I've cared for many trench injuries like this with soldiers."

"She has," Stalling said.

"You may work here," Fleck said, "but I have a few conditions."

Anna clasped her hands.

"First," Fleck said, "you need to be willing and capable of boarding a veteran who is selected to undergo training. There are limited government housing options and, if needed, my workers need to be prepared to provide board."

Anna's mind raced. *Certainly, Norbie would be willing to take in a veteran. Would Bruno have any concerns?* "Of course," she said, burying her thoughts.

"Second," Fleck said, "I would like for you to recruit another person to join you. I, of course, will need to approve the worker you recommend. Operating this school will soon be far more than my current staff can handle."

"I will," Anna said, even though she was uncertain she could convince another person to join her.

"Be here at seven a.m. tomorrow," Fleck said. "And before you leave, tend to the dog. There are medical supplies inside." He turned and walked onto the obstacle course.

"Good luck, Fräulein Zeller," Dr. Stalling said. "I'll inform the hospital and will make arrangements for your transfer of employment."

A mixture of excitement and trepidation swelled inside her. "*Danke*, Dr. Stalling."

He nodded and left.

Anna carefully placed her arms under Nia's belly. She lifted the shepherd, frail and light for a dog that should have weighed at least twenty kilograms, and carried her inside the building. A faint scent of straw and old manure filled Anna's nose. She placed Nia in a stall that had once been used for a horse, and then located a medical bag that contained antiseptic and soap. She filled a chipped, enamel bowl with water, which she pumped from a well, and then washed Nia's paws.

The dog whimpered but made no effort to move.

Anna carefully cleaned between the dog's nails, the webbing raw and red, and then applied antiseptic.

Nia flinched.

"I'm sorry." Anna stroked Nia's head. "It burns, but it will help fight the infection."

The cadence of Nia's breath slowed, and her muscles relaxed.

Anna finished rinsing Nia's paws with antiseptic. With no bandages or rags, she used her skirt to dry the pads. She cupped a handful of water to her mouth. But Nia, lacking the strength to raise her head, produced a feeble lick and closed her eyes.

"The war is over for you," Anna whispered. "I'm going to make you well, and someday you'll be a guide dog."

Anna stroked Nia's protruding ribs, which felt like a washboard covered with fur. She removed Norbie's lunch of potato and bread from her purse, and then stashed the food under a bit of straw near Nia's nose. *I don't know what they'll feed you, but you need all the nourishment you can get.* She left for home, eager to tell Norbie the news of her new job, as well as to find a way to recruit another employee, but all she could think about was saving Nia.

CHAPTER 7

OLDENBURG, GERMANY—JULY 19, 1916

At sunrise, Anna dressed and went to the kitchen, where she lit a wood stove and toasted a bit of black bread. With her mind imbued with thoughts of Nia, she'd barely slept. *I hope she was able to eat*, Anna thought, picking at her bread. She regretted not offering to bring Nia home with her, despite that Fleck, who appeared to be a rule-following ex-military man, would likely not allow a dog to leave the premises. *I'll try when he sees that I'm a good worker.*

The house was quiet, except for ticking coming from the first-floor workshop, and the snores emanating from Norbie's upstairs bedroom. With a bit of time before heading to work, she retrieved a piece of paper and pencil.

My darling Bruno,
Much has transpired since my last letter.
Do you remember my correspondence about
a doctor who planned to establish a guide
dog training school in Oldenburg? Well, I've
accepted a position at the school. Or, more
precisely, my offer to work was granted. Either
way, today is my first day of employment,
and I'm beyond elated to begin working with
shepherds.

Do you think I've gone mad? I realize that I know little about dogs, but my experience as a nurse has awakened me to the obstacles that battle-blinded men will face when returning home from war. I believe, with every fiber of my heart, that shepherds will provide veterans with hope, comfort, and independence. I want be part of a solution to help them regain their lives. Although I have reservations about leaving the hospital, I feel this is something I must do.

I pray that you are safe. Please write when you can.

Your fiancée,

Anna

P.S. The school received a former ambulance dog who returned from the front in horrible condition. Her name is Nia. My first endeavor will be to make her well.

Anna sealed the letter in an envelope and placed it on the kitchen table. She was eager to check on Nia and begin her first day of work, but she was also pleased to bring along her friend Emmi. Yesterday, after leaving the guide dog school, Anna had gone directly to the hospital. She'd told Emmi, while she was taking her break in the garden, about her new job, and that she was charged with recruiting another person to work at the school. Before Anna had inquired as to Emmi's interest, Emmi clasped Anna's hands and asked, "May I join you?"

Anna was overjoyed with Emmi's offer. Even after she told Emmi about the hours, the lesser pay, and the brusque demeanor of Rolf Fleck, Emmi's determination to join her didn't waver. "Ewald works with ambulance dogs at the front," Emmi had said. "I'm certain he'd be honored for me to work with guide dogs." Anna was glad that Emmi would have the full support of her husband, and she wondered, although briefly, how her Bruno would feel about her abrupt change in profession. Before the end of the day, Stalling had made arrangements for the hospital to transfer both of them to the guide dog school. Emmi, who was a highly regarded and competent nurse, would no doubt be welcomed back to the hospital, if she chose to do so. But for Anna, who relied on her ability to comfort and care, rather than technical skills, the change in employment might be permanent.

"Good morning, Anna," Norbie said, stepping into the kitchen.

"Sleep well?" Anna asked.

"*Ja.*" Norbie ran a hand through his mussed, gray hair and yawned. He looked at the pendulum clock on the wall. "You're up early."

"Emmi should be arriving soon," Anna said. "I thought it would be wise to show up early on the first day of work."

"I'll make coffee for you and Emmi," he said.

"There's no need," Anna said.

"I insist," he said, retrieving a tarnished copper coffeepot.

"Okay," Anna said. *There's no changing Norbie's mind when it comes to hospitality for visitors, even ones who will only be staying a minute.*

A knock came from the front door. Anna descended the stairs to Norbie's workshop. A few minutes later, Anna, Emmi, and Norbie sat at the kitchen table with cups of steaming brew. A roasted, wood-like scent permeated the air.

"Thank you, Norbie," Emmi said, clasping her cup.

"It's made from tree bark," Norbie said. "Save your gratitude until after you tasted it."

Emmi chuckled.

"To Anna and Emmi," Norbie said, raising his cup as if it was filled with wine. "May your work mend the lives of those who cannot see."

Anna's heart swelled. "*Prost,*" she said, clinking their cups. She sipped. The hot, bitter brew warmed her belly.

Emmi drank. "It's quite good, Norbie."

Norbie grinned. "How's Ewald?"

"That's kind of you to ask," Emmi said. "His spirts are good. I wrote him last night to inform him of the guide dog school."

"He'll be impressed," Norbie said.

I hope Bruno is as excited about the school as I am. Anna shifted in her seat and pointed to her letter on the table. "Vater, do you have time to mail my letter to Bruno?"

"Of course," Norbie said.

A grandfather clock sounded in the workshop. Seconds later, a barrage of rings, dongs, clangs, chimes, and bells erupted, signaling 6:00 a.m.

Norbie, who prided himself with creating accurate timepieces, shook his head and sighed. "No matter how many adjustments I make to the pendulum disk, that confounded grandfather clock always strikes early or late."

"I'm sure you'll find a way to fix it," Anna said. She finished her coffee and turned to Emmi. "We should get to work."

Emmi swigged her drink. "*Danke* for the coffee, Norbie."

"After the war," he said, "I'll make you and Anna a breakfast of real coffee and cake."

"Sounds delightful," Emmi said.

Norbie hugged Anna. "You'll do great," he whispered.

Anna smiled and released him.

As Anna and Emmi descended the steps, a ticktock chorus rose to a crescendo. They maneuvered through the workshop, cluttered with clocks, and exited through the front door. As they walked over the uneven, cobblestone street, an anxiousness filled Anna's stomach. She wondered if Nia's feeble paws would improve, and if Fleck would accept Emmi as her recruit. *There's nothing I can do about it until I get to work.* For the duration of their walk, Anna told Emmi about Nia's condition, all the while hoping that they could save her.

They arrived at the guide dog school twenty minutes early. Anna had expected that they'd might be the first to arrive, but the door to the building was open. Inside, she found Fleck, walking along the stalls, as if he were inspecting the dogs.

"*Hallo*," Anna said.

Fleck turned and placed his clipboard under an armpit. "You're early. I thought I told you to be here at seven."

"I . . ." Anna swallowed. "I didn't want to be late."

"Tomorrow, arrive at seven," he said. "It's important for the dogs to have a precise schedule."

"*Ja*, sir," Anna said.

Emmi nudged her.

Anna swallowed. "This is Emmi Bauer."

"It's a pleasure to meet you, sir," Emmi said.

Fleck nodded.

"Emmi's the finest nurse at the hospital," Anna said. "She's willing to work here."

Fleck looked at Emmi. "Did she tell you about the pay and the potential need for you to board veterans?"

"*Ja*," Emmi said.

Anna's eyes drifted to Nia's stall, but she couldn't see her. She hoped that she was standing.

"Did Dr. Stalling arrange for both of you to transfer from the hospital to the school?" he asked.

"He has," Anna said.

"Follow me," Fleck said. He approached a series of wooden stalls and pointed, using his clipboard. "One at a time, you will attach a leash to a dog, and then take it—individually—to relieve itself. There is a section of grass behind the barn that is marked."

"Okay," Anna said, noticing that several additional dogs had been delivered, all of which were standing in their stalls and wagging their tails. She glanced to Nia's pen and her heart sank. Nia, her chest slowly rising and falling, was on her side, in the same position where Anna had left her.

Fleck looked at Anna. "You may tend to her later, when the other dogs are training."

"*Ja*, sir," Anna said, dreading the time that would need to pass before she could go to Nia's aid.

"After all the dogs have relieved themselves," Fleck said, "you will feed them and give them fresh water. The bowls are in each of their pens. There is a bin of feed, of which you will give them precisely one level scoop. It will be more efficient if one pumps the water from the well, and the other carries the filled buckets to their bowls."

Emmi nodded.

"Thirty minutes after they have eaten, take them outside again—individually—to relieve themselves. Then attach a harness to each of the dogs." He pointed to a row of harnesses with an attached handle. "You will be shuttling dogs to trainers on the obstacle course. While the men are working with them, you will clean pens and scoop droppings in the yard."

A foreboding knot tightened in Anna's gut. She glanced to Emmi, who was staring into a pen.

"Between shuttling dogs to trainers and cleaning pens, you will provide medical and hygiene care for the dogs who are not working. I'll have a trainer instruct you on how to properly cut their nails."

"Will you—" Anna swallowed and clasped her hands. "Will you need our help with training the dogs?"

Fleck furrowed his brows. "*Nein.*"

Anna swallowed. "I thought that our duties might include—"

"You were mistaken," he interrupted. "Have the dogs ready for when the trainers arrive." Fleck turned, his boots scraping over the ground, and left the building.

I'm such a fool, Anna thought.

Emmi retrieved a leash.

"Emmi," Anna said. "I'm so sorry."

"For what?" Emmi asked.

"I thought our work might include training dogs," Anna said, her words sounding a bit absurd said aloud. "Are you upset with me?"

"Of course not." Emmi placed a hand on Anna's shoulder. "Based on Ewald's stories of ambulance dogs, I assumed that guide dogs would be trained by military veterans. Also, I thought I could do this job because it would be similar to the role of a nurse."

"How so?" Anna asked, relieved that Emmi was not disappointed in her.

"It is the physicians who perform surgery and decide if a limb needs to be amputated. We, as nurses, clean the wound, feed the infirm, and change the bedpans."

"I'm glad I didn't mislead you," Anna said. "But I feel foolish for believing we might work with dogs and their partners."

"You're not a fool," Emmi said. "You're a dreamer, and it's one of the things I admire most about you."

Anna smiled, despite the disillusionment about her duties. "I want to introduce you to Nia."

"We need to get to work," Emmi said.

Anna peeked through a window. "Fleck is smoking a cigarette. We arrived early, so we have some extra time."

"I don't know," Emmi said tentatively. "We might get in trouble."

"It will only take a second," Anna said. "I want you to have a look at her so you can give some thought to how we should care for her paws."

Emmi glanced to the window.

"Please," Anna said.

"Okay," Emmi said.

They entered Nia's pen and kneeled beside the dog. Near her head was gnawed bits of bread and potato.

Nia slowly opened her eyelids. She attempted to stand but whimpered and flopped onto her belly with her chin pressed to the ground.

Anna stroked the dog's back. "It's okay, Nia. This is Emmi. She's going to help me take care of you." She gently lifted the dog's front right paw.

Emmi grimaced. "Damn trenches." She stroked Nia's head, and then examined the remaining paws, all of which were inflamed with redness and blisters between the pads.

Anna kissed Nia on the head and whispered, "We'll be back to feed and care for you soon." Despite her heart telling her to stay, she forced herself to go about their duties.

For the next hour, Anna and Emmi accompanied dogs to do their business. She presumed that Fleck required that dogs be taken individually, similar to the daily experience they would encounter when they were partnered with a blind veteran. Working together at the hospital was beneficial, Anna believed, as they alternated turns pumping water and carrying buckets of water to fill bowls. They used the same tandem approach for feeding the dogs. The food in the bins was chopped turnips, similar to feed for cattle. And given a burlap sack of whole turnips which sat next to a butcher block and tarnished cleaver knife, Anna assumed that making dog food would soon be added to her list of duties.

Regardless of her disappointment of being confined to canine care and nursing duties, she wouldn't have changed her mind about working here, even if she had known the full scope of the role. The shepherds were sweet and affectionate, as well as incredibly intelligent, given they waited for permission to eat, leave their pen, and go potty. Their coats were thick and soft, and the manner in which they panted with a protruding tongue was simply adorable. It took a concerted effort for Anna not to give in to her urge to hug the shepherds. Also, all of the dogs were female, which Anna and Emmi had deduced from escorting the dogs to do their business.

By the time the trainers arrived for work, each of the dogs were fed, cared for, and wearing their harness, except for Nia, who was curled on the floor of her pen. After a brief introduction by Fleck, who called Emmi "Emilie," the trainers took a group of dogs to the obstacle course. Before Anna and Emmi embarked on picking up dog piles and cleaning pens, they tended to Nia.

"Her paws are bad," Emmi said, kneeling beside Nia. "Especially her front, right paw."

Anna rubbed Nia's head. "What do you think we should do?"

Emmi pointed. "The ground in this barn is damp. It'll make it difficult for her paws to heal."

"Straw?"

"It'll help, but what she needs is a dry, warm place to sleep."

Anna envisioned smuggling her home, and quickly buried her thought.

"Let's clean and dry her paws," Emmi said.

Anna retrieved water and antiseptic. Together they cleaned Nia's paws, and then dried them using a few of Norbie's old handkerchiefs that Anna had stashed in her purse. Afterward, they gave her food and water, but Nia only nibbled a bit of turnip.

"Try to drink, Nia," Anna said, cupping a handful of water to the dog's mouth.

Nia lapped water, and then lowered her head.

For the rest of the day, Anna and Emmi cleaned pens, picked up dog piles, shuttled shepherds to trainers, chopped turnips into dog meal, and made a homemade salve from remnants of a beeswax candle, which Anna applied to a shepherd with a bleeding elbow callus. Between her duties, Anna tended Nia. She managed to get a bit of food into Nia's belly by mashing turnips into a paste, which was easier for her to swallow while lying on her side. Twice, Nia had attempted to stand, but she yelped and flopped to the ground.

"I wish I could take you home with me," Anna said, caressing Nia's head.

Nia raised her eyes. Her tail slowly brushed the ground.

The trainers finished their work in the late afternoon. Anna and Emmi escorted the dogs, one by one, from the obstacle course to the barn, where they removed their harnesses and gave them fresh water. While the trainers congregated outside to smoke cigarettes, Anna and Emmi labored to feed the dogs their evening meal. As Anna scooped a cup of turnip feed from a bin, Fleck entered the barn and approached her.

Anna's skin prickled. "May I help you, sir."

He pointed to the metal cup. "My instructions were to give them one *level* scoop."

Anna looked at the feed, heaping from her cup. "Sorry, sir."

"No food must be wasted," he said.

She pushed bits of turnip back into the bin. She held the cup to Fleck.

"Better," he said.

Anna deposited the food into a bowl. She was relieved when Fleck stepped away. But he didn't leave the barn. Instead, he raised his clipboard and began to inspect each of the pens. *Oh, no.*

Fleck went from pen to pen, examining the condition of each shepherd, as well as the cleanliness of their area. After each inspection, he scribbled onto his clipboard. As he examined the dog with the elbow callus, he asked, "What's on her?"

Anna and Emmi darted to the pen.

"A salve, sir," Anna said.

"Where did you get it?"

"I made it," Emmi said.

He ran a finger over the dog's elbow. "The bleeding has stopped, and she's no longer scratching it."

Anna looked at Emmi and smiled.

"Make more of it," he said. He stepped into the adjacent pen, where Nia was curled with her nose toward her tail. "I see this one hasn't improved."

"She's drunk water and eaten some food," Anna said.

He lifted Nia's front paw and shook his head. "If she's unable to recover soon, we'll need to euthanize her."

A pang pierced Anna's stomach. "She'll recover, sir. We've treated many soldiers with their feet in horrid shape from the trenches."

"This a shepherd, not a soldier," he said.

Anna swallowed. *If she stays here, she might not recover fast enough for him.* She looked at Nia, her eyebrows dancing as her eyes looked from Fleck to Anna. *Harbor your heart*, Norbie's voice crowed in her head. She gathered her courage and said, "The obstacle preventing her quick recovery is this cold, damp ground."

Fleck scraped the earth with the heel of his boot.

"Sir," Anna said. "I am willing to take her home to care—"

"*Nein*," he said.

Anna took a deep breath. Her mind and heart raced. "I realize that you want this dog to recover quickly, but we need a warm, dry environment, which we don't have. You have demands to meet, and I want to help you achieve them. If this shepherd remains here, she'll eat your food, take up space, and you might end up having to euthanize her."

Emmi's eyes widened.

Fleck crossed his arms.

"But if you permit me to take her home, she will not eat your food, and she will not take up space, which I'm sure you will need for incoming shepherds. And I *will* deliver you a healthy dog to train, rather than one to euthanize."

Fleck paused, tapping his clipboard.

Anna fought to keep her hands from trembling. *Oh, God, please.*

"All right," he said.

"Thank you, sir," Anna said. "You won't regret—"

"I want a daily report on her condition."

"Of course," Anna said.

Fleck turned and left.

Emmi approached Anna. "I can't believe you did that."

"Nor I," Anna said, her legs quivering.

Anna and Emmi finished their work. One of the trainers, a man in his late sixties with hairy eyebrows, reminiscent of albino caterpillars, helped them carry Nia to his wagon. Instead of sitting up front, Anna hunkered in the bed of the wagon with Nia's head on her lap. The driver snapped the reins and the wagon jerked forward. As the horses clopped over the dirt road, Anna stroked the dog's ears. "You're going home with me."

Nia nuzzled Anna's hand.

She leaned in and whispered, "I promise to make you well."

CHAPTER 8

LILLE, FRANCE—JULY 19, 1916

Bruno, his boots spattered with mud from the trenches, peered through the carriage window as the train chugged into the Lille station, a mere twenty kilometers from the front. He'd been summoned to meet with Fritz Haber, the head of the Chemistry Section in the Ministry of War, but the purpose of the meeting was not disclosed. A feeling of powerlessness encompassed him, as if he were being swept away by a raging river. *Perhaps I'll be reprimanded for my failure to stop the gas attack at Halluch.*

The last time he'd spoken to Haber, who recruited him to join the gas regiment, was in Ypres, when Germany unleashed the first mass use of poison gas, which resulted in thousands of French casualties. The German Empire was the first to breach the Hague Convention treaty that prohibited the use of poison weapons. But being the first to commit the atrocity hadn't changed the tide of the war. Instead, it fueled the Allied forces to begin using their own gas warfare. And any chance of a swift end of the war, Bruno believed, was gone.

Despite the unfavorable wind conditions at the battle of Halluch, Bruno had failed to influence superior officers to stop the gas attack. The poisonous cloud, which blew back on the German lines, killed over one thousand German soldiers. The trenches and dugouts were full of bodies with blue faces and black lips. Most of the deaths were due to not having gas masks. But some of them, who didn't understand that the gas sinks in the trenches, removed their masks too soon. These men swallowed gas, scorching their lungs, and they choked and hemorrhaged to death.

Although it wasn't his duty, he'd insisted on overseeing the burial of the dead, many of whom were destined to mass graves. However, he arranged for four hundred of the fallen men to be properly buried in a cemetery of a French village called Pont-à-Vendin. But the entombments did little to alleviate a cancerous guilt that grew within him. The screams and gurgles of dying men were etched into his brain like a phonograph disc. And burned into his memories was the image and stench of decomposing corpses, stacked like cords of wood.

There are no words to describe the wickedness of war, he'd thought while writing a letter to Anna. He struggled whether to tell her about what had taken place at Halluch. He longed to confide in her, but he feared that providing transparency about his duties might hurt her or, even worse, ruin her feelings for him. *I will tell her everything on my next military leave. For now, I'll carry the burden alone.*

The train screeched to a stop. Bruno shook the horrid thoughts from his mind and retrieved his leather case, which contained Anna's letters and his personal items. As he stepped onto the landing, a pungent scent of burning locomotive coal filled his nostrils. The German-occupied city of Lille was bustling with troops passing through on their way to the front. Reluctant to face a possible reprimand, Bruno chose to walk, rather than take a carriage, to his meeting with Haber.

The city of Lille, which held much of France's coal and steel industry, was captured in October of 1914. Raw materials, manufactured goods, and food flowed east to support the German Empire. Street signs had been changed to German names. Bars and coffeehouses poured beer for German soldiers. An empty cigarette factory, as well as several unused industrial buildings, had been converted into barracks for soldiers. Also, the empire had taken control of printed publications. A German language newspaper, *Liller Kriegszeitung*, was provided to occupying troops, while a German-created French language newspaper, *Gazette des Ardennes*, produced propaganda to occupied citizens. Additionally, the clocks in Lille were set on German time. The occupation, Bruno believed, had transformed the French city into a German outpost.

As Bruno entered the city center, forty Allied prisoners, haggard and wearing soiled uniforms, were being forced to march through the streets by a group of armed soldiers. Silent French onlookers, comprised of old men, women, and children, stood along the street. It was apparent, to Bruno, that citizens of Lille were not permitted to speak to the prisoners. The ravaged men, their eyes lowered, shuffled their feet. *With the exception of their uniforms, they look like our men.*

As the prisoners passed, Bruno approached a soldier. "Where are you taking them?"

"To a prison in the citadel." The soldier adjusted his rifle on his shoulder.

"Will they be transported to Germany?"

"*Nein*. We march them each day between the citadel and train station." The soldier quickened his pace and joined his group.

Bruno's eyes locked on the prisoners. Shame pricked at his conscience. *We parade them through the city to demoralize them.* He gripped the handle of his case, turning his knuckles white, and took another route to his rendezvous with Haber.

On a prominent street lined with palatial homes, Bruno arrived at a grand, three-story bourgeois house with dormer windows jutting from the attic. Angst grew in his gut as he climbed the stone steps to the entrance, bearing the address in his summons from Haber. He knocked on the door, which had a posting that contained two names: *Gabrielle Lemaire*, which was partially scratched away with pencil, and *Celeste Lemaire*.

A young woman in her early twenties with skin the tone of alabaster opened the door. Wavy auburn hair rested on the lace collar of her navy dress. "Oberleutnant Wahler?"

Bruno removed his cap. "*Ja.*"

"They are waiting for you in the parlor," the woman said in German but with a French accent. "Follow me."

They traveled over a rouge marble floor. The click of their shoes echoed in the hallway. She opened a set of tall, oak-paneled doors. Seated at a table were two officers, both of whom Bruno recognized: Fritz Haber, a bald-headed man with pince-nez spectacles, and Otto Hahn, a mustached officer in his late thirties. Like Bruno, Otto was a chemist who'd been recruited by Haber. However, Otto's duties included hunting for sites on both fronts for gas attacks.

"Bruno." Haber stood and extended his hand.

Bruno, feeling surprised to be called by his first name, shook Haber's hand. He greeted Otto.

"Celeste," Haber said, turning to the woman. "Bring us something from the cellar to drink."

The woman left, closing the doors behind her.

"You're probably wondering why I've summoned you," Haber said, taking a seat.

Bruno put down his leather case and sat. "I assume it's about what happened at Hulluch."

"Mishaps are part of war," Haber said.

Otto nodded, appearing as if he'd experienced accidents with poison gas.

"A change in wind can be impossible to predict." Haber adjusted his spectacles on the bridge of his nose. "And commanding officers, who are ignorant of science, can be quite difficult to persuade."

Bruno's shoulder muscles relaxed.

"I've summoned you to discuss a breakthrough in technology."

Otto's lips formed a smile.

"We've placed phosgene gas in artillery shells," Haber said, grinning. "Otto successfully used the new shells at Verdun."

"Poison shells?" Bruno asked.

"We no longer need to worry about the wind," Otto said. "We can place gas anywhere we want."

"What were the results in Verdun?" Bruno asked, uncertain if he wanted to know the answer.

"On June twenty-second, we gassed French artillery positions with phosgene shells," Otto said. "We estimate between one and two thousand casualties."

Haber placed his fingers together. "Your new assignment will be based in Lille. The phosgene shells will be transported here. You'll be responsible for introducing the new weapons along the front, between Hulluch and Ypres."

Bruno nodded.

Celeste entered the room with a bottle of wine and glasses. She poured drinks for the officers.

"*Danke*," Bruno said.

Celeste's green eyes met with Bruno, and she lowered her head. "Will there be anything else?"

Haber waved her off, and she left the room.

"To surpassing enemy technology and winning the war," Haber said, raising his glass.

Bruno clinked his glass and sipped. *The Allied forces will likely begin using their own poison shells in a matter of months.*

"Our advancement will escalate casualties," Otto said. "It'll break the stalemate on the front."

Haber swirled his drink. "Death is death, regardless of how it is inflicted."

Bruno's skin prickled. A flash of gassed bodies—mouths gaped and faces the color of plum—filled his head.

"I've recently spoken with your *vater*," Haber said.

"How is he?" Bruno asked.

"Well," Haber said. "With government contracts, Wahler Farbwerke is becoming a large company. Your family will be quite wealthy after the war."

Bruno nodded, attempting to recall the last letter he'd received from either of his parents or his half-brother, Julius. He took a drink of wine, attempting to wash away his disappointment from their lack of communication. "How is your wife, Clara?" he asked, eager to change the topic of conversation.

"Dead," Haber said.

Bruno straightened his back. "I'm sorry. When did it happen?"

"Last year," Haber said.

Otto lowered his eyes.

"My condolences, sir," Bruno said. "If I had known I would have—"

"She wasn't well," Haber said abruptly.

Bruno nodded. The room turned silent, and Otto changed the subject to the production of phosgene shells. For the next twenty minutes, they avoided topics of personal matters and only discussed plans for the German Empire to win the escalating chemical warfare race.

Haber finished his wine and stood. "I have a train to catch, but Otto will remain in Lille for a few days to help you get started on your assignment."

Bruno stood and shook Haber's hand.

"Good luck to you." Haber put his cap on his head and left the room. Seconds later, the front door opened and closed.

Otto poured wine into his glass.

"Did I do something to offend him?" Bruno asked.

"*Nein*, he was scheduled to leave. But in the future, I recommend not to inquire about his wife." Otto took a sip of wine. "Clara committed suicide."

Bruno's eyes widened.

"Haber doesn't like to talk about it. There are rumors that she was depressed from Haber's work with chemical warfare. When she learned of the gas attack in Ypres, which killed many thousands, she committed suicide."

"Oh, God," Bruno said.

"She shot herself in the heart with Haber's service revolver. Their twelve-year-old son found her."

Bruno's breath stalled in his lungs.

"Let's not speak of this again." Otto drained his drink and placed the glass on the table. "Celeste will show you to your room. I think you'll find the accommodations of this officers' boardinghouse to be far nicer than the old factory barracks. Once you are settled in, I'll show you the supply depot, and then we'll go to the officers' casino."

Bruno nodded.

Otto patted Bruno on the shoulder and left for his room.

Bruno slumped in his chair and lowered his head into his hands. *What will Anna do when she learns of what I've done? What will she think of my family's role in the war?* His heart ached with regret, and he wished there was something he could do to change the past.

Celeste entered the parlor. "May I show you to your room?"

Bruno raised his head and nodded. He stood and reached, his hand trembling, for his leather case.

"Are you all right, *monsieur?*"

"*Ja,*" Bruno lied.

Celeste gently took the case from his hand. "You'll feel better after some rest."

He followed her out of the parlor and up a winding staircase. For Bruno, each step of the ascent felt harder and harder, as if the weight of the war was pressing on his shoulders.

"I've placed towels and water in your room," Celeste said, opening a door. She sat the case next to the bed.

"*Danke,*" he said.

"If you need anything, *monsieur,* you can find me in the kitchen or my room in the attic." She turned and closed the door behind her.

Bruno collapsed onto his bed. His mind raced with potential ramifications of his actions. He struggled to convince himself that Anna—if she learned of his role in the gassing deaths of thousands of men—would never hurt herself, like Haber's wife, Clara. *But how can I know for sure?* Unwilling to risk ruining his engagement and, most importantly, burdening Anna with knowledge of his sins, he resolved to never divulge the truth.

CHAPTER 9

LEIPZIG, GERMANY—JULY 19, 1916

Alone in his apartment, Max shuffled into the living room and sat in a wool upholstered chair. A recording of Mozart's Piano Sonata No. 7 in C Major played on a horn gramophone, next to a dust-covered Blüthner grand piano. The music resonated through the room, but Max's eardrums—damaged from the shell blast—were unable to register the upper treble clef notes, typically played with a pianist's right hand. For Max, the high-pitched tones disappeared into a muffled, black abyss, as if the piano strings were smothered with a blanket.

Max's doctor had attempted to improve his hearing loss with herbal remedies, which included the consumption of dill tea and the insertion of garlic oil droplets into his ear canals. When these treatments failed, the doctor prescribed an electronically amplified hearing aid, the size of a tall cigar box with a cumbersome speaker that was inserted in his ear. While the apparatus amplified the tones Max could already discern, it did nothing to help him detect high-pitched sounds. The doctor diagnosed him with a permanent, high-frequency hearing loss and informed him that there was nothing further that could be done.

Max refused to give up hope that his range of hearing might improve over time. Each morning, after Wilhelmina left for work at the munitions factory, he sat at the piano. He played ascending scales until the notes—beginning with D-sharp on the second highest octave of the keyboard—became undetectable. Of the seven octaves on an eighty-eight-key piano, Max could only hear five of the octaves. He diligently conducted his daily auditory tests. But as months passed, his range of hearing did not improve, and his dream of composing music, as well as his desire to play the piano, began to fade.

Prior to the war, Max's ambition to be a composer was driven by his passion for the piano, which was fostered by his parents, Franz and Katarina. But now, as a blind veteran, music was one of the few paths for him to gain meaningful employment. The country considered a sightless person to be completely disabled. However, Max refused to be viewed as an invalid or an object of charity. *I will not be a burden to Wilhelmina, nor will I be a blind beggar on the street. I'll find a way to support myself, no matter what I have to do.*

Even if his hearing improved, Max's blindness still created a huge obstacle with mobility. Since his brutal mugging on an unaccompanied trip to the market—which resulted in a concussion, a lacerated scalp requiring six stitches, and having his food and money stolen—he'd relied on Wilhelmina to obtain provisions. While most of the residents of Leipzig were kind, law-abiding, and respectful, the shortage of food and rumors of starvation, due to the British naval blockade, had driven some citizens to commit criminal acts. A blind man carrying a basket of food was an easy target for a group of adolescents with hungry bellies. Despite having been beaten and robbed, Max did not abandon his pursuit to explore the streets. With a new walking cane, which he'd made from an old broomstick, he took trips around the apartment block. Each day he ventured farther and farther over the cobblestone sidewalks, determined to create a cerebral chart of his neighborhood.

The quest for independence, Max believed, required far more than the ability to navigate a few city streets. Therefore, he insisted on preparing meals and cleaning the apartment, despite Wilhelmina's concerns that he might make a mess or burn down the apartment building. With much practice, and the precise organization of food, utensils, and cookware, he was able to prepare basic meals, which mostly consisted of toasted bread, fried potato dishes, and coffee. Soon, she grew tolerant, if not appreciative, of his work. He hoped that by lessening the household burden on Wilhelmina, her affection for him would rekindle. However, little changed between them. Exhausted from extra shifts at the factory, she spoke little during meals and often went to bed early. Their intimacy withered, and Max worried that their prewar days of bliss would never return.

The music stopped. The gramophone's needle scratched over the center of the disc. Max stood. With his hands extended, he located the gramophone and raised the tone arm. As he prepared to replay the recording, a key jostled in the door to the apartment. He flipped a switch, and the turntable slowed to a stop.

Wilhelmina, her coveralls stained with grime, entered the apartment and closed the door. She placed an empty tin lunch pail on the kitchen counter.

He shuffled forward with his hand on the wall. "*Hallo.* Wilhelmina?"

She removed her head scarf. "Were you expecting someone else?" she asked, her voice tired and hoarse.

"*Nein.*" *We used to eagerly embrace when we reunited*, he thought. *My disability and the strain of your job at the munitions factory has created a mountain between us.* "How was work?"

"Same."

"Still have the headache?"

"*Ja.*"

Wilhelmina's work at the factory required her to fill shell cases with explosive. She endured daily exposure to hazardous chemicals without adequate protection. In addition to migraines, she and the munitions women were plagued with chronic colds, anemia, and nausea.

"I'm sorry." He shuffled to her and found her hand. Her coveralls, stained with explosive residue, omitted a sweet, chemical odor. He squeezed her fingers, but she didn't return the gesture. "You'll feel better after you wash and eat. We have a few potatoes. I'll make us latkes for dinner."

She slipped away her hand. "I'm not hungry."

"Then I'll make you coffee." He expected a rebuttal. Instead, he heard the creak of a chair as she sat at the kitchen table. Locating a ceramic jar, he carefully hand-scooped substitute coffee grinds, made from tree bark, into a pewter pot.

Wilhelmina removed an envelope from her coveralls. "You received a letter from the Imperial German Army."

Max's chest tightened. Locating a glass pitcher, he poured water into the pot and checked the fill level with his finger.

"Would you like me to read it to you now or later?"

"Now is fine."

She opened the envelope and read.

13ᵗʰ July 1916
Maximilian Benesch,
You are hereby notified that, as a result
of your visual disability, you are
required to report to the Schützenhof
grounds in Oldenburg for mobility
rehabilitation with guide dogs for the
war blind at 8:00 AM on 2 December 1916
for a period of no less than eight weeks.
Arrangements for your transport will be
forthcoming.
Obergefreiter, Frederick Müller
Department of Veteran Affairs
Imperial German Army

Oh, God. The government's solution to my problems is to send me away to train with a dog. He located a box of matches and lit the stove.

"I didn't know that dogs were used for the blind," Wilhelmina said.

"Neither did I." He paused, reflecting on the ambulance, messenger, and scout dogs that he'd seen at the front.

"Maybe the rehabilitation will help you," she said.

"I don't want to go," he said.

"Why?"

"No amount of therapy can fix my eyes, nor my ears."

"You'll have no choice in the matter," she said.

He shrugged.

"I want you to go," Wilhelmina said. "You need to learn to get around on your own, and a dog might be helpful. At the very least, a dog could provide protection from being attacked and robbed." She tucked the letter into the envelope and approached him. "I'm unable to be a constant caregiver for you; I'm required to work. Besides, this might be your only chance of receiving rehabilitation."

A foreboding ache crept into Max's gut. *If I leave, she might not be here when I return home. And if she's here when I come back from rehabilitation, she might not stay if she feels that a dog can keep me safe.* He buried his thoughts, and he refused to admit to himself that he feared being alone.

She placed the letter in his hand, and then went to the washroom and closed the door behind her.

Max's anguish spiraled. Repairing his fractured relationship with Wilhelmina felt daunting, and he dreaded undergoing any type of government rehabilitation, even one which included the appeal of working with a dog. While he waited for the coffee to percolate, he turned on the gramophone. The piano sonata, absent the high notes, filled Max's ears. He prayed for the strength to endure his torment, but it never came.

CHAPTER 10

OLDENBURG, GERMANY—AUGUST 2, 1916

The clang of an alarm clock awakened Anna. She shifted the alarm switch on the back of the clock, silencing the bells. But muted chimes from Norbie's workshop, two stories below Anna's room, reverberated through the house. She rubbed sand from her eyes, and then looked to the corner of the room where Nia was curled on the floor.

"Good morning," Anna said.

Nia's tail thumped against the wall.

"The guide dog school opens today," Anna said. "You're going with me to work."

Nia raised her head.

"Come," she said, leaning over her bed.

Nia labored to stand. She limped, favoring her front right paw, and placed her chin on the bed.

Anna patted Nia on the head and received a wet lick to her face. She giggled and ruffled Nia's ears. *You're getting better.*

For the past two weeks, Anna looked after Nia. She washed and dried her paws, swollen and infected, and then applied a homemade garlic antibacterial ointment, which was a recipe from Emmi. During the treatment, Nia didn't squirm or kick. Other than an occasional sniff or lick at the pungent concoction between her pads and claws, she was a model patient. But it became clear to Anna, when woken in the night by whines and whimpers, that Nia had suffered far more than trench-damaged paws during her service as an ambulance dog on the front.

"You're safe, and you never have to go back there," she'd whispered, cuddling Nia on the floor.

As days passed, Nia's bad dreams waned but didn't disappear. And seeing Nia's distress made Anna wonder if Bruno might also be suffering from battlefield nightmares, even though his letters, which had dwindled in frequency and content, reassured her that he was of sound mind and body.

While Anna was away at work, Norbie filled in as caregiver. Each day, he wrapped Nia in a wool blanket and carried her down the stairs to his workshop, where he fed her turnip feed, mixed with bits of black war bread. Most of the time, Nia slept at his feet while he tinkered on timepieces. Twice per day, he gently transferred her to the garden behind the workshop to do her business. With Nia unable to stand on her own, he held her under the abdomen to keep weight off her paws. After relieving herself, Nia raised her snout and licked Norbie on the nose. In the evenings, Anna returned home to find Norbie at his workbench and Nia curled at his feet. When Anna inquired as to why Norbie was missing his socks and shoes, he'd wiggled his toes and said, "She likes her tummy rubbed."

Within a week, Nia gained a bit of weight. Her rib cage no longer looked like a washboard covered in fur, and her caramel- and charcoal-colored coat began to shine. She managed to briefly stand on her own, her legs splayed and quivering, before flopping on her belly. But after a few more days of care, she was hobbling to the door to nuzzle Anna when she came home from work. And, judging from a broken pendulum clock that remained in the same state of disrepair on a workbench, Anna knew that Norbie had forgone much of his work to care for Nia. Seeing Norbie's selfless compassion reminded Anna of how he'd cared for her after Mutter died. Now, more than ever, she was grateful to have Norbie as her *vater*.

Anna straightened her bed and dressed for work. She helped Nia down the stairs to the kitchen, where Norbie was reading a newspaper and eating breakfast.

"Good morning," Anna said.

Norbie put down his newspaper. "I made you toast and bark coffee. The brew is better than the last batch, but it still tastes like wood tea."

"*Danke*." Anna poured a cup of coffee, the color of blanched hazelnut, from a pot on the stove. She sat at the table and nibbled on her toasted black bread.

Nia hobbled to Norbie and nuzzled his leg.

He patted Nia and looked at Anna. "Are you sure she's healthy enough to spend a day at the school?" he asked, a timbre of sadness in his voice.

You're going to miss her, Anna thought. "Her paws need more time to heal, but my supervisor wants to see how she's recovering."

Norbie nodded.

Anna had provided Rolf Fleck with daily verbal progress reports on Nia's health. However, after two weeks, his patience on Nia's recovery had grown thin, and he insisted on examining the dog for himself. She hoped that, despite the pressure to produce a supply of dogs for training, he would allow more time for Nia's recuperation.

"Our first veteran arrives today," Anna said. "His name is Paul Feyen."

"That's wonderful news," he said. "Will there be others joining him?"

"Not in the first class," Anna said. "Fleck wants to keep it small to allow time for the trainers to learn and make adjustments."

"When is the next class?" Norbie asked.

"Eight weeks," Anna said. "Enough time for Nia to recover and be enrolled in class."

Norbie rubbed Nia's head. "I have two months to spoil you."

Nia licked Norbie's hand.

"We should treat her like a working guide dog, rather than a pet," Anna said. "We mustn't get too attached to her. It's only a matter of time before she's gone."

Nia's eyes glanced between Anna and Norbie.

Norbie patted Nia and placed his hands on his lap. "Okay."

A bit of guilt fluttered in Anna's stomach. Like Norbie, she'd spoiled Nia with cuddles and naps on her bed.

"Will you be working with the veteran?" Norbie asked.

"*Nein,*" she said, attempting to hide her disappointment. "My duties are limited to assisting trainers and caring for dogs."

Norbie took a gulp of coffee. "They should be allowing you to do more."

"I like my work," she said.

"I'm sure you do," he said. "But I think that you'd make a grand dog teacher. Right, Nia?"

Nia perked her head.

Anna sipped her coffee. Despite her proclamation that she was content with her role, she aspired to be a trainer. She loved everything about guide dogs, and the prospect that these beautiful, intelligent animals were destined to be a prosthesis for the eyes of blind veterans. She took every opportunity to attentively survey the work of trainers. The manner in which they judged a dog's temperament. The assessments and tests they administered to the dogs. Obedience commands. The steps they took to induct an untrained dog to a class-standard canine. Advanced training and obstacle work. But by far the most impressive work, to Anna, was intelligent disobedience training, which was when a guide dog learned to disobey a command for the safety of a handler, such as being ordered to cross a busy street. Each evening, Anna recorded her observations in a journal that she kept at her bedside. Her heart and mind were awakened to the incredible feats that the guide dogs performed and, more than anything, she wanted to be part of restoring a disabled person's life. *Perhaps someday I'll get a chance to train with them.*

Strikes of chimes, bells, and rings erupted in the workshop, and then abruptly stopped.

6:30 a.m. Anna paused, waiting for another strike. "Did you fix the grandfather clock?"

"*Ja,*" Norbie said, smiling.

A loud chime sounded.

Norbie sighed. "Confounded pendulum disc."

"We need to leave." Anna stood and patted Nia. "Ready?"

Nia stood. She raised her lame front paw, giving her the appearance of a hunting dog.

"Don't you want to give her something to eat?" Norbie asked.

"I'll feed her at school."

Norbie pointed. "I packed you a lunch."

"*Danke.*" She retrieved a paper sack from the counter. As she turned, Norbie folded his arms and peered out the kitchen window. His plate was empty of bread, and Nia was licking her snout. "I know what you did."

Norbie patted his belly "She needs it more than I do."

Anna fought back a smile and kissed him on the cheek. She helped Nia down the steps and waited outside until Emmi and a trainer, who was driving a horse-drawn wagon, picked them up. They arrived at the guide dog school at 7:00 a.m., precisely as Fleck required.

In the barn, Nia hobbled from stall to stall, greeting the other dogs. Tails wagged. Sniffing noses poked through the gaps in the stalls. As Anna was dishing turnip feed into tins, Emmi scurried to her and said, "Fleck's coming."

Anxiousness flooded Anna's stomach. She dropped the scoop into the bin.

"Where is she?" Fleck asked, entering the barn.

Anna retrieved Nia, resting near a pen with two shepherds.

Fleck frowned. "She's limping."

She's walking. "Nia is doing much better. She's gained weight and—"

"She can't train if she's lame." Fleck grabbed a leash from a hook and attached it to Nia's collar. He examined each of her paws, and then led her around the barn.

Nia, unable to place weight on her front paw, hobbled over the ground on three legs.

Fleck tossed the leash to Anna. "We don't have the luxury of feeding dogs that cannot work."

I will not let you euthanize her. Anna squeezed the leash, attempting to bury her fear. "She only needs time to recover."

"We do not have time, Fräulein Zeller," he said firmly.

"Herr Fleck," Emmi said, stepping to Anna's side. "It some-times takes months for a soldier's trench-damaged feet to heal. I have no reason to believe that the recovery time would be shorter for dogs."

Fleck smoothed his mustache with his fingers.

"Battle-blinded soldiers are flooding hospitals," Anna said, mustering her confidence. "There will not be enough dogs for them. In the months and years ahead, you might need every dog in Germany."

Fleck retrieved a metal case from his pocket, pulled out a ciga-rette, and lit it.

"Two weeks ago, Nia was unable to walk," Anna said. "She's made tremendous strides with her health. I'll have her ready to train by the next class."

Fleck took a drag and exhaled smoke through his nose. "Pair her with another dog and place her in a stall."

"Okay," Anna said. "But—"

"But what?" he asked, his voice impatient.

Anna swallowed. *Harbor your heart*, Norbie's voice echoed in her mind. "If you want to ensure her recovery, she should con-tinue under my care, day and night."

He flicked ash from his cigarette.

"With all due respect, Herr Fleck," Emmi said, "sleeping on the cold ground might cause a setback with her paws."

"Very well." Fleck looked at Anna. "Since you insist on saving this dog, I expect you to feed her with your own food."

I'm already feeding her our rations, Anna thought, but held her tongue. "*Ja*, sir."

Fleck turned and left the building.

"*Danke*," Anna said.

"You did most of the persuading," Emmi said.

Anna hugged her. "I couldn't do this without you."

"Of course you could." Emmi released Anna and smiled. "But it's nice to feel needed."

The clopping of hooves compelled them to step to the door-way. In the courtyard, a horse-drawn wagon slowed to a stop. The driver helped a man, holding a cane and wearing a gray uniform bare of military insignias, out of the wagon. His eyes were dark and motionless, and scars covered his brows and cheekbones.

"That must be Paul Feyen," Anna said.

"*Ja*," Emmi said. "They always look so young."

Anna nodded.

Nia hobbled to Anna and nudged her hand with her nose.

Anna stroked Nia's head. Her tension eased.

Fleck greeted Paul with a handshake, and then introduced him to the trainers and several guide dogs. A smile spread over Paul's face as he patted a dog.

"You think Fleck will introduce us?" Anna asked.

"Maybe, but I wouldn't count on it." Emmi retrieved a shovel and began cleaning a stall.

Nia stared at the group in the yard.

Anna kneeled to Nia and whispered, "Someday, you'll be helping a veteran like him."

Nia wagged her tail.

She ran her fingers through the dog's fur. "We're going to practice every night. You will learn everything the other dogs are doing. And when you're well, there will be no chance of Fleck expelling you from school."

CHAPTER 11

OLDENBURG, GERMANY—OCTOBER 1, 1916

Anna retrieved a harness from a hook on the barn wall and approached Nia, standing on all four paws.

"You've made good progress over the past two months," Anna said, patting the dog on the head. "But you have much to accomplish to become a guide dog."

Nia wagged her tail.

Anna peeked through a warped glass window. On the obstacle course, Fleck and the trainers were working with Paul and his guide dog. With the exception of Emmi, who was trimming a shepherd's toenails, she and Nia were alone in the barn.

"Let's squeeze in a little practice," Anna said, placing the harness on Nia.

"You better not let Fleck catch you doing that," Emmi said, peeking over a stall.

"He won't if you do a good job as a lookout," Anna said.

"Okay, but make it quick." Emmi scooted her stool near a window and resumed grooming the shepherd. The sporadic sound of toenail clips filled the air.

Anna placed a series of buckets and a shovel over the floor. She fetched a walking stick and tied a blindfold over her eyes, blacking out light. Clasping the handle of the harness she said, "Forward."

Nia padded ahead, veering around a bucket to give Anna ample clearance, and then navigated around the remaining obstacles.

Anna gave a downward and backward jerk on the handle.

Nia stopped.

Anna removed her blindfold, kneeled, and stroked Nia's back. "Good girl."

Nia swished her tail.

Emmi stood from her stool and pretended to clap her hands.

Anna's chest swelled with pride.

For the past several weeks, Anna worked with Nia each evening and on her days off from work. Most of her free time was consumed with healing Nia's paw and her surreptitious training. Using a homemade harness, which Norbie constructed from scrap leather and metal tubing, she taught Nia to navigate a mini obstruction course, made from chairs and broken clock remnants, in Norbie's workshop. After Nia mastered the skill of guiding Anna, blindfolded and holding a walking stick, to ascend and descend the steep stairs of their three-story home, they ventured outside. The trainers typically used blindfolds and sticks to simulate the behavior of a blind person, but Anna refrained from using the items in public. She feared that news of her training might reach Fleck, who had strict rules on assigning instructors to dogs. Although the homemade harness was rather unique, she believed that she could, if questioned by Fleck, provide the excuse that she was merely taking Nia for exercise, which was part of her and Emmi's responsibilities at the guide dog school.

Together, Anna and Nia traversed the cobblestone streets of Oldenburg. Mimicking the actions of the trainers, Anna taught Nia to stop at curbs, both up-curbs and down-curbs, as well as to navigate crowded streets, all the while giving ample room to avoid pedestrians. Her training did, however, come with mistakes. On one occasion, Nia attempted to cross a road in front of an oncoming wagon, and to prevent the collision Anna jerked backward on the harness and said, "*Nein*. Bad dog." Anna disliked giving reprimands, which were tactics used by the trainers, but it enabled Nia to learn how to safely guide a partner across the street. Also, after some trial and error, Nia learned to disobey Anna's commands to go forward when encountering traffic or excavation on sidewalks. Although Nia was intelligent and eager to please, her learning curve for guide dog training was shortened, Anna believed, by her ambulance dog experience.

Despite regaining use of her front right paw, Nia often limped—as if she had a thorn stuck deep in her pad—when subjected to consecutive hours of training. Anna worried that Nia's frail paw was a chronic ailment that might never go away, but neither she nor Emmi expressed concern to Fleck. Instead, they predicted that Nia would, in time, make a full recovery.

Based on Anna and Emmi's favorable prognosis of Nia's condition, Fleck permitted Nia to begin working with trainers. But after a few hours of drills the dog's paw began to rise, and Fleck had her removed. Although he was impressed with Nia's performance on the obstacle course, he viewed her as feeble. As days passed, Fleck grew reluctant to include Nia with training, which hindered her ability to form a bond with any of the trainers. Anna knew, from her time at the school, that it was crucial for a trainer and a guide dog to form a strong partnership. This relationship was critical, since it enabled the trainer to create trust between the dog and a blind veteran.

Nia was the odd dog out, like a fragile child who was shunned by classmates to participate in a hopscotch game of *Himmel und Hölle* (Heaven and Hell). Therefore, Nia spent much of her time in the barn, lying with her chin on the ground, while Anna and Emmi shuttled healthy dogs to and from the obstacle course. Anna yearned for Fleck to allow Nia more time with the trainers, but as summer turned to autumn and the war raged on, time was running out for Nia.

"Let's try this again," Anna said, glancing over the makeshift obstacle course inside the barn. She covered her eyes with the blindfold, and then clasped the handle to Nia's harness. "Forward."

Nia padded ahead, veering away from a bucket.

Anna tapped her stick over the ground, searching for obstacles.

"Fleck is coming!" Emmi hissed.

Anna's skin turned cold. She dropped the harness handle.

Struggling to remove her blindfold, she tripped over a shovel and fell. A twinge shot through her forearms. She pulled down her blindfold and worked to remove Nia's harness.

Emmi darted to Nia and unfastened a buckle.

Nia licked Anna's ear.

"Not now," Anna whispered, loosening the harness.

The clack of jackboots grew.

Anna's pulsed pounded. She slipped off Nia's harness, shot to the wall, and placed it on a hook.

Emmi tossed the walking stick and shovel into a stall. She turned to Anna. Her eyes widened. "Blindfold."

Anna removed the blindfold hanging from her neck, and shot her hands behind her back.

Emmi clasped Nia's collar, and they ducked into a stall.

"Fräulein Zeller," Fleck said, entering the barn.

"*Ja*, sir," Anna said, straightening her spine.

"Dr. Stalling and members of the Ambulance Dogs Association will be arriving this afternoon for a reception in honor of our first graduate. There will be a photographer, so I want things to be in order." His eyes locked on the buckets on the floor.

Anna's mouth turned dry.

"You can start by cleaning up this mess."

She nodded.

"Find Frau Bauer, sweep out the back of the building, and then clear the field of dog piles."

"Of course, sir." Anna squeezed the blindfold.

He turned and left.

Anna exhaled, feeling as if she'd come within inches of a speeding train.

Nia poked her snout through a gap in the stall.

Emmi stood from her hiding spot. "Maybe you should limit your obstacle training to Norbie's workshop."

Anna nodded.

In the afternoon, over a dozen members of the Ambulance Dogs Association, including Dr. Stalling, arrived at the school. There was a demonstration with trainers and shepherds on the obstacle course. Afterward, a brief ceremony, lacking cake or celebratory drinks, was held in the barn to recognize Paul Feyen, the first graduate of the guide dog school. Although Anna and Emmi had limited interaction with Paul, due to Fleck's strict protocol on roles and responsibilities, they'd gotten to know him by caring for his shepherd. Paul was gentle and soft-spoken. He worked tirelessly with Fleck and the trainers, and he developed an affectionate bond with his shepherd. He'd come to Oldenburg a broken man who'd been blinded by an exploding shell. Now, he would be leaving with confidence, a loyal companion, and the means to live an independent life. Despite her supporting role, Anna was grateful to play a part in shaping his future. And as Paul posed for a photograph with his dog, a sweet black shepherd with rather large, bat-like ears, Anna beamed with pride.

"Fräulein Zeller," Dr. Stalling said, approaching Anna. "How are you?"

"Well, Doctor," Anna said. "And you?"

"Splendid." He gestured to Paul, patting his dog. "It's a new beginning."

"For both of them," she said.

"Indeed."

"The world's first guide dog school," Anna said. "Congratulations."

He smiled. "This would not have been possible without everyone's effort." With eyes filled with gratitude, he looked at Anna. "*Danke* for your service."

"It's an honor."

"How are you adjusting to your new work?" he asked.

"Good," she said, despite her longing to train shepherds.

"The hospital staff often inquires of you and Emmi. If either of you should ever wish to return, please let me know."

Anna's role as a nurse felt like a lifetime ago. *I was quite bad at giving injections and measuring medicine.* "That's very kind of you, Doctor, but I'm quite happy here."

"I'm glad," he said. "Here at this school, we are restoring sight with living mobility aids."

Through the corner of Anna's eyes, she saw Fleck approaching. Her heart rate spiked.

"Excuse me, Dr. Stalling," Fleck said, stepping to them. "May I have a word with Fräulein Zeller?"

Her skin prickled.

"Of course." Stalling tipped his hat to Anna, and then mingled into the crowd.

"Come with me," Fleck said.

She swallowed, and then followed him outside.

"I have a problem," he said, turning to her.

Oh, no. Anna clasped her arms.

"Several veterans will be arriving in Oldenburg for training," he said. "There's an issue with a boarding assignment for one of the men."

"Oh." Anna's shoulder muscles relaxed. "My *vater* and I have plenty of room—"

"I wasn't finished," he said.

"Sorry, sir."

"A trainer, whom I will not name, prefers not to have one of the veterans in his home." Fleck retrieved a cigarette from his pocket but made no effort to light it. "Because he's a Jew."

A man fought and sacrificed his eyes for our country, Anna thought, *yet he's not permitted to sleep in a trainer's home because of his religious faith.* A burning bile stirred inside her.

"If the other trainers express a similar reservation, he will stay with me. I have no apprehension of having a Jew in my home. However, before I attempt to realign the boarding arrangements, I wanted to inquire if you would be willing to board him."

Anna was glad to hear that Fleck, if needed, was willing to house the man, but she was disheartened to know that a trainer was intolerant of Jews. She wondered, although briefly, if Fleck was worried that other trainers, if asked, would express similar concern. Burying her thoughts, she looked at him and said, "Of course. He can stay with me."

"Do you need to speak with your *vater*?"

"*Nein*," Anna said. "Like me, he will be honored to have him in our home."

"I'm glad this is acceptable." Fleck placed his cigarette back into a silver case, and then rejoined the reception.

Anna entered the barn. With her eyes, she glanced to the trainers and wondered how anyone who nurtured the blind could harbor anti-Semitic beliefs. She hoped that this was an isolated case,
and that Fleck would have no tolerance for prejudiced behavior
from the trainers. Having lost her desire to celebrate, she slipped
away to a stall where Nia was curled on a pile of straw. She kneeled
and stroked the dog's back.

"You wouldn't treat someone badly because they were different, would you?" Anna whispered.

Nia nuzzled Anna's leg.

Anna ran her fingers through Nia's fur. *If people were more like
dogs, maybe the world would be blind to bigotry.* She patted Nia until
the congregation dispersed.

CHAPTER 12

LILLE, FRANCE—OCTOBER 1, 1916

Bruno, his uniform speckled with dried mud and blood, exited the train at the Lille station to begin a two-day leave. On the horizon, a scarlet sunset created the illusion that the western front had been set ablaze. Despite leaving the battlefield, twenty kilometers away, screams and shellfire echoed inside his head.

It had been two months since he'd left Lille to train regiments on the use of the German Empire's new weapon—gas artillery shells. Under the close supervision of Haber, Bruno schooled artillery units on the use of chlorine and phosgene shells, which looked much like regular explosives, except for the green cross painted on the base of the shell. Because chlorine omitted a detectible green gas, as well as a strong pineapple and pepper odor, phosgene had become the poison of choice. Being a colorless gas with a smell like musty hay, phosgene was less detectable than chlorine. Also, phosgene was far more deadly due to its power to react with proteins in the alveoli of the lungs, destroying the blood-air barrier, leading to suffocation. However, phosgene did have a flaw; it could sometimes take up to two days for symptoms of the poison to manifest. Therefore, an enemy soldier could continue to fight until they drowned from the fluid in their lungs. Haber, who was determined to win the chemical arms race, assured Bruno that chemists would soon be devising deadlier variations of poison gas.

Death is death, regardless of how it is inflicted, Haber's voice had chimed in Bruno's head as he watched colossal guns fire gas shells toward enemy lines. It sickened him to think that he had sold his soul to Haber. Equally, he was revolted by the fact that his family's business was profiting from producing nocuous weapons for the government. There was little he could do, he believed, but fight to survive the war and pray that Anna would never learn of the atrocities he was ordered to commit.

The suicide of Haber's wife, Clara, weighed heavy on Bruno's conscience. Like a festering sore that would never heal, Bruno feared that Anna would someday discover what he'd done. *When we marry and move to Frankfurt, how will I keep my war duties and my family's role in supplying the army with poison gas a secret?* He was plagued with horrid dreams of Anna—her eyes filled with tears— raising his Imperial German military revolver, and then placing the tip to her breastbone. Each night, he woke with his body trembling and his clothes saturated with cold sweat. He thought that the visions would subside with time, but as each day passed and showers of poison shells rained down on the enemy, his feeling of dread escalated.

Fear of hurting Anna was not the only thing that had shaken Bruno. His new assignment, which led him along the French and Belgium front, often placed him under enemy shellfire. The German artillery guns, which fired both explosive and gas shells, were a prime target of British, French, and Canadian forces. Eight days ago, Allied forces initiated a bombardment while Bruno was training a group of soldiers on the proper handling of phosgene gas shells. As screaming bombs hailed down from the sky, Bruno grabbed a soldier by the arm and leaped into a bunker. An explosion quaked the ground. Bruno, compelled to aid yowling men, emerged from the bunker and discovered a massive crater where a howitzer once stood. Chunks of iron and mutilated bodies covered the ground. He dragged a soldier, who was moaning and clasping his rib cage, into the bunker. Using his hands, Bruno applied pressure to a hole in the man's chest, where he was missing several ribs. A steaming shard of metal protruded from his hip. Bruno shouted for a medic, but his voice was dwarfed by the bombardment. As minutes passed, the metallic smell of blood grew, and the soldier's whimpers dwindled. He held the man until he bled out.

Bruno, attempting to shed the macabre images from his mind, made his way through the streets of Lille. As he passed a café, boisterous chatter of drunken German soldiers permeated the air. Most of the soldiers, staying in Lille while on their way to or from the front, sought bars and brothels. But Bruno, weary and hungry, craved the sequestered sanctuary of the bourgeois house that Haber had arranged for him. Although he was required to inspect railway shipments of gas shells during his brief military leave, he planned to spend much of his time in his room.

As he turned a corner, the grand, three-story home came into view. Near the front gate, the woman caretaker, whom he recognized by her svelte stature and auburn hair, was speaking with two soldiers. *Celeste.* A memory of the woman serving wine to Haber flashed in his head.

One of the soldiers, a mustached and broad-shouldered sergeant, clasped Celeste's arm and pulled her to his chest.

Bruno's skin turned warm. He squeezed the handle of his leather case and quickened his pace.

"*Non*," Celeste said, pressing her palms to the man's tunic.

"Leave her alone," Bruno ordered.

"Go to hell," the sergeant said, his back to Bruno.

The second soldier, a corporal with a jagged scar on his lower lip, turned his head. His eyes locked on the insignias on Bruno's uniform, and he slapped his comrade on the shoulder.

The sergeant released Celeste. He turned, and then snapped to attention. "I am sorry, sir. I wouldn't have spoken to you like that if I had known you were an officer."

Bruno approached the sergeant. An odor of sweat and beer permeated his nose. *Drunken bastard.* He fought away the urge to strike him. "She works for Germany."

The sergeant's eyes filled with fear.

"She billets officers," Bruno said. "Perhaps you would like to explain to them why you are harassing a woman who cares for them."

"I—I am sorry, sir."

"I am not the person you should be apologizing to."

"My apologies, *fräulein*. I meant you no harm."

Celeste lowered her head.

"Return to your barrack," Bruno ordered. "If I should see either of you on the streets of Lille again, you will be severely punished."

The soldiers saluted and left.

"*Merci*, Herr Wahler," Celeste said, looking at Bruno. "However, I am perfectly capable of taking care of myself."

He nodded, feeling abashed by the soldiers' conduct.

"Come inside," she said. "Your room is prepared."

Bruno followed her into the house and shut the door.

Her eyes gravitated to bloodstains on the sleeves of his jacket. "I'll prepare you a bath, *monsieur*. The tub is in a room next to the kitchen. Leave your dirty uniform, and I'll clean it."

"Okay."

"Will you be going out for dinner?"

"*Nein*."

"I'll prepare something to eat."

"That will not be necessary," he said.

"I'll place something in the parlor, in the event you are hungry later." She turned and headed toward the kitchen.

Bruno scaled the stairs, boards creaking under his boots, and entered his room, which contained a four-poster bed and a stand with a porcelain water bowl. While he waited for the tub to be filled, he removed a stack of Anna's letters from his leather case, slumped in a chair, and read.

> Bruno,
> I miss you, my darling. I pray for your safety and for the war to end. Convincing myself that time and distance are the only things keeping us apart is an arduous endeavor. Do you know when your leave will be? Perhaps I could persuade my supervisor to grant me time away from work. If so, could we visit your family? The longer we are engaged without me meeting your parents,

the more I worry that they will not approve of me.

Bruno shifted in his seat. *If she learns the truth about my duties and family's role in supplying poison gas, her feelings for me will change.* He hoped that by the time he was awarded his two-week leave, he'd find a solution to the dilemma.

Nia is recovering, but she continues to refrain from placing weight on her right front paw. I'm anxious for you to meet her, assuming you arrive home before she's assigned to a veteran. Nia is lovely, affectionate, and incredibly intelligent. Norbie spoils her with attention. I'm smitten with her, and I'm afraid I'll be heartbroken when she departs.

Bruno rubbed stubble on his chin, pondering how different Anna and Norbie's relationship was to that of his own family.

Good night, for now, my darling.
Anna

I wish things could be different for us. He put away the letter, and then retrieved a straight razor and clean uniform from his case. In a small, windowless room off the kitchen, he bathed in a tarnished copper tub. Although the water was cold, it was far better than his last bath in an old wine barrel, of which the water was used, over and over, by over a dozen officers until the water turned the color of the trenches. Using a chunk of lye soap, which omitted a strong ammonia odor, he washed his oily hair and body. He scrubbed until his skin turned raw but was unable to cleanse the horrid visions that lingered in his brain.

Dressed and clean-shaven, he followed an aroma of sizzling sausage to the kitchen, where Celeste was standing by a stove. His stomach ached with hunger.

"Have you changed your mind about eating?" Celeste asked. Using a fork with two long tines, she rolled sausage over a hot pan.

"*Ja*," Bruno said. He left the kitchen and sat at a table in the parlor. A moment later, Celeste delivered a plate of sausage and roasted potatoes, and then retrieved a bottle of wine from the cellar.

"Will there be more officers staying with you this evening?" he asked.

"*Non, monsieur.*" She poured wine into a glass.

"*Danke.*" He took a sip. The wine was dry and crisp, with a hint of toasted vanilla. "Have you eaten?"

"I will have something after I clean your uniform." She placed the bottle on the table.

A decision burned inside him. He craved solitude, yet he wanted to know more about what life was like for Celeste and the citizens of Lille. Before he changed his mind, he stood from his chair and said, "Would you like to join me?"

She clasped her hands. "I only made enough for you."

"I'm not that hungry," he lied. "We can share the food."

She glanced to the wall, as if she were pondering his offer, and then nodded. She retrieved a plate setting and wineglass, and then sat, draping a napkin over her lap.

Bruno cut the sausage in half. He placed it, along with a helping of potatoes, on Celeste's plate and poured wine into her glass.

She forked a bit of potato.

He chewed a piece of sausage. Containing spice and fat, it was far more savory than the dry field sausage which tasted like baked leather. "It's good."

She nodded with her eyes lowered.

For several minutes, they ate without speaking. Utensils clicked against porcelain plates.

His mind raced with what to say. "Do you often encounter ill-behaved soldiers?"

She took a drink of wine. "More often than I would like."

"I'm sorry."

"*Merci.*" As she attempted to cut her sausage, the knife slipped from her fingers and clanged against the plate.

"Do I make you uncomfortable?"

"*Non*," she said, her eyes avoiding him.

"Your German is quite good. Where did you learn to speak it?"

"When I was a young, my parents took me and my younger sisters on summer vacations in Switzerland."

A childhood memory of Bruno's *mutter*—abandoning him with nannies and spending months at a time in a Swiss chalet—flashed in his head. He buried the image and asked, "Is your family in Lille?"

"Paris," she said. "It's where I'm from."

"Oh," he said. "Why are you in Lille?"

She paused, rubbing a finger over her glass.

"It's okay, if you don't want to tell me." He forked a piece of potato, crusted with bits of caramelized onion. "You're an exceptional cook. It's been many months since I've had something—"

"I was visiting my aunt Gabrielle when the Germans invaded Lille," she said, looking up from her plate. "We were unable to make it out of the city." She sipped wine. "This is her home."

"It's grand," Bruno said. "I assume it caught the attention of the army to billet officers."

"*Oui*," she said.

"Where is Gabrielle?" he asked.

Celeste squeezed the stem of her glass with her fingers. "She was taken away."

"Why?"

She took a gulp of wine. "A few months ago, twenty thousand women and girls were rounded up by the Germans and relocated to rural areas of occupied France."

Oh, no. A wave of repugnance flooded his body.

"They're coerced to perform farm labor to feed your country." She took a jagged breath. "Many of the women were dragged away, kicking and screaming, by soldiers with bayonets."

He ran a hand through his hair, attempting to comprehend the enormity of the mass roundup. *The British naval blockade is depleting Germany's food supply, and now we're resorting to forced labor to feed our people.* Despite the dire circumstances, he detested his country's solution to nourish a starving population.

She took a swig of wine, as if to gather her courage. "To shame and degrade the women, the Germans forced them to undergo gynecological examinations."

A revolting shock surged through him. "I—I'm deeply sorry," he said.

Her hands trembled as she pushed away her plate.

"I wish there was something I could have done."

"If you'd been here during the roundup, could you have stopped it?"

"*Nein.*" He refilled her glass as his mind struggled to find the right words. "You were fortunate not be taken."

"Luck had nothing to do with it." She crossed her arms. "A *hauptmann*, who had billeted here, arranged for me to remain in the house as caretaker on the condition that I be his courtesan."

Oh, God.

Her eyes welled with tears.

He gripped the table. "Did he hurt you?"

"Not anymore." She rubbed her hands, as if she were spreading ointment. "He was killed at the front."

Bruno's veins flowed with disgust. *Atrocities are not limited to the battlefield. I cannot begin to imagine the suffering that you've endured.* "You must hate us."

Her eyes met his. "*Oui.*"

"I don't blame you," he said, his voice fading to a whisper.

She dabbed her eyes with a napkin. "I say too much."

"It's okay."

She took a deep breath and exhaled. "If you're willing, *monsieur*, tell me something about you."

"I'm from Frankfurt," he said, his mind still reeling from Celeste's story. "Prior to the war, I was a chemist in my father's ink and dye business."

She sipped wine. "Are you married?"

"I have a fiancée in Oldenburg. Her name is Anna. We met after I sustained an injury on the front. She was a nurse who mended my wounds."

Celeste smiled.

"Do you have someone waiting for you in Paris?" he asked.

She shook her head. "Only my *maman*, papa, and sisters. I miss them terribly."

"You'll see them after the war."

She ran her finger over the table. "But I'm afraid that they'll think different of me."

"Why?"

"I'm a collaborator," she said. "In Lille, I'm the former mistress to a fallen enemy officer. I'm viewed no differently than the French prostitutes who work in the German brothels. Regardless of which side wins the war, my family will eventually learn of what I've done, and they'll disown me."

"They'll understand." *You collaborated to survive.* He appreciated Celeste's trust in him, and her courage to speak candidly. But most of all, her fear of being rejected by her family resonated with him. As if by reflex, he said, "I worry that Anna will spurn me, too."

Her eyebrows raised. "May I ask why?"

He swirled his wine, pondering if he should continue. Fueled by alcohol and Celeste's display of vulnerability, he looked at her and said, "Because of the horrible things I've done."

"It's war," she said. "She'll forgive you for what you did."

A flash of gassed corpses, their faces blue and bellies bloated. *Death is death, regardless of how it is inflicted*, Haber's mantra replayed in his head. "I do not believe that will be possible."

She smoothed her skirt and placed a hand on Bruno's fingers.

His skin tingled.

"Perhaps after the war," she said, "we'll find absolution for our sins."

Bruno nodded.

"Good night, Herr Wahler. *Merci* for inviting me to join you." Celeste stood and carried the plates to the kitchen.

Bruno finished the last of the wine, and then went to his room. Shaken from his conversation with Celeste, he was unable to sleep. He retrieved a pencil and paper from his case to write a letter to Anna, but the words never came.

PART 3

INTERMEZZO

THE TURNIP WINTER

CHAPTER 13

OLDENBURG, GERMANY—DECEMBER 2, 1916

Anna, bundled in a knee-length wool coat with Nia at her side, waited in anticipation for a battle-blinded veteran named Maximilian Benesch to arrive at the Oldenburg train station. She knew little about him, except that he was a Jewish soldier from Leipzig who was blinded while fighting at the front. She'd spent the past few days organizing the kitchen and spare bedroom, as well as rearranging living room furniture, to create a conducive environment for the visually impaired. Even Norbie, who was fond of the clutter in his workshop, had pushed away workbenches and display cases to create a straight path between the storefront door and the stairs to their upper-floor home.

The evening train was running late. To occupy her time, she retrieved an envelope from her purse. She unfolded Bruno's letter, his first correspondence in over two weeks, and read it for the second time.

> *Dearest Anna,*
> *I'm sorry for my lack of communication, my love. I've been deterred with training artillery troops and traveling to and from an armament depot in France. It pains me*

*to think that you might be worried about
my safety. I hope you will forgive me. In the
coming weeks, I promise to find a way to
write more frequently.*

Anna patted Nia. *I miss receiving his letters, and the poems he wrote
for me when we first met.* Guilt swelled up in her heart. *It's selfish of
me to crave attention when he's fighting for survival.* She shook away
her thoughts and continued reading.

*The death and shelling can cause one to
go mad. I am fortunate that my duties allow
me a reprieve from the fighting at the front.
I gaze at your photograph often. Thoughts
of you protect me, like a shield, from the
emotional stresses of war. I long to hold you
in my arms, and to begin our life together
when the war is over.
    The Wahler family business is thriving,
despite our country's suffering, and it will
provide us a comfortable life. After the war,
we'll have no financial worries, my darling.
We'll purchase a grand home in Frankfurt
to raise a family. The rationing will be over,
food will be plentiful, and we'll eat until we
grow old and fat.*

Anna took a deep breath and exhaled. She assumed that she
would move to Frankfurt after the war. But they hadn't discussed
her work at the guide dog school. *How can I leave Oldenburg when
so many dogs will be needed to for battle-blinded soldiers?* She stroked
Nia's ears and decided to worry about it later.

*There is the possibility that I will be
granted leave in the coming months,
perhaps in January. If so, I will return to*

*Oldenburg, and we will celebrate the new
year together.
  Affectionately,
  Bruno*

A train whistle blew. Anna folded the letter and placed it inside her purse. Wheels screeched over steel rails. Thick puffs of steam and smoke, like miniature storm clouds, spewed from the locomotive. The train slowed to a stop and the vapor dispersed. Carriage doors opened and passengers exited, one by one, onto the landing.

Tired and hungry from her day working at the guide dog school, she stood on her toes and scanned the crowd. An acrid scent of burnt coal filled her nostrils. "Do you see him?" she asked, glancing at Nia.

Nia perked her ears.

The throng of people, a mixture of civilians and military personnel, scattered through the station. After most of the passengers had disembarked the train, a soldier emerged from a carriage. Walking backward down the steps, he helped a man—holding a walking stick and wearing a charcoal-colored military trench coat—from the carriage.

"There," Anna said. She clasped Nia's harness and approached the men. "*Hallo*. Maximilian Benesch?"

"*Ja*." Max released the soldier's arm, and then placed the tip of his walking stick on the ground. "Please, call me Max."

"I'm Anna." She paused, debating whether she should attempt to shake his hand and decided against it when he clasped his walking stick with both hands, like a sheepman unwilling to part with his crook. Unlike many soldiers who sported mustaches or beards, Max was clean-shaven, save a bit of stubble on his chin and slightly uneven sideburns. He was tall and lean with pronounced cheekbones. Dark brown hair, a bit long for a soldier, hung from under his cap.

"Here's your luggage." The soldier, appearing as if he was running late for an engagement, placed a leather suitcase at Max's feet. "Good luck to you."

"*Danke.*" Max stared ahead.

The soldier tipped his cap to Anna and left.

Nia sniffed Max's leg and wagged her tail.

He shifted his weight.

"This is Nia, a soon-to-be guide dog," she said. "Would you like to pet her?"

He hesitated, cupping the top of his stick with his hands.

Maybe he's tired from the trip. "You'll be working with guide dogs for the next two months. I think it is best that we properly get acquainted." She gently clasped his hand and shook it, noticing his firm but gentle grip. "I'm Anna Zeller, your host while you train in Oldenburg."

The lines in his face softened. "It's nice to meet you, Anna."

She placed his palm on the dog's head. "This is Nia."

Max stroked the dog's ears and smiled. "*Hallo*, Nia."

Nia looked up and panted, her tongue hanging from her mouth.

"Will I be working with her?" Max asked.

"*Nein*," Anna said, attempting to hide her disappointment. "Nia's not quite ready for training. Rolf Fleck, the supervisor, will decide which shepherd will be assigned to you." She looked at him. "It's a twenty-minute walk to my home. Would you like to hold my arm, or would you like to clasp the handle to Nia's harness?"

Max picked up his suitcase and tapped the stick to the pavement. "I'm accustomed to using this."

He'll soon be walking with a guide dog; no need for me to put him to work tonight, she thought.

Anna, providing verbal directions, guided Max through the train station. Outside, they traversed the sidewalks, illuminated by a dull, flickering glow of gas streetlamps. Frigid air turned their breath into mist. She attempted to initiate conversation, but Max—focused on navigating the craggy cobblestone—provided cursory responses to her questions. They spoke little, other than for guidance on the route, until they neared Anna's street.

"What's wrong with Nia?" Max asked.

Anna squeezed the harness handle. "She's recovering."

"It sounds like she's limping," he said, slowing his pace.

Anna glanced to Nia, favoring her right front leg as she padded over the sidewalk. "Her paws were injured while serving as an ambulance dog at the front."

"I'm sorry," he said. "Trenches?"

"*Ja*," Anna said. "How did you know?"

"Even with leather boots and frequent changes of socks, the mud wreaked havoc on men's feet. I assume the trenches were even worse for dogs."

Anna slowed her pace and patted Nia's back. "Her front paw becomes tender after prolonged walks. However, she's getting better." *But not fast enough for Fleck.*

He stopped and inhaled, as if he were catching his breath. "It's okay, Nia. I sometimes get fatigued, too."

Nia glanced to him and limped ahead.

"Here we are," Anna said, reaching the door. She undid the lock with a key from her purse and guided Max inside. Ticktocks thrummed in her ears.

Max perked his head.

"My *vater*, Norbie, is a clockmaker," she said. "We live above his workshop."

He nodded and placed his stick to his chest.

She led him upstairs to the kitchen, where Norbie was warming up leftover soup for dinner. A sulfuric turnipy smell, much like overcooked cabbage, filled the air. "Vater, this is Max."

"*Hallo*." Norbie covered a steaming pot with a lid and approached Max. "I'm Norbie."

Max put down his suitcase and extended his hand.

"Welcome to our home," Norbie said, shaking his hand. "We're happy to have you stay with us."

"*Danke*," Max said.

"How was your trip?" Norbie asked.

"*Gut*," Max said.

Anna removed Nia's harness. The dog hobbled to Norbie to receive a rub under her chin, and then settled on the floor. *You'll feel better tomorrow*, Anna hoped. She took Max's coat and cap, and hung them on a rack near the stairs. "Do I have time to give Max a quick tour before dinner?"

"Absolutely," Norbie said. "I'll keep the soup warm."

Anna, like a boardinghouse host, led Max through the kitchen, pointing out the location of cupboards, stove, sink, table, and chairs. Entering the living room, she said, "On the left is a sofa and an upholstered chair, followed by a small table with a gramophone. In the corner is a *kachelofen* (tiled stove). We're low on coal, which you likely noticed by the chill in the house. You might need to wear layers to sleep."

Max nodded.

"Please, feel free to explore as much as you like."

He shuffled forward, lightly tapping his stick, and located furniture.

"You're approaching a bookcase," she said. "I was informed that you might have received instruction on reading braille. I acquired a few books through the hospital. I hope you like them."

"*Danke*. I'm sure I will." He glided his fingers over books and moved on.

"Piano."

Max paused, resting a hand on the keyboard. He tapped a few keys, producing a twangy resonance.

"It's badly out of tune, I'm afraid. It hasn't been played in years." A dull ache rose in Anna's abdomen. "It was my *mutter*'s. She died when I was a child."

"I'm sorry," Max said.

"*Danke*," she said. "Do you play?"

"I used to, but not anymore."

"Maybe you'll want to try again during your stay."

"*Nein, danke*." He removed his hand from the piano. "Where would you like me to put my things?"

"Upstairs." She led him to a third-floor spare room, which contained a bed, nightstand, and a chest of drawers. "The water closet is at the end of the hall. Please make yourself comfortable and take as much time as you need. Come down to the kitchen when you are ready to join us for dinner."

He put down his suitcase. "All right."

Anna closed the door, and then descended the stairs to the kitchen.

"Is Max settling in?" Norbie asked, placing spoons and napkins on the table.

"*Ja.*" She retrieved bowls from a cupboard and placed them on the counter. "He seems a bit sad. I know he's been through a lot, but I expected him to be enthusiastic about being here."

"Leaving his home might be difficult for him," Norbie said. "It might take some time for him to adjust."

Anna nodded.

Fifteen minutes later, Max descended the stairs to the kitchen. Nia hobbled to him and nuzzled his leg.

"Looks like you made a friend," Norbie said.

Max nodded and patted Nia.

They sat at the table—Max between Norbie and Anna—with steaming bowls of turnip soup and three thin slices of black war bread. Norbie said a brief prayer, requesting a swift end to war and famine.

"It's kind of you to share your food with me," Max said.

"You're quite welcome," Norbie said. "Anna's a remarkable cook. She can make a delectable soup from ugly turnips and scraps of potato peels."

"Vater exaggerates," Anna said, feeling appreciative for his sweet words. She took a spoonful of soup, bitter and lacking flavor.

Max took a sip. "It's good."

Anna smiled.

Norbie blew on his soup. "Anna mentioned that you are from Leipzig. Do you have parents living there?"

"*Nein,*" Max said. "They're dead."

Her breath turned shallow. "I'm sorry."

Max nodded.

"My condolences." Norbie sipped soup.

"Anna told me about your wife," Max said. "I understand that she enjoyed playing the piano."

"Very much so," Norbie said. "Helga played beautifully, and she sang like an angel."

"She sounds wonderful," Max said.

An image of sitting on her *mutter*'s lap at the piano flashed in Anna's head. She buried the memory and took a bite of soup.

"Do you live with someone in Leipzig?" Norbie asked.

"My fiancée, Wilhelmina."

"She must be happy for you to attend guide dog training," Anna said, feeling relieved to hear that Max wasn't living alone.

Max gave a small nod, and then took a bite of bread.

"Anna is engaged, too," Norbie said.

"Bruno," Anna said. "He's an *oberleutnant* at the front."

"Congratulations," Max said, his voice sincere.

For the rest of dinner, Anna spoke about Emmi, Dr. Stalling, Rolf Fleck, the trainers, and the shepherds at the guide dog school. And while she was telling Max about Paul Feyen, the first graduate of the school, her eyes gravitated to Nia, who was under the table with her chin on top of Max's boot. *She likes him.*

"Anna's a talented trainer," Norbie bragged.

She lowered her spoon. "I'm a nurse turned canine caregiver." *But someday I'll find a way to be a trainer.*

"You're far more than that," Norbie said. "You've taught Nia to follow commands, and she can guide you through town with your eyes closed." He patted Max on the shoulder. "My daughter underestimates herself, Max. She's a remarkable nurse and trainer, and someday Nia will make a faithful companion for a veteran."

Nia raised her head from Max's shoe.

"Thank you for dinner," Max said. "I'd like to wash the dishes."

"I usually wash and Anna dries," Norbie said.

"Please, I insist." Max stood and placed his napkin on the table.

"Very well." Norbie stood and pushed his chair to the table. "If you should need me, I'll be in the workshop trying to fix a grandfather clock that refuses to strike on time." He placed a hand on Max's shoulder. "The hourly chimes might keep you awake. But after a few nights, I'm quite certain you'll grow fond of them."

"I'm sure I will," Max said.

Anna cleared the table. She filled the sink and provided Max with a dishcloth. Working in tandem, Max washed and Anna dried.

"Norbie is quite supportive of you," Max said, handing her a bowl.

"*Ja,*" Anna said.

"You're lucky to have him."

Anna smiled. She wiped the bowl and placed it inside a cupboard.

He washed spoons and rinsed them in water.

Anna's mind raced. There was much that she wanted to know
about Max. *What happened to your parents? How were you injured
at the front?* Instead, she settled on a question that she believed
would be less intrusive. "What were you doing before the war?"

Max removed his hands from the water. "I was a pianist."

"Oh," Anna said.

"I graduated from the Royal Conservatory of Music of Leipzig.
I was starting a career as a classical pianist with plans to become a
composer when the war erupted."

"But you don't play anymore," Anna said, recalling his comments while tapping the keys of her *mutter*'s piano.

"True." He handed her a bowl.

"Why?" she asked. "Were your hands injured?"

"Ears."

Anna's eyes widened.

"A shell explosion damaged my eardrums."

Her skin turned cold.

"I'm no longer able to hear high-pitched sounds," he said, his
voice doleful. "It's impossible for me to detect the upper octaves
of a keyboard."

Oh, God. "I am so sorry."

He nodded and scrubbed a pot.

"Is there anything that can be done?"

"I'm afraid not."

Anna's heart sank. She finished drying the dishes, and she
showed Max, per his request, the precise location of where she
and Norbie stored kitchenware.

"Would you like to join me in the living room?" Anna asked.
"Perhaps you could try out one of the braille books, or I could read
to you."

Nia stood and wagged her tail.

"I'm a little tired from the journey. I think I'll go to my room."
He paused, fiddling with a button on his shirt. "But first, I'd like to
tell you something. And I hope you don't take it the wrong way."

She clasped her hands. "Okay."

"The work that you and the school are doing sounds incredible, and I'm certain that many battle-blinded men will be eternally thankful for your efforts to help them." He placed his hands into his trouser pockets and shifted his weight. "But I've lost far more than my sight. My life was stolen from me at the front. There is no way to restore my hearing and, without it, I have no chance of regaining a career as a pianist, let alone a composer. I did not come here on my own accord; I've been ordered here by the government. I realize that I'm extremely fortunate to have been given one of the few slots at the school, but I have misgivings about the school's ability to repair a lost future."

Anna's mouth turned dry.

Nia padded to Anna and nuzzled her leg.

"I do not mean any disrespect, and I hope you are not upset with me. I merely want to be forthright with you."

Anna, attempting to dispel her angst, ran her fingers through Nia's fur. "Please, you mustn't quit. After a few days of training at the school, you'll feel better about things."

"I didn't mean to imply that I was going to quit," he said. "My intent is for you not to be surprised or disappointed when this doesn't work out for me."

"Promise me that you'll at least give it a try."

"I will," Max said. "Thank you again for dinner." He ran his hand over the wall to locate his stick, and he shuffled up the stairs.

Anna's eyes welled with tears. She sat on the floor and cuddled Nia.

Nia licked Anna's cheek.

"We must find a way to help him," Anna whispered. She wiped her eyes and hugged Nia. "Somehow, we need to show him that his life is worth living."

CHAPTER 14

OLDENBURG, GERMANY—DECEMBER 3, 1916

Anna rolled over in bed and turned off the alarm clock, silencing clanging bells. An uneasiness stirred inside her. For much of the night her mind reeled with thoughts of Max, and she'd gotten little sleep. She rubbed her forehead, attempting to bury her worry. *His spirits will improve once he begins working with shepherds.*

"Nia," she called, dangling her arm over the bed.

She waited for the click of toenails over the hardwood floor, typically followed by a wet lick to her hand, but nothing came. She lifted her head, propping her elbows on the mattress. The door was ajar and Nia's blanket was bare. *She's probably in the kitchen with Vater.*

She got out of bed, the cold floor sending a chill through her bare feet. She dressed for work, adding extra layers of clothing beneath her wool dress, and then knocked on Max's door.

"Come in," Max said.

"Good morning," she said, opening the door. Max, wearing his uniform except for his boots, was sitting on a neatly made bed with Nia curled at his feet. Her eyes widened. "Good morning to you, too, Nia."

The dog's tail thumped the floor.

"She pawed at my door last night, so I let her in," he said. "I hope it was okay."

"Of course." She eyed his clothing. "Are you wearing long underwear?"

"*Nein*," he said, staring toward a wall.

"You'll be outside in the cold for much of the day. I suggest adding a layer of clothing. If you need extra garments, you can borrow some of Norbie's clothes."

"I have some in my suitcase."

"We leave for school in thirty minutes," she said. "When you're ready, come downstairs for breakfast."

"All right."

"Coming, Nia?"

Nia yawned, emitting a faint, high-pitched whine. She padded to Anna, and then followed her down the stairs.

Anna entered the kitchen, where Norbie was placing toasted black bread and a pot of bark coffee on the table. "Thank you for getting up early to prepare breakfast." She hugged him, noticing his shoulder blades protruding from beneath his sweater. *You've lost more weight.*

He released her. "I wanted to surprise you with a nice meal, but all we have is a hunk of bread and turnips. I wish we had a bit of plum jam to hide the sawdust taste of the bread. It'd be nice for Max to have a decent breakfast for his first day of school."

Anna nodded. Potatoes were scarce, and people were surviving on turnips, which were traditionally used to feed animals. Her heart ached with the thought of people, especially children, perishing from malnutrition. She shook away her thoughts and gestured for her *vater* to take a seat at the table. "There's something about Max that you should know."

Anna told Norbie about the damage to Max's ears from a shell explosion. "Before the war, he was an aspiring pianist. His range of hearing is compromised, and he's unable to detect the upper octaves of a keyboard."

"Oh, my," Norbie said. "He must be devastated."

Anna nodded. "He's given up on his dream of becoming a composer, and I'm worried that he'll abandon his guide dog training."

"Fate has brought Max here." He looked into his daughter's

eyes. "I can think of no one better than you to help him regain his spirit."

Anna smiled, feeling grateful for her *vater*'s confidence in her.

Max came to the kitchen a few minutes before they had to leave, allowing little time to eat. After a thirty-minute walk over frost-covered streets and sidewalks—of which Max preferred to use his walking stick and Anna's verbal instructions, rather than allowing Nia to guide him—they arrived at the barn at precisely 7:00 a.m. Anna, shivering from the cold air, ushered them inside.

"*Hallo.*" Emmi attached a harness to a German shepherd and approached them.

"Max," Anna said, rubbing her glove-covered hands, "this is Emmi."

Max removed his cap and nodded.

"It's a pleasure to meet you," Emmi said.

Nia greeted the shepherd with a sniff to her nose, and then wagged her tail.

Anna touched Max's arm. "The trainers and trainees will be here in an hour. Do you think you can make a fire while Emmi and I tend to the dogs?"

"*Ja,*" he said.

She guided him to a cast-iron stove that Fleck had installed at the back of the barn. It was used to warm the staff during their breaks. Like Anna, who cared for Nia in her home, some of the trainers had begun taking some of the dogs home in the evening due to the falling temperature.

She handed him an ash shovel and a metal pail. "You can empty the ash in here. The wood is stacked to the right of the stove, and matches are on a shelf in front of you."

Max kneeled and began cleaning the stove.

Anna removed a dog from its pen, attached a harness, and walked outside. She met up with Emmi, who was taking a shepherd to do her business in the yard.

"How's it going with boarding Max?" Emmi asked.

Anna frowned. "Not so well."

"What's wrong?" Emmi asked.

Frigid wind nipped at Anna's neck. She adjusted her scarf, and then told Emmi about Max's hearing loss and former profession as a pianist. "He's sad and depressed, and he barely spoke during our walk."

"Oh, my," Emmi said, her breath turning to mist.

"I think he might give up," Anna said.

"I doubt that Dr. Stalling and Fleck—or the government for that matter—would permit him to leave."

"Perhaps," Anna said. "But I was referring to his determination to carry on."

Emmi place a hand on Anna's shoulder. "Anyone boarding with you has no chance of quitting."

"*Danke*," Anna said.

Anna and Emmi took the dogs, one by one, to the yard to do their business. Afterward, they fed them, including Nia, in the barn. To replenish the food bin, Anna removed partially frozen turnips from a burlap sack and chopped them with a meat clever. *Dogs and Germans now eat the same food*, Anna thought, tossing hunks of turnip into the bin.

The clack of horse hooves grew outside the barn, and then stopped. A moment later, Fleck entered with a shepherd at his side.

"Good morning, Herr Fleck," Anna said.

He tipped his cap and looked to the back of the barn, where Max was placing logs into the stove. "Maximilian?"

"He goes by Max," Anna said.

"Escort him outside. I want to introduce him to a veteran who is boarding with me." He smoothed his mustache and crossed his arms. "In the future, I expect you or Emmi to be tending to the stove, not a veteran."

Anna looked at him, his wool coat absent a trace of dog hair despite working with shepherds. "*Ja*, sir."

For the morning, Anna and Emmi shuttled shepherds to and from the obstacle course, where trainers conducted basic training exercises with six veterans, including Max. Anna was disappointed, but not surprised, that neither Fleck nor the trainers had made the effort to introduce her or Emmi to the veterans. *We'll get to know them over time*, she thought, cleaning out a pen. She went about her duties, more determined than ever to find a way to further her contribution toward the rehabilitation of blinded men.

While the trainers and trainees were congregated around the stove to take a lunch break, Anna and Emmi went outside to eat. Anna removed sliced turnip, wrapped in a napkin, from her purse and gave a piece to Emmi.

"Here," Emmi said, breaking a piece of black war bread in half and giving it to Anna.

From their position by the door, they had a clear view to the obstacle course, where Fleck was working with Max.

Emmi nibbled bread. "Why are Fleck and Max forgoing their lunch?"

"I don't know," Anna said, watching Max struggle to navigate with a shepherd around a wooden barrel.

"He's performing terribly," a gruff voice said.

Anna turned.

A sixty-year-old trainer named Waldemar stepped into the doorway and rubbed his elongated, spade-shaped chin. An unruly gray mustache ran from his upper lip to his earlobes. "He has trouble grasping our instruction on basic dog handling techniques."

"A shell explosion compromised Max's range of hearing," Anna said.

"He hears our commands just fine," Waldemar said. "I think he suffers from low intelligence. Or maybe his brain was damaged by that shell."

Anna's pulse spiked. She stuffed her food into her coat pocket. "I can assure you that his cognitive skills are quite intact."

"It's only his first day," Emmi added.

Waldemar furrowed his brows. "I can't believe that we're squandering training on a Jew."

Anna's skin turned hot.

Emmi clasped Anna's arm, as if to prevent her friend from confronting Waldemar.

Anna slipped from her grasp and approached him. "Max sacrificed his sight while fighting for our country. He deserves to be here, as much as any other battle-blinded veteran."

Waldemar pulled a cigarette from his pocket and lit it. "It doesn't matter. He'll be lucky to last a week before Fleck sends him home." He took a deep drag and blew smoke in her face.

Anna fought back a cough and stood her ground.

Waldemar shook his head, and then walked away.

"Are you all right?" Emmi asked, stepping to Anna.

"*Ja.*" Her legs trembled. "I think I know which trainer refused to have Max board in his home."

Emmi nodded. "You were absolutely right to confront him, but please be careful. Waldemar could make it difficult for you and Max, and he might be able to persuade Fleck to expel him."

"I will," Anna said, wondering if her rebuttal to Waldemar had created unnecessary attention to Max.

Emmi looked at Anna. "I wish I had your mettle. I'd love to be able to speak my mind like that."

"You have far more courage than you think."

Anna hooked her arm through Emmi's. With their appetites curbed by Waldemar's anti-Semitic outburst, they took a walk around the grounds. For the rest of the afternoon, they tended to the care of shepherds. Nia, who was still viewed as lame, received less than an hour on the obstacle course with a trainer, and she spent most of the day curled near the stove. Often, Anna peeked out the window to check on Max. She hoped that his dog handling skills would improve, and that his initial poor performance would soon be forgotten. But her hopes were dashed when the trainers finished their work and Fleck called Anna aside.

"Is everything all right, Herr Fleck?"

He shook his head. "Max did not respond well to training."

Anna's chest ached. "I'm sure he'll do better tomorrow."

"He lacks focus," Fleck said. "I informed him that if does not display that he wants to be here, I'll have no choice but to fill his spot with someone else. Dr. Stalling has quite a long waiting list of veterans in need of a guide dog."

Anna swallowed. "Why are you telling me this?"

He smoothed his mustache. The lines in his face softened. "I thought you could have a talk with him."

"*Ja*, sir," Anna said, feeling relieved that Fleck was not deter-mined to expel Max.

"Also, I want you to be prepared to take on another boarder, in the event that things do not work out for Max."

She nodded.

Fleck turned and left the barn.

Anna and Emmi finished caring for the dogs and they, along with Nia, met up with Max, who was hunkered on a wooden crate outside the barn. Under a setting sun, which painted the sky in ribbons of navy and magenta, they walked toward town. Max spoke little, despite their attempts to engage him about his day. Becoming frustrated with Max's solitude, she insisted that he hold the handle to Nia's harness, something she wished she would have done sooner. *Maybe if I had required him to walk with Nia from the train station, as well as to school, he wouldn't have had such a horrible first day.*

Reaching the outskirts of town, Emmi said her goodbyes and gave Nia a pat on the head. She turned onto a cobblestone street and disappeared from sight.

Anna and Max, with Nia between them, continued their walk. Alone with him, she thought he might begin to open up. Instead, he shuffled along the route, making no effort to talk. With each step, her patience waned.

"I understand you had a rough day," she said.

Max adjusted his grip on the harness. "*Ja.*"

"Would you like to tell me about it?"

"*Nein.*" He walked, tapping his stick over the ground.

"You're going to have to make more of an effort if you want to continue training."

"I know."

"They'll expel you if you don't show them you want to be here."

Nia paused at a curb.

"Why did she stop?" Max asked.

"Curb," Anna said.

He tapped his stick until he found the obstruction, and then stepped onto the sidewalk.

Anna's frustration swelled. "What happened, Max?"

"Nothing."

She clasped the handle to Nia's harness and gave a backward and downward jerk. "*Halt.*"

Nia stopped. She panted, her breath producing a mist in the frigid air.

Max lowered his head.

"You promised me you'd try."

He rubbed his face with a glove-covered hand. "That's not it."

"Then what is it?" Anna touched the sleeve of his coat. "Please, tell me."

He took a deep breath and pulled an envelope from his coat pocket. "This morning, I found this in my suitcase."

A foreboding ache grew in her gut.

He held out the envelope. "Will you read it to me?"

She led him and Nia to a public bench near St. Lambert's Church— its neo-Gothic spires towering toward early evening stars—and sat. A horse-drawn carriage passed by; the clopping of hooves faded into the night. Under the flickering glow of a gas streetlamp, she removed her gloves and opened the envelope. Her anxiousness grew. She'd read scores of letters to maimed soldiers at the hospital, but this one, she worried, might have far different consequences.

"Are you sure you want me to read this?" she asked.

He nodded. "I think I know what it's about, but I need to know for sure."

She unfolded the letter and read aloud.

Dear Max,
I always thought that our love would last forever. No matter what hardship we faced, whether it be illness, poverty, or trauma, I had believed that our bond was unbreakable. However, I had not fathomed the devastation a war could bestow upon us.

Anna trembled. She squeezed the paper between her fingers to steady her hands.

The loss of your sight has shattered both of our hearts. Since your return from the front, I've prayed for the strength to cope with your blindness. But my despondency has grown like a cancer, and I rue that I am not capable of providing you the care and warmth you so deserve.

A wretched ache grew beneath Anna's sternum. She paused, loosening her scarf, and then continued reading.

My ability to give and receive affection is fractured, and I believe that no amount of time will allow it to heal. I feel dead inside. I will not be here when you return home. I regret not having the nerve to tell you this before you left, but I know of no other way. Please know that I'll always think fondly of you and the endearment we once had. I pray that your rehabilitation will restore your soul and enable you to have a life of your own.
  Wilhelmina

"I'm so sorry," Anna said, tears welling in her eyes.
"*Danke,*" he said.
Nia padded to Max and placed her chin on his lap. She stared at him but didn't wag her tail.
He rubbed Nia's head.
"Are you okay?" Anna asked.
He nodded. "Our relationship was over the day I came home from the front. My blindness changed everything between us. It was naïve of me to think that with time, and me gaining mobility, our fondness for each other would rekindle."
She wiped her eyes. "You knew this was coming, didn't you?"
"Not the letter. But I didn't expect her to be at the apartment when I came home."
Anna looked at him, his face filled with melancholy. "I'm so

sorry you had to spend the entire day with the letter in your pocket." *No wonder you couldn't concentrate at school.* She folded the letter, placed it in the envelope, and gave it to him. "I could have read it for you this morning when you discovered it."

He slipped the envelope into his coat pocket. "I didn't want to ruin your day."

His fiancée has rejected him, and he's worried that he might dampen my spirts. Her heart ached. He'd lost everything—family, fiancée, sight, range of hearing, and his passion for music. To make matters worse, he would have no one when he returned to Leipzig. They sat silently on the bench, with Nia taking turns to nuzzle their hands, until the biting cold compelled them to leave.

CHAPTER 15

OLDENBURG, GERMANY—DECEMBER 4, 1916

Using his left hand, Max clasped the handle of a harness attached to a German shepherd named Gunda and stepped onto the frozen ground of the training course. On the opposite side of the dog was Waldemar, the trainer who had been assigned by Fleck to work with him. Stationed around the course were teams comprised of a blind veteran, guide dog, and trainer.

"We're going to practice the basic guide dog commands that we covered yesterday," Fleck called to the men. "This afternoon, you'll switch dogs and trainers. This will help me determine which shepherd is a good match for you—and which partner is a good match for the dog."

Waldemar leaned to Max and muttered, "Clasp the handle overhand, not underhand."

The man's sour breath pervaded Max's nose. He adjusted his grip.

"Trainers," Fleck said. "You may begin."

"Do you remember the commands?" Waldemar asked.

"*Ja,*" Max said. His mind raced, recounting each of the commands. *Halt. Forward. Back. Right. Left.*

"Well, what are you waiting for?" Waldemar asked.

"Forward," Max said. He felt a tug as the dog walked ahead. The pace of the shepherd was consistent with the other dogs that he had worked with the day before, however, he couldn't help noticing how different it felt from his predawn walk with Nia and Anna.

Anna had insisted that Max get in extra practice before school, and she'd awakened him extra early. They ate breakfast with Norbie, who had set his alarm clock to prepare coffee and fried turnip. And while Norbie climbed back into bed for a bit more sleep, Anna, Max, and Nia traversed the still streets of Oldenburg.

Like an old friend who anticipated one's thoughts, Nia guided him through town—to the train station, around St. Lambert's Church, and to a pond near Oldenburg Palace. Anna spoke nothing of Wilhelmina's letter, and nor did he. Although he was saddened by his failed engagement, he was relieved to have resolution. *It's better to end it now than when I return home,* he'd thought, shuffling over a snow-covered path. But with the end of his relationship came a simmering dread. *I'm going to be isolated and lonely, unless I receive a canine companion.* He'd made his way to the training grounds, accompanied by Nia and Anna, with a newfangled resolve to do everything he could to graduate from guide dog school.

"Pick it up," Waldemar grumbled.

"*Schneller,*" Max said to the dog.

They quickened their pace. Boots and paws padded over the ground.

"How long have you been working with shepherds?" Max asked, attempting to generate a conversation.

"Long enough," Waldemar said.

Max probed further, but it soon became clear to him that the trainer had no intention of speaking to him, other than to give orders.

Under the direction of Waldemar, Max and Gunda traveled over the course, making several left turns, right turns, and stops. Eventually, Waldemar steered them away from the obstacle area. They entered a trail, which cut through a barren field. The sound of the other trainers' voices faded, and then disappeared. Lumps of frozen earth and exposed rock made it difficult for Max to walk. Using his right hand, he tapped his walking stick in an attempt to locate obstacles.

"Where are we going?" Max asked.

"Never mind where we're headed," Waldemar said. "Keep your focus."

Maybe this is meant to mimic the difficulty of cobblestone streets. But why not do this in town? He buried his thought and continued walking.

Several minutes later, Waldemar requested him to direct the shepherd to stop, and then to back up.

"*Halt*," Max said, giving a backward and downward jerk on the harness handle.

The dog stopped.

"Back."

The dog and Max slowly stepped backward. The heel of his boot struck something hard, and he tumbled onto his backside. A sharp twinge shot through his tailbone.

"Watch where you're stepping," Waldemar said, his voice filled with irritation.

"Was that your foot?" Max asked.

"*Ja*," he said.

Max stood and dusted snow from his clothing. *How did your foot get behind me?*

Waldemar glanced to Fleck and the trainers, who were far away and out of earshot. "You did badly yesterday."

"*Ja*," Max said. "I will do better."

Waldemar approached the dog and patted its back. "Gunda is having trouble bonding with you. She's the most amenable shepherd in the group, and I'm concerned that none of the dogs will grow attached to you."

Max pressed his lips together.

"Maybe you're not cut out for this," Waldemar said. "You might want to think about resigning before Fleck has you removed."

Max's blood turned hot. "I won't quit." He clasped the harness and stared ahead.

For the rest of the morning, Max worked with Waldemar, who criticized him on his commands and maneuvers. He was relieved when he and the veterans were given lunch, courtesy of the military, which consisted of black bread and a field sausage. Huddled around the barn stove, the veterans ate their food. Despite his hunger, Max only consumed the bread, and he stashed the sausage in his coat pocket. *I'll give it to Anna and Norbie.*

Max contemplated telling Fleck about what happened with Waldemar, and he quickly dismissed the idea. Based on his experience, nothing good came from a Jewish soldier complaining up a military chain of command, and he believed it would be the same for a Jewish veteran. At the front, Jews were often given the more dangerous assignments, such as patrolling for enemy activity or conducting raids on Allied trenches. Also, they were routinely assigned the less appealing duties of removing mud from the trenches, digging tunnels, and carrying away the dead. And while stationed at Ypres, Max had witnessed a Jewish soldier named Konrad express dissatisfaction to an officer about a sergeant singling him out, because of his ethnicity, to empty rat-infested latrines. Konrad was relieved of latrine duty but was permanently assigned to a unit—consisting mainly of Jews and insubordinate soldiers—to conduct nightly repairs to barbed wire in no-man's-land. Konrad lasted four nights until his body, ravaged by machine-gun fire, was found tangled in barbed wire, like a fly in a spider's web.

Max resolved to keep his mouth shut. *I'll take everything Waldemar gives me, until I graduate or I'm kicked out of school.* For the afternoon, Max rotated with the other trainers, who were far different from Waldemar. Although they were strict with their manner of instruction, they were kind and supportive and, during breaks, they expressed genuine interest in Max by asking personal questions and chatting like equal comrades. And it became clear, to Max, that Waldemar was prejudiced against him because of his Jewish ethnicity.

Waldemar influencing Fleck to remove him from training wasn't Max's only problem. He struggled to create a working rapport with any of the shepherds. Although he liked them, and he assumed that they were tolerant of him, none of them were like Nia, who was gentle and smoothly carried out his commands, despite a slight limp in her gait. He hoped that his lack of focus on his first day of training hadn't tainted how the dogs viewed him. For the rest of the day, he diligently followed instruction, like he'd done when he was taught to play the piano as a child.

With renewed determination—fueled by Anna's kindness, as well as to prove Waldemar wrong—he practiced his commands with the shepherds, again and again.

At the end of the day, the trainers and veterans left, except for Max. While he waited for Anna to finish her duties, he sat on a crate outside the barn. A frigid wind stung his cheeks, compelling him to flip up his coat collar. Although he was tired and cold, he was eager to hear Anna's voice, and to walk home with her, Emmi, and Nia. Having endured hours of commands, he longed for a cordial conversation. Minutes later, the barn door squeaked open. A patter of paws approached and he received a wet lick to the face.

"*Hallo*, Nia," Max said, wiping his nose.

"How was training?" Anna asked.

"Better," he said, not wanting to disappoint her.

"I'm glad," Emmi said.

Anna paused, slipping on her leather gloves. "I told Emmi about Wilhelmina. I hope it was okay."

"It's all right," he said.

"I'm sorry, Max," Emmi said.

"*Danke*," he said.

They walked to town with Max holding Nia's harness. Unlike the day before, he initiated conversation by asking questions about their duties and experiences with shepherds. By the time Emmi took a separate route to her apartment, he'd learned about her nursing work with Anna, her husband, Ewald, who served as a medic at the front, and how Anna recruited her for the school. Based on Emmi's kind words about Anna, he determined that they were not only close colleagues but best friends.

Arriving home, Anna made a dinner of sautéed, diced turnip mixed with old bread crust. Max gifted Anna and Norbie the sausage that he'd stashed in his pocket, but they insisted that they share it. So, Anna chopped the sausage into bits and added it to the food. Finishing their meals, Max and Anna washed the dishes, and they settled into the living room where Norbie was sorting through a stack of phonograph discs.

"Max, do you mind if I play something lively?" Norbie asked. "The sausage has renewed my energy."

"*Nein*," Max said, feeling glad to have made a contribution to the meal. He tapped his walking stick over the floor until he located the sofa, and then sat.

Nia curled near Max's feet.

"You might regret your answer to Vater's question," Anna said, joining him on the sofa.

"Why?" Max asked.

Norbie grinned. "I do believe my daughter is jealous of my singing." He selected a disc, placed it on a gramophone, and lowered the tone arm.

The needle scratched over the disc, and a reedy, organ-like sound of an accordion filled the air.

Max turned an ear toward the gramophone.

A choir of children, singing an upbeat melody, joined the accordion accompaniment.

A *children's song*, Max thought, surprised by Norbie's choice of music. Despite his ears unable to detect the high notes, he soon recognized the tune about a boy who journeys into the world and returns as a man to his family. "I sang this song in kindergarten."

"Me too," Anna said.

"'Hänschen klein,'" Norbie said. "It's a masterpiece." He tapped his foot to the beat of the music and sang the lyrics in a vibrato tenor voice, which was flat and out of tune.

Max smiled, admiring Norbie's uninhibited enthusiasm.

Anna nudged Max with her elbow and lowered her voice. "Surprised?"

"*Ja*," he said.

Norbie lifted the needle from the disc. "Join me."

"I don't remember the words," Max said.

"You'll learn them quickly, my boy," he said. "Anna?"

She nodded, reluctantly.

He lowered the needle.

Max listened to Norbie and Anna sing. Unlike her *vater*, Anna's soprano voice was pure and with perfect pitch, like a finely tuned violin.

Nia's tail thumped the floor.

"Sing," Anna said to Max.

Max breathed the words. A memory of playing the piano and singing along with his military comrades flashed in his head. Their celebration with schnapps and song had pacified their pain. And like his friends, Norbie and Anna were using music to provide a temporary reprieve from the war. Millions of soldiers had been killed or maimed. Food shortages had placed civilians on the brink of starvation. There were only reasons for Germans to mourn, Max believed. But despite a turbulent world and hunger gnawing at their bellies, Norbie and Anna had mustered the fortitude to carry on. For the moment, Max's mind drifted from the war, Wilhelmina, and his blindness. A swell of fervor rose in his chest, and he sang the final verse.

"Bravo!" Norbie said, clapping his hands. He raised the tone arm on the gramophone but left the disc spinning.

Nia raised her head and yawned.

"I don't sing that bad," Norbie said, patting the dog.

Anna shifted in her seat. "You might be a tad flat."

"Nonsense." Norbie stepped to the piano and tapped a key, which produced a sharp, twangy resonance. "La-la-laaaa," he sang, adjusting the pitch of his voice. "Maybe I'm a little off."

Anna chuckled.

Nia squinted her eyes.

"Max," Norbie said. "What do you think?"

"I like your singing," Max said, not wanting to hurt his feelings. "You perform with gusto."

Norbie beamed, and then put on another recording.

For the evening, German folk music resounded from the gramophone. Norbie sang. Anna, Max, and Nia listened.

Norbie stretched his arms, and then turned off the gramophone. "That was fun. But I'm getting tired."

Anna stood and kissed him on the cheek. "I'll take Nia outside before I go to bed."

"Okay," Norbie said. "Sleep well, Max."

"You too," Max said, standing from the sofa.

Norbie patted Nia, and then climbed the stairs. His footsteps faded and a door clacked shut.

"You have a wonderful *vater*," Max said.

"*Danke.*"

"I think he enjoyed singing that children's song the most."

"*Ja*. My *mutter* sang 'Hänschen klein' to me when I was a small child. He plays that phonograph when he misses her."

Max clasped his hands. "Do you mind if I ask how she died?"

"Cancer." She sat on the sofa and patted the space next to her. He sat.

"Mutter died when I was five. She'd been sick for over a year."

"I'm sorry."

"She was far too young." She glanced to the piano. "Her illness didn't stop her from doing what she loved. Some of my fondest memories include sitting on her lap as she sang and played the piano. She had a beautiful voice."

"So do you."

She smiled. "Maybe, if you're comparing me to Vater's singing."

He chuckled.

Nia stood and placed her chin on the sofa between them.

Anna rubbed her snout. "He sings off key, but he doesn't care. And I enjoy listening to him."

"With the proper tools, I could tune your piano for you. Of course, I'd need your help with tuning the upper octave keys."

"*Ja*," she said. "That would be lovely."

Nia nudged Max with her nose, and he ran a hand over her ears.

"I'm really sorry about Wilhelmina's letter." Anna took a deep breath. "How are you?"

A dull ache grew in his abdomen. "I'll be all right."

"I'm glad that today was better for you."

A flash of Waldemar's voice and sour breath filled his head. He nodded.

"How are the trainers treating you?" she asked, as if she could read Max's thoughts.

"Okay," he said, not wanting to burden her with his problem.

"Do you have a favorite shepherd?"

"Not yet," he said.

"Too bad Nia's paw isn't healed," she said.

"Maybe I should defer school and come back when Nia is ready to train with a veteran," he jested.

"That would be nice. Unfortunately, veterans only have one chance at training. There are hundreds in need of a guide dog."

If I don't pass, I'll be on my own, he thought.

"Well," Anna said, "we better get some sleep. I'll be getting you up early again tomorrow to practice with Nia."

"Why?"

Anna paused, wringing her hands. "I overheard one of the trainers make a disparaging remark."

An angst grew in his belly. "About me being a Jew?"

"*Ja,*" she said. "I think he's the reason you're boarding with me."

"Waldemar?"

"How did you know?"

"Let's just say that he isn't easy to work with," Max said.

"Perhaps we should inform Fleck."

"*Nein,*" he said. "In the military, little good can come from a Jewish soldier protesting to superiors about anti-Semitic behavior. I expect it to be the same with veterans. Besides, I can handle Waldemar."

"All right," Anna said. "But we're not taking any chances. You're going to need to be at the top of the class, and that means you'll need more practice time than the others. Be prepared to wake at five a.m."

"Okay." He rubbed Nia, located her collar, and stood. "How about I get a little extra practice by taking Nia outside to do her business?"

Anna smiled. "Downstairs, make a right to the back door leading to the garden. I'll leave my bedroom door cracked open for her when she comes upstairs."

Max, guided by Nia, made his way to the stairs. At the threshold he paused. "*Danke* for your help, and the nice evening. It's been a long time since I've enjoyed listening to music."

"I'm glad," she said.

Nia guided Max to the garden, dormant and covered in a layer of fresh fallen snow. The dog padded over the ground. A moment later, Nia nudged his hand, and then guided him inside and upstairs to his bedroom.

Max kneeled and whispered, "Good night, Nia."

The dog licked his face. She walked, her toenails clicking over the hardwood floor, to Anna's partially open door and slipped inside.

In his room, Max undressed and crawled into bed. Wind whistled through a crack in the window frame. Unable to sleep, his mind stirred with thoughts of training. He dreaded working with Waldemar, but he needed to withstand the man's wrath to pass training. *If I'm kicked out, or if Fleck deems me to be an unsuitable match for any of the shepherds, I'll be alone.*

To bury his angst, he turned his thoughts to Anna. *She's kind, committed to helping the blind, and she refuses to allow me to fail. I'm fortunate to be boarding with her and Norbie.* He slowly drifted toward sleep with the echo of Anna's and Norbie's voices singing "Hänschen klein" in his head. But he was roused by the sound of scratching. Opening his door, Nia trotted inside and plopped on the floor next to his bed.

"Does Anna know you're here?" he whispered.

Her tailed brushed the floor.

CHAPTER 16

LILLE, FRANCE—DECEMBER 6, 1916

Bruno, cold and sleep deprived, emerged from his bunker after a night of fierce enemy shellfire. The artillery guns had paused, but echoes of shockwaves reverberated through his blood and bone. An acrid scent of cordite lingered in the air. He buttoned his wool trench coat and squelched through a muddy trench leading away from the front lines. Although he was glad to have a two-day reprieve from the fight, he was reluctant to leave the front. Haber had summoned Bruno to meet with him to jointly inspect a supply of phosgene shells that had been delivered to a supply depot in Lille. But Bruno suspected that Haber, who usually delegated such menial tasks, had far more crucial matters to discuss. And the prospect of seeing Haber resurrected Bruno's sense of foreboding. *If Anna learns of my secret, our relationship will be over.*

Winding through the trench, he encountered a group of soldiers carrying a mixture of shovels, wooden clubs, and bayonets. Along a trench wall was a piece of cord that was strung between two stakes, like a miniature clothesline, from which dozens of dead rats hung by their snake-like tails.

Hunting, he thought.

Rat infestation, which spawned disease, was a secondary battle that raged in the trenches. Unlike the battlefields where there were breaks in fighting, the rats tormented soldiers by day and night. Trench rats were large, the length of a man's forearm not including the tail, and their bellies were bloated. They bred rapidly and were well fed from discarded food tins, human waste, and nips of flesh from sleeping soldiers. However, most of the rats' food supply came from no-man's-land, where they feasted on corpses of fallen soldiers.

"There!" a soldier pointing a club shouted.

A large rat, bearing its sharp, yellow incisors, squeaked and scurried into a dugout.

Bruno, his boots squelching in mud, passed the rat hunters and turned into an adjacent trench.

He expected the conditions to improve as he moved away from the front. However, as he approached a clearing, the air turned thick with a stench of burning flesh. He covered his nose and mouth with his sleeve and pressed on, but the fetor grew worse. Soon, he arrived at the source of the odor. Where a first aid tent once stood was a smoldering mass of canvass and charred corpses. Given the amount of burned remains, the triage station appeared to have contained approximately thirty injured soldiers. Distraught medics scoured the grounds, placing hunks of blackened flesh and shredded limbs into burlap bags. *Oh, dear God. The poor bastards didn't make it out of their stretchers.* His body trembled. He fought back the urge to vomit and quickened his pace.

Bruno, with horrid images of burned bodies lingering in his head, hitched a ride in a transport lorry to Lille. At midday, he arrived at a large ammunition warehouse, and was greeted by Fritz Haber.

"Bruno." Haber placed his cap under his armpit. A fine sweat gleamed on his bald head.

"*Hallo*, sir." Bruno shook his hand.

Haber adjusted his pince-nez spectacles and scanned Bruno's clothing, spattered with dried mud. "I see you've come directly from the trenches."

"*Ja*," Bruno said. "I didn't want to be late."

"*Gut.*" He put on his cap. "My train leaves soon, and I have much to tell you. Follow me."

The depot, which had been a foundry before the war, contained thousands of phosgene shells—painted with a green cross—which were stacked in piles, reminiscent of partially constructed pyramids. Since his last visit to Lille, an enormous supply of shells had arrived at the depot.

Haber gestured to an aisle, the length of a passenger ship, with shells stacked on both sides. "The Imperial German Army has plans for artillery units to increase the usage of chemical weapons."

Bruno swallowed, wondering how much of the poison in the room was manufactured by his *vater*'s company, Wahler Farbwerke, and how many thousands of men would die excruciating deaths. He buried his thought and nodded.

Haber placed the tips of fingers together, as if he were holding an invisible ball. "Soon, I expect one out of every three shells fired upon our enemy to contain gas."

"That is good news, sir," Bruno lied. "*Danke* for coming to Lille to personally show me the supply, and to inform me of my expectations."

"That's not the reason I summoned you," Haber said.

Bruno straightened his back.

"At our last meeting, I promised that our chemists would be devising an arsenal of more lethal weapons." His bespectacled eyes met Bruno's. "Two of my top chemists, Wilhelm Lommel and Wilhelm Steinkopf, have developed a new chemical derived from sulfur mustard."

"Congratulations, sir."

Haber nodded. "It's a blister agent that creates debilitating chemical burns to the skin and eyes, as well as bleeding and blistering within the respiratory system."

Bruno's blood turned cold. A flash of gassed corpses, skin the color of plum, filled his head.

"Large-scale production of the sulfur mustard has begun," Haber said. "It'll be ready for use as a weapon by summer, and I would like you to implement its use."

A burn rose inside Bruno's esophagus. "I am honored, sir."

Haber placed a hand on Bruno's shoulder. "I believe this new weapon, like no other, will instill fear in our enemy. It will break their morale. It's only a matter of time before we win the chemical arms race, and the war."

"*Ja*, sir."

Haber removed his hand from Bruno's shoulder. "I've spoken with your *vater*. He's quite pleased to have his son disperse shells that contain agents from his factory."

Bruno nodded. He was saddened but not surprised that his *vater*, as well as his *mutter*, hadn't written him a letter in months. *If Vater was gratified with my military service, he certainly has made no effort to tell me.*

"Well," Haber said, adjusting his cap on his head. "I must leave, but I will be in communication with plans for our new weapon. In the meantime, you have plenty of phosgene shells to distribute." He turned and left, the clack of his jackboots echoing through the building.

Bruno stared at a stack of shells. He took in gulps of air, attempting to calm his nerves, but a deep-seated memory of his recruitment by Haber surged in his head.

As part of his indoctrination to the Disinfection Unit, Bruno, as well as several other candidates in consideration for the special squad, had been summoned by Haber to a discreet research facility of the Kaiser Wilhelm Institute. They were led to a room with a sealed glass panel that provided a view into a concrete chamber, which contained a small lab monkey in a cage. With little explanation, other than they were to witness an experiment, Haber nodded to a chemist wearing a white lab coat. The man released a valve on a gas cylinder, from which a lead pipe ran into a wall. A green-yellow vapor spewed into the chamber. Candidates peered through the glass. The animal screeched and convulsed. Bruno, sickened and horrified, struggled to contain his composure. Through the corner of his eyes, he saw Haber, observing the reaction of the candidates. *He wants to make certain we are insensitive to the experiment, and that we won't be a problem for the Disinfection Unit,* Bruno had thought. He bit the inside of his cheek, hoping the pain would hide his shock. After the experiment, one of the candidates, who'd winced and lowered his head, was immediately dismissed and escorted from the facility. And months later, Bruno learned that Haber's tests were not limited to primates. While in a bunker under shellfire, a fellow officer of the Disinfection Unit, who had drunk a bottle of schnapps, disclosed that he'd witnessed Haber and his chemists conduct toxic gas experiments on rats, guinea pigs, and farm animals.

Bruno lowered his head into his hands. A wave of shame engulfed him. He hated what he'd done, and he wished that he had the fortitude to rebuke Haber. But if he did, he might be shot. At the very least, he'd be viewed as disloyal and reassigned to a battlefield combat role with a high fatality rate, and he'd be shunned from the Wahler family. *There is no way out of this hell. I've made a pact with the Devil, and my fate is eternal damnation.*

Bruno, his soul ravaged, forced himself to go about his duty. He ordered a group of soldiers to conduct an inventory of the phosgene shells, and he left the ammunition depot. To attempt to rid himself from his dismay, he walked the streets of German-occupied Lille, but visions of grotesque, gassed bodies replayed in his head, over and over. At sunset, he arrived at the officers' boardinghouse.

Celeste opened the door. "Oberleutnant Wahler, please come in."

Bruno stepped inside and removed his cap. "*Hallo*, Celeste."

She scanned the mud on his boots and coat, and then looked into his eyes, surrounded with dark circles. "Are you all right, *monsieur?*"

"*Nein.*" He ran a hand through his oily hair. "Do you have anything to drink?"

Celeste nodded. She took his coat, slipped away, and then returned with a small fluted glass containing a clear liquid.

"Schnapps," she said, giving him the glass.

"*Danke.*" He gulped the drink; the alcohol warmed his throat and stomach.

She took the empty glass. "Would you like a basin of warm water or a bath, *monsieur?*"

"A basin is fine," he said. "I didn't bring a change of uniform."

"I have a supply of extra clothing. You can wear something else while I clean your uniform."

He nodded.

"Come to the parlor after you've washed. I'll give you something to eat."

"That will not be necessary." He turned and began to ascend the stairs.

"You said that the last time you were here," she said, looking up at him.

He paused, placing a hand on the banister.

"You'll feel much better after you've eaten."

"All right."

Bruno washed, shaved, and put on a clean shirt and pants, which Celeste had placed by his door. Carrying his dirty uniform, he went downstairs and was drawn to the kitchen by an aroma of sautéed shallots. Celeste, standing by a stove, stirred a pan with a wooden spoon.

"It smells good," he said.

Celeste glanced to him. "Place your uniform in the corner. Your food will be ready in a few minutes." She placed two plump sausages into the pan. The meat hissed and crackled.

"Will there be others joining me?" he asked.

"*Non.* Two men are billeting here tonight, but they've chosen to eat at the officers' casino."

A memory of his dinner with Celeste flashed in his head. "Have you eaten?"

She rolled the sausage. Oil spattered. "I'll eat after I clean your clothes."

"That's what you said the last time I was here."

She smiled, and then nodded.

He took a seat at a small wooden table with two chairs.

"It's much nicer in the parlor," she said, dividing the food onto plates.

"Here is good," Bruno said, "as long as it's okay with you."

Celeste nodded. She placed the food, napkins, and silverware on the table, and then retrieved a bottle of white wine, corkscrew, and glasses.

Bruno stood and slid back her chair.

"*Merci,*" she said, sitting.

Bruno opened the wine, poured two glasses, and sat. "To an end to war," he said, raising his glass.

She clinked his glass and sipped her wine.

He took a bite of sausage, rich with fat and salt.

"Did you have bad day, *monsieur?*"

He took a swig of wine, crisp and citrusy, and then nodded.

"I'm sorry," she said, cutting her sausage. "Would you like to talk about it?"

He shook his head, but his mind drifted to their last conversation. *She'd survived by becoming a mistress to a German officer, who is now dead. Her aunt, one of thousands of Lille women rounded up by the German military to farm the French countryside, was taken from her home. Celeste confided in me, and I'd said little.* A surge of selfishness swelled within him. He put down his fork and said, "My unit requires me to perform hellish duties."

She looked at him. "I can see the burden on your face."

He swirled his wine. Although he'd never spoken to anyone about the emotional toll of his work, he felt he could trust her. "I feel like my soul is rotting away."

"I'm sorry," she said. "Please remember that it is not your fault. War compels soldiers to perform terrible acts."

But I have committed war crimes. He gulped down his wine and refilled his glass. "What I've done is far worse than most men."

Celeste slid her hand toward his, but stopped short of touching his fingers. "Do you regret doing these things?"

"*Ja.*"

"Then all is not lost."

Bruno looked into her eyes. "I pray you are right."

She lowered her hand to her lap. "Have you confided in your fiancée about this?"

He shifted in his seat. "*Nein.* If she learns of my duties, it will be over between us."

"Maybe your fate will be better than you believe it to be."

"Perhaps," he said, despite a dread gnawing at his gut.

She took a deep breath. "I know how you feel. After the war, my family will spurn me, too."

"You collaborate to survive," he said. "They'll forgive you."

"I wish you were right," she said. "But I believe it will never happen."

Bruno nibbled his food. "We come from different worlds, but we share a similar dilemma."

Her eyes met his. "*Oui.*"

They turned their conversation away from the war, and for the remainder of the meal they discussed fond prewar memories. He learned that Celeste was raised in a prosperous Parisian family, given her private schooling and holidays in Switzerland and the French Riviera. Although he was cautious with revealing details of his military experience, he told her about his childhood, his chemistry studies at Ludwig-Maximilians-Universität, and his *vater*'s expectations that he would join the family ink and dye business after the war.

"You will have a burgeoning career when you go home," Celeste said.

"*Ja.*" Bruno finished his wine. "But I wish I could do something else with my life."

"Like what?"

"I'd prefer any profession that does not work with chemicals," he said, his head buzzing from alcohol. "If I had it to do over again, I would have loved to have studied art or literature at the university. It would have compelled me to pursue a life of my own, rather than follow in the footsteps of my *vater.*"

"It's never too late to take a different path."

"True. However, I've done things that cannot be changed, things that will forever couple me to—" *War atrocities.* He refilled his glass and took a long gulp.

"It's all right if you don't want to tell me," she said. "Maybe you could write your fiancée about it."

He shook his head.

"I understand." She gently touched his sleeve. "Sometimes, it's okay to keep a secret."

Bruno's skin prickled.

She removed her hand and poured wine into his glass. "Secrets are not lies."

His pulse quickened. "I suppose you're right."

Celeste's lips formed a flirtatious smile. She crossed her legs; the hem of her skirt rose, revealing a bare calf.

His eyes wandered.

She lowered her voice. "Maybe you don't have to give up what you need in order to have what you want."

He swallowed.

She ran a finger over the rim of her glass.

Bruno, his conscience clashing with his desire, forced himself to drain his drink and stand. "I should go."

"Are you sure?" she asked, tucking strands of hair behind her ear.

"*Ja,*" he said. "*Danke* for the food and conversation."

She stood. "You are quite welcome."

"Good night, Celeste."

"Sleep well, *monsieur.*"

Alone in his room, Bruno's pain and loneliness swelled. Despite the risk that his conversation with Celeste could lead to something he would regret, he wished he would have stayed with her. Part of him felt guilty for divulging things that he hadn't revealed to Anna in his letters. *It's easy to speak with Celeste because there's no risk of her rejecting me because of my role in the Disinfection Unit,* he rationalized in his head. The wine that he'd drunk exacerbated his craving for solace. Unable to sleep, he lit a candle and sat in a chair. But as minutes passed his restlessness spiraled.

A knock came from the door.

"Come in," he said, standing.

Celeste, carrying a stack of folded clothing, entered the room. "I saw light coming from under your door. I hope I'm not disturbing you."

"Not at all," he said.

She extended her arms. "I cleaned the mud from your uniform."

"*Danke.*" He approached her and took the clothing, their fingers touching and slipping away. His skin tingled.

She looked at him. Candlelight flickered in her green eyes.

His pulse accelerated.

"Will there be anything else?" she asked, her voice soft.

He shook his head.

"If you should need me, I'll be in my room." She turned and

left, glancing to him as she passed through the doorway. Wood creaked on the stairs that led to her attic bedroom.

Bruno tossed the clothing onto the bed. His mind and heart raced. *How will I face Anna? But when I return to the front, I could be killed at any moment by shellfire or an Allied gas attack.* Smothered with pain and dread, he desired comfort, regardless of the consequences. Before he changed his mind, he retrieved the candle and left his bedroom. His heart rate rose as he climbed the stairs. At the landing, he found her waiting for him.

Celeste took the candle from him and placed it on a dresser. She turned to him and slowly unbuttoned her blouse.

His breath quickened.

Candlelight glowed over her porcelain-like skin. She gently clasped his fingers and placed his palm to her chest.

He felt her heart pounding beneath her sternum. A subtle scent of lilac perfume filled his nose. He pulled her close and closed his eyes as her lips approached his own.

CHAPTER 17

OLDENBURG, GERMANY—DECEMBER 8, 1916

Anna, hoping to catch a glimpse of Max, peeked through the partially opened barn door. On the snow-covered obstacle course, each of the trainers were paired with a veteran and a shepherd, while Fleck supervised the instruction. Max, who was being guided over a log barrier by a shepherd, was partnered with Waldemar.

Anna sighed. "I wish he was paired with someone else," she whispered to herself.

Nia, sitting near Anna, perked her ears.

After a week of training, each of the blind veterans—except for Max—had been permanently assigned a guide dog. It wasn't due a lack of effort on Max's part, Anna believed, given that he'd practiced before and after school with Nia, which helped him improve his dog handling skills. However, Fleck was not yet convinced that Max and a shepherd had formed a bond. To Fleck, it was crucial for both the handler and dog to develop mutual trust, the foundation for their life together after leaving Oldenburg. Therefore, Fleck rotated Max with dogs and trainers in a quest to find the right match.

But three days ago, the number of viable guide dogs was significantly reduced due to an outbreak of kennel cough, a canine infectious tracheobronchitis. Every dog that was housed at night in the barn had become infected, and they were immediately quarantined at a shelter with the Ambulance Dogs Association. Fortunately, the ill dogs would likely make a full recovery, and none of the shepherds that stayed with trainers were sick. However, it left only two viable dogs for Max—Gunda, who was under the care of Waldemar, and Elfriede, who housed with Fleck. For the past few days, Fleck had frequently blown a whistle that he'd begun carrying in his pocket to signal for Anna to rotate dogs for Max. And as of this morning, Fleck had yet to decide which dog was best suited for him.

"Anna!" Emmi called from the back of the barn. "I need help."

Anna turned and ran to the rear door, where Emmi was kneeling beside Elfriede, a black and silver German shepherd lying on her side. Blood covered her left hind paw. "Oh, my," she gasped.

Nia cantered to them.

Emmi lifted Elfriede's paw, revealing a badly torn toenail. "I was bringing her inside and somehow her toenail got stuck between planks of wood."

Anna glanced to the open doorway, where trainers had placed boards, due to heavy snow accumulation, to create a path inside the building. "I'll get the medical supplies." She darted away and returned with bandages, antiseptic, and a bowl of water.

Emmi dipped the dog's paw into the bowl. Blood swirled in the water.

"How bad is it?" Anna asked, kneeling.

"The toenail has been ripped off," Emmi said, examining a bloody stump of tissue.

The dog trembled.

"You'll be okay, girl," Anna said, stroking the dog's head.

Emmi gently cleaned the dog's paw and applied pressure with a cloth. Once the bleeding slowed, Anna applied antiseptic to the wound.

The dog flinched and whimpered.

Nia inched close and licked the shepherd's face, like a mother caring for her puppy.

Elfriede relaxed and brushed her tail over the ground.

"You're a good nurse, Nia," Anna said.

Nia opened her mouth and panted, creating the appearance of a smile.

Emmi bandaged the paw and helped the dog to stand. It hobbled on three legs, unable to place weight on her hind leg, and then flopped on her side.

"She'll be okay in a few days," Anna said.

"*Ja*," Emmi said. "But Fleck will be angry with me."

"It was an accident," Anna said. "Besides, Fleck is always upset about something. It's his nature."

"But Fleck cares for Elfriede in his home. He's become quite protective of her." She glanced to the dog. "He might discharge me."

"He'll do no such thing," Anna said. "You're an incredible caregiver for the shepherds, and you're as smart as any veterinarian. If it wasn't for your insistence that each of the trainers take a guide dog home in the evening, rather than have the dogs sleep in communal pens in the barn, it's quite possible that all of the dogs would have contracted tracheobronchitis."

"*Danke*," Emmi said. "But it doesn't change the fact that Gunda is the only healthy dog left for Max."

Waldemar works with Gunda, so Max will be stuck with Waldemar for the duration of training. Anna rubbed her neck. "It'll work out."

Emmi nodded.

Fleck's whistle sounded.

Anna's skin prickled.

"I'll tell him," Emmi said.

"*Nein*." Anna retrieved a harness from a hook on the wall. "I have to go out there anyway. I'll tell him that we were both walking Elfriede when she injured her foot. He can't afford to discharge both of us."

Emmi's eyes widened. "I thought you said that I have nothing to worry about."

"You don't," Anna said, hoping she was right. She approached Elfriede and stroked her side. "Do you think you can walk outside so we can show Herr Fleck your paw?"

Elfriede struggled to stand. She whined and settled on her belly.

"That's okay, girl," Anna said.

Nia padded to Elfriede, and then looked at Anna. She tilted her head, holding eye contact.

Anna's mind raced.

The shrill of Fleck's whistle pierced the air. "Fräulein Zeller!"

Anna's heart rate spiked. *Harbor your heart*, her *vater*'s words echoed in her head. Before she changed her mind, she slid the harness on Nia.

"What are you doing?" Emmi asked.

Anna buckled the harness. "Fleck needs another dog, so I'm giving him one."

"But he doesn't think Nia is physically ready for training."

"The worst thing that can happen is that he sends Nia back to the barn," Anna said, hoping to hide her uneasiness.

Emmi took a deep breath. "All right, but I'm not letting you go out there by yourself."

"Okay." Anna slipped on her gloves and patted Nia. "Ready, girl?"

Nia wagged her tail.

As they left the barn, cold air stung Anna's face. She squeezed the harness handle, attempting to suppress the trepidation building in her chest. As she approached Fleck and Waldemar—their backs to Anna—she overheard their vigorous conversation.

"Gunda doesn't care much for Max," Waldemar said.

Fleck crossed his arms. "Why is that?"

"With all due respect, sir, I don't think Max is capable of bonding with a shepherd."

Anna's blood pressure rose. She slowed her pace and glanced to Max, who was taking a break with the other veterans and trainers who were huddled near a grouping of birch trees.

Fleck stroked his mustache. "What is your recommendation?"

Waldemar glanced to Max and lowered his voice. "Send him home. There are blind veterans who are more deserving of a guide dog."

Oh, no. Anna's mouth turned dry.

Fleck paused, grinding the heel of a boot into the snow. "Let's give him one more chance with Elfriede."

"Herr Fleck," Anna said, interrupting.

Fleck turned and frowned. "Where's Elfriede?"

"Her toenail got stuck between the boards leading to the back door of the barn," Anna said.

"She lost an entire toenail, sir," Emmi said, stepping forward. "Exposed nerves are quite painful. It'll be several days before she can train in the ice and snow."

"Damn it," Fleck grumbled. He looked at Nia. "Why did you bring her?"

Anna swallowed. "I thought that you'd need another dog."

Fleck lit a cigarette. He took a drag and blew smoke through his nostrils.

Anna, attempting to maintain her confidence, stroked Nia. Through the corner of her eyes, she saw Max leave the group and walk, tapping his cane, toward them.

"All right," Fleck said.

Anna's heart leaped.

Waldemar furrowed his brow. "But Nia is lame. She'll be limping within an hour of training."

"Excuse me, sir," Max said, shuffling toward their voices. "I've been practicing with Nia in the evenings, and I'd like to give her a try on the obstacle course."

Waldemar glared at him.

Max stopped near Fleck. "Nia's limp doesn't bother me. I'm a bit slow myself; I sometimes get winded." He tapped his cane to his chest. "Gas, you know."

"*Ja*," Fleck said. He puffed his cigarette and looked at Waldemar. "Give Nia a go."

"Sir," Waldemar said. "I, as well as the other trainers, have spent little time with Nia. She has not been properly instructed. It'd be better to try again with Gunda."

"But you just told me that Gunda wasn't working out," Fleck said, his voice impatient.

Waldemar's face turned red.

"Herr Fleck," Max said. "Anna has been instructing me and Nia on the same techniques used by the trainers. With your permission, I would like to work with Anna on the course."

Anna's eyes widened.

Fleck looked at her. "Is this true?"

"*Ja*," Anna said. "While doing my duties, I often get a chance to observe the trainers. I merely modeled your techniques with Max and—"

"No wonder he performed poorly," Waldemar interrupted. "She's not a trainer, she is an inferior nurse who couldn't hold her position at the hospital."

Anna's skin turned hot. She struggled to hold her tongue.

Fleck flicked ash from his cigarette. "Anna, take Max and Nia onto the course."

A jolt shot up her spine.

"Sir," Waldemar said.

Fleck looked at Waldemar. "Rotate in with the other trainers to give them breaks."

"But—"

"That's an order," Fleck said.

Waldemar stuffed his hands into his coat pockets and walked away.

Anna took a deep breath. "*Danke.*"

"Save your gratitude, Fräulein Zeller," Fleck said, firmly. "This is temporary, until Elfriede or one of the other shepherds recovers. If you fail to perform to my expectations, I will not hesitate to remove you from the grounds. Do you understand?"

"Of course, sir," Anna said.

Fleck tossed his cigarette and made his way onto the course.

"What are you waiting for," Emmi whispered, her eyes beaming. "Get out there."

Max extended his arm. "Shall we?"

Nia wagged her tail.

Anna guided his hand to the harness. With Nia between them, they walked onto the course. Eyes of the trainers fell upon them. She felt like a stagehand who'd been asked to fill in at the last minute for the leading role of an opera. Her heartbeat pounded in her eardrums. She squeezed the handle of Nia's harness to keep her hand from shaking.

"Don't worry," Max said, as if he could sense her nervousness. "You'll do great."

"What makes you so sure?" she asked.

"I've worked with every trainer and shepherd at this school." He nudged her with his elbow. "If I'm honest, you and Nia are the finest duo here."

Anna's confidence swelled.

For the next few hours, the trainers worked with the veterans and their dogs. Anna ignored glares from Waldemar and focused on aiding Max and Nia. She dreaded that Fleck might bark orders to perform a task that she was unfamiliar with, but she was relieved to find that she knew most of them. And for the drills that she hadn't observed, such as maneuvering over a series of uneven log barriers that was recently constructed, Max helped her along by describing what the other trainers had done. By afternoon, Nia began to favor her right front paw and, soon after, she began to limp. Fleck's glances grew more frequent. Her fear mushroomed. She prayed for Nia to have the stamina to continue working, and that they wouldn't be dismissed. Hour after hour, they labored on the course until Fleck glanced at his wristwatch and blew his whistle, signaling the end of the day's training.

Max rubbed Nia's back. "Well done."

Nia raised her chin and peered at him.

Anna exhaled, her breath misting in the frigid air. She ruffled Nia's ears. "You made it."

The walk home from school took longer than usual. Nia's pace was slow due to her tender paw, which had been aggravated by prolonged exposure to the frozen ground. But the limp in her gait didn't seem to dampen the dog's spirits, considering that she wagged her tail on the way to town. Anna had planned to join Emmi to check on the ill dogs that were recovering at the ambulance dog shelter, but Emmi insisted that she go alone.

"It's on the way to my apartment," Emmi said. "I'll take care of them tonight."

"Are you sure?" Anna asked.

Emmi nodded. "Go home and get warm. You, Max, and Nia have been working outside for most of the day. Besides, you must be excited to tell Norbie about getting a chance to train."

"I am," Anna said. "But it's temporary. Fleck will have Nia and me removed from the course as soon as the other shepherds are well."

"Perhaps," Emmi said. "But as much as I enjoy working with you, I'm counting on you and Nia to remain on the training course."

"I'll try not to disappoint you," Anna said.

Emmi grinned. "I still expect to see you at seven a.m. Your new role does not provide a reprieve from chopping feed and picking up dog piles."

Anna chuckled.

"Max," Emmi said. "Please take your trainer and guide dog home."

"Will do." Max patted Nia's side.

Emmi turned and walked away.

"Forward," Max said to Nia. She padded ahead, guiding him around a mound of shoveled snow.

Anna glanced to Max. A dusting of frost covered his cap. "Thank you for sticking up for me. If it wasn't for your endorsement, Fleck would not have permitted Nia or me to work with you."

"You're welcome," he said. "But I didn't do it out of pity."

"Waldemar?"

"*Nein*, although it's nice to have a break from working with him. You're as good or better than the other trainers, and you're far more pleasant to work with." He tapped his cane over cobblestone. "You and Nia deserve a chance to train."

"You sound like my *vater*."

"I'll take that as a compliment, assuming you are not referring to Norbie's singing."

She smiled, her cheeks feeling numb from the cold air. "Working with Nia, the best dog in all of Deutschland, makes me look good."

He gave a tug on the harness handle. "*Halt*."

Nia stopped, raised her right front paw, and panted.

"Why are we stopping?" Anna asked.

He turned to her. "You're not giving yourself enough credit. Nia is an incredible guide dog, but you have a gift, Anna."

She looked at him. A glimmer of light from a gas streetlamp flickered over his stubbled face.

"This afternoon on the obstacle course," he said, "I kept thinking about all the good you and the school are doing for battle-blinded soldiers. You're not merely pairing them with a shepherd to give them companionship and independence—you're restoring their lives and giving them hope."

Tears welled in her eyes.

"I can tell that you want to be trainer; I feel your passion for guide dogs each time you work with me and Nia. And I believe Emmi is right—you must strive to remain a trainer."

"It's Fleck's decision, not mine," she said.

"You're right," he said. "But even if Fleck decides to remove you from your substitute role, you must never give up on your dream."

Anna wiped her eyes with her sleeve. *He's lost so much, yet he's encouraging me to pursue my aspirations.*

"How about a pact?" he asked, extending a gloved hand. "I'll do my best to graduate from guide dog school, and you do everything in your power to remain a trainer."

"Agreed." She shook his hand.

Nia raised her snout, her eyes peering back at them.

Anna released his hand and patted Nia. "You're in this pact, too, Nia. I'm expecting you to show Fleck that you're worthy of being a guide dog." *And someday you'll be assigned to Max.*

Arriving at home, Anna—despite being chilled, tired, and hungry—was excited to tell her *vater* about the day. They entered Norbie's workshop, void of light except for a glow coming from under a crack in the back door.

"Vater!" Anna called.

"Outside," he said, his voice muffled.

Anna opened the back door. In the garden, a small snow-covered space that was surrounded by a brick wall, Norbie was on his hands and knees. Beside him was a lantern, spade, and hand trowel. Ice beads clung to his beard.

"What are you doing?" she asked.

"Digging for food." Norbie attempted to stand and grimaced.

Anna dashed to him and helped him to his feet.

Nia led Max into the garden.

"Why?" Anna asked, dusting snow from his clothing.

Norbie, his eyes filled with sadness, looked at Anna. "I went to pick up our rations and was told that they were out of food."

Oh, God. "How long?"

"They don't know," Norbie said. "I'll try again tomorrow. But in the meantime, we only have a couple turnips for us to eat." He glanced to a row of leafy stalks, which were partially covered in snow. "I was saving the winter leeks to separate and replant in the spring, but I decided to dig them up for us to eat. The ground is frozen. It took me over an hour to collect a couple of meager plants."

Anna clasped his hands. "You're shivering, and you have icicles in your whiskers. Let's go inside."

"I'll be a little while longer," Norbie said. "I barely have enough for a watery soup."

"I'll do it," Max said, stepping forward. He removed his gloves, reached into his pocket, and handed Anna a small package wrapped in newspaper.

She lifted a corner of the paper, exposing a hunk of bread and a field sausage. Her heart sank. "You can't keep giving us your lunch."

"The military gives me more than I need." He turned toward Norbie. "My time in the trenches has turned me into a skilled digger. How many do you need?"

"*Danke*, my boy." Norbie patted Max on the shoulder. "A few more would be splendid." He led Max to a row of winter leeks, handed him the garden tools, and then went into the house.

Anna paused, watching Max hack away at the frozen ground with a garden trowel. The winter was unseasonably cold, as if Mother Nature was bestowing her wrath in response to the war that ravaged her Earth. A shiver ran down her spine. *What if there are no rations available tomorrow, or the day after that?* The dormant leek bulbs in their miniscule urban garden would not be enough to augment their depleted rations. Her excitement to tell Vater about her day vanished, replaced with a fear of not having enough food to survive the winter.

"Take Nia inside," Max said, scraping at frozen soil. "I can find my way upstairs."

"All right." Anna clasped Nia's harness and led her inside.

In the kitchen, Anna removed Nia's harness and bundled her in a blanket. She attempted to check her paws, but the dog playfully rolled in the blanket, as if she were drying herself after a bath. Assured that Nia's sore paw was not causing her too much distress, Anna lit the wood stove and prepared a bowl of lukewarm water for Norbie to thaw his numb fingers, and a pot of boiling water to make soup. She chopped the frozen leeks and a turnip and tossed them into the pot. Thirty minutes later, Max entered the kitchen with a handful of leeks, which she diced and added to the soup.

Dinner was served well after 9:00 p.m., a time when they were usually preparing to go to bed. On the table were bowls of leek soup and a plate with Max's leftover field sausage and bread.

"It's good," Norbie said, tasting his soup.

"It needs cream and potato," Anna said.

Max took a bite. "I like it. You're a remarkable cook to make savory soup out of dormant leeks."

Anna appreciated their efforts to compliment her on the food, but she couldn't stop thinking about the dwindling food supplies, due to the British naval blockade, and the rumors that many Germans would die from starvation before spring. *Famine has become a weapon.* A fusion of hunger and dread gnawed at her stomach.

"Have you told Norbie?" Max asked.

"*Nein,*" she said, staring at her soup.

"Tell me what?" Norbie asked.

"It's nothing," Anna said. "It can wait until tomorrow."

"Anna and Nia trained with me," Max said.

A smile spread over Norbie's face. "That is glorious news." He leaned to Anna and hugged her. "I'm so proud of you."

Anna's angst faded. "*Danke.*"

"Why didn't you want to tell me?" Norbie asked.

"I'm worried about us not having enough rations," she said. "What if the British blockade doesn't end."

"Everything, including war and blockades, eventually ends," Norbie said. "If rations continue to be sparse, I'll find a way to get us food, even if I have to barter every one of my clocks and time-pieces to get us through winter." Norbie patted her hand. "Now, tell me about your day."

You always have a way of making terrible things tolerable, Anna thought. She took a bite of soup, bitter and bland, and for the next several minutes she told him about Fleck permitting her and Nia to temporarily train with Max until healthy shepherds became available.

Norbie beamed. "This calls for a celebration." He stood, opened a china cabinet, and retrieved crystal wineglasses.

"What are you doing?" Anna asked.

"I'm going to pour us drinks for a toast."

Anna furrowed her brows. "But we don't have any wine."

Norbie looked at her. "Do you remember what wine tastes like?"

She nodded, feeling confused.

"*Gut*." He poured water from a clay pitcher into the wineglasses. "To Anna, Max, and Nia," he said, raising his glass. "And their success with guide dog training."

Anna clinked their glasses and took a sip of water.

"Ah," Norbie said. "That's a fine Riesling."

"*Ja*," Max said. "Citrusy and sweet. What year is it?"

Anna smiled.

Norbie pretended to examine a label on the pitcher of water. "1913."

"A fine year," Max said.

"Let's have some sauerbraten and spätzle," Norbie said. He carved the small, shriveled field sausage with a paring knife and placed the bits of meat onto their plates with a thumb-size piece of black bread.

Max sniffed his food. "Smells divine."

Norbie chewed a bit of dry sausage. "It's delicious but not quite as tender as my wife, Helga's, sauerbraten. Her recipe called for the meat to be marinated—in a secret family recipe of wine, herbs, and spices—for seven days."

A childhood memory of Anna and her *mutter* pouring pretend tea for dolls flashed in her head.

Max nibbled his bread. "The spätzle is mouthwatering, but it's not quite as tasty as my *mutter*'s recipe. Her spätzle called for a rare variety of nutmeg—grown on a secret spice island—and eggs from hand-fed ostriches."

Norbie chuckled. "That's the spirit."

They're creating an imaginary dinner to help us feel better. She fought back tears and took a spoonful of soup.

With a bit of encouragement from Norbie, Anna joined the childish make-believe game. As the meal progressed, they attempted to outdo each other with the usage of delectable words and far-fetched recipes. Anna forgot about the war, British naval blockade, and threat of starvation. Long after dinner was finished, they chatted at the table, like a family after a holiday meal. The scant amount of food had done little to curb the grumble in her belly, but Vater and Max had filled her heart with hope.

CHAPTER 18

OLDENBURG, GERMANY—DECEMBER 9, 1916

Anna, anxious to read a letter that she received from Bruno, finished her evening chores and went to her bedroom. Although she was exhausted from working outside in the cold for most of the day, her heart thrummed as she opened the envelope.

> *Dearest Anna,*
> *I have much I need to tell you, my darling. However, I will save most of my words for when I see you. The military has granted my leave for January, and I should know the precise dates in the coming days.*

Thank Goodness! She took a deep breath to calm the quiver in her hands.

> *I hope this letter finds you well. I am hearing rumors that the Royal Navy blockade is creating severe food shortages in many German cities. I pray that this is not the case for Oldenburg. Are you getting enough to eat?*

Anna's mind flashed to the bowls of watery turnip and leek soup that they'd eaten for the past two days. With the exception of Max's veteran rations that he'd insisted on sharing with her and Norbie, they'd consumed only soup and bark coffee.

The fighting and death are taking a toll on me. I tell you this not to alarm you, but to vent my vexation. I often remind myself that war compels one to do unthinkable things. However, affirmations do little to diminish the guilt that rages inside my chest. I'm plagued with worry about my actions in this war, and I hope that you will someday forgive me.

"Of course," she whispered, feeling heartbroken for him. As a nurse, she'd witnessed the aftermath of the mutilation that took place on the front. But she could not begin to imagine what it would be like to be forced by the military to fight, let alone kill, another human being. She wished that there was something that she could do to ease his anguish, and that the bloodshed in Europe would come to an end.

I long to hold you in my arms and forget the past. I have credence that things between us will be as they once were. I'll write to inform you of my arrival. Perhaps you can arrange to take time away from work while I'm on leave.
Affectionately,
Bruno

A mixture of excitement and melancholy stirred within her. She was elated by the news that Bruno would soon be home, but his remorseful words had shaken her core. *He's hurting. I'll find a way to help him when he's home. But Fleck will never give me time off from work while boarding and training Max.*

The past two days were arduous for Anna. The other trainers had spoken little to her, as if they didn't believe a woman, especially one who lacked a military background, had earned the right to train dogs. Through the corners of her eyes, she'd frequently seen Waldemar, glaring at her from the sidelines of the obstacle course. And Fleck had criticized many of her training techniques, most notably the manner in which she instructed right shoulder work—the capacity for Nia to leave ample room for Max on his right when passing fixed objects such as signposts and benches.

"Your right shoulder work is pitiful, Fräulein Zeller!" Fleck had shouted. "You need to make certain your dog protects its handler from head to toe!"

Anna, her nerves rattled, had made adjustments with Nia. Throughout each day, Max provided words of encouragement, which she greatly appreciated. But being on the obstacle course, as opposed to watching from the sidelines, revealed her flaws and how much she needed to learn in order to become a competent instructor. Although she worried that Fleck might reconsider his decision to allow her to temporarily train, and that Nia might be removed from the course when the other dogs were healthy, she refused to give up on her quest to be a guide dog trainer.

The sound of a solitary piano key resonated from the living room. She straightened her back and listened. The tone faded, and the same note was played again. Driven by curiosity, she placed Bruno's letter in a drawer and descended the stairs to the living room.

Max, standing at the piano with the front panel removed to expose the strings and tuning pins, tapped a key. A twangy resonance filled the room.

"I think it's sharp," Norbie said, standing beside Max.

"I believe it's flat," Max said.

Nia, lying in the center of the living room, thumped her tail.

"Are you sure?" Norbie asked.

"*Ja*," Max said.

"It's definitely flat," Anna said, approaching them.

"Ah, Anna," Norbie said. "Max is going to tune your *mutter*'s piano."

"That's very kind," she said.

"We don't have a tuning key," Max said, "but a wrench from Norbie's toolbox should work well as a substitute."

"How is Bruno?" Norbie asked.

"He's coming home on leave," Anna said, hesitant to disclose details of Bruno's emotional turmoil.

"Wonderful," Norbie said. "When will he arrive?"

"Next month," she said. "He doesn't yet know the date."

"That is grand news," Max said. "I'm happy for you."

Anna's mind flashed to Bruno's contritely worded letter. *After enduring hardships of war, he's worried that things might not be the same between us.* She buried her thoughts and stepped to Max. "May I help you tune the piano?"

"Sure," Max said. "It will go faster if someone can strike the keys while I adjust the tuning pins."

"I can do it," Norbie said.

Anna fidgeted with a sleeve of her sweater. "I think Max might need someone to know the notes on the keyboard."

"The ability to play a few chords would also be helpful," Max said.

"Oh," Norbie said, a timbre of disappointment in his voice. "Anna can read music, so maybe she's a little better suited than me for the job. But if you need an extra opinion on whether a key is sharp or flat, you can find me tinkering in my workshop." He rubbed Nia's belly, causing the dog to roll over on her back and thump her tail, and then descended the stairs to his workshop.

"What would you like me to do?" Anna asked.

Max gestured for her to sit on the piano bench. "You can start by striking the middle C, and hold the key down so I can locate the hammer."

Anna sat and struck the key. A flat, twangy tone filled the air.

He glided a hand inside the piano until he located the pressed felt hammer. He followed the string to the tuning pin, and then turned it clockwise with the wrench. The pitch sharpened.

"Is it difficult for you to tune a piano without a tuning fork?" she asked.

"Not really," Max said. "But I'll need to rely on your ears for the upper octaves."

She struck the key again. "I hope I can do a good job."

"You will," he said. "You sing in perfect pitch. I'm sure you'll have no trouble with directing my adjustments."

Anna smiled. She gazed at the network of metal wires. "How many strings are there?"

"There are typically two hundred and thirty strings on a piano with eighty-eight keys."

"Oh, my," she said. "I guess I never paid much attention to how many strings were hidden inside the piano. How long will it take to tune?"

"A couple of hours," he said. "But without my sight, it might take a little longer."

"You're lucky that I filled in for Vater," she said. "He's unaware that he's a bit tone deaf, and you might be up all night, debating whether a string is flat or sharp."

He chuckled. "I don't mind. Norbie is great fun."

"*Ja*, he is," she said, grateful for her *vater*, as well as Max's kind words.

"Middle D," he said.

She pressed the key.

He located the hammer and string, then adjusted the tuning pin.

"Are all of the strings flat?"

"Most will be," Max said. "Due to humidity, they tend to turn flat in the winter and sharp in the summer." He ran his hand over the inside of the piano and paused, his fingers resting on a raised metal manufacturer's emblem.

"Is something wrong?"

"It's a Blüthner piano," he said. "I thought it might be one based on its clarity and rich warm sound." He ran a fingertip over the crown and raised name on the emblem—Julius Blüthner. "My *vater* was a piano maker for Blüthner in Leipzig."

Anna's eyes widened. "Could he have worked on this one?"

"Maybe," he said. "How old is it?"

"I'm not exactly sure," she said. "I think my *mutter* purchased it around thirty years ago."

"He would have been working at Blüthner then, but there were other piano makers." He rubbed his chin. "It's nice to think that he might have made this one."

She looked at him, his face turned somber. *He's asked many questions about my* mutter, *but I've made little effort to learn about his family.* Her chest tightened. "It was insensitive of me not to inquire about your parents. I'm sorry."

"It's okay," he said.

"Would you consider it to be intrusive of me if I asked what happened to them?"

"*Nein.*"

She patted the space on the bench next to her.

Nia, still lying on her back from her belly rub, peered with her head upside down toward Anna.

He sat and took a deep breath. "My parents, Katarina and Franz, were originally from Vienna, but they moved to Leipzig when my *vater* began his career as a piano maker. They were on holiday, celebrating their wedding anniversary in Kotor, a coastal town in Montenegro, when war was declared."

Anna clasped her hands.

"Instead of fleeing Kotor, they volunteered to help with refugees from Bosnia and Herzegovina, who were also coming back home from holiday. A few weeks later, in August of 1914, they boarded an Austro-Hungarian passenger ship called the *Baron Gautsch.*" He paused, running a hand through his hair. "On the voyage from Kotor, the ship ran into a minefield laid by the Austro-Hungarian Navy."

Her skin turned cold.

"One hundred and twenty-seven passengers and crew members died in the sinking of the ship, including my parents."

"Oh, my God," she whispered.

He swallowed. "My parents' bodies were never recovered."

Her heart ached. She placed a hand on his arm. "I'm so sorry."

He nodded.

She slid her hand to her lap.

"They were wonderful parents," Max said. "My *mutter* was a singing teacher who occasionally performed at the Leipzig Opera. My *vater*, of course, played the piano. Our home was filled with laughter and song."

"They sound lovely," she said.

A smile formed on his face. "My earliest memories were of Vater teaching me to play scales, while Mutter sang along in her beautiful mezzo-soprano voice."

"I now understand why you pursued becoming a pianist and composer," Anna said.

He nodded. "My parents supported my musical aspirations, but they never forced me to practice. I played the piano because I loved it. And after my first childhood recital, I knew that I wanted to be a professional pianist."

"What happened?"

"People applauded." He peered toward the ceiling, as if he were replaying memories in his mind. "I felt immense satisfaction to give others joy."

Anna smiled.

"I practiced every day, and as I improved my piano skills, my *mutter* began to tell me that I was destined to perform at the Great Hall of the Musikverein in Vienna. Have you ever been there?"

"*Nein*," Anna said. "What is it like?"

"Perfect acoustics," Max said. "It's one of the finest concert halls in the world. And it's incredibly beautiful, with towering ceilings ornately decorated in gold." He looked toward her. "Someday, you need to go there."

"I will," she said, wondering if a postwar German Empire would provide her the opportunity to experience such luxuries.

"Eventually, I went on to study piano at the Royal Conservatory of Music of Leipzig. Surrounded by gifted tutors, my skills ascended. I began to dream that I might someday perform in the Great Hall of the Musikverein, just like my *mutter* had predicted. And as I developed my craft, I began to compose piano concertos." He fiddled with the wrench. "But the war changed things for me."

Anna drew a jagged breath. "Maybe there's a chance for you to play again."

He shook his head. "You'll see why when we tune the upper strings." He rose from the bench. "We should probably get back to work. I don't want to keep you up all night."

"I don't mind," she said.

He placed his hands inside the piano. "You'll feel differently tomorrow, when Nia is nudging you to stay awake on the obstacle course."

Nia swished her tail.

For the next thirty minutes, Anna tapped keys and Max adjusted tuning pins. Lacking a damper stick, which was needed for keys with multiple strings, Max improvised by using an old postcard to isolate strings. Key by key and string by string, they tuned the piano. As they ascended the keyboard, Anna observed how Max increasingly struggled to hear the sounds.

"The notes are turning faint and fuzzy," he said.

Anna tapped the key harder.

He resorted to placing his ear to the top of the piano to register the pitch, and a few strings higher he shook his head. "You'll have to direct me from here."

Anna's heart sank. "Okay."

Relying on Anna's guidance on pitch, Max tuned the upper registry strings. And when they began working on the lower half of the keyboard, which Max could hear well, his ardor returned.

"I was thinking about Fleck's comments on your right shoulder work," Max said, tightening a string.

She straightened her spine. "And—"

"In my opinion, your right shoulder work is excellent. Nia has yet to guide me into a pole, tree, wagon, door, or any other fixed object."

Anna tucked loose hair behind her ear, then tapped a key.

Nia, roused by hearing her name, stood and sat beside Max.

He rubbed Nia's fur. "I think Fleck is being tough on you to show the others that he's not taking his decision to allow you to train lightly."

"I don't know," she said, shifting in her seat. "I have lots to learn."

"Everyone does," Max said. "Fleck and his men are new to training shepherds to be guides. Prior to establishing the school, they were working with ambulance dogs, and none of them had worked with disabled veterans."

Anna's confidence bloomed. "I hadn't thought of it that way."

"You're doing a splendid job. Keep doing what you're doing and Fleck will eventually realize that you're the best trainer in school." He looked toward Anna. "And that you and Nia are irreplaceable."

Nia panted and wagged her tail.

"*Danke.*" She fought back tears welling in her eyes. "You're doing well, too. I'm sure that Fleck will permanently assign you a shepherd, and I hope it is Nia."

"Me too." He stroked Nia's ears. "But—"

"What?"

"You and Norbie are fond of her, and she's attached to both of you. I hate the thought of taking her away from her home."

He's facing the possibility of a future alone, and he's worried about everyone but himself. "Nothing would make us happier than for Nia to be with you."

He nodded reluctantly.

"I do, however, expect you to send us letters to keep us apprised on how Nia is doing. And you should know that when Norbie and I begin to miss her, which will happen quite often, we'll be coming to visit her in Leipzig."

He smiled. "I think that seems more than fair."

They finished tuning the remaining strings. Max replaced the cover on the piano and sat beside her on the bench. Placing his hands on the keyboard, he played a few scales and chords.

"What do you think?" he asked.

"It sounds beautiful. My *mutter* would have been proud to play a piano so finely tuned."

"I'm glad."

"I wish I had kept up playing the piano. I can barely remember my chords, let alone play a song." She looked at him. "It seems such a waste to allow it to sit idle."

He paused, resting fingers on the keys.

She hoped that her comment might influence him to attempt to play, perhaps a few more chords or a melody on the base clef keys. Instead, he rose from the bench.

"I should probably get some rest," he said.

"*Ja*," she said, feeling disappointed. "Thank you again for tuning the piano."

"You're welcome." He patted Nia and shuffled toward the stairs.

"Don't you want to take Nia with you?"

"I can find my way," he said. "Besides, Nia will be sneaking into my room later."

Anna chuckled.

Nia's tail brushed over the floor.

"Good night," he said.

Anna, reluctant to leave the piano, hugged Nia and stroked her fur. *It must be horrible for him to fix an instrument that he's no longer able to play. Yet he did it for us, and in honor of Mutter.* Her chest felt like a gutted, hollow gourd, and she was saddened to see him leave when there was so much more that she wanted to know about him. *He's easy to talk with, and he makes me feel like I'm deserving of being a guide dog trainer.*

Nia gave Anna a wet lick on the cheek.

She kissed Nia on the head and whispered, "I wish this piano had a thousand strings to tune."

CHAPTER 19

OLDENBURG, GERMANY—DECEMBER 12, 1916

Max, standing on a snow-covered street with his coat pockets filled with an assortment of Norbie's repaired watches, patted Nia with a gloved hand. "Are you up to making a few more stops?"

"Are you talking to Nia or me?" Anna asked, standing beside him.

"Both," he said, his breath misting in the frigid air.

"I'm okay." She put down her bag—which contained several small clocks and timepieces, as well as four beets and two turnips—and examined Nia's paw. "She hasn't limped much, and her pads look to be all right."

"Good," Max said, feeling relieved. "Perhaps you could direct me to the homes with the largest gardens."

"Straight ahead," Anna said.

"Forward," Max said, gripping the harness.

Nia padded ahead.

For the past few days, Max had worked with Anna and Nia under the close supervision of Fleck on the school grounds. He'd diligently worked to improve his skills, not merely for himself but to show Fleck that Anna and Nia were worthy of being on the training course. *Elfriede and the dogs with kennel cough will soon recover, and Fleck needs to see that Nia and Anna are doing a superior job.* Each day, his dog handling techniques improved, and his bond with Nia grew. At times, it felt effortless for him to be guided by Nia, as if the dog could sense his thoughts before he gave a verbal command. Today, he was eager to continue working with Nia and Anna on the obstacle course, but Fleck had surprised them and the entire class by giving them the afternoon to train in town.

Each group—comprised of a trainer, veteran, and shepherd—spread out through town. Some traveled to parks or gardens near Oldenburg Palace, while others made their way to the train station or the marketplace. But when Anna had asked him where he wanted to go first, he surprised her by saying, "Home."

Due to the dwindling supply of rations, Norbie had spent much of his time trying to barter his timepieces for food. He'd had little success for the past two days, save a bronze pocket watch that he'd traded for a half-loaf of molded bread. With little to eat, Max had dug up more winter leeks from the garden for soup. He hated that he was eating what little food they had and, even more, that he had no means to contribute, other than his military-issued lunches, toward their nourishment. So, when Fleck gave them the afternoon to work independently, he'd convinced Anna that they should offer to help Norbie with bartering his timepieces. While Norbie took a break from the bitter cold to tinker in his workshop, Max, Anna, and Nia canvassed the more affluent streets of Oldenburg. They'd knocked on dozens of doors. Most of their solicitation ended in failure, but they'd managed to sell a woman's silver watch in exchange for a few beets and turnips.

"Maybe we should go to the train station," Anna said. "I haven't seen any of the other trainers, and I'm worried we might get in trouble."

"We won't get in trouble," Max said. "We're training—we just happen to be carrying a few of Norbie's timepieces to trade for food while we practice our drills."

"Norbie appreciates your help, as do I," Anna said. "But what if Fleck catches us? He'll think we've abandoned our work."

"It won't be a problem," he said. "Think of how pleased Norbie will be when we come home with food."

"You're right," she said. "But we've already collected more than Norbie did in two days."

"It's my salesmanship," Max said, nudging her coat.

Anna chuckled. "Are you sure about that?"

It's good to hear you laugh. "Perhaps Nia is the better peddler. Without her, I doubt people would warm up to the idea of parting with their food, even if we were offering gold bullion."

"She's irresistible," Anna said, rubbing the dog's head.

Nia swished her tail.

"Let's keep going," he said.

"All right," she said. "But not much longer. The sun is setting and it'll be dark soon."

They knocked on the doors of several more homes, all with no success. Either the residents hadn't yet returned home from work, or they refused to answer the door. Climbing the steps to a large row house, Anna rang a mechanical bell. As footsteps grew from inside the house, Max and Nia nudged their way forward. The door cracked open.

"May I help you?" an elderly woman's voice asked.

Max removed his cap. "*Hallo*, I'm Max, and this is Anna. I realize that rations are scarce, but we wanted to inquire if you might be willing to trade a bit of food in exchange for a clock or watch."

"*Nein*," the woman said.

"They're quite exquisite," Anna said. "They've been refurbished by my *vater*, Norbie Zeller."

"He's the finest clockmaker in Deutschland," Max added, recalling stories of Norbie's accomplishments. "He's worked on the town's most prized timepieces, including the clock towers in Oldenburg Palace and St. Lambert's Church."

The woman paused, her eyes peeking around the door. "Are you with that dog school?"

"*Ja*," Anna said. "Max is a veteran in training, and Nia is a guide dog."

The woman opened the door and tightened a black wool shawl around her shoulders. "She's a beautiful shepherd. Would it be okay for me to pet her?"

"Of course," Max said, despite that they were not supposed to allow people to pet shepherds while they were working.

The woman, her veined hand quivering, stroked Nia's fur.

"Such a gorgeous dog. I had one like her when I was a child. Her name was Herta. She'd walked with me to school every morning."

Nia peered up at the woman.

"Herta sounds lovely," Anna said.

"I'm sorry," the woman said, rubbing Nia's back. "What are you selling again?"

"Timepieces," Anna said. She removed a small mantel clock from her bag.

Max plucked a pocket watch from his coat and extended his hand.

"I don't have much need for timepieces," she said.

Max's shoulders slumped.

"But they are beautiful, and I think I have enough food to get me through winter. Would you consider a couple of pickled preserves for your clock?"

"*Ja,*" Anna said.

The woman slipped away and returned with two jars of pickled beets. She gave them to Anna and took the clock.

"You are very kind," Anna said.

She nodded, and then looked at Max. "Good luck to you, young man."

"*Danke.*" Max extended his arm. He felt the woman shake his hand and slip away.

The woman entered her home and closed the door.

Max clasped Nia's harness and descended the steps to the sidewalk. Although he was thankful for the woman's food, a swell of indignity rose within him. He hated charity, even though they were technically bartering for food. *Someday, when I return home to Leipzig, I will find a way to support myself, no matter what I have to do.*

Anna joined Max and examined a jar of pickled beets. "I'm so glad we came. Norbie will be—"

"What?" Max asked.

"You're supposed to be working, Fräulein Zeller," a gruff male voice said.

Waldemar. Max's pulse accelerated.

"I—" Anna stashed the jar into her bag.

"We *are* working," Max said.

Waldemar gripped the harness to his dog, Gunda. "How can you be training when you're hawking for food?"

Damn it. Max's mind raced. "It was my idea. I insisted on bartering a few items while practicing guide dog maneuvers. Anna and her *vater* are out of rations, and I was trying to help them."

"It doesn't matter," Waldemar said. "You've violated Fleck's directive—and his trust. Instead of training, you've been going door to door for the entire afternoon begging for food."

He's been following us. Max's skin turned hot.

Anna swallowed. "I can explain—"

"Take it up with Fleck." Waldemar stroked his wooly gray mustache. "I expect that he'll dismiss you when you arrive at work tomorrow."

Anna crossed her arms.

Max shuffled forward. "It's all my doing."

Waldemar smirked. "If I were you, Max, I'd pack my bags tonight." He turned and walked away with his dog.

"Oh, God," Anna breathed.

"I'm sorry," Max said. "It's all my fault."

"No, it's not," she said. "I agreed to it."

Nia nuzzled Anna's leg.

"He's probably on his way to see Fleck," Anna said. "I'll likely be terminated, and you might be kicked out of school."

"*Nein*." Max shuffled to her. "Fleck will do no such thing."

"How do you know?"

"Waldemar is just trying to cause trouble. He resents having less responsibility in the class, and I think he's lost much of his credibility. Fleck will not dismiss you."

"Are you sure?" Anna asked.

"*Ja*," Max lied, hoping to alleviate Anna's concern. "I'll talk with him and clear things up for us."

"Maybe we should locate Fleck's home and speak with him tonight," Anna said.

"Do you know where he lives?"

"*Nein*."

"Then we'll talk with him in the morning." He extended his arm and found her shoulder. "In the meantime, I don't want you worrying about things."

"All right."

Max slipped his hand away, clasped Nia's harness, and said, "Forward." He felt a tug from Nia as she padded ahead. The sound of boots crunching snow filled his ears, and the weight of timepieces jostled in his coat pockets. He spoke little as they traversed the cobblestone streets toward home; his thoughts steadfast on finding a way to convince Fleck not to reprimand Anna. *If someone needs to be blamed, it will be me.*

In his room, Max sat on his bed with a braille book of poetry titled *Phantasus* by Arno Holz. He lifted the cover, releasing a sweet, musky scent of ink and paper, and ran his fingertips over the lines of raised dots. But Holz's vivid imagery did little to diminish his apprehension. By persuading Anna to combine training with bartering for food, he might have ruined her chances of continuing to work with him and Nia. In his determination to acquire nourishment for Anna and Norbie, who had graciously welcomed him into their home and fed him, he hadn't stopped to think that Waldemar might see them exchanging timepieces for food and inform Fleck that they were not training. The other trainers, Max believed, would have understood. He didn't regret helping Anna, but he did rue that he didn't go knocking on doors after working hours. And Anna's fate, as well as his, might rest on their ability to convince Fleck to accept their word over Waldemar's.

Norbie had been delighted that they'd come home with jars of pickled beets and vegetables, and neither he nor Anna, given her silence during dinner, wanted to dampen Norbie's spirits by telling him about their run-in with Waldemar. With the added beets to their diet of turnip and leek soup, they would have enough, if they reduced the portions, to last them a few days. Hopefully by then, the city's supply of rations would return to normal. But deep down, Max feared that the availability of food would get worse with winter.

The patter of Nia's footsteps in the hallway grew, and the ajar bedroom door squeaked open. Toenails clicked over the hardwood floor, and Max received a gentle nudge to his elbow.

Max placed down his book. "*Hallo*, Nia."

Nia panted.

Max slid onto the floor and leaned his back against the bed. He patted his thigh and the dog flopped onto his lap. He'd much rather have Nia jump onto his bed, but Fleck's protocol did not permit guide dogs on furniture while they were training. And considering he'd broken enough rules for one day, he thought it would be best to follow orders. "If I get to bring you home with me," Max said, scratching Nia behind the ears, "you'll be allowed to sleep in a bed or nap on a sofa."

Nia's tail swished over the floor.

"Does that sound good?"

Nia's tail thumped harder.

He rubbed her side. *You'll have all of the comforts of a home if you live with me. But first I need to convince Fleck that we're worthy of each other.*

His fondness of Nia had grown exponentially since he'd arrived in Oldenburg, and the despondency that swallowed him, like a foundering boat on a sea, had slowly lifted. Although his heart still ached from Wilhelmina's rejection of him, he felt—perhaps for the first time since being told by a doctor that he would never see again—that his life was worth living. And no matter how difficult it would be to find a path to create a life of his own, he felt that he had the strength to go on with Nia at his side.

"You're a remarkable dog, Nia." He ruffled her ears. "How did you get to be so kind and smart?"

Nia playfully wriggled on her back.

"Did Anna teach you?" He paused, resting a hand on her belly, and lowered his voice. "I made a mess of things for her."

Nia's eyebrows raised.

"I need to find a way to fix things for her with Fleck." He ran his fingers through her fur. "What should I say to him?"

Nia gently placed a paw to Max's arm.

You seem to know my thoughts and feelings. I wish I knew what you're thinking.

Nia squirmed but made no effort to leave his lap.

He rubbed her chin.

The dog licked his hand.

Max smiled. "I'll figure something out."

The pluck of piano keys rose from the living room.

Nia rolled onto her belly and stood.

More keys were played, creating a simple chord. *Anna*, Max thought, getting to his feet. He paused, debating whether he should go back to reading or join her. But considering he'd botched things up this afternoon and he didn't want her to go to bed worrying about her job, he brushed his clothes and turned toward the sound of Nia's panting. "How about we join her?"

Nia left the room and scampered down the stairs.

Forgoing his cane, he glided his hand along the walls and banister to the living room. The floorboards creaked under his weight, and the piano chords stopped. "I thought you might have already gone to bed."

"*Nein*," Anna said, sitting at the piano. "It's a little early to sleep."

"Is Norbie in his workshop?"

"*Ja*," she said, patting Nia. "He's putting together more timepieces to barter."

Max's chest tightened.

"Is my tapping on the keyboard disturbing your reading?" she asked.

"Not at all," he said. "May I join you?"

"Sure."

He extended his arm and searched for the sofa.

"Could you sit beside me?" she asked. "I have a few questions about chords."

Max shuffled toward the sound of her voice and sat beside her at the piano bench. He placed his hands on his lap.

"I've forgotten some of the chords," she said, playing a lower octave C major chord.

"Which ones would you like to learn?"

"All of them," she said.

"So that you can learn to play pieces?"

"Maybe someday." She struck the chord again. "Until then, I'd like to listen to my *mutter*'s piano while it remains in tune."

"Okay," Max said. "Try a D major—D, F-sharp, A."

Anna located the keys and—using her thumb, middle, and pinkie fingers—played the chord.

"Nice," Max said. "How about E-flat major—E-flat, G, B-flat?"

She played the chord.

"You're a natural."

Anna chuckled. "I'm only pressing the keys that you tell me."

"Perhaps, but you know where to find them." He paused, rubbing his knees. "I'm sorry about what happened today."

"It's all right."

"Are you worried about Fleck?" he asked.

"Not really. Besides, it's worth it to make sure Vater has food."

"I'll make things right with Fleck," Max said, hoping to hide the wane of confidence in his voice.

"We will." She played the chord.

Max's mind raced, searching for something to talk about, other than Fleck. "What type of music does Bruno like?"

Anna's fingers slipped from the keys.

"Does he like classical music or does he prefer folk songs, like Norbie?"

"I don't know," she said, her voice hesitant.

"Oh," Max said, feeling like he'd stumbled into a sensitive topic.

"It's just that—" Anna took a deep breath. "Our courtship was brief, and with the war and having a mere two weeks of leave per year, we haven't had the opportunity to spend much time listening to music."

"I understand," Max said. "You'll have plenty of time after the war."

"*Ja*," she said, her voice soft.

"How did you meet?"

"I mended his broken arm while working as a nurse at the hospital."

"And he was smitten with you," he said.

"I guess so," Anna said. "He stayed in Oldenburg during his recovery. We got to know each other and grew close."

"Tell me about him."

"Bruno is sweet," she said. "He wrote me poems while he was recovering from his injury. It's the reason we courted."

Max smiled. "A poet."

"Well, not exactly." She paused, running a finger over a key. "He hasn't written a poem in quite some time."

"The front has a way of temporarily stealing one's zest," Max said, hoping to lift her spirits. "I'm sure you'll receive enumerable poems and love letters after the war."

"*Danke*, Max."

"What else drew you to Bruno?"

She took a deep breath.

"I'm sorry," he said. "Am I being intrusive?"

"Not at all," she said. "I was just thinking. He has many qualities that I wish I had."

"Like what?"

"Confidence, competence, intelligence—"

"I disagree," Max said. "You have all of those qualities." *You're the most brilliant and brave person I know.*

"That's lovely of you to say," she said, "but you didn't know me when I was working as a nurse. I had trouble with measuring medicine, and I had a reputation of administering the most painful injections of any nurse in the hospital ward. Once, I even missed a man's arm and injected his mattress with morphia."

Max chuckled. "I think you've found your calling with training shepherds."

She smoothed her skirt with her hands. "I guess I was attracted to traits in Bruno that I didn't see in myself. Also, his upbringing is quite different from mine. His family owns a manufacturing business in Frankfurt, and he plans to someday run the company."

With Bruno's family wealth and influence, why hasn't he arranged to acquire food? A bit of resentment smoldered in Max's gut. He shook away his thought and said, "I assume you'll leave Oldenburg."

"Eventually," she said.

He wondered how Anna felt about having to give up her dream of becoming a guide dog trainer, but decided it might be meddlesome to ask. "Bruno's family must be quite proud of the work that you're doing, and I bet they're overjoyed for you to move to Frankfurt."

"I haven't met them," she said, a timbre of disappointment in her voice.

Max swallowed, feeling as if he had fallen in a tar pit.

"Bruno wants to introduce me to his parents in person."

"They'll love you," he said.

"You really think so?" she asked.

"I know so."

She smiled and clasped her hands.

He felt her shift her weight on the bench. *I've inquired enough about her personal life.* "Let's try a chord that's a bit more challenging: A-flat minor—A-flat, C-flat (B), E-flat."

Anna played the chord, striking an incorrect key. A clashing resonance filled the air. "Sorry."

"May I?" he asked, gesturing toward her hand.

"*Ja.*"

He glided his hand over the keyboard, and then gently placed her fingers over the correct keys. "Okay."

She played the chord.

"Perfect," he said.

"Could you try to play something for me?"

An uneasiness stirred in his gut. "*Nein.*"

"Why?"

"I can't hear the upper keys," he said. "You saw what happened when we tuned the piano."

"Of course," she said, "but I've been giving this a lot of thought. Do you remember our turnip soup dinner when you and Norbie pretended to drink fine wine and eat delectable foods to cheer me up?"

"*Ja.*"

"During your game, my brain resurrected memories of what a Riesling wine tastes like. And I discovered that I could recall the savory flavor of sauerbraten, down to the precise taste of meat marinated in cognac and raisins." She turned toward him. "Did you remember the tastes, too?"

"I did," he said, crossing his arms. "But my limited range of hearing is different."

"I disagree," she said. "If our brains can remember taste, there's no reason we cannot recall sound. I think you can build a tone memory bridge to play the piano."

"It's not that easy," Max said. "The upper registry is a silent void to me."

"It's not to me," Anna said. "Or an audience."

Max took a deep breath, attempting to dispel the tightness growing in his chest.

Anna gently placed a hand on his arm.

His tension eased.

"You told me that you gained immense satisfaction by giving others the joy of music," she said. "It's why you became a pianist."

He nodded.

"Please," she said softly.

Nia padded to Max's side and brushed against his leg.

"Are you in this, too?" he asked.

The dog wagged her tail.

He turned toward Anna. "You're not going to give up on this, are you?"

She slipped her hand from his arm. "*Nein.*"

"All right," he breathed.

Max moved closer to Anna to center himself over the keyboard. He sifted through his memories, visions of recitals flashing in his head. He considered several adagio tempo pieces that would venture to, but not focus on, the high octave keys. After a bit of thought, he decided on Concerto No. 3 in D Minor, Movement II by Johann Sebastian Bach. He positioned his hands over the keyboard, took a deep breath, and played a solitary D key slowly in repetition, like a slow heartbeat. The solitary notes progressed to a dyad—a two-note chord—and on to a minor chord. As the pulse of chords continued, he played, using his right hand, a delicate melancholy melody. Images of his parents in the front row of a Leipzig concert hall surged through his brain. He imagined himself as he was before the war, a robust man with hope and aspiration. As the theme ascended to tones that his damaged eardrums could not detect, he fought back the urge to stop. His pulse quickened as he struggled to conjure the missing sounds. But gradually, he began to fabricate absent pitches within his head. The concerto grew to a crescendo, the vibration of the piano reverberating through his hands, blood, and bone. Minutes later, the piece drew toward the end, growing slower and softer. He finished, his fingers holding down on the keys, as the tones faded, and then disappeared.

The sound of Norbie's clapping hands pierced the air. "Bravo!"

Max slipped his hands from the piano.

"Magnificent, my boy," Norbie said. "I heard your music in my workshop and I came upstairs. I hope you don't mind."

"Not at all," Max said. He turned to Anna. "How was it?"

Anna, her eyes pooled with tears, leaned to him. "It was the most beautiful thing I've ever heard."

CHAPTER 20

LILLE, FRANCE—DECEMBER 12, 1916

In his room at the officers' boardinghouse, Bruno put on his uniform, which Celeste had cleaned and pressed. Using a military-issued grooming kit, he shaved, trimmed his thick mustache, and combed his hair. He placed his personal items into a leather case and left his room. As he descended the grand staircase of the bourgeois home, a sense of disquietude encompassed him. Instead of going off to the ammunition warehouse—where, for the past several days, he had supervised the procurement and shipment of phosgene gas shells—he was returning to the fight. He'd received orders from Haber to escalate the rate of gas shells along the front, while they waited for the new chemical weapon—derived from sulfur mustard—that Haber predicted would change the tide of the war.

"I packed you some food," Celeste said, peering up at him from the foyer.

A twinge of guilt pricked at his stomach. He descended the remaining stairs, his jackboots clacking on French oak flooring, and approached her.

"It's sausage and dried fruit," she said, extending a paper-wrapped package.

"*Danke.*" Bruno took the food and placed it into his bag. He paused, looking into her emerald-green eyes. Flashes of their intimacy flared in his head. "I wish there was a better way to leave things between us."

"It's all right," she said. "What we had was comfort. Nothing more."

It was more than that. You gave me affection and soothed my pain. "I don't know when I'll be back."

"Until we meet again, I will hold you in my prayers." Celeste gently placed a hand to his cheek.

His skin tingled.

"Take care of yourself," she said softly.

He slid her hand from his cheek, and then kissed her palm. "Goodbye, Celeste."

"*Adieu.*" She slipped away and disappeared into the parlor.

Bruno, a flurry of emotions swirling inside him, left the house and made his way to the train station. He'd arrived in Lille in a vulnerable state, and Celeste had given him succor in his hour of need. He loathed being unfaithful to Anna, and he expected his amour to be limited to one night of passion. But each evening in Lille, he'd succumbed to his desire to seek solace in her touch and affection. It wasn't unusual for soldiers, especially in Lille where the occupied town was filled with brothels and street prostitutes, to seek the company of a woman. He'd attempted to rationalize that his moments of weakness would be forgotten after the war. *But how will I look at Anna and not feel ashamed for what I've done? How would she feel if she knew about Celeste?*

For most of Bruno's life, he'd detested his parents' promiscuous behavior. His mother spent an inordinate amount of time alone at the family chalet in Switzerland, and Bruno was quite certain that his father had another mistress, if not more. It sickened him to think that he was repeating the cycle of his father, as if he'd inherited a trait that precluded him from being faithful.

Despite his anger with himself for his actions, he didn't blame Celeste for their affair. Like him, she was alone and suffering. And Celeste, a former courtesan to a fallen German officer, feared that her family in Paris would rebuke her for being a collaborator with Germany. *She is doing what she needs to survive,* he'd thought as she slept with her head on his chest, her breath flowing in waves over his skin. Celeste had asked nothing from him, other than his affection, and he'd done the same. They were, Bruno believed, two people pacifying their war-driven psychological pain through intimacy.

Twenty kilometers from Lille, Bruno arrived at an ammunition depot, behind the reserve line of the front. In the distance, German and Allied artillery cannons boomed. A familiar odor of expelled gunpowder penetrated his nostrils, turning his stomach sour. His thoughts of Celeste and Anna faded and were replaced by his allegiance to the Fatherland. He reported for duty, and then he went off to inspect the ammunition depot, only to find that the large supply of phosgene shells and mortars, which he had arranged to be shipped from Lille, had not been put to use.

Bruno, his veins pumping with irritation, went to an officers' bunker and located the highest-ranking available officer—Major Brandt.

"Sir," Bruno said, saluting the major. "I'm Oberleutnant Wahler. I'm responsible for transporting phosgene shells to this section of the front. May I ask why the shells have not been put to use?"

The major—a thin, middle-aged man with hooded, bloodshot eyes—took a gulp from a flask. "Kainz, the general of artillery, has ordered the use of only high-explosive shells."

Bruno's skin turned hot. "I'm here to implement the orders of Fritz Haber, head of the Chemistry Section in the Ministry of War, to increase the rate of phosgene shells."

The major shook his head. "I'm under the orders of Kainz, and we'll continue to fire high-explosive shells until he informs me otherwise."

"Perhaps General Kainz is not yet aware of the German Empire's plans," Bruno said. "Would you like to confer with him, or shall I arrange to speak with the general myself."

"He went to the front line to gain a better view of how mortar fire was penetrating the Allied trenches, and he got stuck there when the French commenced a sustained bombardment." The major took a swig from his flask. "That was twenty-four hours ago. He's likely hunkered in a dugout waiting for the bombardment to end."

Damn it. "Is it possible for me to get a message to General Kainz?"

"*Nein,*" the major said. "I will not risk the life of a messenger during a bombardment. You'll have to wait until the firing ends."

But that will be when the Allies commence their attack. An attack always follows a sustained bombardment. His chest muscles tightened. "Then I will deliver the request to General Kainz."

"You're a fool," the major grumbled. "You'll be under heavy shellfire before you reach the support lines."

The major's words stung Bruno. But the weight of his sins, combined with his hope that Haber's chemical weapons would eventually bring an end to the war, compelled him to step to a table with a trench map. "Sir, with all due respect, I *will* reach the general. And I would appreciate if you would show me the area of the line where he would likely be seeking shelter."

The major paused, taking a sip from his flask. He approached Bruno, and then placed his finger on the map. "Here."

Bruno scanned the diagram, memorizing the location.

"It will be easy to find, but hell to get there." The major drew a deep breath and exhaled.

A smell of schnapps filled Bruno's nose. "*Danke,* sir."

"Good luck, Wahler."

Bruno saluted and left. With nothing more than a service pistol and trench coat, he made his way toward the front line. A rumble of explosions filled the air, like a continuous roar of thunder. In the distance, fountains of earth spewed toward a clouded sky. In his haste to leave, he'd failed to bring a respirator, and he hoped that the enemy bombardment would not include a gas attack.

At the reserve line he encountered a hail of enemy shellfire. A large section of the trench had been blasted away, leaving mounds of dirt, rock, and mutilated bodies. *Oh, God.* He hunkered into a cavity, which had been carved into the side of the trench, and took in gulps of air. He gathered his courage and sprang from his pit. He ran, his boots squelching in the muck, until he reached the support line trench. The proximity and intensity of explosions grew. His heart rate spiked, and a concussive blast toppled him to the ground. Stunned, he crawled on his hands and knees and rolled into a dugout. Under the flickering glow of a *Hinden-burglicht*, several soldiers helped Bruno to his feet and checked him for wounds.

"You're a lucky bastard," a gaunt-faced soldier said, pointing to a rip near the hem of Bruno's trench coat. "You almost took a shell splinter."

Bruno ignored the comment and grabbed a canteen, which was hanging from the side of a bunk. "How far is the trench that will lead me to the front line?"

"Fifty meters," a soldier said.

Bruno guzzled water.

A blast quaked the earth. Bits of rock and dirt showered down from the ceiling of the timber-lined dugout. A man wailed.

Bruno turned. In the corner was a soldier, no more than eighteen years of age given his lack of facial hair, trembling and wriggling on the floor as if he was having a seizure.

"Henri," the gaunt-faced soldier said. "He's gone mad."

Hysteria, Bruno thought. *He's been driven insane by cannonade.*

A bomb exploded, rumbling the dugout. The young soldier whimpered and arched his back, like he'd been given an electrical shock.

"Try wrapping him in blankets," Bruno said. "And put plugs in his ears." He turned and approached the exit.

"Are you sure you want to go out there?" one of the soldiers asked.

"*Nein*," Bruno said, peering to the trench. "But I need to find General Kainz."

Before he lost his nerve, Bruno fled the dugout and slogged through muck. From dugout to dugout, he maneuvered through the winding trench. Reaching an intersection, he stepped over the upper torso of a fallen soldier with a gaping jaw and intestines strewn over the mud, and then made his way forward. He buried his fear and forced his legs to move faster. Minutes later, he reached the front line and the shellfire stopped.

He leaned against the wall of the trench and sucked in air, attempting to cool the burning in his lungs. German soldiers, carrying rifles with bayonets, emerged from dugouts and crouched along the fire step. Some prayed, while others removed personal belongings from their pockets. A soldier, his hands trembling and struggling to affix his bayonet, bent over and vomited onto the ground. The shrill of whistles, followed by the barking of machine guns, pierced the air. Pistol-wielding officers ordered the men to attack. Soldiers climbed out of the trench and into battle, but scores of the men—killed or maimed by a hurricane of bullets— tumbled back into the trench.

God help them. Bruno staggered through the wounded and dead, as well as the soldiers waiting for their turn to go up and over into no-man's-land.

"Where's General Kainz's dugout?" Bruno shouted to a group of soldiers.

A man pointed. "Hundred meters!"

Bruno, determined to reach the general, slogged ahead. But as he narrowed in on the location of the dugout, screams and gunfire erupted from within the trench. His blood turned cold. He turned and saw French soldiers, wearing horizon-blue-colored uniforms and carrying rifles, appear at a bend in the trench. *They've broken through!*

Bruno's heart rate soared. In one swift motion, he removed his pistol from its holster and discharged his ammunition, felling two soldiers. Bullets whizzed near his face. He turned and sprinted, all the while attempting to reload his weapon, only to encounter dozens of French soldiers pouring into the trench from above. Within seconds, the German line was overwhelmed. With no other option of escape, he scampered up the side of the trench and crawled toward the German lines. A barrage of bullets split the air, inches above his body. He pressed his chin to the dirt and pushed ahead.

Meter by meter, he clawed and kicked his way over mud, shrapnel, and corpses. Bullets flared above his head. *I'll never make it to the support trench—it's too far!* Forty meters into his crawl, his hands reached a void in the earth, and he tumbled into a large shell crater, its basin filled with knee-deep, frigid water. He got to his feet, his drenched coat weighting him down like a lead blanket. He dug his hands into his pockets, and then into the water, but was unable to locate his pistol. As he began to climb out of the hole, German machine guns erupted from the support trenches. A swarm of bullets ripped the air above him. Realizing that his odds of avoiding both enemy and friendly gunfire were remote, he crouched at the side of the crater and waited for the fighting to diminish.

A French soldier, carrying a rifle, plunged into the hole.

Bruno, his adrenaline surging, shot up.

The Frenchman's eyes locked on Bruno. He charged forward with a bayonet.

Bruno dived, feeling the blade scrape his side, and crashed into the basin. As the Frenchman swung around, Bruno sprang up from the water and tackled the man onto his back. Gripping the rifle in both hands, he overpowered the Frenchman, who was smaller and younger that Bruno. He pressed the barrel of the rifle over the man's neck, sinking his head under the water.

The Frenchman flailed his legs. Bubbles streamed from his nose and mouth.

Bruno's pulse pounded in his ears. But as the man's body weakened, Bruno hesitated, releasing pressure on the soldier's throat.

The Frenchman raised his head above the water. He choked and gasped for air.

"I'm taking you as prisoner," Bruno said. "But I'll kill you if you cause any trouble."

The Frenchman sucked in deep breaths.

"Do you understand?"

The Frenchman nodded.

Bruno exhaled, and then lifted the rifle.

The Frenchman lunged and sank his teeth into Bruno's hand.

Pain flared through Bruno's arm. As the Frenchman attempted to snatch the bayonet, Bruno slammed the rifle over the man's trachea, pinning him beneath the water.

The Frenchman thrashed his limbs. But as seconds passed, his energy evaporated and his body turned still.

Bruno, his legs quivering, sloshed to the side of the trench and collapsed. He placed the rifle over his lap, and then applied pressure to his bleeding hand. He peered toward the edge of the crater and waited for more enemy soldiers, the machine-gun fire to cease, or a German counterattack. But long after sunset none of them had come.

Although he'd killed hundreds, if not thousands, of Allied troops as a member of the Disinfection Unit, he'd never truly felt the consequences of his actions until now. Killing a man with his bare hands had shaken him. Echoes of the soldier's gurgles filled his head. He wondered if the man had a wife and children, which compounded his agony. French rockets shot up light flares with attached parachutes. The crater's water became illuminated, revealing the submerged body of the Frenchman, and then faded away as the flare floated to the ground. Bruno, cold and gutted, lowered his head to his knees and he wished for an end to it all.

At sunrise, a German counterattack reclaimed the front-line trench that had been lost to the Allies. A scout unit, comprised of three soldiers, located Bruno in the crater. They helped him, weak and shivering, to his feet and gave him sips of warm coffee from an insulated flask. As the soldiers were aiding him out of the hole, he hesitated.

"Wait." Bruno turned and waded into the frigid water. He reached inside the French soldier's coat, the body stiff with rigor mortis, and retrieved a wallet. Inside a soggy leather flap was identification, *Soldat 1.eme—Jules Bonnet,* and a worn family photograph of the Frenchman and a woman who appeared to be his wife, holding a baby in a lace dress and bonnet. His hands trembled. *God, forgive me.* He placed the soldier's wallet into his pocket, and then slogged out of the shell hole, making a silent vow to do something for the man's family after the war.

CHAPTER 21

OLDENBURG, GERMANY—DECEMBER 13, 1916

A wintry gust bit at Anna's cheeks as she stepped through the threshold of Norbie's workshop. She squinted, shielding her eyes from blowing snow, and turned to Max.

"It's going to be a rough walk to school," she said. "It's snowing heavily, and there's several inches on the ground."

"We can make it." Max wrapped a scarf around his neck, tucking the ends into his wool coat, then patted Nia's side. "Ready, girl?"

Nia gave a whole-body shake, as if she'd been given a bath, and then stood at attention with her chin up.

Max clasped the handle to Nia's harness. "Forward."

Nia padded ahead, her paws sinking in the snow.

Anna locked the door behind her. She paused, watching Nia guide Max over the dark, predawn street. *This might be our last day of training together. Fleck is going to terminate me or, at the very least, demote me.* A lump formed in the pit of her stomach. She'd rehearsed her explanation for bartering for food—when she was supposed to be training—but it likely didn't matter. Fleck was a stickler for rules, punctuality, and precise technique with his trainers. She held little hope that Fleck would understand or take pity with their lack of rations. If anything, she hoped that she'd be able to persuade Fleck that it was she, not Max, who had failed him.

Although she'd slept little, it wasn't due to fretting over saving her job. She'd spent much of the night awake in bed, buried under layers of blankets to keep warm, thinking about how beautifully Max played the piano. He'd only performed the one piece, but the angelic resonance of the strings replayed over and over in her head. She was overjoyed that Max might be on his way to regaining his ambition to play music. Even if her days of training were over, it was worth it, knowing that she and Nia played a small part in Max's journey to be a pianist. *With Nia's help, Max will live a life of independence doing what he loves most.*

A few streets away, they met up with Emmi, whose thick wool scarf was wrapped around her face, leaving a slit for her eyes.

"It's a day like this that makes me happy to be inside cleaning kennels, rather than playing on the obstacle course," Emmi jested.

"*Ja,*" Anna said. *After meeting with Fleck, I might be working with you in the barn, or searching for a new job.*

"Good morning, Emmi," Max said.

Emmi adjusted her scarf to uncover her face. "Hi, Max."

"How's Ewald?" he asked, staring ahead.

"That's sweet of you to ask," Emmi said. "I received a letter from him last night. His spirits are good, and he expects to be home on leave in the summer."

"That's wonderful," Max said.

Emmi glanced to Anna. "Any news from Bruno?"

Anna's shoulder muscles tightened. "*Nein.*"

"I'm sure you'll hear from him soon," Emmi said.

Anna nodded. She shuffled her boots through unplowed snow. To the east, the horizon glowed behind ashen clouds.

Emmi, as if she were attempting to change the subject, dusted snow from Max's coat. She turned to Anna and grinned. "You're slacking on your job, Anna. Max is turning into a snowman."

Anna lowered her head.

Emmi's smile faded. "What's wrong?"

"I created a mess of things for Anna," Max said.

"You did not," Anna said.

"It was my idea," Max said, turning toward Anna.

Emmi furrowed her brows. "What are you talking about?"

Anna drew a deep breath, cold air stinging her nostrils, and then looped her arm through Emmi's. As they walked toward school, she and Max told Emmi about bartering Norbie's timepieces for food, and their encounter with Waldemar.

"Oh, no," Emmi said. "Waldemar followed you for the entire afternoon?"

"I think so," Anna said. "I'm sure he has informed Fleck. I'll likely be relieved from my duties when we arrive at school."

"You won't be let go," Max said. "I'll talk with him. I'm sure he'll be reasonable about the situation."

"*Ja*," Emmi said. "You'll smooth things over with Fleck; you always do."

"I hope you're right," Anna said, walking ahead. "But if things work out poorly with Fleck, I might need to speak with Dr. Stalling about returning to the hospital."

Emmi nudged Max, and then picked up a handful of snow. She packed it with her gloved hands and tossed it, striking the back of Anna's knit cap.

A clump of snow dropped inside Anna's collar, freezing her bare skin. She turned, slipping on ice. "What was that for?"

"You worry too much," Emmi said.

Anna, as if by reflex, grabbed a handful of snow and hurled it. But it missed Emmi, who ducked, and struck Max in the face.

Max crouched to a knee and lowered his head.

"Oh, no!" Anna dashed to him and placed a hand on his shoulder. "I'm so sorry. I didn't mean to—are you okay?"

Max sprang up, laughing, and dumped a large ball of snow onto Anna's head.

"Trickster!" Anna said, packing a handful of snow.

Emmi chuckled, then received a snowball to her shoulder from Anna.

Within seconds, the trio—like a group of schoolchildren on a snow holiday—were chucking snowballs, pelting each other's coats. Max, with the aid of Nia, who pointed him in the general direction of Anna and Emmi, landed several hits. Anna's angst evaporated under a hail of snowballs and, for the moment, she forgot all about Fleck, her hunger, and the war.

Max tossed a snowball, landing short of Anna's feet.

"Come on, Max!" Anna shouted. "Is that all you got?"

Max waved, and then sucked in air to catch his breath.

Anna dropped her snowball and approached him. "Are you all right?"

He nodded. "I'm out of snowball fighting shape."

"If the winter continues to be like this," Emmi said, extending her hand to catch snowflakes, "you'll get plenty of exercise with me and Anna."

A muffled clopping and squeak of wagon wheels grew from behind them.

Anna turned. Through the falling snow, a horse-drawn wagon appeared. On the bench and holding the reins was Fleck. Sitting next to him was his dog, Elfriede. *He's early.* She dusted her and Max's coats, attempting to hide evidence of their snowball fight.

Fleck tugged on the reins and the wagon slowed to a stop. "Get in."

Anna swallowed. "All of us?"

"*Ja,*" he said.

Max slipped off his gloves, removed Nia's harness, and the dog leaped into the bed of the wagon, where she padded forward and greeted Elfriede with a sniff.

Anna, Max, and Emmi climbed into the bed of the wagon. Fleck tugged on the reins, and the wagon pulled away.

Anna waited for Fleck to say something, but he silently steered as the horse plodded toward school. *Let's get it over with*, she thought, staring at the back of Fleck's snow-dusted coat. She wondered, although briefly, if she should address the issue head-on with Fleck. But she didn't want to put Emmi in jeopardy of getting caught in Fleck's crossfire. And considering Max's silence, she believed that he might also be thinking the same thing. So, she leaned back, allowing icy flakes to patter her face, until they arrived at school.

They jumped down from the wagon. The horse snorted, its hot breath misting in the frigid air.

Anna motioned to Emmi to enter the barn.

Emmi nodded and slipped inside.

Fleck tethered a leash to Elfriede, who was no longer favoring her paw with the injured toenail.

"Elfriede looks much better," Anna said, desperate to break the silence.

Fleck flapped his cap against his coat, dusting away snow, and placed it on his head. His eyes met Anna's. "I'd like to have a word with you and Max—inside."

"*Ja*, sir," she said.

Anna, Max, and Nia entered the barn, where Emmi was preparing a fire in the cast-iron stove.

Emmi looked at Anna and silently mouthed, "It'll be okay."

Anna gave a subtle nod.

Rusted iron hinges screeched as Fleck closed the barn door. Anna's skin prickled.

"Fräulein Zeller," Fleck said, facing her, "I assume that you are aware that Waldemar has come to me with a concern about you and Max.

She clasped her gloved hands. "*Ja*, sir."

"Herr Fleck," Max said, shuffling forward. "It was all my doing. I insisted that Anna permit me to barter for food while we were training."

"You'll get your chance to say your piece, Max," Fleck said. "First, I'd like to hear from Fräulein Zeller."

Max slipped off his gloves and placed them in his coat pockets. "Of course, sir."

"We're nearly out of food, sir," Anna said. "I'm not sure if we'll have enough to last us until the supply of rations in Oldenburg are restored. My *vater*, Norbie, has had little success with trading his timepieces for food." Her stomach fluttered. She drew a deep breath, preparing herself for what she was about to say. "I thought that by enlisting Max and Nia to barter timepieces, people would be more, how shall I say, *sympathetic* to our need."

Emmi, her eyes wide, dropped a stack of wood. "Sorry," she blurted.

Fleck crossed his arms.

"That's not true," Max said. "Anna is attempting to take my

blame to save me from possibly being removed from training. It was me, not Anna, who insisted on bartering the timepieces." Using his thumb and forefinger, he rubbed the smooth leather handle to Nia's harness, as if it were a worry stone. "Anna and her *vater* are nearly starving, yet they share what little food they have with me while I board in their home. It's not fair; I receive military-issued lunches to sustain me, and they receive nothing. I wanted to help."

Oh, Max. A flash of him digging frozen leeks from the garden filled Anna's head.

Fleck sighed. "It's admirable of you to want to aid Fräulein Zeller and her *vater*, but Waldemar is right. You should not have been conducting personal tasks while training in town. When I give an order, I expect it to be followed. You're fortunate to have been selected for this program. There are countless blind veterans we can replace you with who will have no trouble adhering to my instructions."

Max gently placed his hand on Nia's head, and the dog leaned in to him.

Anna's heart sank. "Please, Herr Fleck, don't let Max go. He deserves to be here."

Fleck looked at Anna, then pointed to the shepherds' feed bin. "If you needed food, why didn't you pilfer turnips?"

"I—" Anna said, surprised by his question. "I would never take the shepherds' food. They barely have enough to eat, and they need their strength to train."

Fleck smoothed his mustache, and the lines in his face softened. "How much food do you have at home?"

"Sir?" Anna said.

"Tell me exactly what you have left to eat," Fleck said.

"With the exception of some winter leeks in the garden, we have a few beets and turnips, enough to last a few days."

"Follow me." Fleck glanced to Emmi, who was eavesdropping by the stove. "You too, Frau Bauer."

Emmi tossed a handful of kindling into the stove and joined the group, gathered by the turnip bin.

Fleck retrieved a burlap bag, hanging on a hook. "Frau Bauer, how many days until you're out of food?"

"Three," Emmi said.

Fleck loaded the bag with turnips and handed it to Max. "Put it under the bench in my wagon. You can divide it up after work."

"*Danke*, sir," Max said. He clasped Nia's harness, and the dog guided him out of the barn.

"But sir," Anna said. "What will the dogs eat?"

"We have a few more days until the shepherds with kennel cough return to the barn. In the meantime, I'll arrange to get more turnips through the Ambulance Dogs Association." Fleck shook his head in disgust. "The military and support units get food, while Germany's people are left to starve."

Anna blinked back tears. "I don't know how to repay you."

"You can start by following my orders," he said firmly. "And to never permit a veteran to deviate from my protocol."

"I will, sir." She clasped her hands to keep them from trembling. "Does this mean we're not being terminated?"

"Not today." Fleck walked toward the door.

A mixture of relief and curiosity stirred within her. "Sir, may I ask how you knew that I hadn't taken turnips from the bin?"

He paused, lighting a cigarette from his pocket. "I conduct frequent inventories of our supplies. I know precisely how many scoops of chopped feed that can be produced from a sack of turnips." He took a drag on his cigarette and blew smoke through his nose. "If you were stealing food, I'd know about it."

Give them each one level scoop, Fleck's voice echoed in Anna's head.

"And to be clear," Fleck said, "if you or Max should have another error in judgment, I will remove you from this school."

"*Ja*, sir."

Fleck left, his jackboots thumping on the frozen ground.

Anna wiped her eyes with the sleeve of her coat.

Emmi approached Anna and placed an arm around her shoulder. "I can't believe he gave us food."

"Nor I," Anna said.

Emmi gave her a squeeze. "Best we get to work."

Anna and Emmi went about their morning chores until the trainers arrived with their assigned veterans and shepherds. While a few of the trainers, armed with shovels, cleared paths on the obstacle course, Anna approached Max and Nia.

Nia nuzzled Anna's side.

"How did it go with Fleck?" Max asked.

"Neither of us are terminated, at least for today."

"*Gut*," Max said. "Do you see Waldemar?"

"Fleck's talking to him by the barn, and Waldemar doesn't look happy."

Max nodded. "I appreciate your efforts to protect me, but in the future, I suggest not stretching the truth with Fleck."

Anna clasped Nia's harness, the dog wagging its tail between them. "You risked everything to help me."

Max placed his gloved hand upon Anna's. "That's what friends do. Right?"

Friends, Anna thought. "*Ja.*"

Fleck blew his whistle, signaling for the group to line up on the course.

Max slipped his hand away and clasped the harness.

For the morning, they performed training walks with turns and artificial obstacle work. The snow grew heavier and the temperature plummeted, but Fleck didn't give them a break. Instead, he pushed them harder, as if he were leveraging the horrid weather conditions to harden the veterans, as well as their shepherds, for the difficult future that lay ahead of them. By afternoon, Nia's bad paw grew tender and she began to hobble. Anna expected that Fleck might replace Nia with Elfriede, now that the dog's toenail was healed. But Fleck permitted Nia to stay on the course. And for the rest of the day the trio of Max, Anna, and Nia trained with the other groups, while Waldemar, his face filled with contempt, stood on the sidelines.

Chapter 22

Oldenburg, Germany—December 18, 1916

Anna, Max, and Nia entered Norbie's workshop to a toll of chimes, dongs, and clangs. Shivering, Anna and Max unbuttoned their coats and loosened their scarfs, while Nia greeted Norbie at his workbench.

"You're home early," Norbie said, ruffling Nia's ears. In front of him was a mantel clock, its back opened to expose internal gears, and an array of intricate tools that gave Norbie the appearance of a doctor performing surgery.

"It's bitter cold," Anna said, rubbing her hands together. "Fleck was concerned about everyone getting frostbite, so he gave us the remainder of the afternoon off."

The chimes stopped, revealing an underlying chorus of tick-tocks.

"That's the second time this week that he's curtailed training," Norbie said.

"*Ja*," Anna said. "Fleck says that if the weather continues to be dangerously cold, he'll need to delay graduation for the veterans."

Max peered in the direction of Norbie. "How do you feel about getting stuck with me for another week or two?"

"That would be splendid," Norbie said. "However, I'll need to start charging you board."

Anna's eyes widened. "Vater."

"It's okay," Max said. "I don't have much, but I'd be happy to pay you what I have."

Norbie grinned. "Would you agree to me waiving your rent in exchange for evening piano performances?"

Max smiled. "I think I can make that work."

Nia's tail batted the workbench.

Anna approached her father, squeezed his hand, and silently mouthed, "*Danke*."

For the next few days, Max played the piano in the evenings, performing soul-stirring pieces by Frédéric Chopin, Johannes Brahms, Wolfgang Amadeus Mozart, Claude Debussy, Antonio Vivaldi, Ludwig van Beethoven, Joseph Haydn, and Richard Wagner. Max had played each composition from memory, constructing mental tones for the pitches that were outside of his range of hearing. Their living room with an audience of three, including Nia who lay near Max's feet, had been transformed into a diminutive concert hall. And she was appreciative that her father was encouraging Max to play. *Soon*, Anna thought, *he'll resurrect his dream of becoming a professional pianist.*

A solo grandfather clock chimed.

"Confounded pendulum disc," Norbie muttered. "That clock is always off; I'll work on it later. Come upstairs and get warm. I'll make you coffee to take off the chill."

Upstairs, they gathered in the kitchen where Norbie made a pot of substitute coffee. Max covered Nia, wriggling on her back like she was scratching an itch, in a thick wool blanket.

Norbie poured each of them a cup of the steaming brew, and as Anna was taking her first sip he said, "A letter for you arrived from Bruno. I put it in your room."

Anna's heart rate quickened. She lowered her cup to the table.

"Go read your letter," Max said. "Norbie and I will prepare dinner. Okay, Norbie?"

"Of course." Norbie looked at Anna. "Take your coffee to your room so you can drink it while its hot. It'll taste like tar if it's cold."

Anna nodded, and then went to her room where a letter was neatly propped against her pillow. She placed her cup on a bedstand, removed her boots, and sat on the bed. She opened the envelope and unfolded the letter.

> *Dearest Anna,*
> *How are you, my darling? Today, I heard more rumors about the dwindling food supply back home. Are you receiving enough bread and potatoes? Hopefully, shipments of supplies are getting through to Oldenburg. If not, I'll search for a means for you to acquire food.*

Anna leaned against her headboard and covered her legs with layers of blankets. It felt like ages since she'd tasted black war bread, let alone fried potatoes. For the past several days, they'd eaten little more than turnips, thanks to Fleck's generosity, and winter leeks that Max had dug up from the dormant garden. She wondered if Bruno's family in Frankfurt, whom she was anxious to someday meet, was having the same difficulty with acquiring rations.

> *I plan to arrive in Oldenburg on the evening train on the 23rd of January to begin my military leave. It's been trying, beyond anything I've ever had to endure, other than the fighting and death at the front, to be away from you. I crave to be with you again, my love. Perhaps you'll have success with taking a leave from your work while I'm home. Tell your supervisor that the dogs can train on their own for a few weeks. Maybe we could take a trip to Frankfurt to see where we will build a life after the war.*

Anna squeezed the paper between her fingers. Despite her eagerness to visit Frankfurt and meet Bruno's family, she couldn't abandon Max, Nia, and her responsibilities at the guide dog school. *I can't leave. Not now. Maybe not ever.* She took a deep breath, dispelling the thought from her mind.

> *To answer your question as to whether I like music, the answer is yes. I don't have a favorite style or composer, but I do find German marches to be quite invigorating. After the war, we'll attend as many performances as you wish. I am a bit curious, though. What prompted you to ask such a question?*

A memory of her conversation with Max flashed in her head. *I was embarrassed that I didn't know what type of music Bruno liked. At least I now know that he likes marches.*

> *Dreadful images of the acts that I've committed for the Fatherland haunt me in my dreams. Do you believe that all sins can be forgiven? I pray for absolution, both from God and you. I'm sorry to end this letter with such a dire tone. I promise to leave my unrest behind when I come to Oldenburg, and all will be right between us.*
> *Affectionately,*
> *Bruno*

Oh, poor Bruno. Anna, her chest aching, folded the letter and placed it in the envelope. *I wish I could do something to ease his pain.* She clasped her hands and said a silent prayer for him, and then curled under her blankets like a child seeking comfort, until a growing scent of cooked turnip prompted her to return to the kitchen.

"Anna," Norbie said. "I thought we could have an early dinner to create more time to listen to Max play the piano."

"Sounds wonderful," Anna said, attempting to set aside her

worry about Bruno. She looked at Max, standing by the stove and flipping what looked to be a pancake in a hot iron skillet. "What are you making?"

"Turnip latkes," Max said. "I had some help; Norbie grated the turnip and leek. I don't know how they'll taste without egg, spice, and oil to fry them in, but I thought it would be something different for you to eat." He turned the remaining latkes over by locating them with a finger and flipping with a spatula. "How's Bruno?"

Her breath turned shallow. "He's safe, but his spirits are low," she said, deciding to leave out the details.

Max turned toward her. "He'll be all right."

"Harbor your heart," Norbie said, hugging her. "I have faith that Bruno will return home safely from the war."

I needed that. Anna released him. "He'll be here on leave beginning the last week in January."

"That's splendid news," Norbie said. "Max, you'll get to meet Bruno, assuming your graduation is delayed."

"I hope so," Max said. "I'm looking forward to meeting him."

Anna, an uneasiness running through her legs, sat at the table while Max and Norbie, both of whom insisted that Anna relax, served dinner. She buried her worries as Norbie said grace, including a special prayer for food to be bountiful, an end to war, and for Bruno to arrive home safely.

"I hope you don't mind me making a latke for Nia," Max said, placing a small plate on the floor. "I thought it would be all right, considering most of our meal came from the shepherds' food supply."

"Not at all," Anna said.

Nia sniffed her latke, and then gobbled it in one bite.

Max stroked Nia's back. "I hope everyone likes it as much as Nia."

Anna nibbled her food. "It's excellent."

Norbie ate a forkful of turnip. "You're a first-rate cook, Max."

Max smiled.

They ate their meal while Norbie told stories about Anna and his deceased wife, which he narrated with much fondness and enthusiasm. *His love for Mutter has never faded*, Anna thought, eating crumbs from her plate. Although she was a bit embarrassed about a variation of a tale—in which Norbie claimed that Anna had won a lead role in a secondary school play, when in actuality she'd only be given a few lines to speak—she loved to hear her father talk of the past and, most of all, witness his seemingly limitless ardor for his family.

After dinner, Anna and Max washed and dried the dishes, and then everyone retired to the living room. For nearly two hours, Max played piano pieces. It was clear, to Anna, that Max had found a way to re-create the missing tones within his head. His fingers glided over the keyboard, filling the room with music. Anna's disquietude about Bruno, war, and starvation disappeared and, for the moment, she was lost in a tranquil sea of song. And when Max played Prelude in E Minor by Frédéric Chopin, she was overcome with emotion, her eyes filling with tears.

"Bravo!" Norbie said, standing from his seat as Max finished. He clapped his hands. "Take a bow, Max!"

Nia nudged Max's arm with her nose.

Max, his face appearing flushed, gave a small bow.

"That was heavenly," Anna said, wiping her eyes.

"*Danke*," Max said. "I'm glad you liked it."

"You're crying," Norbie said, looking at Anna.

"You are, too," Anna said, pointing out tears on Norbie's cheeks.

Norbie wiped his face. "Oh, so I am." He stepped to Max and placed a hand on his shoulder. "My boy, you've turned me into a weepy mess."

"Sorry," Max said. "I do, however, have something that might lighten your mood." He sat, placed his hands on the keys, and played Norbie's favorite children's folk song.

"'Hänschen klein,'" Norbie said, beaming. He tapped his foot, proudly singing the verses out of tune.

Anna covered her mouth with her hand, attempting to contain her amusement. She gazed at Max. *That's so sweet of you to play that song for him.*

After the piece was over, Norbie thanked Max for his musical performance and gave Anna a hug good night. Humming the tune to "Hänschen klein," he climbed the stairs to his bedroom.

Anna approached Max at the piano. "You made his night by playing that song."

"Which one?" Max asked. "Prelude in E Minor or 'Hänschen klein'?"

Anna chuckled. *It feels good to laugh.*

Max turned toward her. "Are you tired?"

"*Nein*," Anna said, despite her exhaustion.

He slid over on the bench and patted the space beside him.

She sat, placing her hands on her lap.

"Thank you for encouraging me to play," he said.

"You're welcome," Anna said. "But I'm sure you would have found a way to resume your art with or without me."

"I don't know," he said. "I was stuck in a mental, muddy morass, and you helped me to imagine hearing the undetectable notes."

She paused, touching a piano key. "You're the most talented pianist I've ever heard."

"That's very kind of you to say." He nudged her with his knee. "Would it be impolite of me to ask how many piano performances you've attended?"

"Not many," she said, "But I've listened to lots of professional pianist recordings on Norbie's gramophone, and you are by far the best."

"I'm honored." Max drew a breath, placed his fingers on the keyboard, and he began to play.

The solemn, slow tempo piece began with gentle chord progressions. Anna's breath slowed, and she closed her eyes. An image of tranquil waves lapping on a pebble shore filled her head. "It's beautiful," she said softly. "I'm unfamiliar with this one. Chopin?"

"Benesch."

She turned to him. "Yours?"

Max nodded. He played a few more bars, then slowed to a stop.

"When did you compose it?"

"I haven't, yet. It's a melody that I hear in my head when—" He placed his hands on his knees. "When you, me, and Nia are training."

Anna smiled. "Play it again."

Max performed the intro to the piece. "Like it?"

"Love it." She stood from the bench.

"Where are you going?"

"I'm getting something to write with."

"Why?"

"Because composers need to record their work." She darted to her room and returned with a pencil and pad of paper.

"There's no need," he said as she sat beside him.

"Yes, there is." She placed the pad on her lap and drew blank piano staves. "I'll work to get some proper staff paper. In the meantime, we'll make our own. You'll need to go slow. I can read music, but I've never recorded it on paper."

"You're not going to give up on this, are you?"

"*Nein.*" She rolled the pencil between her fingers. "How many movements will there be in the piece?"

"There are typically three movements in a piano concerto," he said, "but I was thinking that this would be a suite with five individually composed movements."

"What is the title?"

"I don't have one," he said, shifting in his seat.

"You must call it something," she said. "What were you thinking of when the music came to you."

He rubbed stubble on his chin. "Light. I envisioned darkness giving way to a glorious, warm light."

"*Light Suite?*"

"*Ja.*"

"*Light Suite* is a beautiful title," she said.

"The piece I was playing was the first movement, Prelude."

"*Prelude to Light,*" she thought. "Key?"

"C-sharp minor."

Anna scribbled on the top of the paper.

Light Suite
1. Prelude to Light C-sharp minor

For over an hour, alternating between the base and treble clefs, she recorded the notes per Max's direction. Whole notes. Half notes. Quarter notes. Eighth notes. Bar lines. Ties. Slurs. Crescendos and diminuendos. At the bottom of the paper, she stopped to rest her fingers, which had begun to ache from squeezing the pencil.

"Thanks for being patient with me," Anna said, rubbing her hand.

"How about we pick up tomorrow?" he asked.

"But we've only written a few bars."

"We have plenty of time to finish before I leave."

I wish you didn't live so far away, she thought.

He stood and extended his arm.

She clasped his hand, allowing him to help her from the bench, and then his fingers slipped away.

"Nia," Max said. "Let's go outside before you go to bed."

Nia stood and yawned, sticking out her tongue.

"You're tired," Max said, kneeling and rubbing the dog's cheeks. He paused, looking toward Anna. "May I ask you something personal?"

It's about Bruno. "Of course," she said tentatively.

"What do you look like?"

"Oh," Anna said, feeling surprised.

"I know what Nia looks like from giving her brushings, and Norbie has provided me a good description of the caramel and charcoal-color patterns on her coat." He stood, resting his hand on Nia's head. "I know the timbre of your voice, the smell of your clothing, and sound of your footsteps. I have a picture of you in my head and was wondering if I was right."

"Well—" Anna fiddled with a loose thread on her sweater.

"I'm sorry," he said. "It was intrusive of me to ask."

"It's okay. I was thinking of how to describe myself." She stepped forward and patted Nia, who swished her tail over the floor. "I have shoulder-length, light blond hair." *When it's clean.* "And my eyes are blue."

"Nose, cheeks, ears," he said.

"*Ja*, I have all of them all."

Max chuckled. "I was hoping you would be a little more specific."

"Here." Without thinking, she clasped his hand and placed it to her cheek.

He gently, and respectfully, glided his fingertips over her face.
Her breath caught in her chest.

"You have a dimple on your chin."

"Mutter had one, too," Anna said. "She was beautiful."

He lowered his hands to his side. "So are you."

Anna smiled. Her mind raced, searching for a response. "Am I the same as you had imagined?"

He nodded. Extending his hand, he located Nia's collar.

"Would you like me to join you with taking Nia outside?" Anna asked.

"*Nein, danke.*" He walked with Nia to the stairs, then paused. "I had an enjoyable evening, Anna."

"Me too," she said. "Good night."

Max and Nia disappeared down the stairs. The door to the garden squeaked open and closed.

Anna went to her room, where she put on another layer of clothing. The temperature outside had plummeted, given the thick layer of frost that covered her window. She extinguished her lamp, got in bed, and buried herself under layers of blankets. Soon, the patter of paws and the shuffle of boots grew in the hallway, then disappeared into Max's room. *I miss having Nia in my room, but I'm glad that she and Max have bonded.*

Alone, her mind turned to Bruno's letter, sending a surge of dismay through her veins. She prayed that he'd find peace, and she resolved to do everything she could to help him when he arrived home. *Everything will be fine when we're together,* she tried to convince herself. Desperate for solace, she turned her thoughts to Max's composition, the melody playing over and over again in her head. But soon, all she could think about was how her skin tingled as his fingers explored her face.

CHAPTER 23

OLDENBURG, GERMANY—DECEMBER 19, 1916

Max, guided by Nia, walked with Anna and Emmi through snow squalls on their journey to school. He gripped the handle to the dog's harness, feeling the sway of her body as she plodded through the snow. Their conversations were muffled, due to gusting winds that compelled them to cover their faces with scarves. Reaching the barn, cold and shivering, they shuffled inside.

"Fleck will surely limit your training time today," Emmi said, closing the door.

Anna stomped snow and ice from her boots, and then loosened her scarf. "*Ja*. I can't feel my toes. He won't want to take the chance of anyone catching frostbite."

I hope so, Max thought, shuffling to the cast-iron stove. *Each day that graduation is delayed gives me more time with Anna.*

With extended arms he located the stove, kneeled, and began to insert wood and old newspaper. Neither the windburn on his cheeks, nor the hunger in his belly—due to the meager portions of turnip he'd eaten for the last several days—dampened his spirits. For most of the night, as well as their morning slog to school, his mind had been on Anna. In less than three weeks, he'd gone from a battle-blinded veteran, who'd nearly given up on his will to live, to a man with hopes and dreams. And, Max believed, it was all because of her.

It was Anna's perseverance and compassion that had saved Nia, who was now saving him. With Nia at his side, he would break the shackles of dependency. He could do almost anything with a guide dog, he thought, including travel on trains and the navigation of unfamiliar streets and cities. His confinement to an apartment— or at most a radius of a few city blocks—was now expanded to all of Deutschland, perhaps even all of Europe, assuming there wasn't a war and that he'd someday earn enough money to travel. Although the guide work that Nia performed was essential for his quest for independence, it was her affection and companionship that was most important to him. He cherished their time at home, when Nia lay at his feet, cuddled with him on the sofa, or gave him an occasional lick to his cheek. In return, he'd brush her fur and rub her belly, all the while telling her what a smart, good dog she is. They'd become close partners, and he hoped that Fleck would, in the end, overlook Nia's feeble paw and allow her to go home with him.

He was deeply grateful to Anna. She'd given him far more than dog handling skills and the chance of having Nia as his guide. She and her *vater* had welcomed him into their home and treated him like family. She'd empathized with his injuries, the death of his parents, and his failed engagement, yet she didn't allow him to dwell on his misfortune. Day by day, she'd urged him to carry on, and his heartbreak gradually transformed to hope. Despite his initial skepticism, her encouragement for him to imagine high-pitch notes had worked, rekindling his passion to play the piano. And Anna had reminded him of the root reason that he'd performed as a musician: to give others joy and an escape from the hardships of life. *It doesn't matter that I can't hear the high tones*, he thought while playing "Clair de lune" by Claude Debussy. *What matters is how an audience feels when listening to the piece.* His fondness for Anna had bloomed, perhaps into something more than friendship. However, he knew that nothing more would ever come of it.

The door screeched open, and wind blasted the interior of the barn.

Fleck, Max thought.

"Are you finished with your chores?" a gruff voice said.

Waldemar. Max tossed wood into the stove. *He's early.*

"Almost," Anna said, sweeping out a stall. "Where is Herr Fleck?"

"He was summoned to a meeting with Dr. Stalling and directors at the Ambulance Dogs Association." Waldemar puffed his chest. "He put me in charge for today."

Irritation rose in Max's chest.

"Did Fleck say how long he wanted us to work in these conditions?" Anna asked.

"*Nein*," Waldemar said. "But he did request for me to arrange for indoor work. Finish your chores and get outside. You're training in town."

Max shut the door to the stove and stood.

"Frau Bauer," Waldemar said. "After you're done with your work here, Fleck wants you to go to the ambulance dog shelter and check on the shepherds with kennel cough." He looked at Anna. "He plans to put them back into rotation with the veterans, which means that you and your lame dog will likely be back in the barn."

Max clenched his hands.

Waldemar turned and left, leaving the door open.

Frigid wind gushed into the barn, and Emmi darted to the door and shut it.

Max shuffled to the sound of Anna's sweeping broom. "We can handle Waldemar for a day. He's jealous of you and is trying to get under your skin. If Fleck's intentions were to replace you and Nia, he would have done so days ago with his dog, Elfriede."

"I suppose you're right," Anna said.

"Go," Emmi said. "I'll finish the work here, and then leave for the shelter."

"Are you sure?" Anna asked.

"*Ja*," Emmi said. "I'm glad you'll be working indoors."

"You too," Anna said.

Max, Anna, and Nia went outside where Waldemar—his coat collar turned up to block the wind—was sitting in his wagon with his dog, Gunda. As Anna approached the bed of the wagon, Waldemar turned and said, "What do you think you are doing?"

"I thought you were going to give us a ride to town," she said.

"You're mistaken," he said.

He waited here to spurn us from getting in his wagon. Max clenched his jaws. He shuffled forward, gliding his gloved hand over the side of the wagon, and peered in the direction of Waldemar's voice. "I realize that you might not want to provide someone like me a lift in your wagon. But give Anna a ride to town; it's freezing. I'll meet her there. Nia and I know the way."

"*Nein,*" Waldemar said. "The walk will give both of you extra practice, which you sorely need."

"May I have a word with you, alone?" Max asked.

"It's okay," Anna said, stepping to Max. "Let's go."

Waldemar tugged on the reins. The horse snorted and propelled the wagon forward. "Get moving, or you'll be late."

"Where are we meeting?" Anna called.

"St. Lambert's!" Waldemar shouted. The wagon traveled down the road and disappeared into the dark, predawn snowfall.

"Bastard," Max breathed.

Nia, as if she could sense Max's vexation, leaned against his leg.

"Thanks for trying to help," Anna said.

"I don't like the way he treats you."

"And I hate his bias toward you," she said. "But there's nothing we can do about it for now." She tightened her scarf and nudged Max. "Let's go."

Max gripped Nia's harness. "Forward."

Nia padded ahead, guiding him through the snow.

Wind bit at Max's face. "Maybe we'll catch a wagon ride with another trainer."

"This is the only road leading to the school," she said. "Waldemar arrived early, like Fleck. He timed it perfectly for when the trainers and veterans would be en route. He'll tell each of them to turn around and head back to town before they reach us."

Damn him. Max lowered his head and shuffled forward.

On a normal day, the one-way walk from school to town was thirty-five minutes. But given the wind and snow, blasting the front of their bodies, it took them nearly fifty minutes to trudge their way to the center of town.

"Waldemar is standing outside of the cathedral," Anna said, her teeth chattering. "It'll be warm inside. It's a magnificent church, and you'll enjoy climbing the stairs to the balconies."

"Sounds good," Max said. He continued forward until Nia guided him to a stop.

"You're late," Waldemar said.

"Are the others inside?" Anna asked, ignoring his comment.

"*Ja*," Waldemar said. "But you'll be working at the train station."

"Why?" Max asked.

"I didn't think it would be appropriate for a Jew to train in a Lutheran place of worship, so I've made alternate arrangements for you."

Ire surged through Max's veins. "You could have told us your plans before we left the school grounds." He stepped toward Waldemar and felt Anna clasp his arm.

"What time shall we finish at the train station," Anna said.

"Sundown," Waldemar said. "In the interim, I'll be checking in on you."

"Come on, Max," Anna said. "The way is straight ahead."

Max buried his angst and commanded Nia to proceed forward. Once they were out of earshot he said, "I should have argued with Waldemar to allow us to join the others."

"It wouldn't have done any good," Anna said. "He dislikes you because you're Jewish, and he loathes me because I am a woman, infringing upon his work."

"Maybe I should speak with Fleck," he said.

"I doubt that Fleck—or the pastor of our church, for that matter—would condone banning you from the cathedral because of your faith. But we need to pick our battles, Max. I don't want to take a chance of you not graduating because we disobeyed Waldemar's orders when he's acting as a substitute supervisor." She rubbed the sleeve of his coat. "Like you said, it's only for one day."

"But it'll be cold for you and Nia at the train station."

"At least we'll be shielded from the wind," she said. "Today, we'll follow orders, and soon you'll be leaving Oldenburg with Nia."

A memory of serving on the front filled Max's head. Regardless of his education and combat training performance, he'd been given a low rank position because he was a Jew. Now, Anna was struggling to succeed in a role that was dominated by men. *We're both fighting to be viewed as equal.* He tightened his grip on the harness and trekked through the snow.

Arriving at the train station, they went straight to work. Although the structure provided cover from the wind and snow, the temperature remained frigid. To protect Nia's frail paw, they took periodic breaks on a wooden bench, where they placed the dog on their laps and warmed her pads with their bare hands. Since Max did not receive his usual military-issued lunch, which he presumed was at St Lambert's, Anna insisted that he eat half of her lunch, a leftover turnip latke that Norbie had packed for her. Regardless of their fatigue and hunger, they pressed on with training, practicing left turns, right turns, and avoidance of obstacles. Nia excelled at carriage work—when Max told her to "find the seat"— and she shined with intelligent disobedience work by successfully refusing to follow Max's commands to place him in danger of falling off the ledge of the platform. Waldemar checked in on them twice to make sure they were working and, while doing so, made disparaging comments about their dog handling techniques. But Waldemar's contempt didn't rattle Max as it did before. The isolated training had turned out to be blessing, all because he had more time with Anna and Nia.

After training, they arrived home to a dark, empty home. Anna, still wearing her coat, lit a lamp, and placed it on the kitchen table.

"Norbie is running errands and will be home late." She removed her leather gloves and blew on her fingers. "We were saving our small stash of coal for later in the winter, but I think we're going to need it tonight. Would you mind making a fire in the *kachelofen*?"

"Not at all," Max said, unbuckling Nia's harness. He ruffled the dog's fur, and then ran his hand along the living room wall until he found the tiled stove. He removed hunks of coal from a tin bucket and placed them into the stove by stacking on a layer of kindling, arranged like a small wooden pallet. He stuffed in paper and lit it, using a box of matches he'd located by the bucket. *I so appreciate the latitude to do things on my own*, Max thought. *Unlike Wilhelmina, Anna and Norbie don't fret about me accidentally setting the house on fire.*

"I'm boiling water in the kitchen," Anna said, entering the room. "I'll prepare you a washbasin."

"*Danke*," Max said. "But you wash first. Your teeth were chattering; the hot water will take off your chill."

"Are you sure?"

"*Ja*," Max said. He patted his lap, and Nia sprang to him. "I have a dog to keep me warm."

Anna smiled. "All right."

While Max waited for the tiled stove to radiate heat, he remained in his coat and cuddled with Nia on the sofa. He took in a few deep breaths, attempting to alleviate the tightness in his chest. *The brumal air makes my lungs feel like they're being squeezed in a vise.* "How are you feeling?" he asked, rubbing Nia's ears.

Nia panted.

He gently rubbed Nia's right front leg. "Is your paw okay?"

Nia leaned back her head and gave him a wet lick to the chin.

He chuckled. "I guess so."

Twenty minutes later, Anna entered the room and approached him. "Ready for your washbasin?"

Max nodded. He stood, unbuttoned his coat, and slid his cap from his head.

"When was the last time you had your hair cut?"

Max ran a hand over his head. "I can't remember."

"Come to the kitchen," she said. "I'll cut your hair."

"It's not necessary," he said.

"Norbie never goes to a barber. I trim his hair and beard, and he's never complained about my work, even when I nearly snipped off his earlobe."

Max fidgeted with the cuff of his coat sleeve.

Anna giggled.

She's kidding. "All right."

Minutes later, Max was leaning over the kitchen sink as Anna gently saturated his hair with warm water. Using lye soap, which omitted an ammonia-like smell, she lathered his hair. The touch of her fingers over his scalp sent tingles down his neck and spine. His heart rate quickened.

"Am I getting soap in your eyes?"

"*Nein*," he said.

She rinsed his hair and gently dried it with a towel, then sat him in a chair with the towel draped over his back and shoulders. Using a pair of scissors and a comb, she began to trim his bangs.

Anna's breath caressed his face. His skin prickled. "How long have you been cutting Norbie's hair?" he asked, attempting to distract his thoughts.

Anna snipped strands of hair. "Since I was in grammar school. He made the mistake of mentioning that my *mutter* had cut his hair. I offered to do it for him, and he accepted."

"I'm not surprised." Max shifted in his seat.

"Hold still."

He felt the cool steel of the scissors against his forehead, then the sound of snips as she cut along his bangs and temples.

For twenty minutes, Anna combed and cut his hair, while Nia—sitting in the corner—batted her tail against the wall in response to their intermittent conversation. As Anna trimmed around his neck, the clack of Norbie's footsteps grew in the stairway.

"*Hallo*," Norbie said, entering the kitchen and placing a bag on the counter.

Max's face flushed. "*Hallo*, Norbie."

"I'd keep very still if I were you," Norbie said. "I once sneezed during a haircut, and she nearly severed my earlobe."

"That was a long time ago," Anna said. "And it was only a tiny nick that barely bled."

"I thought you were joking about Norbie's ear," Max said.

"*Nein*," Anna chuckled. "I've never been very good with sharp objects, especially the hypodermic needles that I injected while working as a nurse." She removed the towel and dusted hair from his neck.

Max smiled, running a hand through his clean, trimmed hair. "Feels good. *Danke*."

"You're welcome." She turned to Norbie. "Would you like a trim while I have the scissors?"

"Not tonight," Norbie said. "I have a few things that I want to show you. A small food shipment arrived in Oldenburg, and I waited in the ration line for three hours." He removed a half-loaf of bread from the bag and placed it on the counter.

Anna gasped, covering her mouth.

"What is it?" Max asked.

"Black bread," Anna said.

"And one egg," Norbie said, carefully removing a brown egg from his coat pocket. "It'll make your turnip latkes even more delectable, my boy."

A wave of relief rolled through Max. *Anna and Norbie will have food for a few more days.*

"It turns out that bartering timepieces is a lot easier if you're not seeking food." Norbie rummaged in the bag and handed a stack of papers to Anna. "I traded an old watch to a music store owner in exchange for blank staff paper. I hope it's the kind that you wanted."

"It's perfect," Anna said, examining the paper.

A memory of Anna recording his piano composition on scratch paper flashed in Max's head.

"I told him about your composition," Anna said. "I hope you don't mind."

"Not at all," Max said.

Anna peeked in the bag and smiled. "This is for you, Max. Hold out your hands."

Max accepted what felt like an elaborate candlestick holder, until he explored it with his hands. *A nine-branched candelabrum.* "Menorah?"

"*Ja,*" Norbie said. "Anna thought that you might want to celebrate Hanukkah, so I paid a visit to an old friend who is the rabbi of the Oldenburg synagogue. According to the Jewish calendar, tonight is the lighting of the first candle."

"This is incredibly thoughtful and generous," Max said. "How can I repay you?"

"You and Nia can join me on a trip to the forest to bring home a silver fir tree for Christmas," Norbie said. "And you can continue playing the piano. This house hasn't sounded this beautiful since my wife, Helga, was alive."

Max nodded. "It's an honor to play Helga's piano."

Norbie drew a jagged breath. He sniffed and wiped his eyes with a handkerchief.

After many years, his heartache is still raw. Max wondered, although briefly, how long it would take for his own heart to heal from the death of his *mutter* and *vater.* And if he would ever experience the boundless, unconditional endearment that his parents had. He shook away his thoughts and said, "I'll make dinner tonight—I insist."

After a meal of turnip latkes, containing egg and black bread crumbs, they settled in the living room. For the first time in days, their bellies didn't ache with hunger. Anna inserted two partially used candles into the menorah, which she placed on a table near the window. Max lit the candle in the middle, the shamash. He said a silent blessing, and then used the shamash to light the candle on the right side of the menorah. Max—rejuvenated by nourishment and, even more, Anna and Norbie's warmth—took a seat at the piano. For two hours he performed classical concertos and suites, as well as a several folk songs—including "O Tannenbaum"—which Norbie sang until he grew tired and went off to bed.

Alone with Anna, Max made room for her on the piano bench, where they sat thigh-to-thigh. Beneath the bench, Nia curled at the heels of their feet. With his mind and heart on Anna, Max began to play "Prelude" from the piano suite called *Light* that they'd worked on the night before. Bar by bar and with much repetition, Anna recorded the composition on the new staff paper. The process was tedious and slow. But Anna didn't seem to mind, and neither did Nia, given the occasional swishes of her tail from beneath the bench.

As the candles on the menorah burned low, Anna leaned her head to Max's shoulder and yawned.

Max paused, resting his hands on the keys. "Tired?"

"A little."

"You should go to bed."

"Not yet," she said, her voice soft. "I was wondering—do you know what the second movement of the suite will sound like?"

"I think so." He inhaled, taking in the scent of her hair. "Would you like to hear it?"

"I'd love to."

Nia's tail thumped the floor.

Max reflected on his time with Anna and Nia. *I feel alive*, he thought. Drawing upon the flurry of emotions swirling inside him, he positioned his hands over the keys and played.

Chapter 24

Lille, France—January 14, 1917

At the front—twenty kilometers from Lille—Bruno conducted an inventory of phosgene gas artillery shells, identifiable by a green cross, that were stacked like cords of wood. Fifty meters away, German artillery cannons exploded, again and again, sending shockwaves through his body and filling his nose with an acrid scent of smokeless powder propellant. Behind the artillery line was a vast dump containing thousands of discarded shell casings. As he counted the armament, using a clipboard and pencil to records the results, it became increasingly clear that he had influenced Kainz, the general of artillery, to escalate the usage of phosgene. *One out of every three shells fired upon the enemy contains poison gas*, Bruno thought, scribbling a tally on his paper. *Haber will be pleased.*

General Kainz hadn't been hunkered in a dugout on the front line during the Allied bombardment, as Major Brandt had led Bruno to believe. Instead, the general had been in a reserve line bunker planning an offensive attack with a group of officers. The major had been intoxicated and ill-informed, but Bruno had only himself to blame. He was a fool for thinking he could reach the front line under heavy Allied shellfire. In the time since his senseless mission to contact the general, Bruno carried the wallet of the fallen French soldier—whom he drowned in knee-deep rainwater of a shell crater—in his coat pocket. The man's identification, as well as the water-stained photograph of his family, was an incessant reminder to Bruno of his sin, and the promise he'd made to do something for the man's wife and baby after the war. *If I hadn't tried to reach the front during the bombardment, he might still be alive, somewhere on the other side of no-man's-land*, he'd often wondered. *But if he was alive, more German soldiers might be dead.*

It was strange, Bruno thought, to be haunted by the act of suffocating one man in self-defense when he'd killed hundreds or, more likely, thousands of men due to his role in the Disinfection Unit and the Imperial German Army's escalating chemical warfare program. In an attempt to rationalize his actions, Bruno resorted to repeating Fritz Haber's mantra silently in his head. *Death is death, regardless of how it is inflicted.* But the affirmations did little to lessen Bruno's guilt. Instead, it deadened his denial that he, Haber, and the German Empire were the ones who'd broken the Hague Convention treaty, which prohibited the use of chemical weapons. And in doing so, they'd opened Pandora's box.

The Allied forces had not only retaliated with creating their own chemical warfare capability, they'd also begun to master its use. The French and British were now estimated to be producing many thousands of tons of chlorine and phosgene. And Bruno had witnessed the devastation of the Allies' capability when he was called upon, two days ago, to examine a section of the front line where infantry troops had suffered a large loss of life.

Bruno had been met at the front line by an inexperienced infantry officer, Hauptmann Fischer, who feared that the enemy had unleashed a more advanced chemical weapon. The *hauptmann's* concern was based on the fact that all of the men had died before they could reach their respirators. The forty-meter section of trench was littered with scores of corpses, which were awaiting transport to a mass grave. The men were young, new recruits, given their lack of facial hair and the untattered condition of their uniforms. *They're barely older than boys*, Bruno thought, staring at a dead, blond-haired soldier with a contorted mouth and skin the color of eggplant. "Chlorine gas," he'd told the infantry officer. Unlike the *hauptmann*, Bruno had seen this tactic performed by Allied artillery before. In the first attacks, the Allies sometimes

used lachrymatory gas shells or clouds of harmless smoke. And
hours later, the Allies performed a second attack with lethal chlorine gas, designed to surprise complacent German soldiers who'd
removed their respirators. Bruno—sickened by the preventable
loss of life—schooled the officer on Allied tactics, then squelched
his way out of the corpse-filled trench.

Due to the escalating death toll of battle-hardened officers, the
training for German soldiers had deteriorated in the years since
the war began, leaving many units ill-prepared to fight. Additionally, the military's once plentiful food supply had plummeted, although senior officers and special roles, like Bruno's assignment in
a chemical warfare unit, continued to have access to better rations.
Front line soldiers had gone from eating hearty bread with savory
pieces of saveloy, to bits of boiled turnips, turnip stew, and dirty
carrot tops. And with the men's hunger came fatigue, which was
soon followed by poor morale. He'd watched young, bright-eyed
men arrive at the front eager to fight for the Fatherland. But within
a year of experiencing death and terror, the men—if not killed or
maimed—had grown old, their eyes dark and void of spirit.

As Bruno recorded his final tally of shells, a runner, his boots
and coat spattered with mud, approached him.

"Oberleutnant Wahler?" the runner asked, his breath producing a mist in the cold air.

"*Ja*," Bruno said.

"This is for you, sir." He handed Bruno a slip of paper, saluted,
and then left.

Bruno unfolded the message.

```
Oberleutnant Bruno Wahler is hereby
summoned to meet with Fritz Haber, head
of the Chemistry Section in the Ministry
of War, at 4:00 p.m. on 14th January 1917.
Location: Officers' boardinghouse, Lille.
```

Bruno rubbed the stubble on his chin. *A meeting with Haber on
short notice cannot be good.* He glanced at his watch and realized

that he'd need to leave immediately to have a chance to arrive on time. He darted to his dugout, where he found a letter addressed to him with Anna's handwriting on his bunk. He placed the letter and his personal items into a leather case, and then made his way to a field hospital, where he hitched a ride in an ambulance that was headed to Lille. Bruno sat in the back on the floor, between double bunks of cots that held four injured soldiers, the worst of whom was a man with a severed leg from which brown pus oozed through the bandaged stump. A foul stench of gangrene pervaded Bruno's nose. To distract himself, he retrieved Anna's letter from his case and read.

> *My darling Bruno,*
> *I pray that you are safe, and that this letter finds you in good health and spirit. It's thoughtful of you to ask about the food supply in Oldenburg. Potatoes have been unavailable for months, and deliveries of supplies to the city are irregular, at best. Norbie did, however, acquire black bread this week. My supervisor has given us some turnips, which were to be used to feed guide dogs. I'm grateful for his generosity, but I worry that our gift of turnips will cause shepherds to go hungry.*

You're a kind soul, Anna, Bruno thought. *But I hope that you will not place a dog's well-being above your own.*

> *I'm excited to see you, Bruno. I'm using a calendar to cross off the days until your arrival. It feels like ages since we've been together. I know it is foolish of me to fret, but I sometimes wonder if I will look the same to you. I'm a bit thin and overworked, and I hope you will see me as you did before.*

Of course I will. The ambulance struck a rut, bouncing Bruno from the floor. He steadied himself by stretching out his legs and continued reading.

> *I regret that I will be unable to take off time from work while you're here. Norbie and I are boarding a blind veteran named Max, and I'm needed at the guide dog school. Graduation for the current class of veterans has been delayed due to cold weather, and I'm in the midst of training with Max and his shepherd, Nia. Please know that I'm anxious to visit Frankfurt and meet your family. I hope you understand, and that you'll pass along my disappointment to your family. I assume you'll still want to visit them while you're on leave.*

I will not be seeing my parents, Bruno thought. *I haven't even written them about my leave.*

> *I'm delighted to hear that you like music. The reason I asked is that Max is a magnificent pianist. He plays for Norbie and me in the evenings, and he's working on a composition that I am recording for him on staff paper. You'll like Max and Nia. I've told Max about you, and he's very much looking forward to meeting you.*

"*Wasser,*" a soldier moaned. He lifted his hands, trembling and wrapped in field dressings. "*Wasser.*"

Bruno located a canteen in a medical supply box, dribbled water into the man's mouth, and then returned to reading his letter.

> *It breaks my heart to know how horrible you feel about having to fight. The front is*

*a wretched place, and I pray each day for
the senseless slaughter to end. You're doing
what you are forced to do. I understand
that you do not have a choice in the matter,
and I hope that you realize this, too. And in
response to your question in your last letter,
the answer is yes, I do believe that all sins
can be forgiven.*
    Your fiancée,
    Anna

Exoneration of my crimes may not be possible, Bruno thought. Moans and whimpers grew as the road condition deteriorated, shaking the soldiers' battered bodies in their bunks. He struggled to bury his anguish, as well as shut out the pain and suffering that reverberated inside the ambulance. And for the rest of the journey, he closed his eyes and lowered his head onto his knees.

Despite his attempt to be punctual, he arrived in Lille over an hour late, due to the ambulance getting stuck twice in the mud. Reaching the officers' boardinghouse, Bruno—his chest swirling with dread—climbed the stairs and knocked. Seconds later, delicate footsteps grew from inside, and the door swung open.

"Bruno," Celeste said. She greeted him with a kiss on both cheeks. "Haber is in the parlor."

He paused, looking into her eyes. "How are you?"

She smiled. "I am well. And you?"

"I'm all right," he lied.

"It's good to see you," she said.

"You too."

She glanced at his leather case. "Will you be staying?"

"I don't know," he said. "I packed in the event Haber requires my presence in Lille."

"I'll place it in your room." She took his coat and leather case, her fingers brushing his hand.

An image of their bare bodies—entwined as one—flashed in Bruno's head, sending a twinge of guilt through his abdomen. He slipped his cap from his head and held it to his chest. "I wish

I would have said more when I left. I feel bad about how I left things between us."

She placed the case in front her, as if she was creating a barrier between them. "We can talk later. Haber's waiting for you."

Bruno nodded. He made his way to the parlor, where Haber was sitting at a table with a newspaper and a half-empty bottle of wine.

Haber lowered his paper and frowned. "You're late."

"I'm sorry, sir. I came as soon as I received your message."

"You're a mess," Haber said, looking at Bruno's mud-covered boots.

"I hitched a ride in an ambulance, which got stuck in mud. The driver needed my help to push it out, and to unload and reload the injured soldiers."

"I expect you to leave the menial tasks to others," Haber said. "You have more important matters to tend to."

"*Ja*, sir," Bruno said.

Haber gestured to a chair.

Bruno sat.

Haber adjusted his pince-nez spectacles and peered at Bruno. "I was hoping to have our meeting over a glass of wine, but it's too late for that now. My train leaves soon."

"Perhaps we can have a drink together another time, sir."

Haber took a gulp of wine, then nodded.

"Sir, how is the development of the sulfur mustard weapon coming along?" Bruno asked, hoping to change the subject to something other than his tardiness.

Haber's brows softened. "*Gut*. The agent, which we hoped would create severe chemical burns, as well as bleeding and blistering within the respiratory system, is turning out to be far more potent than we expected."

A burn rose in Bruno's esophagus. He swallowed and said, "That is good news, sir."

"I want *you* to launch its use in July."

"It will be a privilege."

A slim smile formed on Haber's face.

"Have you selected a site to use the mustard gas?"

Haber placed his fingertips together. "Ypres."

Where we conducted the first gas attack. A memory of a green chlorine cloud, floating over no-man's-land and asphyxiating hundreds in its path, surged inside Bruno's brain. He gripped the arms of his chair, attempting to hide his disgust. "You've put much thought into selecting the location. I have no doubts that the new agent will be a success, and I appreciate you keeping me informed."

"You're welcome, Bruno, but that's not why I've summoned you."

He leaned forward.

"It has come to my attention that you've become reckless," Haber said.

Bruno's shoulder muscles tightened.

"Is it true that you attempted to reach the front line in the midst of a heavy enemy bombardment?"

Bruno shifted in his seat. *He knows.* "That is correct, sir. I had been trying to reach Artillery General Kainz to persuade him to use gas shells, rather than solely rely on high-explosives. It turned out that the general was not at a front-line dugout, where I was told he would be."

"Do you wish to die?" Haber asked.

"*Nein*, sir."

"Then act like it," Haber said firmly.

"*Ja*, sir."

Haber swirled the wine in his glass. "I need you to remain alive. You're needed to launch my new weapon, which will put fear into our enemy and lead the empire to victory."

Bruno nodded.

"You have much to live for, Bruno. Your *vater* is becoming enormously wealthy from his supply contracts for the Imperial German Army. After the war, you'll have a prestigious position at Wahler Farbwerke, and you'll have a luxurious life."

Unless we are convicted and hung for war crimes, Bruno thought.

"I want you to stay in Lille to oversee the distribution of phosgene shells until you begin your military leave," Haber said. "Get some rest in Germany. When you return to the front, your mind and body will be refreshed to execute the next stage of Germany's chemical warfare."

"I'll be ready, sir," Bruno said.

"*Gut.*" Haber drained his wine and looked at Bruno. "Out of curiosity, were you able to influence the general to increase the use of gas?"

"*Ja,*" Bruno said. "The ratio of gas to high-explosive shells is one in three."

Haber stood and placed a hand on Bruno's shoulder. "Well done."

"*Danke,*" Bruno said, struggling to contain his repulsion from Haber's touch.

Haber retrieved his coat from the back of his chair and left.

Bruno, relieved for Haber to be gone, drew a deep breath and exhaled. He retrieved an extra glass that had been placed on the table and filled it with white wine. He gulped it down, barely noticing its rich, fruity taste, and then refilled the glass. For several minutes he sipped Haber's wine and waited for the alcohol to deaden his pain.

Celeste, carrying a cup with rising steam, entered the parlor. "Am I disturbing you?"

"*Nein,*" Bruno said, slumped in his chair.

"Tea." She placed the cup in front of him. "It might make you feel better than the wine."

He straightened his back and looked at her. "*Danke.*"

"Will you be staying?" she asked.

"*Ja.*"

"I'm glad." She tucked loose strands of hair behind her ears. "Would you like me to prepare you something to eat?"

"Maybe later." As he lifted the cup, his hand trembled, spilling tea on his tunic. He put down the drink and brushed his clothing. "Sorry. My nerves are frayed."

"It's all right." Using a napkin from the table, she gently dabbed his clothing.

His eyes met hers.

She paused, resting her hand on his chest.

He clasped the napkin, but instead of taking it, his fingers gravitated to hers. His heartbeat quickened.

She moved closer, her knee touching his leg.

While seated, he placed his hands on her hips, then slid his palms to the base of her back. Pulling her to him, he placed his cheek to her breastbone.

"You're safe here," she said softly.

He drew a breath, taking in a scent of lilac perfume. Her heartbeat fluttered beneath his ear.

She gently ran her fingers through the back of his hair.

He squeezed her, feeling their bodies mold together. *I cannot do this*, he tried to convince himself. But his mind and heart—tired and ravaged—desperately desired comfort, regardless of the ramifications. *I'll be different after the war*, he resolved within himself. He stood, his hands gliding over the back of her dress. Their lips met, and his pain slipped away.

On Bruno's seventh consecutive morning of staying in the boardinghouse, he rolled over in bed to the warmth of Celeste. Under a dull glow of predawn light, coming from a gap between the curtains, he watched her chest slowly rise and fall with the rhythm of her breath. Unlike previous days, when he would work at the ammunition depot and spend evenings with Celeste, today would be the end of their time together. In a few hours, he would depart for his two-week military leave in Oldenburg, Germany.

A strange mixture of guilt and indebtedness churned inside him. His time with Celeste had eased his trepidation and helped him forget, although temporarily, about the wicked acts he'd committed on behalf of Haber and the Imperial German Army. Each of the past several evenings they'd slept together in his room. But their intimacy was far more than physical pleasure, Bruno believed, considering it was their conversations that had kept them awake until the early hours of the morning. They'd talked of the past, and they'd discussed what they wanted their lives to be like after the war, even though they both knew that they would take divergent paths. And each night, under the glow of candlelight, Celeste read aloud *Alcools*, a collection of poems by Guillaume Apollinaire. Initially, she'd translated the French to German for him, but he preferred her to recite it in French, so he could get lost in the cadence and timbre of her voice. He'd grown close to

Celeste. She was kind, understanding, and beautiful. What they had, Bruno believed, was more than companionship but less than devotion.

Bruno caressed Celeste's bare shoulder with his thumb.

She stirred and opened her eyes. "Good morning," she whispered.

"How did you sleep?" he asked.

"Well." She rolled to him, nuzzling her head to his chest.

He pressed his lips to her hair.

"I have something I'd like to ask you before you leave."

"All right."

"Do you love her?"

He drew a breath. "I do."

She ran a finger over his chest, as if she were tracing his ribs. "Will you remember me?"

He sat up and looked into her eyes. "Forever."

They embraced, their foreheads touching together. She kissed him on the cheek, and then slipped out of bed.

"Come downstairs," she said, putting on her dress. "I'll make you breakfast before you leave for the train station."

He nodded.

She slipped on her shoes and left the room, closing the door behind her.

Bruno climbed out of bed. He quickly dressed, packed his leather case, and went downstairs, all the while hoping to gain a few more minutes of time with her. He entered the kitchen to the sound of meat sizzling in a hot iron skillet. A scent of frying bacon filled his nose.

"It smells good," he said, approaching her.

She turned and pressed a hand to her stomach.

"Are you all right?"

Her face went pale. She cupped a hand to her mouth and dashed to the sink, where she leaned over and vomited.

"May I help?"

"Leave me," she said. "I'll be fine."

Ignoring her plea, he placed a hand on her back, feeling her muscles contract as her stomach heaved.

She took in several deep breaths, and her body relaxed. Celeste, her eyes bloodshot, stood and faced him.

Bruno retrieved a dish towel and handed it to her.

She wiped her mouth.

Bruno swallowed. "How long have you been feeling ill?"

Her hands trembled. "The past three mornings."

He clasped her fingers. "Are you—"

Celeste's eyes welled with tears. "I think I'm pregnant."

CHAPTER 25

OLDENBURG, GERMANY—JANUARY 23, 1917

Anna, accompanied by Max and Nia, stood on the landing as the evening train chugged into the Oldenburg station. Her heart rate quickened as the train's wheels screeched over steel rails. Although she was excited to see Bruno, an uneasiness stirred inside her. *It's been so long since we've been together. I hope things will be the same between us.* In an attempt to bury her worry, she removed her leather gloves and ran her fingers through Nia's fur.

Nia looked up at Anna and panted, her breath misting in the cold air.

"You're a good girl, Nia," Anna said.

The dog swished her tail.

"Do you see him?" Max asked, as the train hissed to a stop.

Anna scanned the passengers seated next to the carriage windows. "Not yet."

The carriage doors opened and passengers, a blend of civilians and soldiers, descended upon the landing.

Anna stood on her toes, but was unable to see through the growing crowd of people. She left Max and Nia, and then wriggled through the throng, like a spawning salmon fighting a current. But within a few minutes, the passengers filtered out of the station, leaving the landing empty except for Anna, Max, and Nia.

Anna's shoulder muscles tightened. "He's not here," she called to Max.

"Forward," Max said to Nia. They walked toward Anna. He tapped his cane over the ground. "*Halt.*"

Nia stopped.

"I'm sure he is fine," Max said. "It's not unusual for train schedules, especially routes to and from the front, to be delayed."

"*Ja,*" Anna said reluctantly.

"Are you all right?"

"I'm disappointed," Anna said, deciding not to include her uneasiness of reuniting with Bruno. *I'm going mad. We're engaged, and I should be overjoyed to see him.*

"I'm sorry," Max said. He extended his elbow. "Let's go. We'll celebrate tomorrow, when Bruno is home."

"*Danke.*" Anna clasped Max's arm, and she walked with him and Nia out of the train station.

Over the past few nights, Anna had prepared the house for Bruno's arrival. She'd scrubbed the floors, cleaned the windows, and washed the sheets. To spruce up the kitchen, she placed old wildflowers—which had been hanging upside down to dry on a hook in Norbie's workshop since last summer—in a ceramic vase on the table. Unlike Bruno's last visit, when he'd resided in a local boardinghouse while they courted, Norbie insisted that Bruno stay with them. However, her *vater* expected that Bruno would take his room, and that he would sleep in his workshop. "You will share a bed on your wedding night," Norbie had said, unfolding a cot beside a workbench. She admired, as well as appreciated, her father's etiquette, especially since he likely deduced that she'd already been intimate with Bruno, given the amount of time she'd spent in his boarding room during his last military leave.

She had planned to give up her virginity when she was married, but things changed when she met Bruno. He was charming, attentive, and made her feel comfortable. Eventually, she accepted his invitation to meet him at his boardinghouse room, where he confided in Anna about his fear of returning to the fight, and his desire for emotional support and intimacy. Anna's heart ached for him. As a nurse, she'd heard many stories of soldiers making appeals to their girlfriend or fiancée for sexual relations. The war had placed enormous strain on men at the front, as well as women who were struggling to survive at home, and traditional sexual norms, Anna believed, were beginning to decay. Regardless, she politely declined Bruno's request on the basis that they should wait until they were wed. But as days passed, and his time to return to the fight drew near, she accepted his invitation.

We're engaged to be married, Anna had rationalized, slipping into his bed. *I want us to experience being together should something dreadful happen to him at the front.* For Anna, the sexual intercourse was awkward, and it was more painful than pleasurable. *What I've done cannot be undone*, she'd thought curled next to him. Although she didn't regret her decision, she hoped that the next time that she and Bruno would be intimate would be on their wedding night.

Norbie's sleeping arrangements for Bruno's visit weren't ideal, but she assumed that Bruno would be amenable to her *vater*'s request. However, with her guide dog obligations, she was relieved to know that she wouldn't have to sacrifice time away from Max and Nia to be with Bruno. It was crucial, Anna believed, for her to remain focused on her training responsibilities, especially since Fleck now had other shepherds that could replace Nia. Last week, the dogs that had contracted canine infectious tracheobronchitis returned to the group, thanks to Emmi's herbal remedies to reduce their coughing and expedite their recovery. Anna was happy to see all of the dogs, healthy and wagging their tails, back at school, despite her fear that she and Nia could be replaced at any moment by another trainer and shepherd. But, to her astonishment, Fleck continued to allow them to work with Max. Although Fleck hadn't committed to permanently assigning Nia to Max, Anna believed that the pair would remain together as long as *she* didn't make a mess of things. Hour by hour, and day by day, she trained them on obstacle avoidance, traffic work, navigation of unpaved country roads, traffic crossings, and space training to ensure that Nia was providing enough room for Max's height and width. Anna followed Fleck's directions to precise execution, and she was determined— more than ever—for Max to graduate and take Nia home.

Training, however, had been complicated by the winter weather, which remained unseasonably cold. The temperature rarely rose about freezing, and piles of snow and ice covered the sidewalks, making navigation hazardous for the veterans and their shepherds. Therefore, Fleck had modified the schedule to work partially indoors at the *Rathaus* (town hall) and St. Lambert's Church. But unlike Waldemar, who'd refused to permit Max to enter a Lutheran place of worship, Fleck had not raised the issue of Max being a Jew. Anna was delighted for Max to explore the castle-like church, and to experience the smell of the ancient timbers and echoes of their voices in its vast space. And Max seemed exceptionally proud when he and Nia climbed the colossal clock tower, despite him having to stop to catch his breath, to place his hands to the giant ticking timepiece that Norbie kept in working order.

Although things were progressing well at the guide dog school, that was not the case for Oldenburg's food supply. The shipments of rations, which consisted mainly of turnips and black bread laced with sawdust, were infrequent at best. The citizens of Oldenburg had turned haggard with dark, sunken eyes and protruding cheekbones. There were rumors that people, particularly the elderly and very young, were dying of starvation. And based on Emmi's interaction with a hospital nurse—who spoke of emaciated patients, too far gone to digest mashed turnip and broth, dying in their beds—she believed that the stories were true. The meager rations they received were not enough to keep them nourished. And if it wasn't for Max sharing his military-provided lunches, as well as Fleck giving her another sack of turnips, Anna would not have the strength to train.

Anna, Max, and Nia arrived home from the train station long after sunset. Cold and hungry, they entered the kitchen, where Norbie was preparing dinner.

"Bruno wasn't on the train," Anna said, taking off her coat.

"I'm sorry." Norbie removed a pan from the stove, and then hugged her. "The trains are about as dependable as my confounded grandfather clock."

She squeezed him.

"He'll arrive on the morning train," Norbie said.

"*Ja*," she said, feeling appreciative for his reassurance.

He released her and smiled. "I made turnip cutlets. We'll save one for Bruno."

"*Danke*," she said.

They ate dinner and, like they did each night, settled in the living room. Max played the piano, a medley of classical and folk pieces, until Norbie grew tired and went to bed. Afterward, Anna gathered a pencil and staff paper and joined Max at the piano.

"It's been a tiresome day," Max said, resting his hands on the keyboard. "Let's skip working tonight. You'll be more rested for training—and to see Bruno."

"*Nein*," Anna said, scooching next to him on the bench. "We need to finish your composition."

"It can wait," he said facing her.

"I'd rather work." *If I go to bed, I'll only worry about Bruno. I'll feel better here with you.* "But you're welcome to rest if you're too worn out to play."

"I'm all right," he said. "I've been rehearsing the next movement of *Light Suite* in my head. Would you like to hear it?"

"I'd love to," she said. "Your music is captivating; it makes me forget about the war."

"Then I'll play until dawn, or until a peace treaty is signed, whichever you prefer."

Anna smiled.

He placed his hands over the keys and played. The movement began with beautiful, yet sad, diatonic chord progressions.

An ominous feeling washed over Anna. She closed her eyes and imagined a fragile paper boat floating in a vast sea.

With his right hand, Max added a flowing, delicate melody to the chords. His fingers danced over the keyboard, and the music grew more intense.

For several minutes, Anna listened to the piece, which Max played effortlessly, as if he'd rehearsed it for years. The music stopped, which was followed by a few seconds of silence, then the thumping of Nia's tail on the floor.

"What do you think?" he asked softly.

Anna took a deep breath and opened her eyes. "It's magnificent."

"Do you really think so?"

"I do."

"I have some changes to make," he said, "but what you heard was essentially the music that has been percolating in my brain for the past few days."

"I wouldn't change a thing." Echoes of the piece replayed in her head. "At the beginning, I felt alone and sad. But as the movement progressed, I had hopeful feelings, like there was a reason to fight on, in spite of turbulent times."

Max placed a hand to his chin, as if he was contemplating her reaction to the piece.

"*Ja*," Anna said. "I felt—hope."

"I'm glad." He placed his hands on his lap and turned to Anna. "What is it that you hope for?"

She took a deep breath, pondering his question. "An end to the war. Bountiful food for Germans. Bruno to be safe." Anna fiddled with her sleeve. "And for you to have Nia as your guide."

"Those are all very good things, but they are hopes that you have for others. What hopes do you have for yourself?"

"Well, for starters, I hope that Fleck will continue to permit me to train."

"He will," Max said. "He'd never allow the best trainer in Deutschland to leave the school."

She grinned.

"What other hopes to you have?"

A childhood memory of Norbie and her *mutter* holding hands flashed in her brain. "To someday have the type of relationship my parents had—filled with laughter and affection."

Max smiled. "Would you like to have children?"

"*Ja*," she said. "Two."

"Very precise."

She chuckled. "I guess so. With me being an only child, I'd always wanted a sibling."

"Me too," he said. "You and Bruno will have a good life."

She nodded, despite a faint foreboding in her gut. "What hopes do you have?"

"That you'll train enough guide dogs for every blind person in Germany to have one."

"I'll do my best." Anna nudged him with her elbow. "But I was referring to something you desire for yourself."

He drew a breath. "Nothing else."

"There must be something that you yearn for," she said.

He turned toward her. "I've already received my wishes—you've helped me resurrect my passion to play the piano, and you've given me Nia."

"That's sweet of you to say," Anna said. "What about having a person to share your life with?"

He shook his head.

"I know it might feel a bit soon to be considering this now, after what happened with Wilhelmina, but you have your future ahead of you."

"I'd once hoped for that, but I'm not sure if that will be an option for me."

"It still is," she said. "You're kind, handsome, and a brilliant pianist. Someday, you'll perform at the Great Hall in Vienna, and loads of women will be seeking to gain your attention. You'll have lots of opportunities to meet the right person."

Max played with a button on his shirt.

"You're blushing," Anna said, noticing a slight redness in Max's face.

"So I am," Max said. He stretched his arms, and then positioned his hands on the keyboard. "How about we record a bit of music before we're too tired to stay awake?"

"All right," Anna said, feeling a bit disappointed to end their conversation.

For hours, Max played while Anna recorded notes onto staff paper. Like the previous movement, they worked in small increments, repeating each bar of music over and over, until they were both satisfied that the notes were accurately recorded. Consumed with transposing the piece to paper, they worked until a ruckus of clock chimes sounded in Norbie's workshop.

Anna silently counted the tolls. "It's midnight."

Max stood and extended his hand. "Time for you to go to bed."

Anna clasped his hand and rose from her seat. His hand slipped away, and then she placed the draft of the composition in a storage compartment in the piano bench.

"Come, Nia," Max said. "I'll take you outside."

Nia stood and stretched, arching her back.

"Good night, Anna," Max said, clasping Nia's harness.

"Sleep well."

Anna extinguished a lamp, turning the room black. As she felt her way along the wall, the sound of Max tumbling down wooden steps sent her heart rate soaring. *Oh, no!*

Nia barked.

Anna, her blood turned cold, shot to the stairwell. "Max!" She peered down into the blackness of Norbie's workshop and waited for his reply. But all she heard was Nia's whines.

CHAPTER 26

OLDENBURG, GERMANY—JANUARY 24, 1917

Anna darted down the stairs to the workshop, void of light. "Max!" she cried, kneeling and extending her arms. She felt a lick to her hand from Nia, and then located Max, his body face-down on the floor.

Oh, God! Her heart pounded against her rib cage. "Max, can you hear me?"

Nia whimpered.

She examined him for injuries by gently running her hands over his spine, neck, and head. "Max," she said, her voice quavering.

He groaned.

"Can you talk?"

"*Ja*," he wheezed.

Nia's tail whipped back and forth, striking Anna's side.

Anna felt him attempt to get up. "Wait. Are you hurt?"

"My mouth tastes like copper," he said. "I might have a bloody nose."

"Any other pain?"

"*Nein.*"

Thank God. "Let's rest a moment." Anna helped him to a sitting position on the floor, then she sat behind him with her legs straddled. "Lean back."

Max rested his back to her chest. He labored to remove a handkerchief from his pocket, then wiped his nose. "I'm all right. It's merely a nose bleed."

Anna drew a jagged breath and exhaled. She wrapped her arms around him, feeling his diaphragm rise and fall. "You could have broken you neck." Hot tears pooled in her eyes.

"I didn't," he said.

Nia curled onto their feet, as if she felt the need to protect them.

"What happened?" she asked, leaning her cheek to his shoulder.

"As I descended the stairs, I became light-headed. I must have missed a step and stumbled."

"Have you become dizzy before?"

"*Nein.*"

"How much did you eat today?"

"Enough."

"Are you eating any of your military lunch?"

"A little."

Anna's heart ached. "You can't be giving us all of your food. You're training all day, and you need every morsel they give you to keep your strength."

"You need extra nourishment, too," Max said.

"But I'm smaller than you."

"*Ja*, but you and Norbie need more than turnips and occasional pieces of black bread," he said. "We're in this together. Remember?"

She wanted to argue with him, but instead she tightened her arms around him. "You nearly frightened me to death."

"I'm sorry." He placed a palm over her hand.

She nuzzled to him.

Floorboards squeaked from above them, and a light flickered in the stairwell.

"Anna, Max!" Norbie, wearing his bedclothes and a coat, descended the stairs with a cupped hand protecting the flame of a candle. "I heard a clamor. Are you all right?"

Anna felt Max's hand slip away.

"*Ja*," Max said. "I took a tumble down the steps." He carefully stood, and then helped Anna up from the floor. Candlelight flickered over his face.

Anna took the handkerchief from Max's hand and dabbed a bit of blood from a nostril. "Your nose doesn't look broken."

"*Danke*," Max said, retrieving his handkerchief. He turned toward Norbie. "I'm sorry to have awakened you."

"Not at all, my boy," Norbie said, placing a hand on Max's shoulder. "Are you sure that you're okay?"

Max nodded. He reached his hand and located Nia, then stroked the dog's head. "None of this was your fault, Nia. You did a good job of helping me find the banister. It was me who was not being careful."

Nia nuzzled against his leg.

"How about I take you outside?" he said, rubbing the dog's ears.

"I'll come with you," Anna said.

Max shook his head. "I appreciate your offer, but soon I'll be on my own. I'm likely to have many tumbles and mishaps in my future, and it's probably best if Nia and I learn to work through them on our own."

"All right," Anna said, the truth stinging her.

"*Danke* for your help, Anna," Max said. "And Norbie, I appreciate you coming to check on me."

"You're welcome," Norbie said.

Max clasped Nia's harness, and together they exited through the door leading to the garden.

A blast of frigid wind prickled Anna's skin. Her heart prodded her to wait for him to return and climb the stairs, but her brain understood that Max was right—it was best to allow him to recover from his accident on his own. Reluctantly, she scaled the two flights of steps with Norbie, where they said a second good night and went to their separate rooms. She dressed for bed, adding an old wool sweater to help keep her warm, and then crawled under several layers of blankets. Minutes later, the shuffle of boots and the patter of paws grew in the hallway, followed by the creak of a door. *Thank goodness.* Anna, her veins still flooded with adrenaline, whispered two prayers: one for Bruno and another for Max. But long after she'd gone to bed, she remained awake, reliving Max's fall and the fear—of him being injured or worse—that had shaken her core.

Three days passed, and Bruno had not arrived in Oldenburg, nor had Anna received a letter or telegram to inform her of his whereabouts. Both Norbie and Max had reassured her that the journeys of soldiers from the front were often met with delays, and that Bruno would eventually arrive. But with the passing of time, her worry spiraled. To distract her mind, she buried herself in guide dog training and each evening she stayed up late, until she could no longer keep her eyes open, transposing Max's composition.

In addition to consuming herself with work, Anna strived to make certain Max was getting added nourishment to prevent more episodes of fatigue. Because Max remained intent on sharing his military rations with her and Norbie, Anna resorted to stealthy methods of altering portion sizes. At meals, she gave Max the biggest turnip cutlet or an extra ladle of leek soup. But when Max insisted on helping her carry their plates of food to the table, he'd discovered—by examining slices of black bread with his fingers—that he was receiving a larger portion of food. Therefore, she'd resorted to slicing Max's black bread at twice the thickness as the others, then compressing his slice with her hand to create equal depth. *Same size but twice the density. He'll get a bit more nourishment, even though the bread contains wood pulp.*

Her attempts to battle Max's weariness by giving him more food had worked. For the past few days, despite grueling obstacle course training and canvassing many kilometers of cobblestone streets in the cold, he hadn't had another incident of dizziness, although he did, at times, require moments to catch his breath. "Gas, you know," he'd often say to Anna while pausing to suck in air. It wasn't unusual for the veterans to have ailments in addition to their blindness. In fact, many of the veterans in class had other afflictions, including a man who tottered when he walked due to embedded shrapnel in his leg, and another veteran who required training on the opposite side of his guide dog due to nerve damage in his left arm. And Anna was disheartened to think that the veterans, even after they'd regained their independence through a guide dog, would still be battling maladies long after the war was over.

At the end of a tedious day of training, Anna, Max, and Nia walked to the station and waited for the evening train to arrive. And like the days before, the passengers exited the carriages and mingled out of the station, leaving the trio alone.

An ache grew in Anna's stomach. "I'm worried that something bad has happened."

"He's fine," Max said, stepping to her with Nia.

"How do you know?"

Max paused, as if he was carefully choosing his words. "Our military is proficient with promptly notifying families of unfortunate events. Bruno's parents would have informed you if something had happened."

She drew a deep breath.

"Also, the military often changes dates of one's leave on short notice. He's probably already written you a letter to inform you of when he'll be home."

"I hope so," she said. She hooked her arm around his elbow. "Let's go."

They left the train station and walked home. Reaching the front door to Norbie's workshop, they stomped snow off their boots, and then entered. Anna locked the door and turned to go upstairs, but a savory aroma caused her to freeze.

Nia, her nostrils twitching, raised her snout toward the ceiling.

"Oh, my," Anna gasped. "What's that wonderful smell?"

Max sniffed, then smiled. "Norbie's frying sausage."

Oh, my! Food has reached the city! She imagined foreign supply ships breaking through the British naval blockade. Her eyes flooded with tears. She shook away her thoughts and dashed upstairs to the kitchen, where Norbie was stirring a skillet of sausage and onions.

"You acquired meat!" Anna said. "How did you get it?"

Norbie, holding a wooden spoon, approached her and grinned. "Bruno."

Anna's eyes widened.

"*Hallo*, Anna," a deep voice said.

Anna's breath stalled in her lungs. She turned and saw him,

dressed in his military uniform and standing in the living room. Her body trembled. "Bruno!"

Bruno swept her into his arms and hugged her.

She squeezed him, feeling the bristles of his mustache tickle her neck.

He kissed her, and then wiped tears from her cheeks.

"Thank God, you're home," she said, placing her hands against the breast of his tunic.

"My leave was set back a couple of days," he said. "I didn't have the means to contact you. I hope my absence didn't cause you distress."

Anna sniffed back tears. "You're here now, and that's all that matters."

Max and Nia entered the kitchen.

Anna slid her hands from Bruno's chest. "This is Max."

"It's nice to meet you," Max said, extending his hand.

Bruno glanced at Max's blank, staring eyes, and then shook his hand. "You too."

"And this is Nia," Anna said, stroking Nia's fur. "She's a guide dog and, hopefully, she'll go home with Max after training."

"She will," Norbie chimed in.

Bruno tentatively approached the dog.

"It's all right," Anna said. "You can pet her."

Bruno gave Nia a pat on the head, and then slid his hands into his front pockets.

"Anna is an incredible trainer," Max said. "She's the best in the group."

Anna smiled.

"Bruno," Norbie said. "You must go to the guide dog school to observe. You'll be impressed when you see them train."

"I'm sure I will." Bruno paused, stepping away from Nia, and pointed to the stove. "I brought dry sausage and onions from an officers' boardinghouse in France. It's all I could gather before I left."

"It's a blessing," Anna said. "*Danke.*"

Norbie dished sliced sausage and caramelized onions onto

plates, and they sat at the table with Max next to Norbie, and Anna next to Bruno. Norbie said grace, giving thanks for Bruno's safe arrival and his gift of food.

Anna took a bite of sausage and chewed, savoring the rich, gamey flavor. She wondered, although briefly, how long it'd been since she'd eaten meat. Burying her thoughts, she glanced to Bruno. His eyes were surrounded by dark circles, and the hair near his temples had turned gray. *You'll eat and sleep and forget about the war.*

"The sausage is delicious, Bruno," Norbie said.

"*Ja,*" Max said. "It's generous of you to share your food."

Bruno nodded and forked a hunk of sausage.

Anna, despite her head buzzing with a flurry of things that she wanted to ask, refrained from overwhelming Bruno with too many questions. Based on her experience as a nurse, she knew that it often took soldiers some time to acclimate to life away from the war. And considering the way Bruno's eyes remained fixated on his plate, she assumed that it might take a while for him to adjust to being home. *He'll engage when he's ready.*

"Bruno," Norbie said. "I wish you could have seen Nia when Anna brought her home."

Bruno looked up from his food.

"Nia had been trained as an ambulance dog, but she injured her paws at the front." Norbie glanced at Nia, curled on the floor, and he lowered his voice, as if he were sheltering his words from a child's ears. "She was deathly thin and couldn't walk, and she was on the verge of being euthanized. Anna saved her, and now she's a guide dog."

"That's not entirely true," Anna said. "You and Emmi helped."

"Nia is lucky to have you, Anna," Max said.

Bruno placed down his fork and clasped Anna's hand. "So am I."

"*Danke,*" Anna said. She felt him squeeze her fingers, and then slip away. Desiring to change the subject to something other than herself, she said, "Max is a brilliant pianist."

"*Ja,*" Norbie said. "He's been performing for us every night."

He turned his eyes upward, as if looking to heaven. "Helga would have loved to have heard him play."

"Helga?" Bruno asked, forking a bit of onion.

He doesn't remember my mutter's *name.* Anna's heart sank.

"She was my wife," Norbie said.

Bruno looked at Norbie. "Please forgive me. I do remember stories of her from you and Anna. I understand she was a lovely woman. I'm tired and my brain is not working well."

"It's all right," Norbie said.

Bruno turned to Anna. "I'm sorry."

She placed her palm on his hand and nodded.

Their conversation dwindled and they finished eating their meals, with each of them saving a bit of their sausage to augment their rations for the rest of the week. Although Anna offered to help clear the table, Max and Norbie insisted on washing and drying the dishes, allowing her and Bruno time alone in the living room.

"How was your travel?" Anna asked, sitting beside him on the sofa. She smoothed her skirt over her knees.

"*Gut.*" He turned to her. "You look beautiful."

"*Danke,*" she said, still feeling hurt from his failure to recall her *mutter*'s name. *I need to let it go.* "Will you be going to Frankfurt to visit your parents?"

"*Nein.* I plan to spend my military leave with you."

"I hope they will not be upset with me for monopolizing your time," she said.

"They won't," he said.

She looked at him. "It feels strange not having the opportunity to meet them."

"It's temporary," he said. "After the war—when we're living in Frankfurt—you'll see them often, perhaps more frequently than you would like."

How can I leave the school when there are so many veterans who will be in need of a guide dog? She buried her thought and said, "I assume Vater has already invited you to stay here with us."

"He did, and I accepted. But perhaps in a few days, I could get a room at the boardinghouse, like my last visit. It will give us time to be alone."

Anna wiggled her toes inside her boots, attempting to dispel divergent feelings rising in her chest.

"I've missed you," he said.

"I've missed you, too, and I want us to have time together." Her heart rate accelerated. "But I'm unable to take time away from work, and I should be here for Max and Nia. I've made a commitment to them, and the guide dog school."

Bruno rubbed stubble on his jowls.

"Are you upset with me?"

"*Nein.*" He held her hand and looked into her eyes. "I want things to be the way they were."

"Me too." *But what if it's not the same?*

Bruno caressed her hand and paused, touching her bare ring finger.

"If I had known when you were arriving," she said, "I would have worn my engagement ring. I usually store it in a keepsake box while I'm working, but I'll wear it while you're here."

He nodded, and then glanced toward the sound of chatter in the kitchen. "We have much catching up to do, and it would be nice for us to have privacy."

"We can create a bit of privacy here," she said.

"We will," he said. "But in the event that we can get away, even for a few hours, I'll have a room available for us."

Anna picked at a loose thread on her sleeve, then nodded.

Norbie and Max—guided by Nia—entered the room but didn't sit.

"We thought that we'd say good night before we head off to bed," Norbie said.

Anna straightened her back. "But it's early."

"The rich food has made us sleepy," Norbie said, rubbing his belly. "Right, Max?"

"*Ja,*" Max said.

"But you haven't played the piano," Anna said. "And we need to work on finishing your composition."

"Tomorrow," Max said. "Tonight, you and Bruno will catch up on lost time."

"*Danke*," Bruno said.

"You're welcome," Max said. "But could you do me a favor?"

"Of course," Bruno said.

"I want you to take my room instead of Norbie's."

Norbie turned to Max. "But I've already made plans to sleep on the cot in my workshop."

"I insist." Max patted Nia, standing next to him. "Besides, it'll make it easier for me to take Nia out to the garden to do her business."

"Are you sure?" Norbie asked.

Max nodded.

"I appreciate that," Norbie said. "My back isn't what it used to be."

A swell of gratitude filled Anna. *It's sweet of him to think about Vater.*

"Is that all right with you, Bruno?" Max asked.

"It is," he said.

Minutes later, after Norbie and Max had gone to bed, Anna and Bruno sat side by side on the sofa. To catch Bruno up on her life, she told him about Dr. Stalling, Emmi, and Fleck, as well as the challenges that she and Max encountered with Waldemar, including his refusal to allow them to train inside a church.

"Your letters didn't mention that Max was a Jew," Bruno said.

Anna shifted in her seat. "I didn't think it would matter to you."

"It doesn't," Bruno said. "I'm merely surprised that he wouldn't be housed with a Jewish family. Even at the front there are separate chaplains—*Feldrabbiners* (field rabbis) serve the Jewish soldiers."

"All of the blind veterans are boarding with trainers, none of whom are Jewish." She crossed her arms. "I'm honored to have Max stay with us."

"I'm glad that he's been a suitable guest."

Anna's shoulder muscles tightened.

"I could speak to your supervisor about Waldemar, if you like."

"I would prefer that you didn't," she said. "It might make things more difficult for Max and me. Fleck doesn't condone Waldemar's behavior, but he tolerates him because there are few trainers, and we're expecting larger groups of battle-blinded veterans to arrive in Oldenburg. I appreciate your offer, but for now, I think we can deal with Waldemar on our own."

"All right." He moved close, his leg touching her knee.

She drew a deep breath and gestured to the gramophone. "Would you like to listen to music?"

"Only if you do."

"I do," she said, hoping the music would ease the awkwardness of their reunion.

Bruno stood and went to the gramophone, where he sorted through a box of records. After making a selection, he placed the disc on the gramophone and lowered the tone arm. Static hissed and, a few seconds later, a boisterous beat of bass and snare drums filled the air. After a few bars, the beating drums were joined by a brass band, comprised of trumpets, baritones, and tubas.

"We have lots of music choices," Anna said, "including several piano suites that you might enjoy."

Bruno sat, placing his arm around Anna. "I didn't recognize the names of the songs, except for the military marches."

A memory of Max's question flashed in her head—*What type of music does Bruno like?*

"Did I pick the wrong record?" he asked.

"*Nein*," she said, not wanting to disappoint him.

He pulled her close.

"I think we should take it slow," she said.

"Of course." He caressed her cheek with his thumb, then eased back on the sofa.

She rested her head on his shoulder. *It's irrational of me to be on edge. I'll feel better about things tomorrow.* But the longer she sat with Bruno, listening to the oom-pah rhythm of deep brass instruments, the more she yearned to be with Max at the piano while Nia thumped her tail on the floor beneath their bench.

CHAPTER 27

OLDENBURG, GERMANY—JANUARY 28, 1917

Max, struggling to concentrate, traveled over a series of logs on the obstacle course with Nia. Anna followed closely behind them while Fleck, scribbling notes onto a clipboard, sat on a stool near the barn. For much of the morning, Anna had been silent, other than to provide instruction. Even on their walk to school, she'd said little to him or Emmi, other than to inform her friend that Bruno had arrived in Oldenburg. *Something is troubling her,* he thought, locating a felled log with his cane. *When she's ready to talk, I'll be here for her.*

With his mind on Anna, Max made several mistakes through-out the day, including a near fall while navigating a simulated up-curb, made from bricks, which earned him a lecture from Fleck on being attentive while training. Thankfully, Nia guided him flawlessly, with the exception of some hobbling due to her frail paw, otherwise he would have made far more errors. He thought that Anna would become more talkative as the day wore on, and that her spirits might improve if Bruno came to the school grounds to observe as Norbie had suggested. But as far as Max could tell, Bruno had not arrived. And as hours passed, her solitude grew worse.

Max, unable to contain his concern, turned toward Anna and asked, "Would you like to talk about what's bothering you?"

Anna glanced to the other groups, all of whom were out of ear-shot. "Nothing is bothering me."

"You're quiet," he said.

"I'm merely tired."

He continued his walk with Nia. "How was your evening with Bruno?"

"Fine."

He waited for her to say more, but only heard the crunch of snow beneath her boots. As he debated in his head whether to probe further, she quickened her pace and reached his side.

"Well, if I'm honest," she said, "our conversation was a bit un-comfortable at times."

"Oh," he said. "I'm sorry."

"He seemed distracted, with the exception of gaining time away together, which is not an option considering my work. Some of the things that I'd written him about in my letters were forgot-ten, and I was hurt that he didn't remember—" She drew a deep breath. "Never mind."

Your mutter, he thought. "Helga?"

"*Ja*," she said, her voice soft.

"That must have been rough for you to hear."

"It was."

Max recalled the somber timbre of Bruno's voice. The man's dour tone reminded Max of the many despondent soldiers that he'd encountered in Ypres who were on the brink of being broken by war. He wondered if Anna or Norbie had recognized the same thing, or if his combat experience, combined with his reliance on hearing due to blindness, had made him more keenly aware of Bruno's mental state.

"It takes time for one to adjust from being at the front," he said. "I'm sure you already know this from your work at the hospital, but it might feel different when you're in the thick of it."

"True." She walked with him and Nia around a pile of snow.

"One day, a soldier is fighting for his life, and two days later—after a year of witnessing death in hellacious conditions—he's back home, sitting at the kitchen table. To a soldier, the change in environment is a shock. Your head is foggy and your emotions are numb, as if your brain was injected with anesthetic."

"You sound like you're speaking from experience," she said.

"I am," he said. "And I can tell you that things can get better with time."

"I hope so."

"They will," he said. "I believe that good things happen to people with good hearts—and yours, Anna, is made of gold."

"You're sweet." She clasped Nia's harness, placing her hand next to Max's. "Speaking of good things, it was lovely of you to sleep on the cot in the workshop instead of Norbie."

"I'm glad to do it."

"Did the ticking and chiming of clocks keep you awake last night?"

"*Nein*," he said. "But the march music is still stuck in my head."

"I'm so sorry," she said.

He nudged her arm. "I was kidding."

"Oh." She chuckled. "Tonight, I'll insist that we play something more relaxing."

"It's all right," Max said, slowing his pace. "There's nothing wrong with a person having a different taste in music. It makes me happy to hear Norbie sing 'Hänschen klein'—the more out of tune the better."

Anna glanced at Max and smiled.

"My friends at the front loved military marches." A flash of playing a piano, while his comrades sang and drank schnapps, filled his head. "My friend, Otto, once told me to stick to playing marches because people would pay to hear them."

Anna leaned in.

He drew a breath, taking in her scent.

"You certainly know how to make a woman feel better," she said. "I'm going to miss you when you leave."

His chest ached. "I'm going to miss you, too." *More than you will ever know.*

Her hand slipped away from the harness, and the space grew between them.

Max, attempting to contain his feelings, patted Nia and quickened his pace. They completed two more laps around the obstacle course. And with each step and maneuver, all he could think about was how lucky Bruno was to have Anna.

"Oh, no," Anna said.

"What is it?" Max asked.

"Waldemar is coming."

"Where's Fleck?"

Anna glanced around the course. "I don't know."

The crunching of bootsteps grew. Hairs raised on the back of his neck. He tugged on the harness and said, "*Halt.*"

Nia stopped and panted.

"Fleck wants to see both of you," Waldemar grumbled.

"What about?" Max asked.

"It's likely concerning your poor performance," he said. "Fleck has been scribbling notes about you on his clipboard all day."

Max's face turned hot. Fearing that a rebuttal could potentially get Anna in trouble, he gripped Nia's harness and held his tongue.

"Where's Fleck?" Anna asked.

"The barn." Waldemar scratched at his scraggly, gray mustache and looked at Max. "I always knew that Fleck would eventually come to his senses and expel you from training. However, I'm surprised that you lasted this long." He turned and walked away.

"Don't listen to him," Anna said. "He's only trying to annoy you."

"He's doing a damn good job of it." Max stroked Nia's back. "Well, let's see what Fleck wants."

Inside the barn, Nia guided him toward the area of the woodstove. As he felt the warmth of the fire begin to radiate over his face, he commanded Nia to sit.

"Herr Fleck," Anna said. "I understand that you'd like to have a word with us."

"*Ja.*" Fleck removed a cigarette from his pocket and lit it. He took a deep inhale and blew smoke.

A burnt scent of tobacco filled Max's nose. He fought away the urge to cough.

"Frau Bauer," Fleck called.

"*Ja*, sir," Emmi said, grooming a shepherd at a nearby stall.

"Please take your dog for a walk," he said.

He wants to speak privately with us. A lump formed in the pit of Max's stomach as he listened to Emmi and the dog leave the barn.

"I've been giving considerable thought to the shepherd assignments," Fleck said. "And I've decided to make a change."

Dread shot through Max. He placed a gloved hand on Nia's head. "With all due respect, sir, I do not wish to have another shepherd. I'd rather go back to Leipzig alone, than to exchange Nia for—"

"Max," Fleck interrupted. "I wasn't finished."

Max nodded.

Fleck took a drag on his cigarette. "As I was saying, I've decided to make a change. Despite your lack of focus this morning, I am permanently assigning Nia to you."

Anna's eyes widened.

Max froze, questioning whether he interpreted the man's words correctly.

"You've worked with most, if not all, of the shepherds," Fleck said. "And I see no need to pair you with another dog, since it's become apparent that you and Nia have formed an inseparable bond."

He swallowed. "Are you saying that she's mine?"

"*Ja*, assuming you finish the rest of training."

"*Dankeschön*, sir," Max said, feeling overwhelmed with gratitude.

Anna kneeled to Nia. "Did you hear that, girl? You're going to go home with Max."

Nia wagged her tail.

"Max," Fleck said. "I trust that your concentration will be better tomorrow."

"It will, sir," he said.

"*Gut.*" Fleck turned to Anna. "Take Max and Nia to town to train for the remainder of the afternoon, and take Frau Bauer with you. Instruct her to go to the ambulance dog shelter. They have a few shepherds in need of paw care. And if it pleases you, you may mention that the supervisor there was quite impressed with her care of the shepherds with kennel cough. He commented to me that he'd rather have Frau Bauer care for his dogs than their former veterinarian who'd been sent to the front."

"Of course, sir," Anna said. "I'll be sure to tell her."

Fleck gave a nod and left the barn, leaving them alone.

Anna threw her arms around Max. "Congratulations! I'm so happy for you!"

He hugged her. "It wouldn't have happened without you."

Her embrace lingered.

He felt the warmth of her breath against his neck. His heart rate quickened. Nia stuck her snout between them, and he felt her arms slip away. Gathering his composure, he smiled and said, "Shall we get back to work?"

"With pleasure," she said.

They gathered Emmi and departed for town, leaving the other groups who were still conducting drills on the obstacle course. Once they were away from school, Anna informed Emmi about Fleck's compliment with regard to her care for the dogs with kennel cough.

"He really said that?" Emmi asked, beaming.

"He did," Max said.

"Like I've been telling you," Anna said, "you're as good as any veterinarian."

"*Danke*," Emmi said. "It's not every day that I receive an accolade for my work. I'll take any praise from Fleck I can get, even if he prefers not to deliver it himself."

"You deserve it," Max said.

"I have more news," Anna said. "Fleck has permanently assigned Nia to Max."

"Oh, my goodness!" Emmi said. "That's marvelous!"

"We still need to pass the rest of the training," Max said, leery that being overconfident would only lead to disappointment.

"I have no doubt that you will graduate," Emmi said. "Soon, you'll be taking Nia home to live with you."

A wave of indebtedness washed over him. "If it wasn't for both of you, Nia and I wouldn't be together. I'm grateful for what you've done for us."

"You're welcome, Max," Emmi said.

Anna blinked her eyes, as if she was fighting back tears.

As Max adjusted his hand on Nia's harness, he heard approaching footsteps.

"Is that him?" Emmi asked.

"*Ja*." Anna ran ahead.

"Who?" Max asked.

"Bruno," Emmi said.

Max's elation faded.

"You came to see us," Anna said, stepping to Bruno.

Bruno nodded. "I was planning to view you from afar, of course. I wouldn't want to make you nervous, or draw unnecessary attention to you from your supervisor."

It's good that he came out in support of Anna, Max thought.

"We're training in town for the remainder of the day," she said. "I'm glad I caught you on our way there."

Bruno placed his hands into his coat pockets. "You look surprised to see me."

"*Nein*," she said. "I'm happy that you came."

"*Gut*," Bruno said.

Anna gestured with her hand. "Do you remember Emmi?"

"*Ja*," Bruno said, looking at Emmi. "You worked at the hospital with Anna."

Emmi nodded. "Welcome home."

It's wrong of me to be envious, Max thought, feeling a bit ashamed of himself. *He seems to care for Anna, and I want what is best for her.* He buried his thoughts and said, "Bruno, how about you follow Nia and me back to town, and you'll see what Anna has taught us to do."

"Lead the way," Bruno said.

Max gave a command to Nia, and the dog pawed ahead.

For the remainder of the afternoon, Anna, Max, and Nia trained on the sidewalks and street crossings of Oldenburg. He and Anna spoke little with Bruno, who followed a dozen or so paces behind them, as if he was making an effort to not interrupt their training. But Bruno's presence did, however, stall conversation between Anna and Max. Instead of carrying on their usual banter, which was often the case when training away from Fleck and the others, Anna once again turned quiet, with the exception of training dialogue. And Max's glorious day, of being awarded Nia, turned bittersweet.

At home, they found Norbie tinkering on a pendulum clock in his workshop, and Anna told him news of Max and Nia's official partnership.

Norbie set aside his tools and hugged Max. "Outstanding work, my boy!"

"*Danke*," Max said.

Norbie released him, and then kneeled to Nia. "I'm proud of you, too!"

Nia licked his nose.

Norbie chortled and wiped his face.

After a dinner of diced turnip with specks of leftover sausage, everyone settled into the living room. Max sat at the piano, Anna and Bruno claimed spots on the sofa, and Norbie hunkered in a chair. Max played several folk songs, which Norbie sang out of tune with excessive vibrato. And all the while he was playing, he wondered if Bruno had the same affinity, as he and Anna, for Norbie's beautifully bad vocals. He received his answer after the third piece.

"Max," Bruno said, "it might be nice to hear something other than folk music. Do you know any marches?"

An impulse to perform another round of "Hänschen klein" surged through Max, and he fought away a smile.

"Max is a classical pianist," Anna said to Bruno. "Maybe he should select a piece that he would like to play."

"I don't mind," Max said, feeling appreciative of Anna's attempt to prevent him from hearing more military marches. He placed his hands over the keys and played one of the marches that his comrades had once enjoyed. Finishing the piece, he turned on his bench and faced them.

"Well done," Bruno said.

"*Danke*," Max said, staring toward the sound of Bruno's voice.

"It reminds me of the songs in the taverns near the front," Bruno said.

"Where are you stationed?" Max asked.

"Lille, France," Bruno said. "But my position keeps me on the move along the western front." Bruno glanced at Anna, sitting beside him. "Unfortunately, my frequent change of location creates delays with the delivery of letters between Anna and me."

Anna folded her arms.

"I understand from Anna that you're an *oberleutnant*," Max said. "Infantry, calvary, artillery?"

"At the beginning of the war, I was with an infantry pioneer regiment, but now I'm in artillery."

"Oh," Max said, thinking it was unusual for a soldier, even an officer, to move from an infantry to an artillery division. "What pioneer regiment were you in?"

Bruno shifted in his seat. "Thirty-six."

Pioneer Regiment 36. Max's mind raced, struggling to recall where he'd heard the name.

"I think that's enough discussion of the war," Anna said.

"I agree," Norbie said. "I suggest we talk about something bright, like our futures and how good our lives will be after the war." He grinned and patted his belly. "When the fighting is over and food is plentiful, I'm going to eat sauerbraten and spätzle until I bust out of my clothes."

Anna chuckled.

It's good to hear you laugh, Max thought.

"How about you, Max?" Norbie asked. "What will you do after a peace treaty is signed?"

Max extended his hand toward the floor. Nia padded to him, and he rubbed her head. "I'll live in Leipzig with Nia, and I'll indulge her with treats and belly rubs."

"That's the spirit, Max," Norbie said. "What else?"

"I'll find work as a pianist."

"And as composer," Anna added. "You're going to be a famous pianist, and we'll come to see you perform in the Great Hall of the Musikverein in Vienna."

Max smiled.

"And what about you, Bruno?" Norbie asked.

"Anna and I will marry," Bruno said. "I'll work at my family's manufacturing business in Frankfurt, where we'll purchase a grand house and—" He paused, rubbing stubble on his chin. "We'll have lots of children."

An ache grew in Max's chest.

Anna glanced to Bruno, then lowered her head.

"How is your family's business doing?" Norbie asked. "In times of uncertainty, I'm sure it's been difficult for your *vater* to keep it afloat while you're away."

"On the contrary," Bruno said. "My *vater* has gained military supply contracts to keep things running. I assure you, Norbie, your daughter will be financially well taken care of."

"What is your family business?" Max asked.

"Wahler Farbwerke," Bruno said. "It's an ink and dye business."

What does the military need with ink and dye? Curiosity stirred in Max's gut. "May I—"

"Max," Anna said, "I'd love for Norbie and Bruno to hear the movements of *Light Suite* that you've finished. Would you mind playing it for us?"

"Not at all, but you haven't shared your aspirations," Max said.

"It's not necessary," she said.

"Oh, but it is," Norbie said. "You must share something that you're looking forward to after the war, even if it is something small."

Anna glanced to Nia. "I'd like to continue to train guide dogs."

A smile spread over Norbie's face.

"Dr. Stalling has grand plans for expanding guide dog training," Anna said. "Maybe someday he'll open a school in Frankfurt."

"That would be good for veterans," Bruno said. "But you'll have no need to work when we are married."

Max clenched his jaw. *It's her choice.*

"True," Anna said. "However, I may decide to train after the war, assuming I'm given the opportunity to do so."

Bruno straightened his back. "Very well, if you like."

She smoothed her skirt with her hands. "Max, could you honor us with your piece?"

"Sure," Max said, feeling proud of Anna for holding her ground. He turned to the piano, positioned his hands over the keyboard, and played. Initially, it felt strange for him to perform his music that was inspired by Anna, who was now sitting next to her fiancé. But as he continued with the piece, emotions of his time with Anna swelled within his heart. Instead of ending his performance with the most recent movement that Anna had transcribed for him, he played the next movement, which he had been rehearsing in his head. And as he finished, he was jolted by the sound of Norbie's applause.

"Bravo!" Norbie said, clapping his hands. "Bravo!"

Max turned on his bench and gave a small bow.

"That was sublime," Anna said. "Is it the next movement of the suite?"

"*Ja*," Max said.

Anna left the sofa and approached him. "Stand."

"Why?" Max asked, rising from his seat.

Anna opened the compartment on the piano bench and retrieved her staff paper. "We're going to record this movement while it's still fresh in your head."

"We can do it later," Max said. "It's getting late, and you'll want to spend time with Bruno."

"Bruno," Anna said, turning to him. "Could you give me an hour to work on this with Max?"

Bruno rubbed his jowls, then nodded.

"Come with me," Norbie said, placing a hand on Bruno's shoulder. "I'll show you a few antique clocks that I'm working to restore, and a confounded grandfather clock that refuses to strike on time."

Alone with Anna, Max played the new movement to *Light Suite*, bar by bar, which she recorded onto staff paper. And as their hour drew to a close, so did the realization that his time with Anna would soon come to an end. *God, I'm going to miss you.* He slipped his hands from the keyboard and placed them on his lap.

"We have a couple more minutes," Anna said.

I wish it was a hundred years. He took a deep breath, his lungs feeling heavy from the chronic exposure to cold air. "May I share a few thoughts with you?"

"Of course."

"I'm glad that you shared your commitment to train guide dogs with Bruno. But when the war is over, and when you're married and living in Frankfurt, it might seem difficult, perhaps even impossible, to pursue your dream. You have a gift, Anna. You're restoring the lives of blind veterans through guide dogs. And it would be a shame if Bruno's plans for your life hindered the pursuit of your true purpose."

"It won't," Anna said. "But I've made a commitment to Bruno, which will eventually require me to move away. And the chance of being a trainer will depend upon a school being established in Frankfurt." She picked at the edge of the piano with a fingernail. "I don't know what else to say."

"You don't need to say anything," Max said. "I simply wanted you to know that I believe in you. If there is anyone who can create a path to train guide dogs, even if it's outside of Oldenburg, it is you."

"*Danke*," she said.

He stood. Nia rose from her place on the floor and joined him.

"Stay," she said. "We have a little more time."

"It's best that you spend it with Bruno," he said. "Enjoy the rest of your evening."

"Good night," she said, her voice soft.

Max clasped Nia's harness and they descended the stairs to the workshop, where he informed Norbie and Bruno that he and Anna were finished working on the composition. He took Nia out to the garden to do her business, and then he settled onto his cot. Music emanated from the gramophone in the living room, sending a wave of restlessness through him. *Anna and Bruno are together.* He slid over and patted the cot.

Nia hopped up and curled next to him.

"We're partners from now on, girl," he said, running a hand over her fur. "When we aren't working, I'm going to spoil you rotten."

Nia leaned back and licked his face.

Max, his mind racing with thoughts of Anna, struggled to sleep. He hoped that Bruno would always be kind and supportive of her, and that nothing would prevent Anna from pursuing her ambitions. Also, he rehashed the evening conversation in his head, in particular a few of Bruno's comments that ignited a wariness within him. *Pioneer Regiment 36 sounds familiar, maybe it's a special unit. Why would an officer be transferred from infantry to artillery? Does the military have a great need for ink? Perhaps it's to dye the uniforms.* He fought to bury his newfound unease. But long after the gramophone music ceased, he remained awake, listening to the ticktock of clocks. And he prayed, for Anna's sake, that his reservations about Bruno were groundless.

CHAPTER 28

OLDENBURG, GERMANY—JANUARY 30, 1917

Bruno, kneeling in the garden, labored to harvest winter leeks while he waited for Anna to come home from work. He hacked away at the frozen earth with a hand trowel, sending throbs of pain through his joints and bones. His intentions were to add sustenance to Anna and her *vater*'s meager diet, which mainly consisted of turnips. And he hoped that by toiling away at the solid ground he would distract himself from the cancerous guilt that consumed his soul. Instead, his isolated act of penitence only exacerbated his torment.

This morning, on his way home from observing Anna train at the school grounds, he witnessed three children, no older than twelve years of age, break into a barn and flee with a handful of looted rutabagas. Rather than attempt to stop them, he'd watched the children—emaciated, with protruding cheekbones and sunken eyes—devour the vegetables as they scurried away through a snow-covered field. Despite the atrocities that he'd experienced at the front, he was shaken by the horrid condition of the children. Although he'd heard the rumors of malnutrition, he had been detached from the daily sight of starvation in Germany. The food shortages were not entirely caused by the Allied blockade, Bruno believed. The empire was also to blame. After all, the army had seized most of the horses, and they conscripted the bulk of the agricultural workforce. Additionally, farming fertilizers were scarce due to diverting nitrogen to produce explosives. *I should have paid more heed to Anna's letters about the dwindling supply of rations. I could have brought more food with me from Lille.* But in his shaken state of leaving Celeste, he hadn't thought to load his leather case with more food.

His travel home from the front had not been delayed as he'd led Anna to believe. The first two days of his military leave were spent with Celeste. Upon learning that she was pregnant, he refused to leave her, despite her encouragement for him to go home. "It's not your problem," she'd said, curled next to him in bed. But it was his predicament, he believed, and it was *their* baby that was growing inside her. Like friends, rather that lovers, they talked through the options for the pregnancy and themselves. At the end of two days, much of which was spent in the confines of his room, they decided that Celeste would have the baby, and that Bruno would provide for her and their child. And Bruno insisted that Celeste move to Germany—in the event that the German Empire was defeated—so that he could care for her and their child in a town near Frankfurt, rather than her be ostracized for having what the French referred to as a "Boche baby." However, Celeste was reluctant to commit to leaving France, despite the risks to her, and the shame that might be cast upon an illegitimate child.

Bruno loathed his father's affairs, and now Bruno had a mistress, too. *I'm repeating the sins of my* vater, he'd thought while consoling Celeste. Before the war, he'd intended to lead a different life from his *vater*, which Bruno hoped would include a lifelong commitment to one woman. Falling for Anna had reaffirmed his conviction. However, the years of killing had ravaged him, and in a fragile state he'd sought comfort from his pain in Celeste's warmth. Months from now they would have a war baby. And for the rest of his life, he would need to live with the consequences of his lapse in faithfulness.

Far more had been compromised, Bruno believed, than his fidelity to Anna. Since he'd foolishly accepted Fritz Haber's recruitment to a special chemical warfare unit, he'd committed unspeakable acts. Thousands were gruesomely killed or maimed by poison gas. Someday, Bruno believed, he would go to hell, if there was such a place. And in the interim, he would live in a purgatory of secrets and lies. To protect himself and the woman he loved, the past and present would need to be compartmentalized—his life with Anna, his care for Celeste and their baby, the atrocities that he'd committed at the front, and his family's role in the German Empire's chemical warfare program. And if Anna were to find out about any of the other facets of his life, he'd likely lose her forever.

As Bruno loosened a frozen leek from the ground, the back door squeaked open.

"There you are," Anna said, entering the garden.

He tossed the leek into a tin bucket, and then stood and hugged her. "How was work?"

"*Gut*," she said, releasing him. "*Danke* for digging up leeks."

He nodded. "There aren't many left. I'll see what I can do to acquire more food."

"We'll manage. Come inside and I'll—" Her eyes locked on his bloodied knuckles. "Your hands."

"I forgot my gloves inside the house," he said.

She carefully clasped his fingers and examined the cuts. "Your hands are shaking."

"I'm cold," he said, hoping to hide that his nerves were shot.

"Come with me, and I'll tend to your wounds."

He followed her to his room, which Max had slept in before moving to a cot in the workshop. She retrieved a basin of water and soap, and placed them on a washstand.

"Soak them," she said.

He inserted his hands, numb from the cold, into the basin.

She cleansed his cuts with soap, turning the water red.

As the numbness began to subside, a prickly tingling ran through his fingers. He looked at her. "You're beautiful."

She shook her head. "I'm thin and ragged."

"Not to me."

"*Danke*," she said, her eyes focused on his hands.

Piano music emanated from the living room.

"He's playing earlier than usual," Bruno said.

"Norbie sometimes talks Max into performing a few pieces before dinner."

He nodded. "Perhaps we could go for a walk."

"I'd like to," she said, "but my legs are exhausted from training all day."

His shoulder muscles tensed. "We haven't spent much time together."

"We will," she said. "Tonight, after I transcribe for Max, we'll sit in the living room and listen to music."

He soaked his hands. "You're with him a lot."

"Of course," she said. "I'm his trainer, and I'm boarding him in our home. We're together most of the time."

"How long will he be here?"

She retrieved a towel from the washstand. "A few more weeks, at least. Graduation is delayed due to the cold weather, and Fleck has not provided a date."

A smidge of resentment smoldered inside him. "I was hoping we could create more time for us."

"We will," she said, a hesitance in her voice.

"When?"

She handed him the towel. "We can stay up late in the living room, when everyone has gone to bed."

"I look forward to it," he said, drying his hands.

She looked at his wounds. "The blood has stopped. I don't think you'll need bandages."

Bruno set aside the towel and lowered his hands, feeling the outline of a key in his pants pocket. Butterflies fluttered in his stomach. "I went to the boardinghouse today, and I secured a room for us."

She looked at him. "I'm not sure if it's a good idea for me to be away."

He stepped to her and placed a hand to her cheek. "I've missed you."

"Me too, but—" She lowered her eyes.

He stepped close. "I know you feel obligated to be here for Max. But it might be good for him to spend more time alone. Soon, he'll move away with his dog."

"It's not that easy," she said.

"It can be." Using a finger, he gently lifted her chin.

Her eyes met his.

His pulse accelerated. He leaned in, drawing his lips toward hers.

Norbie's singing, accompanied by the piano, erupted from the floor below them.

Anna eased back. "We should go."

"Wait." He placed his hands on her shoulders "I know things feel a bit strange between us. You do know that my affection for you hasn't changed."

She drew a breath. "I do."

"The war has been hard on you, and the fighting at the front has taken a toll on me. But time together will mend the distance between us." He caressed her shoulders with his thumbs. "Do you remember how happy we were when we first met?"

She nodded.

He searched through his memories. "I wrote you poems to convince you to spend time with me."

"*Ja.*" A slim smile formed on her face. "They didn't rhyme all that well."

"They were awful, and I'd assumed it was your pity that allowed me to court you." He leaned in, his forehead touching hers. "I'll do whatever it takes to make things as they were."

"I have so much that I want to talk to you about," she said, her voice soft.

"Me too."

"Anna, Bruno!" Norbie called. "Come and join us!"

Anna swallowed. "We should go."

He straightened his back, feeling space grow between them. "Tomorrow, meet me at the boardinghouse after you're finished at school."

"I don't know if I can."

He looked into her eyes. "We'll only be gone a short while. I promise."

"Anna!" Norbie called.

"I need to go," she said.

"Please."

"All right," she said, slipping away from him. She picked up the water basin and left.

He sat on the bed and dabbed his marred hands with the towel. *Everything is going to work out.* A moment later, a piano folk song reverberated through the house and, after a few bars, Anna and Norbie began to sing. Rejuvenated by Anna's promise to meet him at the boardinghouse, he stood, brushed the wrinkles from his uniform, and went downstairs to join them.

Bruno, despite an invitation by Norbie to join them at the piano to sing, chose to sit on the sofa. It surprised him that Norbie, who'd lost a great deal of weight from his last visit, had the stamina to sing. But it soon became evident, to Bruno, that Norbie was attempting to lift his daughter's spirits. *The more horribly he sings, the more she smiles—and he knows it.* He could not imagine either of his parents behaving in such a selfless, kindhearted manner for him, even when he was a child.

After a few songs, Norbie patted Max on the back. "Splendid job, my boy. Your music makes me want to sing for hours. However, it's my turn to cook dinner."

"It's always a pleasure." Max stood from his bench. "I'll help you in the kitchen."

"Rest," Norbie said. "You've trained all day, and I'm starting to feel quite lazy with you preparing much of our food." He turned to Bruno. "Want to help me prepare dinner?"

"I'm not much of a cook," Bruno said, regretting that his upbringing did not include learning to make meals.

"You'll only need to dice turnips and leeks," Norbie said.

"Okay," Bruno said.

"But your hands are scraped," Anna said.

"Oh, I nearly forgot." Bruno glanced at the cuts and dried blood on his knuckles, and then looked at Norbie. "Would it be okay to take a pass tonight?"

"Of course." Norbie peeked at Bruno's hands. "Ouch. Next time, use my gardening gloves; they're on a shelf near the back door."

"I will," Bruno said.

"I'll help you," Anna said. She followed Norbie into the kitchen, leaving Bruno with Max and Nia.

Max, sitting on the piano bench, lowered his hand and patted Nia.

"How long have you been playing the piano?" Bruno asked.

Max turned toward him. "Since I was a child."

"You play well," Bruno said.

"*Danke*," Max said. "My *vater* taught me to play. He used to work at a piano manufacturer."

"What does he do now?"

Max stroked Nia's ears. "He's dead. My parents died at the onset of the war."

"My condolences."

Max nodded. "Are your parents in Frankfurt?"

"*Ja*," Bruno said.

"They must be anxious to meet Anna."

Bruno shifted in his seat. "They are."

"Tell me about them," Max said.

"There's not much to tell," Bruno said. *We barely write each other.* "My *vater*'s life is committed to his business, and my *mutter* travels a lot, or at least she did before the war. They're not, how shall I say, as affectionate as Norbie."

Max nodded, staring toward Bruno. "There are few people in this world like Norbie. He's incredibly supportive of Anna, and he helped save Nia." He patted the dog's side.

Nia wagged her tail and leaned to him.

"What will you do at your family business?" Max asked.

"Research and production. Eventually, I'll run the business with my half-brother, Julius. However, Julius is much older than me so someday the business will be mine."

"Sounds like you and Anna will have a comfortable life," Max said.

"I think we will."

"You had mentioned that your *vater* acquired military contracts," Max said.

"*Ja*," Bruno said.

"I'm curious," Max said. "What does the military do with ink and dye?"

An image of a chlorine gas cloud floating over no-man's-land flashed in Bruno's head. He buried his thoughts and said, "Lot of things."

"Like what?"

Bruno crossed his arms. "Dye for uniforms. Ink for writing. You'd be surprised how many things—from paints to textiles—need colorants."

"I see," Max said, appearing satisfied with the explanation.

Bruno thought about leaving him and going to the kitchen, but he worried that Anna might inquire as to why he'd left Max so quickly. "Enough about me. Tell me about the composition you're working on with Anna."

"Pull up a chair," Max said.

Bruno retrieved a side chair and placed it next to Max's bench, facing the piano.

Max stood, retrieved the staff paper from under his seat, and then gave the draft to Bruno.

Bruno scanned the paper, covered in lines and symbols. "I can't read music."

"It's okay," Max said, sitting. "I'll help you follow along. Look at the top left-hand corner of the first page. I'm going to play the first bar. Follow it like you're reading a book." Max played and stopped.

"Interesting," Bruno said. "I think I saw on the page how the sound of your keys went up and down."

"Precisely," Max said. "I play a bar, and Anna records the notes onto the paper. It's an intricate and time-consuming process, but we're nearly finished with the piece."

Bruno placed the manuscript on top of the piano, then glanced at Max's milky eyes. "Do you mind telling me how you were blinded?"

"*Nein*," Max said. "It was chlorine gas."

Allied bastards, Bruno thought.

"Is poison gas still heavily used at the front?" Max asked.

"*Ja.*" Bruno swallowed. "Where were you injured?"

"Ypres," Max said. "Do you know where it is?"

"I do," Bruno said, recalling his first assignment. "I was once stationed there. However, it would likely have been prior to you."

"Oh," Max said. "When were you there?"

"Spring of 1915."

Max took a deep breath and exhaled. He rubbed his temples, and then placed a hand on Nia, who was sitting beside him.

"So, tell me, Max," Bruno said. "Was it British or French gas that blinded you?"

Max turned toward him. "Neither."

Bruno furrowed his brow. "Canadian?"

"German."

Bruno's mouth turned dry. "How?"

"I was in a front-line trench," Max said calmly, as if he'd rehearsed the story many times in his head. "My unit was informed that the German artillery was going to conduct a forty-eight-hour bombardment. While the men in my unit hunkered in a dugout, I'd decided to walk the trench for a little fresh air before the attack began."

Bruno gripped his chair.

"I was on my way back to my dugout when the bombardment commenced, and the French retaliated with their own shellfire before I could get underground." Max raised his head toward the ceiling, like he was searching through his memories. "In the weeks prior to the bombardment, a special unit installed several thousand metal cylinders along the trench line. They were buried—except for their tops—into the base of the trench. Rubber hoses, attached to cylinder valves, ran up and over the trench to face the enemy lines."

Oh, God. Bruno's breath stalled in his lungs.

"We were never told what the cylinders were for," Max said. "One my friends, Jakob, had jested that the containers contained medicine to kill lice. But we found out what was inside them when a French artillery shell exploded near our dugout, piercing one of the cylinders." Max ran a hand through his hair. "My friends attempted to escape from the dugout, but they were swallowed in a green-yellow vapor. They flailed on the ground with froth spewing from their mouths until they were asphyxiated. I was the only survivor in my unit; I escaped—with scorched lungs and burned corneas—by clawing my way out of the trench."

"I'm sorry," Bruno said.

"*Danke.*"

Bruno's chest ached. "When did it happen?"

"Spring of 1915," Max said. "The twentieth day of April to be precise."

Fear flooded Bruno's veins.

"It appears that you and I were in Ypres at the same time," Max said.

"It seems so," Bruno said.

"Pioneer Regiment Thirty-six, right?"

"*Ja.*"

"What did your regiment do in Ypres?"

Bruno's stomach turned nauseous. "We constructed bunkers."

Max nodded.

Nia stood and placed her head on Max's lap.

Bruno's hands trembled.

Max stared toward him. "Have you ever heard of something called the Disinfection Unit?"

Bruno's blood turned cold. "*Nein.* What is it?"

"The name given to the unit that installed the gas cylinders. I was curious if you'd known about them."

"Never heard of them." Bruno, desperate to end the conversation, stood from his chair. "I'm going to check on Anna and Norbie in the kitchen."

"Sure," Max said.

Bruno turned and froze at the sight of Anna, standing at the entrance to the living room with her hands clasped. "Anna, I didn't hear you come in."

"Dinner is ready," she said.

How long was she there? Bruno thought. "We'll be right in."

"All right." She turned and left.

Bruno, his pulse thudding inside his eardrums, went to the kitchen and took his seat next to Anna at the table. Dinner discussion was sparse, with the exception of Norbie, who attempted to fill the conversational void with fond stories of his late wife, Helga. *I'm so sorry, please forgive me,* Bruno thought, glancing at Max's opaque eyes. *But if it wasn't for a French shell,* he rationalized, *Max would not have been blinded. And if he wasn't injured, he might have been killed in combat.* He struggled to keep the fork in his hand from quivering as he forced himself to eat a turnip cutlet with slivers of leek. And he prayed that he'd convinced Max that his regiment assignment in Ypres had nothing to do with poison gas or the Disinfection Unit.

After dinner, Anna joined Max at the piano to work on his composition, and Bruno excused himself to take a walk outside for some fresh air. He walked, his legs feeling like they were filled with sand, along the icy cobblestone street. Memories of gassed corpses, their mouths contorted and faces the color of plum, played over and over inside his head. Forty meters from the house, his stomach lurched and he vomited onto the snow.

CHAPTER 29

OLDENBURG, GERMANY—JANUARY 31, 1917

Anna, a restlessness growing inside her, walked along the landing of the train station with Max and Nia. Fleck had assigned them to train in town, and she thought that Max might become more talkative as the day progressed. But the longer they worked, the less he spoke. Even last night, he'd cut short their work on the piano composition with the excuse that he was tired. It wasn't unusual to be exhausted, especially with training in the cold and nearly always being hungry. However, his silence—as well as Bruno's reticent behavior, considering he'd gone to bed early rather than stay up with her in the living room—seemed to have begun with the conversation that she partially overheard before last night's dinner.

"Would you like to tell me why you're quiet?" she asked, walking with Nia between them.

Max tapped his cane over the ground. "I'm a bit worn out, and my lungs ache from the winter air."

Nia glanced back but continued padding over the ground.

Anna wondered if something had been said between Max and Bruno to upset them. Her mind raced, attempting to piece together the conversation that she'd interrupted. "What were you and Bruno discussing last night?"

"The war," Max said. "And how I was blinded."

"I'm sure that wasn't easy for you to talk about," she said.

He nodded.

"Did you discuss anything else?"

"His family's business."

She waited for him to say more, but he continued walking and tapping his cane. Her heart rate quickened. "I overheard you say something about a Disinfection Unit."

Max's pace slowed.

"What is it?"

He glanced toward her, and then tugged on the harness. "*Halt.*" Nia stopped.

"Are you sure you want to talk about this?" he asked.

"I do."

He rubbed his face with a gloved hand, and then said to Nia, "Find a seat."

Nia scanned the landing and padded to a wooden bench.

Anna sat next to Max, holding his cane with both hands, and Nia curled at their boots.

"I've been thinking about how to discuss this with you," Max said, staring straight ahead. "What would you like to know?"

"Everything."

"It will be unpleasant," he said. "And it will not be what you want to hear."

A knot formed in her stomach. "I don't care."

"All right." He turned toward her. "But please know that what I say, I say with a heavy heart, and that I only want what is best for you."

"Of course," she said.

For several minutes, Max told her about his conversation with Bruno, including details of how he was blinded by a ruptured chlorine gas cylinder, which was one of thousands of cylinders that were installed in the trenches by a special squad called the Disinfection Unit. Also, he informed her that Bruno and he were both at the front near Ypres, Belgium, at the same time—on the eve of the German military's use of poison chlorine gas, which broke the Hague Convention treaty that banned the use of chemical weapons.

"Oh, God," she said, lowering her head into her gloved hands.

"It's been on my mind," he said. "And I was struggling with how to talk with you about it."

"Is there more?" she asked, raising her head from her hands.

"I'm afraid so," he said. "Would you like a moment before I continue?"

"*Nein*, please finish," she said, dreading what she was about to hear.

"Bruno mentioned earlier in the week that he began the war in Pioneer Regiment Thirty-six."

"*Ja*," she said, looking at him. "But what does this have to do with anything?"

"I've been racking my brain for the past few days, trying to determine why Pioneer Regiment Thirty-six sounded familiar. And while speaking with Bruno last night, I realized that I knew the regiment by another name." He faced her. "It was also known as the Disinfection Unit."

Anna felt like she was punched in the gut. "You must be mistaken."

"It's possible, but—"

"Bruno would have told me if he was ordered to perform heinous acts," she said, interrupting him. Her heart rate spiked. "Did you ask him about it?"

"I did."

"And what did he say?"

"He said his regiment was in charge of building bunkers."

She looked at him, his eyes staring straight ahead. Her skin prickled. "You don't believe him, do you?"

"It's possible that his unit was building bunkers. There are many pioneer units that construct everything from roads to trenches. But there were things Bruno said that I'm struggling to make sense of."

Vexation surged through her. She fought away an impulse to get up and leave. "Tell me what is bothering you."

"First," Max said, "Bruno began the war in the infantry, but now he's assigned to artillery."

"What's wrong with that?" she asked. "I would assume that changes in duties often occur in the military, especially at the front."

"Duties often change, but soldiers, as well as officers, typically remain within the same division." He rolled his cane between his gloved hands. "Poison gas was first released from cylinders by infantry units at the front lines. But now, most poison gas is delivered by artillery shells."

Anna hugged her arms. Her head ached. "What else is troubling you?"

"Bruno's family business is an ink and dye manufacturer, and he commented that his *vater* obtained military contracts."

"I assume that you asked Bruno about this," she said.

Max nodded. "He said that it's for the colorant of uniforms and military supplies."

She looked at him, his head slightly tilted. "You don't believe him, do you?"

"I have some doubts about his story."

"He'd never lie," she said, raising her voice.

Nia stood and nuzzled Anna.

"Everything is all right, girl," Anna said, stroking the dog's side.

"It sickens me to be talking about this," Max said. "I understand how soldiers feel when they are forced to kill by our military. They have no choice, and neither did I when I was on the front. But the ramifications for someone assigned to a chemical warfare unit would be far worse than an ordinary soldier. They'd be horrified and ashamed of their actions, which might be a war crime considering poison gas violates the Hague Convention treaty. And if one refused to follow a command, he'd suffer dire consequences, including the possibility of being shot. But I fear that Bruno's involvement might be deeper than obeying orders."

"This is ludicrous," Anna said.

"I hope it is." Max paused, taking a few deep breaths. "Do you know how ink and dye is made?"

"*Nein.*"

"Neither do I," he said. "But I do know that chemicals are needed to make them. And it takes chemicals to make poison gas."

Images of gassed hospital patients—their eyes bandaged and lungs wheezing—flashed in her head. Her mouth turned dry.

"Did Bruno attend a university?"

"*Ja.*"

"What did he study?"

"Chemistry." Her body trembled. "But science is needed for dye manufacturing. Bruno would never willingly be involved with chemical weapons, and he would have told me if his family manufactured poison gas."

"Based on my experience at the front," Max said, "I have misgivings about his stories. I'm afraid that there might be more to Bruno and his family."

Her head felt dizzy. "I—I can't listen to any more of this."

He extended his hand, as if he were attempting to console her.

She stood and backed away from him. "This is mad!"

"I'm so sorry," Max said. "I pray that my questions are groundless."

"Please stop!" Tears welled in her eyes.

He nodded, and then placed a hand on Nia. "I'll understand if you don't want to be here with me. You can go, if you like. Nia and I can find our way home."

A fusion of panic and denial surged through her. She turned, slipped on a patch of ice, and fell. A sharp pain shot through her hands and knees.

Max sprang from the bench.

"Leave me!" Anna cried.

Max stopped, but Nia padded to her and whimpered.

"I'm all right, girl," Anna said, hugging Nia. Her tears fell onto the dog's coat. She stood and then left—refusing to look back.

For much of the afternoon, Anna walked along the Hunte, a river that flowed northward from Oldenburg, where she thought that she wouldn't encounter Fleck or any of the other training groups. Eventually, her legs grew tired and she sat on the frozen shoreline with her head to her knees. *This can't be happening! There must be a good explanation for everything; Bruno would never lie, and he would have told me if he, or his family, were involved with chemical warfare.* She prayed that Max's concerns about Bruno would turn out to be untrue. But she'd grown to trust Max, and his words had shaken her core.

She desperately wanted to go home and confide in Norbie. But

Bruno was likely at the house, given the time of day, and she didn't want to subject her *vater* to accusations, even if unfounded, that could taint his feelings about her future husband. Instead, she decided that she would talk with Bruno alone at their planned rendezvous. She removed her gloves, unbuttoned the top of her coat, and clasped her *mutter*'s heart-shaped locket. *Harbor your heart.* She repeated her *vater*'s affirmation over and over in her head, but it did little to diminish the wretched ache beneath her breastbone.

Shortly before sunset, she arrived at a three-story brick board-inghouse located a few streets away from the hospital where she'd worked as a nurse. Her heartbeat thumped against her rib cage. She buried her trepidation and entered the front door, where she was met a by a matron, a gaunt woman with gray hair sprouting from under her headscarf.

"I'm here to see Bruno Wahler," Anna said, sinking her hands into her coat pockets.

The woman pointed with a crooked finger to a stairway. "Third floor. Last room on the left."

"*Danke.*"

Her breath turned shallow as she climbed the stairs. She paused at the third-floor landing, taking in gulps of air, and along with it the smell of stale tobacco smoke. Approaching the door, hair stood up on the back of her neck. *It's all a misunderstanding. Everything will be fine.* She knocked. Footsteps grew from inside the room, and the door opened.

"Anna," Bruno said, wrapping his arms around her. "I'm happy you're here."

"I promised," she said, her legs feeling weak.

He released her, shut the door, and then helped her to remove her coat.

The room was much like the one on the second floor, which Bruno had rented during their courtship. It contained a small brass bed with a gray wool blanket, a solitary wooden chair, and a wash-stand, from which a lit candle cast an amber glow over the room.

"I was able to acquire some black bread this afternoon," Bruno said, pointing to a paper bag on the washstand. "I thought we could take it home to share for dinner, unless you'd like to eat some now."

Anna shook her head.

He approached her. "You look pale. Are you feeling all right?" "*Nein.*"

"Please sit." He clasped her hand and led her toward the bed. "I'll get you some water."

"Not now," she said, slipping away from him. She leaned her back against the footboard of the brass bed. "We need to talk."

"What's wrong?"

Nausea rose up from her belly and seized in her throat. "I overheard your conversation with Max last night."

"Oh," he said. "What did you hear?"

She swallowed. "Tell me about the Disinfection Unit."

Bruno's eyebrows furrowed, and then softened. "Oh, that." He attempted to embrace her and she pulled away.

"Please don't," she said, placing her hands in front of her.

"All right." He lowered his arms and looked at her.

"Tell me," she said.

"I know nothing about a Disinfection Unit, other than what Max told me last night," Bruno said, his voice calm. "He claims it was a special unit that installed poison gas in his trench."

"Did you ever hear of it before?"

"*Nein,*" he said. "Max seems to blame this unit for his blindness, even though it was a French shell, which pierced a gas cylinder, that caused the accident." He ran a hand through his hair. "Based on his questioning, he seemed to infer that I had something to do with the installation of gas in his trench."

"Why would he think that?" Anna asked.

"Perhaps it was because I was stationed in Ypres at the time of his injury, and he's now mistakenly associating my regiment with this so-called Disinfection Unit."

"But your regiment did something else in Ypres, correct?"

"*Ja,*" he said. "I led a unit that constructed bunkers. But soon after I was reassigned to an artillery post."

Anna took a deep breath and exhaled.

"His insinuation agitated me," he said. "It's the reason I went for a walk last night. And my time alone helped me realize that there may be more to Max's intentions than merely pointing blame for his blindness."

Anna folded her arms. "What do you mean?"

"I think he has feelings for you."

Anna straightened her spine. "You're mistaken."

"Are you sure?" Bruno asked. "You spend a lot of time together."

An image of sitting next to Max at the piano, her head leaning on his shoulder, flashed in her brain. Her heart rate quickened.

"I cannot begin to imagine how terrifying it might be for Max to face the prospect of living on his own, with the exception of a dog companion." He placed his palms together. "How long has he been here with you?"

"Over five weeks," she said.

"It took me far less than that to fall for you." He moved close. "I think he cares for you, and he dreads being on his own. It might be a catalyst for creating a fallacious impression of me in his head. And he's using it to create a divide between us."

"Max doesn't have feelings for me," she said. "And he'd never deliberately try to hurt either of us."

"How do you know?"

She drew a breath, struggling to provide a rebuttal.

"I wanted to tell you about this last night, but I thought it might upset you." He looked into her eyes. "I wouldn't be surprised if he's already begun telling you stories to create doubt about me."

She lowered her head.

"Oh, no," Bruno said sadly. "He did say something. Didn't he?"

"*Ja*," she breathed.

"I'm so sorry, Anna. I wish I would have talked to you earlier." He gently placed a hand on her shoulder. "I'm not upset, nor do I have any ill feelings toward Max. He's merely grown fond of you. He's hurting inside, and he might be afraid to be on his own."

Her mind struggled to process Bruno's words.

"When we go home," Bruno said, "I'll talk with Max and sort it all out."

"You'll do that?"

"Of course," he said. "Will that make you feel better?"

She nodded.

"*Gut.*" He caressed her cheek with his thumb.

As if by reflex to his touch, she placed a hand to the nape of her neck and clasped the chain to her *mutter*'s locket. *Harbor your heart.* "Can I ask you a question?"

"Anything," he said.

She drew a deep breath. "Why would the army waste the skills of a chemist on building bunkers?"

He paused, looked at her. "Our military places little value on education when assigning men to their posts."

She looked deep into his eyes, seeking any hint that he might not be telling her the truth, and she found nothing. But an ache, deep in the pit of her gut, compelled her to find out for certain, even if she had to mislead him.

"Is there anything else you'd like to know?" he asked.

"There is," Anna said, gathering her courage. "When were you going to tell me that your family's business was supplying the military with poison gas?"

Bruno stepped back, as if he'd been poked with a stick. "What did he tell you?"

"Don't lie to me," Anna said with feigned indignance.

"Max has gone mad!"

"How long did you think you could keep this a secret from me?"

Bruno cocked his head to the side. "There is no secret."

"Then I shall write to your *vater*," she bluffed. "Or perhaps I'll go visit him in Frankfurt to discuss why his son refuses to tell his fiancée the truth about his family's business."

"Anna—"

"Stop the lies!" she cried. "I already know that Wahler Farbwerke is manufacturing poison gas!"

Bruno's jaw muscles tightened.

"If there is to be any chance for us, you need to tell me precisely how you got involved, and what you're going to do about it." She clenched her hands, digging her nails into her palms.

He paused, wiped his face with his hands, and then lowered his eyes. "I didn't have a choice."

Oh, my God.

"A team of chemists, including myself, were recruited by Fritz Haber, head of the Chemistry Section in the Ministry of War, for a special unit." He drew a jagged breath. "I didn't know what it was for. I thought it might be to develop improved explosives. But it turned out to be for the deployment of chemical weapons. There was nothing I could do to leave or change my assignment. And I found out from Haber that my *vater* had entered into military contracts to supply the army with chlorine gas—a by-product from ink and dye manufacturing."

This can't be happening! Anna shuffled over the floor and slumped in the chair. Tears welled in her eyes.

"There isn't a day that goes by that I don't regret what I'm doing," he said.

"Why did you lie to me?" she cried.

"I didn't want to hurt you, and I was afraid of losing you." He kneeled at her feet and placed his hands on her knees. "Things will be different after the war. All will be forgotten. The business will go back to making dye. Our days will be filled with happiness and prosperity—I promise."

Hot tears streamed down her cheeks. "You're committing atrocities."

"It's war," Bruno said. "The British and French are using the same gases."

"It doesn't matter!" she cried. "It's a war crime. You've killed and maimed human beings with poison!"

Bruno stared at her. With a voice devoid of emotion, he said, "Death is death, regardless of how it is inflicted."

She shuddered. A pain pierced her stomach, producing the urge to vomit. "Oh, my God. What has become of you?"

He opened his mouth but made no sound. His hands trembled against her knees.

She stood, pushing him away.

His eyes filled with tears. He lowered his head and wept.

With shaking hands, she removed her engagement ring from her finger and placed it at his feet. She retrieved her coat and left the boardinghouse. Brokenhearted and shattered, she collapsed onto the sidewalk and sobbed.

CHAPTER 30

OLDENBURG, GERMANY—FEBRUARY 7, 1917

Anna entered Norbie's workshop and sat at a workbench, covered with gears and springs from a dismantled grandfather clock. The passing of days since ending her engagement to Bruno had done little to relieve her torment. Norbie and Max were upstairs, and she hoped that her time alone—surrounded by the meditative chorus of ticktocks—would help her forget about him, if only for a little while.

Anna had been devastated when she arrived home from the boardinghouse. She'd confided in Norbie, telling him everything that had happened. Her *vater* was shocked, and he cried along with her until neither of them could produce any more tears. She'd apologized to Max for not believing him, but he only expressed concern about her welfare. He didn't press her to talk, and she felt comforted by his company. And when he ran out of things to say, he'd simply given her a reassuring squeeze on the hand. Also, Max and Norbie invited Emmi to spend evenings at the house to listen to Max play the piano. It was obvious to Anna that they'd invited her best friend to help with consoling her, and she was thankful to be surrounded by everyone she loved, including Nia, who cuddled with her on the sofa.

After she'd ended the engagement, Bruno never returned to the house. Within a few days, when it became clear to Anna that he wouldn't be coming back, she'd placed his leather case, which contained extra clothing and a shaving kit, in a storage closet with plans to dispose of the items later. She wasn't surprised that he didn't want to show his face, considering his confession of perpetrating and aiding chemical warfare, but she was hurt that he didn't make the effort to leave her a note or send her a telegram. *He's horrified and ashamed by his conduct and lies,* she'd thought while darning Norbie's socks. *And so am I.*

Anna turned to the sound of footsteps descending the stairs.

"I made us coffee," Norbie said, entering the workshop.

"*Danke,*" she said.

Norbie placed two steaming cups on the workbench and sat on a stool beside her.

She took a sip. "It's good," she said, despite that she'd lost her taste for food.

"It's a new blend that contains leached acorns."

She nodded.

He took a gulp. "How are you feeling?"

She ran a finger over the rim of her cup. "I feel hurt and betrayed, and I'm disappointed in myself for not knowing more about Bruno and his family's business."

"I'm sorry," he said. "But there was no way you could have known. Bruno didn't fully let you into his life, nor did he foster building a relationship between you and his family. If you hadn't confronted him with the knowledge you gained from Max, he might never have been honest with you. You're a smart woman, and I have no doubt that someday you would have discovered what his family's ink and dye business did during the war, but it might have been after you were married and living in Frankfurt."

Anna's chest ached. She wondered, although briefly, if there were other lies or secrets that Bruno was hiding. *It doesn't matter. It's over between us.*

He squeezed her hand. "I know that you're hurting. But your pain might have been much worse if you learned of this later." He took a sip of coffee. "I'm glad that Max was here to shed light on the truth."

"So am I," she said.

Norbie patted her hand and looked at her. "How does your heart feel?"

"Broken."

"Broken for Bruno or broken for what you both created together?"

"What do you mean?" she asked, feeling confused.

He swirled his coffee. "Are you hurt from the terrible things that Bruno has done? Or are you sad about ending your relationship with him? Or maybe it's both."

Anna contemplated his questions. An image of injured soldiers, their eyes bandaged and gasping for air, filled her head. Tears formed in her eyes. "My heart aches for the thousands of men who will be maimed, blinded, or killed by poison gas."

He removed a handkerchief from his pocket and gave it to her. "Me too."

She dabbed her eyes.

"I'm not surprised that you feel that way," he said.

She sniffed back tears. "Why do you say that?"

"I noticed a difference in your behavior with Bruno," he said. "Compared to his last visit, you didn't sit as close to him on the sofa. There were few hugs or hand holding, and you seldom, if ever, left the house to spend time alone with him. Instead, you made excuses to stay here with me and Max."

She slumped her shoulders.

"I'm telling you this, of course, to make you feel better because I'm your *vater*. However, what I witnessed between you and Bruno leads me to believe that the pain from your broken engagement will not be permanent."

Anna clasped her cup. "You think so?"

He nodded.

"I know my grief is quite different," she said, "but what was it like for you when you lost Mutter?"

"Devastating," he said. "It was the type of heartbreak that never really goes away. Even after all these years, I'm still sad about losing Helga. There isn't a day that I don't wake up thinking about her. It's like I have a splinter deep in my heart that can't work its way out."

She clasped her *vater*'s hand.

He gave her a squeeze. "I understand that things are raw. But I believe, with time, that your heart will heal, and you'll learn to feel affection again. Someday, you'll experience the type of genuine love that I had with your *mutter*."

Anna rose from her stool and hugged him.

Norbie released her and wiped his eyes. "Max is making dinner. How about we join him and Nia in the kitchen?"

Anna nodded. She followed him up the stairs, feeling grateful for her *vater*'s efforts to ease her pain and restore her hope.

The trio ate a dinner of turnip latkes and acorn coffee. Afterward, Norbie went to tinker in his workshop and Anna joined Max in the living room, where he was sitting on the floor and grooming Nia with a brush.

"Need some help?" Anna asked.

"I can handle it," Max said. "But Nia and I would enjoy your company."

Anna sat on the floor with Nia between them.

Nia tapped her tail on the hardwood floor as Max ran the brush over her fur.

"She likes being groomed," Anna said.

"*Ja.*" He paused, locating Nia's front paw. "But having her toenails clipped, not so much."

Nia rolled onto her back and raised her paws in the air.

Anna rubbed Nia's belly. "Her paws might always be sensitive from her time in the muddy trenches."

"You're probably right." He ran the brush over the dog's coat.

She looked at him. "I appreciate you being here for me."

"I wish there was more that I could do for you."

"You've done more than you realize," she said.

"I'm glad." He brushed Nia. "I'm so sorry about everything."

"I know," she said. "And I'm sorry, too."

"For what?"

She swallowed. "Being here with me must remind you of what Bruno did in Ypres, and how you were blinded."

He put down the brush and turned toward her. "I don't blame Bruno for my blindness, nor do I assign responsibility to his family. Even if they hadn't participated in the use or production of chlorine gas, the military would have ordered another officer to lead the installation of gas cylinders at the front. And the military would have procured their poison from another manufacturer. In the end, it wouldn't have mattered."

She greatly appreciated his words, but a deep-seated guilt, if only by association, burned in her abdomen.

"And as for being here with you," he said. "There is no place that I'd rather be."

Anna blinked back tears. *Me too.*

Max finished brushing Nia and disposed of a pile of shed hair in the kitchen garbage. He returned to the living room, running his hand along the wall to guide his way.

"Are you feeling up to working on your composition tonight?" she asked.

"Only if you are."

"I am," she said. "You'll likely be graduating in a couple of weeks. Do you think we can finish it before you leave?"

"I think so," he said, a timbre of melancholy in his voice.

Anna sat at the piano next to Max. With staff paper and pencil in hand, she transcribed his piece while Nia slept under their bench. Bar by bar, she recorded the notes. Her mind gradually drifted away from Bruno, his family, and war atrocities. A calmness spread through her body, suppressing the sorrow in her chest. They worked for hours, drafting the musical composition, and she wished that the piano suite would never end.

CHAPTER 31

OLDENBURG, GERMANY—FEBRUARY 13, 1917

Max, guided by Nia, kicked snow from his boots and entered the school barn, where Fleck had called a meeting with the trainers and veterans. After a morning of obstacle work with Nia—absent Anna, who observed from the sidelines with the other trainers—his feet were nearly numb and his lungs ached from the cold air. He made his way to the woodstove, tapping his cane over the ground.

"*Halt*," Max said, giving a tug on the harness.

Nia stopped, and then sat after Max gave the command.

Max listened to the chatter of men, including Fleck and Waldemar, who were discussing plans to send the veterans to town for the afternoon. He removed his leather gloves and extended his hands toward the heat radiating from the stove. A subtle, sweet smell of burning birch firewood penetrated his nose. As he rubbed his palms together, he felt a soft touch to his arm. *Anna*.

"You did well on the obstacle course," Anna whispered, as if she didn't want the others to hear.

"*Danke*," he said.

"Fleck commented that you and Nia performed the best of all the groups."

Max patted the dog's head. "*Gut* job, Nia."

Nia raised her snout and swished her tail.

"That's not all," Anna said, giving him a nudge with her elbow. "Waldemar was there when Fleck gave the compliment. I'd give anything for you to see the expression on his face."

Max smiled. But proving his and Nia's competence to Waldemar wasn't the only thing that gave him satisfaction. It was the radiant timbre of Anna's voice. *You're regaining your spirit.*

In the two weeks since Bruno left Oldenburg, Anna had gradually begun to shed her grief. She'd been devastated by the most horrible of circumstances, yet she pushed on, day by day, with training him and Nia. Even in the evenings, when they were both tired and hungry, she'd insisted that they carry on with transcribing his piano suite. Anna, Max believed, was the strongest person he'd ever met, and although she had a long journey of healing ahead of her, it was clear that she was on a path to regaining happiness in her life.

"Attention!" Fleck called, stepping to the center of the barn.

Chatter dwindled. Trainers and veterans, along with their guide dogs, gathered around their supervisor.

Fleck stroked his mustache and scanned the group, as if he was making sure everyone was accounted for. "This afternoon, veterans will train alone in town with their dogs. They'll be joined by their trainers as far as the town hall. From there, each veteran and their dog will travel to an assigned landmark to explore. You'll return to the town hall to meet up with your trainer at the end of the day."

Fleck is weaning us away from our instructors and forcing us to be independent, Max thought. Although he was excited to explore the town with Nia, he was disappointed that Anna would not be joining them for much of the afternoon.

Fleck lifted his clipboard and began reading the names of the veterans and their assigned landmark, and when he reached the bottom of the list, he said, "Max, hospital grounds."

Anna leaned to Max and whispered, "You're lucky. It has a large garden to the rear of the building."

I wish you were coming with me, he thought.

Fleck tucked his clipboard under an armpit, lit a cigarette, and said, "I have another announcement." He drew a deep drag. "I've decided on a date for graduation."

Max wrinkled his forehead.

"The twentieth day of February."

He placed his hand on Nia's head. A wave of joy flooded him, and then washed away like a retreating tide. *Only a week left with Anna.*

Fleck puffed his cigarette. "Dismissed."

Max clasped Nia's harness and they exited the barn with Anna. The groups spread out and began walking toward town, but the crunch of approaching footsteps in the snow compelled Max and Anna to stop.

"Congratulations," Emmi said, stepping to Max. "I heard the news."

"*Danke,*" Max said. "But I still need to do well over the next seven days to graduate."

"You will," Anna said.

"How's Ewald?" Max asked, wanting to forget that his time with Anna was drawing to a close.

"He's well," Emmi said.

"I'm sorry that I won't get a chance to meet him this summer when he's home on leave," he said.

"Me too," Emmi said. "Someday, Ewald and I will come to see you perform."

"In the Great Hall in Vienna," Anna added.

"That would be nice," Max said. "But I'd be happy to play in any venue that will have me, and I'd be honored to have you visit me in Leipzig."

Emmi glanced over her shoulder, as if she was concerned that Fleck would notice that she wasn't working. "I better go. Lots of chores to do." She turned and left.

Anna, Max, and Nia walked toward town. Their boots crunched over the snow-covered road, and they adjusted their pace to create distance from the other groups, allowing privacy to speak freely.

"Norbie will be excited to hear the news of graduation," Anna said.

"*Ja.*" *We have little time left together.*

"Do you think we can finish *Light Suite* within a week?"

"I do," he said, "assuming you're willing to put in a few late nights of work."

"Of course," she said.

They walked for several minutes in silence, the news of his impending departure dampening their conversation. Eventually, it was Anna who broke the quietude.

"I've been wondering," she said, walking with Nia between them. "Have you given any thought to staying in Oldenburg?"

His skin prickled. "I haven't considered it."

"With having no family in Leipzig," she said, "I thought you might be open to a change."

His mind raced, and he tapped his cane over the ground.

"Oldenburg is a nice place to live, when there isn't a war, of course. And I'd be here to transcribe your music, assuming you think I'm doing a satisfactory job."

"Your work is impeccable," he said.

"Also, there are people here who care about you."

His pulse quickened.

"There's Norbie, Emmi." She swallowed. "And me."

Max's chest swelled with hope and gratitude. Anna had captured his heart, and he yearned to stay here with her. But far more than his own self-interests, he wanted what was best for her. *I could never let myself be a burden to her.*

He tightened his grip on the harness. "I care about you, too. But you have training to do, and you'll likely be asked to board another veteran with the next class."

"I can help you find a place to live in town," she persisted.

He slowed his pace and turned his head toward her. His shoulder muscles tightened. "As much as I enjoy being here, I think it's best that I give living on my own a try."

She placed her hand on the harness handle next to his. "I'm not asking you to decide today. But please, promise me that you'll give it some thought."

"I will," he said, already knowing what his decision would be.

Minutes later, they arrived at the town hall. The groups split up—with each veteran and his dog venturing off to their assigned landmark—except for Max and Anna.

"Do you remember how to get to the hospital?" Anna asked.

"I know the way to the general area," Max said, struggling to bury his thoughts about Anna's invitation to stay. "I'm sure Nia and I will find it."

"Make sure you explore the garden. Emmi and I used to spend our lunch breaks there. It won't be as nice in the winter, but it'll give you some protection from the wind."

"I will," he said. "What will you do with your afternoon?"

"I'll go home to check on Norbie, and then I'll see about getting rations."

He reached into his coat pocket and removed a small paper bag. "In case you don't have any luck with acquiring food, we can add this to tonight's dinner."

"Oh, Max," Anna said. "You can't keep giving us your military lunches."

He held out the bag.

"You need your nourishment," she said. "Eat it in the hospital garden."

"I'm not hungry," he lied. "Please take it."

Anna exhaled and reluctantly took the food.

"I'll meet you here later," he said.

She slipped the bag into her coat pocket. "Good luck, Max."

He nodded and clasped the harness. "Forward."

Nia padded ahead, and they left Anna behind.

It was more difficult to find the hospital than he'd thought. Although he'd previously traversed the area, he took a wrong turn, and after walking several street blocks in the wrong direction, he resorted to asking for directions from a woman who was shoveling snow from the entrance to her front door. And it occurred to Max that Fleck had expected that the veterans would have trouble finding their destinations. *When I go home, I won't have Anna to rely upon. It'll be up to me and Nia to find our way.*

For twenty minutes, he navigated through unfamiliar cobblestone streets and intersections. Twice, he paused to catch his breath and to make mental notes of his route. Eventually, Max found the hospital, which he verified with an old man with a raspy voice who was smoking a cigarette near the building.

"We did it, Nia," Max said. His veins surged with a sense of pride and accomplishment.

Nia panted and wagged her tail.

They maneuvered their way to the rear of the building. Max increased the tapping of his cane until he found the garden, given the winding path that was bordered on both sides by bushes and dormant flower beds. Relieved to find his destination, he gave the command for Nia to stop. He drew in a lungful of cold air, which stung his throat and produced a cough. Kneeling to Nia, he removed his gloves and warmed her front right paw with his hands.

"You were favoring it on our walk."

Nia nuzzled him.

"Better?"

She licked his nose.

He chuckled, and then stood and put on his gloves. "All right, girl. Let's take a stroll through the garden."

They wandered along the path, absent pedestrians or hospital staff. His boots crunched on the packed snow. Tweets of birds, coming from a nearby tree, decorated the air. Tension eased from his shoulder muscles, and his thoughts turned to Anna.

Two months ago, he'd arrived in Oldenburg a broken man, but Anna had given him hope and restored his will to live. She'd united him with Nia, his companion and living prosthetic for his eyes, and she'd helped him to rekindle his passion for music. By all accounts, Anna had rescued him from the hellish aftermath of war, and he would be forever grateful to her for what she'd done. But his feelings for Anna had grown far beyond the boundaries of friendship. He adored spending time with her—training, walks with Nia, and, most of all, sitting beside her at the piano. Her voice was the first thing he wanted to hear in the morning, and the last thing he wanted to hear before going to bed. Somewhere along the line, he'd fallen for her. And he thought, although he didn't know for certain, that she had feelings for him, too. He'd imagined what it would be like to hold her in his arms and never let her go. But it was far too soon for him to act upon his emotions. *She needs time to heal. And, perhaps, so do I.*

However, things had changed with Anna's invitation for him to remain in Oldenburg. All he had to do was accept her offer. But deep down he had reservations and was torn with making a decision. His heart yearned to stay with her. *I've fallen for her, and I believe she has affection for me. Maybe with time, there might be a chance for us.* But his brain told him otherwise. *I'm blind. She deserves to have a life with an able-bodied man.* He prayed that, in the end, he'd have the strength to do what was best for Anna.

He paused near a tree to catch his breath, and then began a second lap around the garden. But as he tapped his cane around a curve in the path, his head turned dizzy.

"*Halt.*"

Nia stopped.

He leaned on his cane. His breath quickened, and his pulse thumped inside his eardrums. He dropped to a knee and lowered his head. *I should have eaten something.*

Nia licked his face.

"Give me a minute, girl."

"Are you all right?" a woman's voice said.

"*Ja.*" Max stood, using his cane as a brace, and stumbled.

The woman darted to him and clasped his arm. "I'm a nurse. Let's get you inside."

"I'll be all right," Max said. "I merely need a moment to rest."

"*Nein,*" she said. "You're coming with me."

The nurse led him and Nia inside and sat him on a hallway bench. An acidic smell of carbolic filled his nose, reminding him of the field hospital at the front. A cold shiver ran down his spine.

"I'm going to summon a doctor," she said.

"It's not necessary," Max said. "I'll be fine in a moment."

"Stay," she ordered, walking away.

Max ran his hands over Nia's fur. "I'm sorry. If I would have eaten a bit of food, I wouldn't have gotten us in this mess."

Nia licked his hand.

He leaned his back against the wall and rested. A few minutes passed and Max heard the clack of approaching footsteps.

"Maximilian Benesch," an older man's voice said.

"*Ja*," Max said, surprised to hear his name spoken.

"I'm Dr. Stalling," he said. "We've met a few times at the obstacle course."

Founder of the guide dog school. "Of course." Max stood and extended his arm.

Stalling shook his hand. "I understand you were having some trouble in the garden."

"I was a little light-headed," Max said. "I haven't eaten today."

"Oh," Stalling said. "I thought the military was providing lunches for the veterans at school."

"They are."

"Why didn't you eat it?" Stalling asked.

Max paused, wondering if giving away his food might cause problems for Anna, but he wanted to be honest, especially with the man who was responsible for creating the guide dog school. "My host family has little to eat, and I've chosen to allocate my daily military lunches to them."

"Damn naval blockade," Stalling said, shaking his head. "It's very generous of you to give Anna your food."

He knows, Max thought.

"I remember this one," Stalling said, patting the dog on the head. "Nia, right?"

"*Ja*."

Nia looked up at Stalling and thumped her tail, as if she recognized him.

"I was at the school the day Nia arrived. She was in horrible shape. It was Anna who convinced Herr Fleck to try to save her."

Max smiled.

"It looks like she's become a stellar guide dog."

"The best, sir," Max said.

"Well, Maximilian," Stalling said. "Since you're here, how about I get you some warm broth. It isn't much, but it'll warm your belly. And then I'll check you over."

"There's no need, sir. I'm feeling much better."

Stalling placed his hand on Max's shoulder. "Come. I'll join you while you have some broth, and tell you a story about my inspiration to open the guide dog school. I think you'll like it."

"All right," Max said. He clasped Nia's harness and they walked with Stalling down a long hallway. They traveled past a medic, who was pushing a gurney with a moaning patient. Max's heart rate accelerated. A memory of his chlorine-gassed eyes being doused with saline flashed in his head. He buried thoughts of the past and patted Nia. And he hoped that his detour inside the hospital wouldn't cause him to be late for his meeting with Anna.

CHAPTER 32

LILLE, FRANCE—FEBRUARY 15, 1917

Bruno, standing on a hill with a battery of howitzers, raised his field binoculars and scanned the night battlefield. An Allied star shell shot up, illuminating a vast area of no-man's-land, covered in shell holes, barbed wire, and mutilated corpses. The front was still, except for the sporadic bark of machine guns. But everything would change in ten minutes, when the German artillery commenced a bombardment. He lowered his binoculars. A cold sweat formed on Bruno's forehead. His chest felt hollow, as if his heart had been carved out and buried in Oldenburg. He imagined an Allied gas shell exploding near him and—instead of slipping on his respirator—entering the yellow cloud and inhaling the poison.

Bruno, distraught and grief-stricken, had left Oldenburg the evening he confessed his lies to Anna. It was over, he knew, and there was nothing he could say or do that could exonerate him from his heinous acts. *I've already hurt her horribly, and she doesn't yet know about Celeste,* he'd thought while boarding the train. Although he believed that Anna would never do anything to harm herself, he prayed that she wouldn't suffer the same level of despair as Haber's wife. And it sickened Bruno to think that, in his futile attempt to rationalize the use of poison gas, he'd repeated Haber's mantra to the woman he loved. *Death is death, regardless of how it is inflicted.*

His dream of having a life with Anna was shattered. And on his journey back to the front, he'd reflected on their relationship, which had been mainly comprised of absence from each other's lives. Their brief courtship, followed by a spontaneous engagement, had been sustained by letters containing hopes and promises. He'd kept his family's business and his role in the Disinfection Unit a secret. It was naïve of him, he believed, to think that his monstrous acts—which might someday result in him being tried for war crimes—could indefinitely be hidden from Anna. Also, he'd been unfaithful to her, and he would soon father a war baby. Ravaged with shame, he'd attempted to write Anna a letter but the words eluded him. And he hoped that he would someday find the courage to tell her how sorrowful he would always be for hurting her.

Bruno, desperate to alleviate his guilt, wished that he could assign blame to someone, or something, for toppling the first domino of his cascading demise. The war and the constant exposure to death, of course, had taken a toll on him. His *vater* had arranged for him to be recruited by Haber for his special chemical unit, which ultimately led to Bruno gassing hundreds, if not thousands, of soldiers. He'd sold his soul to Haber in order to gain a chance of being seen by his father as equal to his half-brother, Julius, which would give him a place in the family business. Now, he wanted no part of his *vater*'s company, even if the production of chlorine gas to the military stopped at the end of the war. There were people and circumstances that Bruno could fault for his plight. However, he blamed only himself for his sins.

Bruno had spent the remaining days of his military leave in Lille with Celeste, but they did not share a bed. Instead, he remained confined to his room, with the exception of meals and walks with Celeste. Unable to carry the burden of more lies, he'd told her everything that had happened between him and Anna. Also, he informed her of his family's business of providing poison gas to the military, and his role in chemical warfare, which was of little surprise to her given Bruno's association with Fritz Haber, whom she knew well from his visits to her boardinghouse. Although she was appalled by his actions, she didn't rebuke him.

Despite what I've done, she prefers to remain with me because I'm the father of her baby, or she fears being ostracized by her family for being a collaborator. But he didn't care. Celeste, he believed, was his only friend, and she was pregnant. Although it was impossible to make amends for all of his wrongdoings, he was determined to do the right thing for Celeste and their unborn baby. Therefore, he used his remaining time with Celeste to discuss plans for her and their child. And by the time he had to return to the front, he'd convinced her to go with him to Germany after the war. She'd accompanied him to the train station, where he kissed her good-bye and reassured her—despite a foreboding ache in his gut—that they and their child would have lives of fortune and comfort.

"Sir," a soldier said, approaching Bruno.

Bruno turned.

The soldier glanced at his watch. "Two minutes until we commence fire, sir."

"Take your post," Bruno ordered.

The soldier saluted, and then squelched through the mud to take his position at a howitzer. To the rear of the artillery line, there were vast stacks of artillery shells, many of which were marked with a green cross.

How much of my vater's *poison will be dispensed tonight?* Bruno wondered, staring at the multitude of shells.

Instead of seeking shelter in his bunker, Bruno made his way to a clearing, twenty meters behind a cannon. Seconds passed and the battery of howitzers fired, sending shellfire toward the enemy lines. His eardrums pounded. The earth quaked. An acrid smell of explosives burned his nostrils. He watched soldiers load shell after shell into the cannons. Blazing streaks shot through the atmosphere at various angles and trajectories. *The barrels of our cannons are so badly worn that we cannot accurately hit our targets.*

Bruno observed the bombardment, all the while waiting, perhaps even hoping, for the enemy to return shellfire. Soon, Allied forces commenced their retaliation. And while fountains of earth and iron sprayed into the air around him, Bruno remained on the hill, making certain that one in three shells loaded into the cannons contained poison gas.

CHAPTER 33

OLDENBURG, GERMANY—FEBRUARY 20, 1917

Anna, wearing her best Sunday dress beneath a tattered wool coat, accompanied Max and Nia into the barn for the graduation day ceremony. Attendees—comprised of trainers, veterans and their guide dogs, and board members of the German Red Cross Ambulance Dogs Association—gathered near the woodstove. Unlike typical school graduations, there were no diplomas, caps and gowns, or family attendees. The only outsider invited to the ceremony was a photographer, who was setting up a backdrop in a straw-covered stall.

A mixture of joy and sadness swirled within Anna. She leaned to Max and whispered, "You did it."

He looked toward her and smiled. "It's all because of you."

"And Nia," she said, rubbing the dog's ears.

He nodded and patted Nia.

Over the past several days, she'd brought up the subject of him staying in Oldenburg, and each time he'd declined, claiming that he wanted to give living on his own a chance. She admired his mettle, as well as his determination to regain his independence. But selfishly, she didn't want him to leave. *I care deeply for him, and I can't imagine my life without him,* she'd thought while transcribing his piano suite. Although she wanted to act upon her emotions, she'd harbored her heart, as if it were a dormant flower bulb stored in a shed to prevent it from blooming.

They'd went about their final days together, much like they had before. They'd woke early and drunk substitute coffee with Norbie, trained until sunset, ate a turnip dinner with additives from Max's government-issued lunch, and then sat together at the piano to record his composition. Despite their aligned schedules, she'd had few opportunities for personal conversations with him, except during their time at the piano. Fleck had instructed the veterans and their dogs to traverse the city on their own for much of the week, leaving the trainers with idle time. And Anna was disheartened that her final days with Max would entail few walks with him and Nia.

"Gather in!" Fleck called, standing at a makeshift podium made from stacked wooden crates.

Anna joined Max and Nia near the center of the room. Fleck—a structured, ex-military man who valued concise commands over verbose explanations—gave a brief but thorough speech. He announced the names of each of the veterans and their dogs, gave a handshake to each of the men, and then turned the ceremony over to Dr. Stalling for closing words.

The doctor scanned the crowd and placed his hands on the podium. "I thank you, veterans, for your valiant efforts to protect our country, families, and loved ones."

Anna glanced to Max, his blank eyes staring in the direction of the podium.

"I'm indebted for your service," Stalling said. "You've sacrificed much, and the German people will never forget your selflessness to preserve the Fatherland from enemy peril."

Max lowered his hand to Nia's head, and the dog leaned to him.

"Today is a day of renewal and resolve," Stalling said. "You have completed your guide dog training, and I congratulate you. You should feel proud of your accomplishment. And in addition to regaining your own lives, you're paving the way for many battle-blinded men to follow in your footsteps." He removed his eyeglasses and rubbed his eyes. "I pray that your shepherd will be a trusted companion—and a beacon of light to guide your way."

Stalling stepped away from the podium, and the group applauded.

Anna wiped tears from her eyes.

"Are you all right?" Max said, turning toward her.

"I couldn't be happier," she said, her heart breaking.

Dr. Stalling mingled through the crowd and approached Max. "*Hallo*, Max. Anna."

Nia raised her snout, her eyes locking on Stalling, and wagged her tail.

"And you too, Nia," Stalling said, patting her head. He clasped Max's hand and shook it. "Good luck to you."

"*Danke*," Max said. "Anna has given me and Nia all the skills we need to manage on our own. I'm sure you already know this, but Fleck is quite fortunate to have her as a trainer."

"Indeed," Stalling said.

Anna forced a smile. She hadn't told Max that Fleck called her aside yesterday afternoon to tell her that—since Nia was leaving— she would begin rotating between caring for dogs with Emmi and substituting for trainers. Instead of Waldemar being on the sidelines, it would be her. And she hadn't informed Max because she didn't want to dampen his mood on graduation day. *I'll work hard to elevate my status as trainer, and if it doesn't work out, I'll inform Max in a letter.*

"I'm glad things are coming along nicely for you, Anna," Stalling said, appearing unaware of her recent change in duties. "And Max, I wish you and Nia the best in your journey together. Someday, I hope our paths cross again." He tipped his hat and left.

The conversations dwindled, and the crowd dissipated from the barn. Anna said her farewells to the other veterans, and then she, Max, and Nia hitched a ride home in a trainer's horse-drawn wagon. Inside the house, they were greeted by Norbie and Emmi, who had prepared a celebratory meal of acorn coffee, fried turnip, and slices of black bread drizzled with a spoonful of plum butter—which Norbie had bartered in exchange for an antique carriage clock.

With a few hours remaining before Max's train departure, they gathered in the living room. On top of the upright piano was Max's finished composition, *Light Suite*, that Anna had transcribed for him.

"You don't want to forget your manuscript," Anna said, retrieving the stack of papers. "May I place it in your leather case?"

"Of course, *danke*," Max said, taking a seat at the piano.

As Anna inserted the composition into Max's case, the scent of his freshly washed clothing filled her nose. *He's really leaving.* Her chest ached.

"Would you honor us by performing *Light Suite*?" Norbie asked.

"*Ja*," Max said. "But the pleasure is mine." He positioned his hands over the keyboard and played.

A deep sadness swelled within Anna. *We might never sit together at the piano again.* Memories of their shared moments flashed in her brain. The night he opened his heart and revealed how his parents perished in the sinking of the *Baron Gautsch*. The compassionate manner in which he empathized with her having lost her *mutter* at a young age, and how he labored to tune her *mutter*'s piano to honor her memory. The day Max, despite the risk of being removed from school, convinced Fleck to permit her to train him and Nia. His gifts of food to help nourish her and Norbie, and his courage to play the piano, overcoming his inability to hear the high-pitched keys. The tingling of her skin as Max, desiring to know what she looked like, gently glided his fingertips over her face. And the periodic thumping of Nia's tail in response to their voices as they worked on his piano composition. *I'm going to miss him terribly.*

Max played the movements of *Light Suite*, and as he finished, he slipped his hands from the keyboard and placed them on his knees.

"Bravo!" Norbie shouted, his eyes welling with tears.

Emmi clapped her hands. "It's so beautiful."

Anna drew a jagged breath, struggling to maintain her composure.

"I'm glad you like it," Max said.

Norbie wiped his eyes, and then blew his nose into his handkerchief. "Excuse my weepiness, Max. Your piece is most divine, and it stirs up emotions inside me."

"I didn't mean to make you sad," Max said. "But I think I know something that'll cheer you up before I leave." He placed his hands on the keyboard and played.

"*'Hänschen klein,'*" Anna thought. *It's sweet of him to play Norbie's favorite folk song as a departing gift.*

Norbie grinned and joined Max at the piano. He sang the verses, insisting that Anna and Emmi join him. And for the moment, everyone was joyful.

Max finished the song and rose from the piano. "I'm afraid it's time for me to go."

Anna's chest ached. "I'll walk you to the train station."

Max nodded.

Norbie approached Max and hugged him. "I'm going to miss you, my boy."

"Me too," he said, releasing him.

Norbie kneeled to Nia and patted her head. "Make sure Max gives you plenty of treats and belly rubs."

Nia swished her tail.

Max smiled, and then extended his arm in the direction of Emmi.

Emmi leaned in and gave him a squeeze. "Take care of yourself, Max."

"I'll be in good hands with Nia," he said. "I'll keep Ewald in my thoughts and prayers. And keep up the grand work with caring for shepherds—they need you, and so do all of the veterans who will arrive in Oldenburg."

"I will," Emmi said.

Anna retrieved her coat. She fought to steady her hands as she slipped on her gloves.

Max, running his hand along the wall, located the coatrack. He put on his coat and cap, and then picked up his leather case and cane. "Come, Nia."

Nia padded to Max's side, and then followed him and Anna down the stairs.

They spoke little on the way to the station due to heavier than normal pedestrian traffic. Anna held back, allowing Max and Nia to focus on navigating the streets. And at the station, a large crowd of people were standing on the landing. Eager to have a few words in privacy with Max, she led him to an empty bench at the far end of the station.

Anna fidgeted with a button on her coat. "I packed some food for you and Nia. It's in a paper sack in your case."

"*Danke*," he said.

"Do you remember the way from the Leipzig station to your apartment?"

"I think so," he said. "If I have any trouble, I'll ask for directions from someone on the street, and Nia will guide me home."

Anna's shoulder muscles tensed. "Do you have any neighbors in your building who can help you?"

He approached her, following the sound of her voice. "I'll be fine. I don't want you to worry about me."

But I will.

A train whistle blew in the distance.

Anna's breath stalled in her lungs. She kneeled and looked into Nia's eyes. "I'm so proud of you. You've come such a long way, my sweet girl. You have a special job to do, and I know you'll take wonderful care of Max." She blinked back tears. "I'll think of you every day. We'll see each other again—I promise."

Nia nuzzled into Anna.

Anna kissed Nia on the crown of her head, and then stood facing Max. "I'll write you."

"I'll find someone to read the letters to me," he said. "And I'll have them write you back for me."

The whistle blew, closer and louder. Anna's pulse rate quickened.

"I guess this is it." Max leaned in and hugged her.

She squeezed him. Her heart battered her ribs, like a bird attempting to free itself from a cage.

He released her and picked up his case.

A decision boiled in her gut. *Do I say something now, or do I tell him in a letter?* Before she changed her mind, she stepped forward and said, "Wait."

Max stopped.

"Please don't go."

Sadness filled his face.

"It's not too late to change your mind," she said. "Stay here—with me."

"I can't."

She approached him and placed a hand to his chest. "I know you want to live on your own but—"

The train rolled into the station and screeched to a stop.

"I must go," he said.

"But—" Her body trembled. "What I'm trying to say is that I—"

Carriage doors opened and passengers began to climb on board.

Max, as if he sensed her turmoil, placed down his case and clasped her arm. "Everything will be all right."

"No, it won't," she said.

His jaw quivered.

Tears welled up in her eyes. She squeezed the lapel of his coat, attempting to gather her nerve. "I'm afraid of letting you leave and never feeling—for the rest of my life—the way I feel when we're together."

"Oh, Anna," he breathed.

"I know you might think it's far too soon for me to say such a thing, but I began having feelings for you the moment you arrived." She leaned into him. "And I think that you might be fond of me, too."

He ran his hand up her arm and gently touched her face. "You deserve the best, and I want to give that to you. That's why I must go."

Her heart sank.

"You have a wondrous life ahead of you," he said. "Someday, you'll meet someone who will make you forget about everything— the war, Bruno, and me."

"No," she cried. Tears streamed down her face.

A whistle blew, signaling the train was about to depart.

He leaned in and kissed her cheek. "Goodbye, Anna." He slipped away, clasped Nia's harness and his belongings, and—led by Nia—climbed on board a carriage.

Anna, her eyes blurred with tears, watched Max take a seat by a window. The train chugged away from the station, leaving the landing empty except for her. Heartbroken and devastated, she slumped onto a bench and wept.

PART 4

MINUET

CHAPTER 34

OLDENBURG, GERMANY—JULY 17, 1917

Anna pumped a bucket full of water from the school well and carried it inside the barn, where she poured it into a communal trough for a group of thirsty German shepherds. The dogs lapped water and wagged their tails.

"You've worked hard today," Anna said, stroking a dog's back.

"You have, too," Emmi said, chopping turnips into feed at a nearby butcher block. "You haven't sat down all day."

Anna nodded, and then glanced outside to a group of trainers who were taking a cigarette break. Determination burned inside her. *Someday, I'll convince Fleck to allow me to return to being a full-time instructor. He'll eventually realize my success with training Nia wasn't a fluke.* Anna wiped sweat from her brow and went to the well to retrieve more water. She was committed to do whatever it took, even if it meant having to accept a temporary step backward in duties, in order to fulfill her dream of training guide dogs. However, there was another reason she incessantly toiled away, and that was to distract herself from the huge void in her heart left by the departure of Max and Nia.

The past five months had been difficult for Anna. Thoughts and images of him never left her, and memories of his music echoed in her head. She'd thought that the passing of time would lessen her sorrow, but it only exacerbated her yearning to be with him. As promised, she'd written Max at least once a week, and he'd also written to her, although his letters were not as frequent, as if he wanted to be polite yet not mislead her into believing anything further would ever come of their relationship. Regardless of Max's unwillingness to reciprocate her feelings, she missed him immensely. She'd invited him to visit, but he'd declined on the basis that he thought it was best to give Nia more time to acclimate to her new city. And to complicate matters, Fleck remained unwilling to grant her a leave of absence for at least another six months, which dashed her chances of taking a train trip this summer to visit him. *It might be a year before I see him again*, she'd thought while walking a shepherd to a trainer. *Maybe he'll change his mind and visit me.*

According to Max's letters, Nia was doing well with guiding him through the city of Leipzig, although they had many unfamiliar streets left to explore. When Max wasn't working on the piano or running necessary errands, such as obtaining rations, they took walks in a wooded park that was several streets away from his apartment building. Also, he'd reported that Nia's frail paw grew less sore in the warmer months, which delighted Anna. Max's letters were typically factual, rather than emotional, in nature. However, he often ended his correspondence with a bit of humor or uplifting words. "Please inform Norbie that I am, indeed, spoiling Nia with treats and belly rubs," he'd written in a recent letter.

While Nia was adjusting well to her new life, Max was encountering difficulty with gaining work as a pianist. Anna admired Max's resolve to pursue employment, regardless that the government deemed blind veterans as one-hundred-percent disabled. However, there were few musician jobs, if any, available and Max doubted that he would find any type of employment soon. Max did not lament in his letters about not having a job, but she presumed that he was disappointed. And Anna was disheartened that Max, whom she believed was a brilliant pianist and composer, might struggle to find work for many months, if not years.

Even with the passing of seasons, there seemed to be no end to the war in sight. In fact, the fight had grown worse with the United States declaring war on the German Empire after one of their steamers was torpedoed by a German U-boat. It was only a matter of time before many thousands of American troops arrived at the front to battle fatigued German troops who'd been fighting for years. The German newspapers continued to print optimistic reports; however, the rumors of losing the war, and a way of life, had grown rampant. Last week in a ration line, she'd overheard a woman talking about her plans to flee Germany after the war. And Anna hoped that things would never be bad enough to compel her and Norbie to emigrate from their beloved homeland.

Although the war was worsening, the food supply was showing marginal signs of improvement. With the spring and summer harvests, they'd begun adding cabbage and mushrooms to their diet. After subsisting on turnips for months, the new foods tasted rich and were difficult to digest, but she and Norbie were relieved to satisfy their hunger. There were no official government reports, or at least ones that were released to the public, that provided a tally on the number of deaths associated with what people now referred to as the "turnip winter." Many people speculated that the famine, compounded by unseasonably cold temperatures, had claimed many thousands of lives. And Anna believed the rumors to be true given the scores of new graves—the grass sparse and two shades lighter than the other plots—in the Oldenburg cemetery.

"Fräulein Zeller," Waldemar said, entering the barn with a shepherd.

Anna put down her bucket and approached him.

"Tend to this dog," he grumbled, tossing her a leash. "She's infested with ticks."

Anna's face turned hot. She'd seen him on more than one occasion during a smoke break, permitting the dog he was working with to run free near the tree line. "She wouldn't have so many ticks if you'd refrain from letting her do her business in the woods."

"She likes the pines," Waldemar said, scratching his beard. "Besides, removing parasites gives you something to do."

Anna clenched her hands, digging her nails into her palms.

Waldemar snickered, and then turned on his heels and left the barn.

"I don't understand why Fleck keeps Waldemar around." Emmi gave a hard chop with her cleaver, splitting a turnip in half. "He should have kept you on the course and terminated him."

"I'm disappointed in Fleck's decision, too," Anna said. "But I can't forget what Fleck did for us. His gifts of turnips got us through the winter."

"*Ja*," Emmi said, her voice turning soft. She put down her cleaver and joined Anna. "I'll help you check her over. It'll go quickly if we both do it."

Anna and Emmi groomed the shepherd, removing six ugly ticks, and then returned the dog to Waldemar. They finished their afternoon chores and went home. Exhausted, Anna entered her house to the smell of boiled cabbage, and she found Norbie in the kitchen stirring a steaming pot.

"*Hallo*," Norbie said, placing a ladle on the counter. He gave her a hug. "How was your day?"

"Same," she said, releasing him.

"It's only a matter of time before Fleck assigns you another dog and veteran to train," Norbie said, as if he could read his daughter's thoughts. "I have faith in you."

"*Danke*," she said. *You always know what to say to make me feel better.*

Norbie glanced to the counter and stuffed his hands into his pockets. "You received a letter."

Anna's heart leaped. She reached for the letter.

"It's not from Max," he said.

Anna froze, staring at the handwriting on the envelope. *Bruno.* A lump formed in the pit of her stomach.

"You don't have to open it if you don't want to," Norbie said.

"I know." She contemplated throwing away the letter, but she decided to open it, even at the risk of aggravating old wounds. "As much as I dread reading it, I think it's best that I do."

Norbie placed his hand on his daughter's shoulder. "I'll be in my workshop if you need me."

"I'd prefer if you sat with me while I read it," Anna said.

"Are you sure?"

She nodded, and they sat at the kitchen table. She drew a deep breath, attempting to quell her anxiety. Using her finger, she tore open the envelope and removed the letter.

> *Dearest Anna,*
> *There are no words to express how sorrowful*
> *I am for hurting you. I despise myself for*
> *what I've done. It wasn't my intention to lie*
> *or mislead you. I'd naively hoped and prayed*
> *that the unspeakable things I'd done would*
> *somehow disappear when the war ended.*
> *But now I know that the sins I've committed*
> *will follow me forever, and they can never be*
> *forgiven.*

Anna's mouth turned dry. She squeezed the paper between her fingers.

> *When we first met, I was smitten with your*
> *tenderness, honesty, and compassion. I saw*
> *a rare pureness in you that I'd never seen*
> *in another woman. I was envious of the*
> *endearment that you had for your friends*
> *and family, which I had never experienced*
> *with my own relations, and I desperately*
> *wanted to be part of your world rather than*
> *mine.*
> *I'd begun the war believing that it*
> *would all be over in a matter of months.*
> *But months turned to years, and as each*
> *day passed, I sank deeper into my abyss of*
> *transgressions.*

Anna paused, rubbing her eyes, and then continued reading.

> *I regret not having the courage to speak or*
> *write to you sooner. And I say all of this not*
> *to gain your sympathy or your forgiveness.*

*I'm not seeking you to pardon me from my
wrongdoings, nor would I want you to. I
merely wanted you to know how sorry I am
for everything, and that I'll spend my days
working to make amends for what I've done.
   I wish you a lifetime of happiness, and I
pray that the grief I've given you will fade
with time.
   Regretfully,
   Bruno*

Anna folded the letter and placed it in the envelope. She looked
at her *vater*, his eyes filled with concern. "It's an apology letter."

"Are you all right?" he asked.

"I am," she said. "I feel nothing but pity for him, and I hope
that he can find his redemption."

Norbie nodded.

"It feels strange to be emotionally numb toward him," Anna
said.

Norbie patted her hand. "It means you're beginning to heal and
move on with your life."

I hope you're right. She glanced to the pot on the stove. "May I
help you with dinner?"

"It's all finished," Norbie said. "I'll serve the soup in an hour.
It'll give you time to wash and relax."

Anna, knowing she'd never want to read the letter again, disposed of it in the trash. Instead of going upstairs to wash, she was
drawn to the living room where she sat without thinking at the
piano. A swell of loneliness washed over her. She ran a hand over
the empty spot on the bench next to her. *God, I wish Max was here.*

CHAPTER 35

OLDENBURG, GERMANY—JULY 18, 1917

Early morning sun warmed Anna's face as she walked a German shepherd toward the obstacle course, where the trainers were conducting drills with veterans and their guide dogs. Reaching Fleck, she commanded the shepherd to *halt*.

"*Danke*, Fräulein Zeller," Fleck said, taking hold of the dog's harness.

Anna glanced at Waldemar on the obstacle course. "It's going to be hot today, sir. I'd be happy to alternate with trainers to give them a break from the heat."

"Perhaps this afternoon," Fleck said, peering toward the course. "I'll let you know if you are needed."

"*Ja*, sir." Anna turned and left. *I'll never let up. I'll continue to persist until he permits me to remain on the course as a trainer.*

A horse-drawn wagon, driven by a man wearing a dark suit and homburg hat, pulled to the barn and stopped. As Anna approached, the man came into view. *Dr. Stalling.*

"*Hallo*, Anna," Stalling said, stepping down from the wagon.

"It's good to see you, sir," Anna said.

He tipped his hat. "You too. It's been quite some time since I've seen you."

It's because Fleck has me working inside the barn most of the time,

Anna thought, but held her tongue. "I think the last time we spoke was the February class graduation."

"Of course, I remember now," he said. "You'd finished training Max."

She nodded.

"How is he?" Stalling asked.

"*Gut*," she said. "We've kept in touch through letters. He and Nia are adjusting well to his home in Leipzig."

"Oh." Stalling removed his hat.

"However, he's having challenges with gaining employment. He's an incredible pianist, and there's little opportunity for him to work. I'm worried that he might not have a chance to display his talent until after the war is over."

Lines formed on Stalling's forehead. "Did Max mention anything about seeing me at the hospital before he left?"

Anna shifted her weight. "*Nein.*"

"I thought he would have told you," he said, a tone of concern in his voice.

Her heart rate quickened. "Tell me what?"

Stalling paused, wiping his face with a handkerchief from his pocket. He drew a deep breath and looked at her. "In the German Reich, an unauthorized disclosure of a patient's private secrets by a doctor is punishable by law, which may include a fine and imprisonment."

Oh, God. Her mouth turned dry. She placed her hands to her stomach.

"I regret that I'm unable to discuss everything with you," he said. "But from my conversation with Max—unrelated to patient-doctor privacy—I understand that he is quite fond of you. And I do not feel that I'm breaking my oath as a doctor by recommending that you pay him a visit."

"What's wrong with Max?" she asked, her voice quavering.

"I wish I could say more," Stalling said.

She felt helpless. Her mind and heart raced. "I won't be granted a leave of absence until the end of the year."

Stalling shook his head. "That's too long."

Anna's blood turned cold.

"I'll talk with Fleck," he said. "And I'll insist that he permits you to take a leave of absence."

"*Danke*, Doctor," she said. "When should I plan on leaving?"

"As soon as possible."

Dread shot through her. She clasped her hands to keep them from trembling.

"Take care of yourself, Anna." He placed his hat on his head and walked onto the field.

Anna, struggling to control a flurry of emotions swirling inside her, watched Stalling cross the field and approach Fleck. *It must be serious if Stalling wants me to leave so soon. This can't be happening!* As the two men discussed her fate, she said a silent prayer for Max to be all right, and for Fleck to permit her to take a leave of absence. But only half of her prayer was answered when Fleck called her aside and said, "I'm granting your leave, Fräulein Zeller. You may go home and pack your bags."

CHAPTER 36

OLDENBURG, GERMANY—JULY 19, 1917

Anna stood next to Norbie as the morning train chugged into the station. Iron wheels screeched over the rails as the locomotive slowed to a stop. The engine hissed, spewing a black cloud and filling her nose with an acrid smell of coal smoke. A surge of panic flooded her body. She drew in a deep breath, attempting to calm her nerves.

"Are you sure you don't want me to come with you?" Norbie asked.

"I'm sure," she said. "I'll send word to you after I arrive."

"All right," he said. "But I'll be ready to leave at a moment's notice if you need me."

She appreciated his support, and she had no doubt that Norbie, if given the invitation, would take the train with her regardless that he hadn't packed a bag. *I'd love for you to join me, but I feel that I need to see him on my own.* She shook away her thoughts and said, "I didn't get a chance to talk to Emmi, and I'm not sure if Fleck will explain the reason for my absence. Will you speak with her for me?"

"Of course." He gave her a hug. "Tell Max *hallo* for me."

"I will," she said, releasing him.

He looked into her eyes. "Everything will be all right."

Anna nodded, feeling thankful for his reassurance, and then picked up her luggage and climbed on board a carriage. An attendant punched her ticket, which was purchased with money she'd saved from working at the guide dog school, and she located a vacant seat. Minutes later, the train jerked, and then chugged forward. She peered out her window and saw Norbie wave to her from the landing. She pressed her fingers to the glass and watched him disappear.

She leaned back but was unable to rest. Despite sleeping little, if at all, her mind raced with thoughts of Max and her encounter with Dr. Stalling. *What does the doctor know that he's unwilling to tell me? Why didn't Max inform me about his visit with Stalling?* She knew it was something medical and that it was likely serious, otherwise Stalling would not have persuaded Fleck to allow her to leave. She reached to her neck and clasped her *mutter's* locket. "Harbor your heart," she whispered to herself. *Whatever it is that Max is going through, we'll get through it together.*

She retrieved a book from her bag and tried to read, but her brain was unable to focus on the words. Instead, she leaned back in her seat and watched the German countryside flash by her window. She remained awake for the entire seven-and-a-half-hour journey, which included a short delay and a train change in the city of Hanover. Norbie had packed her a lunch of sliced black bread with raw cabbage, but she'd lost her appetite for food. A few hours before sunset, she arrived at the Leipzig station.

The city was far bigger and more populated than her hometown of Oldenburg. The sidewalks were crowded, forcing Anna to weave between throngs of pedestrians. Also, the street crossings were more difficult due to a high volume of horse-drawn wagons and motorized vehicles. And it saddened her to think that Max and Nia had not been given the opportunity to practice their training skills in such a congested urban environment.

She stopped in an apothecary shop and asked the proprietor for directions to Max's street address, which she had from their letter correspondence. Thirty minutes later, she arrived on his street, but she struggled to find his apartment building due to a lack of address signs. She canvassed the area until an old woman, who was sweeping a broom over the front steps of a brick rowhouse, guided her to the correct building.

In the entrance hall, she glanced to a group of metal letter boxes. Her heartbeat quickened as she read Max's name above one of the slots. She sucked in air to catch her breath, and then climbed the stairs to his apartment. She paused, placing down her luggage and rubbing an ache in her elbow. *Please, let him be all right.* She buried her trepidation and knocked.

Paws pattered over the floor inside the apartment. A sound of sniffing emanated from a gap under the door.

Nia. Anna blinked back tears as she waited for Max to answer the door. Seconds passed. Her shoulder muscles tightened. She knocked again. A moment later, footsteps grew inside the apartment.

"Who is it?" Max's voice asked from behind the door.

She clasped her hands. *He sounds the same.* "It's Anna."

Nia barked. Her toenails clicked over the hardwood floor.

She knows that it's me.

A deadbolt unlocked, and the door opened.

Nia lunged to Anna, nearly knocking her over.

"Nia!" she said, kneeling and rubbing the dog's body with her hands.

"Anna, what are you doing here?"

"I came to see you." She kissed Nia on the head, stood to face Max, and froze.

His complexion was ashen with dark circles under his eyes, as if he hadn't slept in days, and his hair was rather long and un-combed. A coarse stubble covered his face and neck.

A pang pierced Anna's chest. *Oh, Max.*

"Why didn't you write to let me know you were coming?" he asked, still clasping the doorknob.

She fought back her angst. "I thought I would surprise you. May I come in?"

He rubbed bristles on his chin, and then lowered his head, as if he'd become self-conscience of his appearance. "Of course," he said, stepping aside.

She retrieved her luggage and entered with Nia.

He closed the door, bolted the lock, and then turned to her, placing his hands to his sides.

He's making no effort to embrace me. Her heart sank.

"Please, have a seat," Max said. "I'll prepare us some coffee."

"Coffee would be nice," Anna said, despite the growing ache in her abdomen. She put down her luggage and sat at a kitchen table.

"How was your train trip?" Max asked, gliding his hand over the counter to locate a tin container.

"*Gut.*"

Nia padded to Anna and lowered her chin to her lap.

"I've missed you, Nia," Anna said, running her fingers through her fur.

"She's missed you, too." Max poured grinds into a coffee-pot and, using his finger as a gauge, added water from a ceramic pitcher.

Anna struggled with what to say, and so did Max, given his focus on preparing the coffee. So, she played with Nia until the brew was ready.

Max placed two cups on the table and sat across from her.

Anna took a sip. "It's *gut.*"

"I'm using Norbie's bark coffee recipe."

"He'd be pleased to hear that," she said.

"How is he?"

"He's well, and he wanted me to tell you *hallo* for him."

He nodded, and then sipped his drink.

Anna stared at him, thin and haggard. *He looks exhausted.* A mixture of fear and sorrow swelled inside her. She squeezed her cup. "How long have you been ill?"

Max's shoulders slumped. "Is it that obvious?"

"*Ja,*" she said. "How long?"

"A while."

Her chest tightened. "Why didn't you tell me?"

"I didn't want you to worry about me."

"You should have apprised me of your health," she said. "I thought we were friends."

"We are," he said.

"But friends confide in each other. Friends help each other in times of need."

Max rubbed his forehead.

"Tell me what happened," she said.

He ran a finger over the rim of his cup.

"Please, I want to know everything."

"All right," Max said. He tilted his head upward, as if he were searching through his memories. "In Oldenburg, I'd begun to have episodes of feeling winded after long walks."

Goose bumps cropped up on Anna's arms.

"I'd had them before, so I didn't pay much attention to them. But toward the end of guide dog training, the short of breath episodes increased, and—on a few instances—they included dizziness. The first occurrence was when I fell down the stairs at your home while taking Nia outside."

An image of Max, lying on the ground in Norbie's workshop, flashed in her head. Her mouth turned dry. "I remember. I thought it was because you weren't getting enough food to eat."

"*Ja*," he said. "That's what I thought, too."

Nia padded to him and placed her head on his knee.

Max gently rubbed the dog's ears. "I found out the real cause of my fatigue the day that Nia and I were assigned to explore the hospital grounds on our own. While we were walking in the garden, I became light-headed. A nurse came to my aid, and she summoned Dr. Stalling."

Anna's hands trembled.

"Stalling was very kind; he insisted on giving me a bowl of warm broth and examining me. After he listened to my chest, he summoned another doctor, who had expertise with treating veterans with gas inhalation." Max took a sip of coffee, as if he was reluctant to finish the story, and then set aside his cup. "The doctor examined me, and I was given a few breathing tests. Afterward, I was informed that I was in the early stages of respiratory failure."

No! Tears welled up in her eyes. She leaned forward and clasped his hand.

He squeezed her fingers. "I'd known, since my treatment in a field hospital at the front, that my lungs were scorched by chlorine gas. The doctors had initially thought that my lungs would heal enough for a normal life. But it turns out that there was far more damage done."

Oh, God. "Were you prescribed a treatment plan?"

He shook his head.

"Have you been assigned a Leipzig-based doctor who can help you?" she asked, refusing to accept his diagnosis.

"Anna," he said, his voice soft. "There's nothing they can do."

"*Nein!*" Anna cried. "There must be something that can be done."

"I'm afraid not," he said.

Tears streamed down her cheeks. "Did Stalling or his colleague tell you how much time you have?"

"Six months to a year."

"Oh, Max," she cried.

He stood and wrapped her in his arms.

Anna sobbed, her body shaking. She remained in his embrace, attempting to come to terms that Max had told her he was dying. She'd encountered terminal cases countless times as a nurse. But nothing could have prepared her, she believed, for learning that she had little time left with the man whom she wanted to spend her life with.

"I was in denial at first," he said, as if he could read her thoughts.

She sniffed, trying to slow the flow of tears.

"When I'd returned to Leipzig, I'd refused to accept the diagnosis. I spent my initial days back home trying to land a job as a pianist, as if finding employment would somehow prove to myself and others that I would be fine. But as days passed, and my breathing became more labored, I came to terms with the truth."

"I'm here for you, Max."

He pressed his cheek to her hair.

"I would have come to take care of you."

"I know," he said. "That's part of the reason I didn't confide in you. I was worried you'd jeopardize your dream of training guide dogs by caring for me."

She released him and placed her palms on his chest. "I don't care. You're what matters."

Nia nuzzled their legs.

"I'm so sorry," he said. "I wish I would have told you earlier."

"It's all right," she said. "I'm here now."

His jaw quivered. "God, I've missed you."

"Me too," she breathed.

"How long are you able to stay?"

"I've been given a two-week leave," she said, her heart breaking. "But I plan to stay as long as you'll have me."

CHAPTER 37

LEIPZIG, GERMANY—JULY 20, 1917

Max clasped the handle to Nia's harness and shuffled out of his apartment. While Anna locked the door behind them, he descended the stairs, stepped outside, and raised his chin toward the sky, feeling the warmth of the sun on his clean-shaven face. *It's going to be a nice day*, he thought. *Please, God, let me have the stamina to make it to the park and back without becoming faint.*

"Which way?" Anna asked, stepping to him.

Max gestured with his cane. "Nia knows the way."

Anna smiled and patted Nia.

"Forward," Max said.

Nia padded ahead.

He tapped his cane and walked. After traveling fifty meters, he grew short of breath and his legs turned shaky, compelling him to slow his pace.

"How about we rest for a moment?" Anna asked.

"*Danke.*" He stopped and took in shallow breaths. "I'm sorry. I hate for you to see me this way."

"There's nothing to feel sorry about," she said. "We can take as much time as you need. Right, Nia?"

The dog wagged her tail.

Max nodded. He paused, inhaling air. His dizziness gradually subsided, and he pressed on.

It took them over twenty minutes, three times what it should have taken, to reach the park. Nia guided him to a bench, where he slumped in a seat. He took in several wheezing breaths, and then unbuckled Nia's harness.

"It's been a while since Nia has had a good run," Max said. "Would you mind giving her a bit of exercise?"

"I'd love to," Anna said. "Come, Nia."

The dog followed Anna onto an earthen path that winded through a lush public garden filled with evergreens.

Max leaned back on the bench. The burn in his lungs faded, and his pulse rate slowed. He took in more breaths, bringing in the scent of pine. A warm breezed caressed his face. And he listened to the sweet timbre of Anna's voice as she played with Nia. *I wish I could join you.*

After a good run and a game of fetch with a stick, Anna and Nia joined Max on the bench. They spoke for an hour, each sharing details of their lives while apart over the past several months.

"Fleck changed my role to a substitute trainer," Anna said. "Much of my duties are focused on caring for shepherds with Emmi."

"Why?" Max asked. "You're the best trainer in the school."

"Fleck didn't give a reason. I assume he thinks my success with training Nia was a fluke."

He held out his hand.

She clasped his fingers.

"You'll train again," he said. "Someday, there will be scores of guide dogs—all across Deutschland—that will have been instructed by you."

"That's a lovely thought," she said.

He entwined his fingers with hers and gently caressed her hand with his thumb.

Nia nuzzled them.

"I feel lucky to have Nia," he said, "especially considering my diagnosis."

"How so?" she asked.

"It would have been easy for Dr. Stalling to have switched Nia's assignment to a healthier veteran. It was kind of him to allow us to remain together."

Anna squeezed his hand.

"I wish you could have seen what Nia accomplished over the past several months." He turned toward her. "She performed admirably. I don't know what I would have done without her."

Nia's ears perked, and she tilted her head.

"But, most of all," he said, "she's been a caring companion."

"I'm glad," Anna said.

Max dreaded bringing their time in the park to an end. He wanted to stay with her, talking and holding hands, but his diaphragm began to feel constricted. Regretfully, he slipped his hand away and rose from the bench. Together, they left the park with Nia between them.

Upon returning to the apartment, Max, who needed to stop twice on the journey home to catch his breath, slumped onto a sofa with his head on a small, decorative pillow. "I'm sorry to be a poor host," he said. "But I think I need to rest."

Anna approached him and gently ran her hand over his forehead.

His muscles relaxed. "Your touch is like heaven," he breathed.

Anna smiled. "Take a nap, and when you wake, I'll have something prepared for us to eat."

He felt her touch fade away, and he drifted into a deep, cavernous sleep.

Max woke to the sensation of Nia's tongue licking his face. He stretched his arms and labored to sit up. "Good girl, Nia. *Danke* for waking me."

Nia gave him another wet lick to the nose, and then padded to Anna.

"How do you feel?" Anna asked.

"Better," Max said, his head a bit groggy. "Is it time for lunch?"

"Dinner."

He rubbed his face. "How long did I sleep?"

"All afternoon," she said.

"I'm so sorry," he said, rising from the sofa.

"It's quite all right. You needed rest."

They sat at the table and ate dinner that Anna had prepared from his leftover turnip latkes, as well as cabbage and bread that she'd brought with her. Afterward, Max—rejuvenated by sleep and food—invited Anna to join him at his grand piano, which took up much of the living room in his modest-size apartment.

"It's beautiful," Anna said, tapping a key. "Did your *vater* make it?"

"*Ja*," he said. "You remembered that he made pianos."

"Of course."

Max felt a strange tug in his cheeks, and he realized that he was smiling, perhaps for the first time in months. He positioned his hands over the keys. "What would you like to hear?"

"I think you already know," she said.

He nodded, and then began playing the first movement to *Light Suite*. Performing on the piano, Max believed, was one of the few remaining things he could do that didn't exhaust him. *I'm unable to take long walks, but I can still give her the gift of music.*

As his hands and fingers glided over the keys, a calmness washed over him. Flashes of his time with Anna, transcribing the piece—bar by bar—onto staff paper filled his head. He felt her warmth next to him, and his loneliness, which had encompassed him since leaving her in Oldenburg, faded away. A deep fulfillment swelled within him, and the emotional wall that he'd created came tumbling down. He played each movement of the piece, and as the resonance of music was replaced by silence, he rose from the piano and extended his hand.

She clasped his fingers and stood.

Nia, lying beneath the bench, gave a high-pitched yawn, then lowered her head back to the floor and closed her eyes.

Max felt Anna move close, her fingers entwining with his.

"I don't want you to sleep on the sofa again tonight," she said.

"But we agreed last night that you would have my bed."

"That's not what I'm saying," she said. "I want us to be together."

Butterflies fluttered in his stomach. He pulled her close, then paused. "I don't know if I'm capable of—" His forehead touched hers.

"It's all right," she breathed. "We'll simply hold each other. I don't want another day to pass with us being apart."

"Nor I," Max said.

Holding his hand, she guided him to the bedroom.

He released her, and then glided his palms up her arms and rested them on her shoulders. His heart thumped inside his chest. He slowly leaned in and their lips met, sending tingles through his body. Patiently, they undressed each other, undoing buttons and buckles. Clothing fell to the floor, and they slipped into the bed and embraced, their bodies melded as one.

CHAPTER 38

PASSCHENDAELE, BELGIUM—AUGUST 15, 1917

Bruno hunkered inside an abandoned church as Allied shellfire rained down on the village of Passchendaele, the last ridge east of Ypres. One side of the stone structure had collapsed from an exploding shell, giving view to a cemetery marred with broken headstones and grave monuments. Several soldiers gathered near a small fire, which they'd created from a wooden lectern. A nearby explosion quaked the church, sending bits of mortar onto Bruno's helmet. His pulse thudded in his ears. A mix of dread and regret churned inside his stomach. *I didn't need to be here.*

Heavy rains had turned the ground soft, causing a section of light rail—running along the front—to collapse into the muck. Therefore, the only way to deliver shells to the last section of the ridge was by pack mules. He could have ordered soldiers to transport the shells, but he eagerly volunteered to lead the men in the mission. Disgusted by the use of Fritz Haber's new chemical weapon, mustard gas, he left the site of the atrocity, as well as the safety of his bunker. And while transporting the shells to the ridge, the Allies unleashed a surprise bombardment, forcing him and his men to abandon the mules and find shelter inside a church.

The preceding month, Bruno's unit had received the first shipments of mustard gas. The shells looked the same as other gas projectiles, except for a yellow cross painted on the side of the casing. On the nights of July twelfth and thirteenth, his unit unleashed the new chemical weapon on British troops. Bruno had hoped that Fritz Haber's promise—that sulfur mustard gas would change the tide of the war—would come true. But Bruno soon learned that this would not be the case when a German patrol captured a dozen British soldiers who were exposed to the mustard poison.

The prisoners were covered with horrific blisters and sores, and many were blinded or coughing up blood. Unlike other poison gases, sulfur mustard was absorbed through the skin, so gas masks were useless, and instead of dying immediately, the prisoners suffered for weeks. A soldier who received a lethal exposure of chlorine or phosgene gas typically died within a couple days. However, the mustard gas was clearly designed to disable rather than kill. And it was clear, to Bruno, that Haber and his chemists had created the poison to inspire terror.

Explosions quaked the earth. A few of the soldiers crawled under pews. But Bruno—his mind and soul ravaged by years of death—climbed steps to a large, ornate wooden altar. He removed a piece of paper, an envelope, and a pencil from the inside pocket of his tunic, next to the identification of the fallen French soldier whom he'd drowned in a water-filled shell hole. He placed the tip of the pencil to the paper and began to write.

> *Vater,*
> *It feels like an eternity since we've corresponded, and I assume this letter will be of surprise to you. My location on the front is weakening under enemy artillery fire, and I believe it is prudent to write in case we do not speak again.*

A shell exploded near the cemetery. Using his sleeve, he wiped a cold sweat from his brow.

> *When I was a child, I longed to gain your affection and approval. And as a*

young man, I hoped to make you proud by accepting Fritz Haber's recruitment to his special chemical warfare unit. I'd once hoped that after the war you would view me as equal to my half-brother and welcome me into the family business. But after witnessing the atrocities of chemical weapons, some of which were made in our factory, I no longer aspire to follow in your footsteps.

I wish you could see with your own eyes the death and suffering that we have inflicted. It was us and the German Empire who unleashed the poison and broke the Hague Convention treaty. We've committed heinous acts against humanity, and if we should lose the war, leaders in Germany's chemical warfare program may be tried for war crimes. I tell you this not to admonish you, but in hopes that someday you and I will seek amends for our transgressions.

In the event that I do not survive this war, I respectfully ask that you honor my service by redirecting the funds of my inheritance that you planned to bequeath to me.

Firstly, I've met a Frenchwoman from Lille named Celeste Lemaire, whom I plan to marry after the war. She is pregnant, and we plan to live in Frankfurt. Celeste has collaborated with Germany, and she is loyal to our cause. If something would happen to me, I implore you to care for her and your grandchild.

Bruno squeezed his pencil, hoping that he would somehow make it back to Lille before Celeste delivered their baby. He buried his thought and continued writing.

Secondly, I've enclosed with this letter the identification to a fallen French soldier. Although I've killed countless Allied soldiers in the name of the Fatherland, this particular death haunts me, and I respectfully request that you do something to provide for the man's family.

Thirdly, I would like for you to make a sizeable donation to a guide dog school that was established in Oldenburg to restore the mobility of battle-blinded veterans. Many of these men were maimed by poison gas, and in some cases the injury was sustained by accidental discharge from German chlorine gas cylinders.

Images of Anna and Max flashed in his head. His hands trembled, and he struggled to steady his pencil.

I pray that you will honor my requests, and that God will forgive us for what we have done.
Your son,
Bruno

Bruno folded his letter and placed it, along with the Frenchman's identification, inside the envelope and sealed it. He stepped down from the altar and listened to the pace of the explosions. *The shellfire might be letting up.* A choice burned in his gut: mail the letter when he returned to headquarters, or send a runner. Before he changed his mind, he approached the soldiers sitting by the fire.

"Jäger," Bruno called.

A thin but muscular young man stood and approached him. "*Ja*, sir."

"I want you to run to headquarters," Bruno said, giving the soldier the envelope. "Place the letter in the post back to Germany."

"*Ja*, sir." The solder stuffed the envelope inside his jacket, sa- luted, and then dashed from the church carrying his rifle.

Bruno watched the soldier disappear through a field, and then sat in a pew and lowered his head. Minutes passed, and as the bombardment stopped, he regretted having sent a runner. *I over- reacted*, he thought. However, an hour later, when he and his men were about to embark on rounding up the pack mules that they'd abandoned, the Allied infantry unleashed the full fury of their shellfire.

Large-caliber projectiles exploded in close proximity to the church. Some of the soldiers scrambled to the rear of the building, while others crawled under pews. The ground rumbled. Explo- sions reverberated through Bruno's blood and bone. With no place to hide, he crouched near the base of a stone wall as the explosions grew closer and closer, as if the angle of the Allied cannons were being incrementally adjusted to narrow in on their location.

A concussive blast knocked him to the ground. He raised his head, his ears ringing from the detonation, and saw that the roof was partially collapsed. A soldier screamed as he struggled to free his crushed legs from under a fallen timber beam. *Nein!* Bruno, determined to aid the soldier, crawled forward over a mass of de- bris. Wood splinters and nails puncturing his hands and knees. Reaching his comrade, Bruno strained—his muscles flaring with pain—to lift the beam. The soldier yowled. And as Bruno gave a final heave, an incoming artillery shell shattered the church's steeple, and tons of stone came crashing down upon them.

CHAPTER 39

LEIPZIG, GERMANY—SEPTEMBER 27, 1917

Anna sat on the edge of Max's bed. She dipped a washcloth into a ceramic basin of lukewarm water, squeezed out the excess liquid, and gently wiped his forehead. With each of Max's shallow respirations, a rattling sounded inside his chest. *He's worse today,* she thought, her heart aching.

"*Danke,*" Max said, his voice hoarse.

"You're welcome," Anna said. She sank the washcloth into the water, and then washed his body, his muscles atrophied from being confined to bed for the past two weeks.

Anna had not gone back to work. After her two-week leave of absence, she'd returned to Oldenburg merely to inform Fleck and Dr. Stalling that she was leaving her position at the guide dog school to care for Max. She'd wanted to resign via telegram, or by having Norbie meet with them to explain her decision. However, Max had insisted that he and Nia would be fine while she was gone, and that he could contact a woman named Magdalena, who'd once been friends with his *mutter*, to help him if he needed anything. She'd only been gone a few of days, but when she'd returned to Leipzig, she discovered that Max's respiration had deteriorated, and she regretted having left him.

Despite Max's fatigue, their initial days of being reunited were blissful. They'd prepared meals together, walked short routes with

Nia, and talked endlessly about everything but the war. She'd read books to him while he cuddled with his dog, and he'd played the piano for her. And in the evenings, they'd retired early to bed, where they lay wrapped in each other's arms. But as each day passed, his breathing grew more labored, and a bluish tint began to appear on his lips and fingernails. Soon, he became too weak to climb the stairs. Confined to the apartment, he played the piano when he wasn't resting. However, a few weeks ago, Max became too frail to leave his bed, and the music ended.

Anna dried Max with a towel and dressed him in clean sleepwear. She picked up the washbasin and carried it to the kitchen. As she disposed of the water in the sink, the front door to Max's apartment opened, and Norbie and Nia entered.

Nia scampered to Anna, where she received a pat on the head, and then ran into Max's room.

"How is he?" Norbie asked, hanging up his jacket.

She approached him. "Not so good."

He hugged her.

"I'm so glad you're here," she said.

"Me too," he said, releasing her.

Norbie had made three trips to Leipzig over the past two months, and when he'd arrived a few days ago and saw that Max was confined to his bed, he'd told Anna that he would remain with her to help. They couldn't afford for her to be out of work and for him to close his clockmaker shop, but Norbie didn't care, nor did she. All that mattered to them was that Max would receive personal care, rather than being placed in a government hospital that would undoubtedly be short-staffed.

"Do you think Max would mind if I check in on him?" Norbie asked.

"I think he'd enjoy your company," she said.

Norbie entered Max's room, followed by Anna.

"*Hallo*, Max," Norbie said.

Max opened his eyes and blankly stared. "Norbie," he said softly. "Please sit."

Norbie sat in a chair beside the bed. "How are you feeling?"

Max tilted his head toward the sound of Norbie's voice. "Better. I was thinking of taking Nia mountain hiking."

"That's the spirit," Norbie said.

Anna fought back tears and patted Nia.

"How was the park?" Max wheezed.

"*Gut*," Norbie said. "Nia chased a squirrel up a tree."

Max's lips formed a slim smile. "*Danke* for being here, Norbie."

"You're welcome, my boy." Norbie removed a handkerchief from his pocket and wiped his eyes.

"I know it's a sacrifice for you to leave your shop," Max said.

"Not at all." Norbie placed a hand on Max's shoulder. "The clocks will stop ticking when I'm gone, but all I need to do is rewind them when I return."

Anna's chest ached.

"Would you like something to eat?" Norbie asked.

"*Nein*," Max said. "But if it's not too much trouble, a cup of your coffee would be splendid. Yours tastes better than mine."

Norbie smiled and blinked tears from his eyes. "Of course." He stood and went to the kitchen.

As Anna turned to follow him, Max patted the side of his bed.

"Stay," he wheezed.

She approached him and sat.

"I should have gone to Oldenburg like you wanted me to." He took in a few breaths. "It was stubborn of me to want to stay here. It's a burden to you and Norbie."

"It's not," she said.

He extended his hand toward her.

She clasped his fingers.

"I don't want you to be sad," he said.

"I can't help it," she said, her voice trembling.

"I'm not afraid of what awaits me." He took in gulps of air.

Tears welled up in her eyes.

"After I'm gone—"

"Oh, Max," she cried.

He caressed her hand. "I want you to live your life. I want you to pursue your dreams, fall in love, and have a family of your own."

"I can't."

"You must." He drew in a shallow breath. "And you will."

She pressed his hand to her lips.

"I wish that things could have been different for us," he said.

Tears streamed down her face. "Me too."

He placed his palm to her cheek, wet with tears. "You're beautiful."

"I'm a mess."

"*Nein*." He ran his thumb over her skin. "To me, Anna, you are flawless."

Overwhelmed with sorrow, she lay down on the bed with him and cried. She wrapped her arms around him, feeling his diaphragm contract. His lips pressed to her forehead, and then he rested his head onto his pillow. Anna, desperate and heartbroken, listened to the whistling of his labored breathing, all the while praying for a miracle.

CHAPTER 40

LEIPZIG, GERMANY—SEPTEMBER 29, 1917

Anna woke and quietly rolled over in bed. Morning sunlight beamed through a crack in the curtains. She paused, watching Max's chest rise and fall, and then carefully slipped out of bed and put on her robe.

"Nia," she whispered.

Nia rose from a blanket, which had been placed on the floor on Max's side of the bed, and padded to her.

Anna and Nia left the room, and she gently closed the door behind her. She crept to the kitchen, doing her best not to wake Norbie, who was sleeping on the sofa, but Nia padded to him and licked his face.

"Good morning, Nia," Norbie said, rubbing the dog's head.

"I'm sorry," Anna said. "I should have made sure that she stayed with me."

"It's all right." He rubbed sleep sand from his eyes and glanced at his wristwatch. "It's seven. I need to be getting up. But first I need to give this one a belly rub."

Nia, as if she understood his words, rolled onto her back with her paws in the air.

Anna smiled. She was happy to have her *vater*'s help and, even more, she was immensely appreciative for his acceptance of her relationship with Max. Not every parent, she believed, would condone their unwed daughter sleeping with a man, let alone entering a relationship with someone who was ill. However, Norbie had expressed no concern or even surprise by the unorthodox arrangement. Since his arrival, he'd displayed nothing but understanding and support for Anna and Max. And for that, she would be eternally thankful.

Norbie made coffee while Anna prepared a bowl of mushed black bread, the consistency of oatmeal, by adding a bit of hot water. She placed a cup of coffee and the food on a tray and carried it to Max's room.

"Good morning," Anna said, setting the tray on a side table.

Nia padded into the room, her toenails clicking over the hardwood floor.

Anna went to the window and opened the drapes, allowing sunshine to flood the room. "It's a lovely morning. Would you like me to open a window?"

Nia whimpered.

Anna turned.

Nia, standing next to the bed, pushed her snout under Max's hand but he made no effort to pet her.

Oh, God. "Max?"

Nia whined. She nuzzled his limp arm.

Anna, her legs feeling like twigs about to snap, approached the bed. She caressed his cheek. "Oh, Max," she cried.

Norbie entered the room and stood at his daughter's side. Tears formed in his eyes.

With trembling hands, she clasped Max's wrist and felt for a pulse but found nothing. Grief-stricken and gutted, she lowered her head to Max's still chest and sobbed.

CHAPTER 41

OLDENBURG, GERMANY—OCTOBER 24, 1917

Anna, carrying a woven basket, entered the garden where Norbie and Nia were standing near a small row of withered plants. She watched Norbie, using the heel of his boot, sink a gardening fork into the earth and pry up a mound of soil. A memory of Max, hacking away at frozen earth to extract winter leeks, flashed in her head. Her chest ached. *God, I miss him.*

Norbie kneeled, crumbled the packed dirt with his hands, and removed several small potatoes. "We'll have more than turnips this winter."

Anna nodded. She helped him harvest potatoes, all the while thinking of her time with Max and wondering if the pain in her heart would ever go away.

They'd buried Max, per his wishes, in a Jewish cemetery in Leipzig, where his parents' grave monument was located. A rabbi had conducted a short yet reflective service, which was attended by a small group of people, most of whom were former coworkers of his parents, given that all of Max's friends were at war. After the service, Anna was approached by an attractive, gray-haired woman holding an envelope who introduced herself as Magdalena, a former friend of Max's *mutter.* "I helped Max with updating his last will and testament," the woman had said. "He didn't have much, but he wanted you to have everything." Anna, her eyes blurred with tears, accepted the envelope. But rather than going back to his apartment to begin the heart-wrenching task of sorting through Max's things, she returned to Oldenburg with Norbie and Nia.

Anna had grieved with Norbie in their home for a week, much like *shiva*, a Jewish seven-day mourning period. But the time and family comfort did little, if anything, to relieve her sorrow. She returned alone to Leipzig the following week to sort through Max's estate, and she was shocked to find that his apartment had been ransacked. Most of the kitchen and living room items were missing, save the grand piano, and his clothes were strewn over the floor. The worst loss, for Anna, was that the manuscript to *Light Suite* was gone. *I should have stayed here and taken care of things for Max.* Anna, filled with blame and heartache, cleaned out Max's apartment, donated his piano to the Royal Conservatory of Music of Leipzig, where he'd gone to school, and left for home.

Anna and Norbie were not the only ones suffering grief. Since returning home, Nia had little interest in playing, going on long walks, or receiving belly rubs. She'd lost her appetite, and her ribs were beginning to show through her coat. Also, the dog often went off to be alone, and most of the time Anna would find her lying on the floor of the bedroom where Max had stayed during his training. Even visits from Emmi, who spent most evenings helping Anna process her grief, did little to raise Nia's spirts. Anna was disheartened by Nia's distress, and she wished that there was something she could do to ease her dog's pain.

Norbie placed down his gardening fork and wiped sweat from his brow. "Would you like something to drink?"

"*Nein, danke,*" Anna said, placing potatoes into her basket.

Norbie nodded and went inside the house.

Anna glanced to Nia, lying in the corner of the garden with her chin on her paws. She stood, walked to Nia—who made no effort to move or wag her tail—and then sat. Anna dusted dirt from her hands, and then stroked Nia's fur. "You miss him, don't you?"

Nia's eyebrows twitched.

"I miss him, too." Anna drew a jagged breath. "Some days, I feel like I can't get out of bed."

The dog blinked her eyes, staring forward.

"I'm thinking that you are feeling the same way." Anna gently rubbed the dog's ears. "It's all right to feel sad. I'm here for you, and we'll get through this together."

Nia raised her head and licked Anna's hand.

Tears welled up in Anna's eyes. She leaned in and hugged her.

"Anna," Norbie said, stepping into the garden. "You have a visitor."

Anna released Nia and wiped her cheeks.

"*Hallo*, Fräulein Zeller," a deep voice said.

Anna's skin prickled. She scrambled to her feet and dusted her clothing. "Herr Fleck."

Fleck removed his cap. "I can come back later if this isn't a good time for you."

"Now is fine," Anna said, attempting to gather her composure.

Norbie looked at Anna. "I'll be inside if you need anything." He turned and entered the house.

Fleck approached Anna. "I'm sorry about Max."

Her chest tightened. "*Danke*."

"How are you?" he asked.

"To be honest," she said, "I'm devastated."

Fleck nodded. "Max was a good man, and it was kind of you to care for him."

Does he know that I was more to Max than a nurse?

Fleck kneeled to Nia and gave her a pat on the head. "How is she?"

"Nia is sad, sir," Anna said. "She has little interest in playing or going for walks, although she complies when she receives a command."

"Understandable. Dogs can mourn a loss just like humans do." Fleck clasped Nia's collar. "Have you tried having her wear her harness?"

"*Nein*," she said.

"Getting her back into a work routine will be good for her."

Oh, no! He's come to take Nia! A jolt of fear shot through her. Consumed with her own grief, she hadn't considered that Fleck would want Nia returned to the school. *It was foolish of me not to think that he would want her back when there are so many battle-blinded veterans in need of a guide dog.*

"Where's her harness?" Fleck asked.

Anna felt sick to her stomach. "Inside."

"Perhaps you could retrieve it."

"Please don't take her, sir," Anna said, struggling to keep her legs from trembling. "Give her a little more time with me. Once Nia's feeling better, I promise to return her."

Fleck looked at Anna. "I wasn't taking her."

Anna's eyebrows raised.

"I thought that by wearing her harness, she'd be reminded of her sense of duty, which might curtail her gloom."

"I'm confused, sir," Anna said. "Why are you here?"

Fleck stood and faced her. "To offer you a position back in the school."

"Oh," Anna said.

"The role would be different from before," Fleck said.

He's not going to let me train, but at least I'll be working with Emmi to care for the dogs. "That would be fine, sir."

"I want you to return as a trainer," Fleck said.

Anna's mouth dropped open.

"However, your role would be to train new trainers," Fleck said. "Stalling is arranging to open several more branches to train guide dogs—Hamburg, Bonn, Dresden, and Münster, among others. We're going to be training hundreds of dogs per year, which means we're going to need many more trainers."

Anna's mind raced, struggling to comprehend everything he was saying.

"I think you and Nia would be a good pair to instruct newly hired trainers," Fleck said. "However, it would mean that Nia would not be assigned to a veteran, and that you'd be required care for her on a permanent basis."

Anna clasped her hands. "It would be an honor, sir."

"*Gut*," Fleck said. "I'll plan on you returning to work on Monday, if that is not too soon."

"Monday will be perfect. *Danke*, sir."

Fleck put on his cap and paused. "Also, you should know that, as of this morning, Waldemar is no longer working at the guide dog school. I've transferred him to a position that does not interact with veterans or shepherds. It's something I should have done long ago."

"*Danke* for informing me, sir."

"I'll see myself out. Good day, Fräulein Zeller." Fleck tipped his cap and left.

Stunned, Anna took in deep breaths, attempting to come to terms with what had happened. She kneeled to Nia and placed a hand on the dog's head. "Did you hear that, girl? We're a team, now. And you're going to live with me forever."

Nia looked up, her eyes meeting Anna's, and she wagged her tail.

PART 5

GIGUE

CHAPTER 42

OLDENBURG, GERMANY—JULY 14, 1919

Anna and Nia finished their day of work, most of which was spent teaching a former ambulance dog handler how to perform traffic work with a guide dog, and then began their journey home. She adjusted her grip on Nia's harness and glanced down at her dog, who was starting to favor her right front paw, due to a laborious day of training.

"You did great today," Anna said.

Nia panted and padded forward.

"When we get home, I'll give you some treats. And I'm thinking that we can convince Norbie to give you a belly rub."

The dog whipped her tail back and forth.

Anna was incredibly proud of Nia. Over the past year and a half, she'd helped Anna train over a dozen new recruits—many of whom were former military dog handlers—to become guide dog trainers. The school, established by Dr. Stalling, had grown with branches in cities all over Germany, and they were now placing nearly six hundred shepherds a year with battle-blinded veterans.

God, I wish Max could see what Nia has done, Anna thought.

Although Anna had worked through much of her sorrow, she felt like a piece of her heart was taken when she lost Max. Her walks to and from work were filled with landmarks that spawned memories of their innermost conversations. The sight of her *mutter*'s piano was a constant reminder of the precious moments they'd shared together. Etched into her brain was the timbre of his voice, the way her skin tingled when he touched her, and the deep feeling of contentment while being held in his arms. And when she closed her eyes and allowed her heart and mind to drift into the past, the melody of his piano suite echoed in her head. She wished that they'd had more time together. *Even a lifetime would not have been long enough*, she'd often thought. But she was deeply thankful to have had Max in her life, and she hoped that her work at the guide dog school would honor his memory.

The war had ended with Germany's formal surrender on November 11, 1918, a few days after Kaiser Wilhelm II abdicated his throne and fled to exile in the Netherlands. It was estimated that three million German men were killed with countless others injured or maimed. And the Treaty of Versailles, which was recently signed by Germany and the Allied nations, blamed Germany for the war and required it to pay reparations. The country was in economic and political turmoil. It might take generations, Anna believed, before Germany and its people would recover from the war. But she was determined to do her part—by restoring the lives of blinded soldiers—to help heal her homeland.

Anna and Nia entered Norbie's workshop, filling their ears with a chorus of ticktocks. She unbuckled Nia's harness, and the dog ran to Norbie, who was seated at his workbench.

"Nia!" Norbie placed down a clock tool and rubbed the dog. "How was your day?" he asked, looking at Anna.

"*Gut*," she said. "How about you?"

"I sold a mantel clock," Norbie said. "And I think I fixed that confounded grandfather clock that never strikes on time."

Anna smiled. *He loves complaining about that clock. He'll be highly disappointed the day it chimes on time.*

"Also," Norbie said, retrieving an envelope from his workbench. "You received a letter from someone in Vienna."

"Vienna?" She took the letter from Norbie and scanned the postage. "I don't know anyone in Vienna."

Norbie handed Anna a small screwdriver, which she used like a letter opener to tear the envelope. She removed the letter and read.

> Dear Fräulein Zeller,
> My name is Felix Weingartner. I'm the conductor of the Vienna Philharmonic, and I'm writing to you in response to a letter and manuscript I received from Maximilian Benesch.

Anna's heart thudded inside her chest. "Oh, my God!"
"What is it?" Norbie asked.
"It's a letter from a conductor about Max's composition! I thought it had been stolen!"
Norbie's eyes widened. "Goodness!"
She leaned to him, allowing him to read with her.

> I extend my condolences on the death of Herr Benesch, and I apologize for the late reply to this inquiry. The package had been set aside while the Vienna Philharmonic was on a brief hiatus due to the war. I've recently had the opportunity to review the composition. I am most impressed with Herr Benesch's *Light Suite* and would like to commission the piece.

Anna's hands trembled. She took in a deep breath, struggling to calm the emotions swelling inside her.

> According to Herr Benesch's letter, you are the inheritor of his estate, which would have the rights to his composition. Assuming the piece remains available, I would like to commission the work to

be included in a concert this upcoming
season at Vienna's Musikverein.

The Great Hall. Tears welled up in Anna's eyes.

The instructions in Herr Benesch's letter
called for you and your guests to attend
the debut performance of his composition.
I hope that this letter finds you well, and
I look forward to your reply.
Sincerely,
Felix Weingartner

Anna, her heart swelling with joy, put down the letter. She
turned to Norbie, his cheeks covered in tears, and hugged him.
"He did it," she cried.

CHAPTER 43

VIENNA, AUSTRIA—OCTOBER 20, 1919

Anna, wearing a formal black dress with her *mutter*'s silver heart-shaped locket, entered the Great Hall of the Musikverein. Beside her was Norbie, dressed in a dark suit, and Nia, who'd recently undergone a good grooming. And walking behind her was her best friend, Emmi, and Emmi's husband, Ewald.

Anna stopped and gazed over the grand concert hall. The space was approximately fifty-meters-long-by-twenty-meters-wide with towering ceilings, from which dozens of crystal chandeliers were hung. The main floor had many rows of seats, which were beginning to fill up with audience members. An ornately decorated balcony wrapped around the entire interior of the structure, most of which was decorated in gold paint and trim. And given the size of the hall and crowd, Anna estimated that there were over fifteen hundred attendees for the performance.

"It's glorious," Norbie said.

"*Ja*," Anna said, butterflies fluttering in her stomach.

Emmi placed a hand on Anna's shoulder. "I've never seen so much gold."

Anna smiled, feeling honored to have the people—and dog—she loved by her side.

Fleck had generously given Anna and Emmi a leave of absence

to attend the debut performance of Max's composition. They'd made the long train journey from Oldenburg to Vienna, where they were provided overnight rooms at a boardinghouse, which had been arranged by Felix Weingartner, the conductor of the Vienna Philharmonic.

Anna was greeted by an usher, who led her and her group up a carpeted staircase. As they reached a private balcony section that overlooked the stage, the usher gestured to a front row of seats, one of which had a letter with Anna's name.

Anna thanked the usher, retrieved the envelope, and then sat between Norbie and Emmi. She stroked Nia's back and said, "Lie down."

Nia settled at Anna's feet.

Anna glanced to the stage with a grand piano. Her breath quickened.

"It'll be all right," Norbie said, as if he could sense Anna's nervousness.

She nodded.

"Felix Weingartner has been quite the host," Emmi said.

"*Ja*," she said, fiddling with the envelope.

Norbie glanced at his watch. "If you like, you have a few minutes to read the conductor's letter before the performance."

Anna opened the envelope and unfolded a piece of paper.

My beloved Anna,
I assume you have a flurry of emotions running through you as you read my transcribed letter that I included with the submission of my composition to Felix Weingartner, and I cannot begin to imagine what you must be feeling by once again hearing the music we created together on your mutter's piano.

Anna cupped a hand to her mouth. Tears flooded her eyes.

"What's wrong?" Emmi asked.

Anna drew a serrated breath. "It's from him."

"Who?" Norbie asked.

"Max." Her jaw quivered.

Norbie's and Emmi's eyes widened. Ewald clasped Emmi's hand and leaned in.

Anna wiped her eyes and continued to read.

I'm sorry that I had to die when our life together had just begun, and I hope that you'll forgive me for departing so soon. Please know that I did everything I could to remain with you. I regret that we will not have the chance to grow old together, but it wasn't meant to be.

I want you to know that my days with you were the best of my life. You restored my passion for life and music, and you gave me Nia, who became my companion and guide. Please know that you've created an imperishable mark on my heart that will go with me to the World to Come.

Oh, Max. Tears streamed down Anna's cheeks. She accepted a handkerchief from Norbie and wiped her eyes.

I want you to move on, my love. You have a wonderful life ahead of you, one filled with a family of your own and loads of shepherds. I'm so proud of you, Anna. You're restoring hope through guide dogs. Live your life knowing that I will always love you, more than you will ever know.

All my heart,
Max

Anna lowered her head into her hands and cried. She felt Norbie and Emmi place their arms around her. She took in deep breaths, attempting to calm her mind and soothe the ache in her chest.

The audience applauded as a man wearing a black tailed jacket and bow tie walked onto the stage and sat at the piano.

"Are you all right?" Norbie asked.

Anna raised her head, wiped her tears, and then looked into his eyes. "I am now."

Norbie smiled.

The applause faded, leaving silence. Norbie and Emmi clasped Anna's hands.

The pianist began to play the first movement of the suite, "Prelude to Light in C-Sharp Minor," which started with somber repeating chords, like rhythmic waves on a shore. And as a delicate melody joined the progression of chords, aesthetic chills tingled over Anna's skin. Memories of sitting next to Max at the piano flashed in her head.

Nia perked her ears and thumped her tail.

Tears of gratefulness filled Anna's eyes. And she knew, deep down, that her and Max's love for each other would live on forever through his music.

AUTHOR'S NOTE

While conducting research for this book, I became captivated by historical accounts of the world's first guide dog school for the blind established in Oldenburg, Germany, in 1916. During World War I, thousands of soldiers, many of whom were blinded by poison gas, were returning home from the front. There are varying accounts of how Dr. Gerhard Stalling, a director of the German Red Cross Ambulance Dogs Association, pioneered the idea that dogs could be reliable guides for the blind. A common element of many of these stories claims that Dr. Stalling and his German shepherd were walking the grounds of a veterans' hospital with a battle-blinded patient. Stalling was called away for an emergency and left his dog with the patient to keep him company. When Stalling returned, the dog seemed to be caring for the blind veteran, which sparked his vision for creating a guide dog school for the blind. The school grew and opened branches in cities throughout Germany, training up to six hundred dogs per year. In addition to supporting German veterans, these schools provided dogs to blind people in Britain, France, Spain, Italy, the United States, Canada, and the Soviet Union. The story of Stalling and the school served as inspiration for writing this story, in which I imagined a German Red Cross nurse named Anna who would begin a quest to become a guide dog trainer.

Prior to writing this book, I knew little about chemical warfare in World War I. It was heart-wrenching to learn about the poison gas atrocities that took place on the western front. In the book, Max—a Jewish German soldier and aspiring pianist—is blinded by a ruptured chlorine gas cylinder on the eve of Germany's first use of chlorine gas. On April 22, 1915, the German army violated the Hague Convention treaty—which prohibited the use of chemical weapons—by opening the valves to 5,700 cylinders and releasing over 150 tons of poison chlorine gas on French troops in Ypres. The German gas unit was first given the name of "Disinfection Unit" for purposes of secrecy. The gas attack resulted in thousands of casualties and, soon after, Allied forces retaliated by developing their own gas warfare capability. I strived to depict the escalating chemical warfare race between German and Allied forces—including the use of chlorine, phosgene, and mustard gases, as well as their delivery systems—which would result in an estimated 1.2 million gas casualties. During the war, German ink and dye businesses produced chlorine gas, which was a by-product of their manufacturing operations. In the story, I created a fictitious company for Bruno's family business called Wahler Farbwerke.

In addition to chemical warfare, my research included the "turnip winter" of 1916 to 1917. Prior to my fact-finding for this novel, I had little knowledge about the British naval blockade, which lasted from 1914 to 1919, that placed Germany under a constant threat of starvation. Due to the blockade, as well as a poor autumn potato crop, the German population subsisted primarily on Swedish turnips or rutabagas—which was typically used as animal feed—as a means of survival during the winter of 1916 to 1917. Malnutrition and disease were rampant throughout World War I, and food shortages contributed to approximately 750,000 German civilian deaths, including an estimated 80,000 children who died of starvation in 1916.

In sharp contrast, the most enjoyable part of my research was on guide dogs. I've always been a dog lover, and it was an honor and pleasure to learn about their training. I spent many hours reading training books and historical records, as well as watching videos on guide dogs. The first guide dog school in Oldenburg trained German shepherds, and Paul Feyen, a battle-blinded veteran, was the first graduate of the school. In the book, I imagined Nia—whom Anna would save from being euthanized—to be a sweet, caring dog who would become a guide and companion for Max.

During my fact-finding, I discovered many intriguing historical events, which I labored to weave into the timeline of the book. For example, the Second Battle of Ypres is when Max is blinded by poison chlorine gas. In April of 1916 at the Battle of Hulluch, the German army launched a gas attack, which blew back over German lines and caused many casualties. In the book, Bruno failed to convince his commander to halt the Hulluch attack due to poor wind conditions. The French city of Lille was under German occupation for nearly the entire war, and I endeavored to reflect the harsh living conditions of French civilians under German rule, including the mass roundup of twenty thousand women and girls who were relocated to rural areas of occupied France for farm labor. I attempted to detail the timeline of events at the Oldenburg guide dog school. Additionally, I strived to depict various types of chemicals and weaponry, and the brutal conditions in the trenches on the western front. Any historical inaccuracies in this book are mine and mine alone.

Since numerous historical figures make appearances in this book, it is important to emphasize that *A Light Beyond the Trenches* is a story of fiction and I took creative liberties in writing this tale. Dr. Gerhard Stalling, Fritz Haber, Colonel Petersen, General von Stetten, and Otto Hahn appear in the story. It was my intent to reveal lesser-known details of Fritz Haber, the head of the Chemistry Section in the Ministry of War. Haber is often remembered as a brilliant chemist who received the Nobel Prize in Chemistry in 1918 for his invention of the Haber-Bosch process, a method to synthesize ammonia. Although his invention was of great significance to the large-scale synthesis of fertilizers and explosives, he is also viewed as the "father of chemical warfare" from his efforts to weaponize poison gases. Additionally, Haber's wife, Clara, committed suicide in May of 1915 by shooting herself in the heart with Haber's service revolver. Her suicide has been a topic of continued speculation. It has been suggested that she opposed Haber's role in chemical warfare, and that she killed herself after learning of his involvement in the first use of chlorine gas at the Second Battle of Ypres, which resulted in enormous casualties.

Many books, articles, documentaries, and historical archives were crucial for my research. *A World Undone: The Story of the Great War, 1914 to 1918* by G. J. Meyer was incredibly helpful with gaining an understanding of events in World War I, as well as obtaining details on key figures and battles. *All Quiet on the Western Front* by Erich Maria Remarque is a masterfully written novel that provided insight into the daily life of German soldiers on the front, and *The Complete Guide Dog for the Blind* by Robbie Robson was of immense help to understand the training techniques used for guide dogs. An article by Monika Baár titled "Prosthesis for the Body and for the Soul: The Origins of Guide Dog Provision for Blind Veterans in Interwar Germany" provided a thorough overview of Germany's enormous challenge of rehabilitating permanently disabled soldiers as a result of World War I. Also, The Seeing Eye guide dog school of Morristown, New Jersey, was a terrific source of information, especially their video library.

It was an honor to write this story. I will forever be inspired by the incredible, loyal guide dogs that improve the quality of life for their handlers, and I'll never forget that eight million people returned home from World War I disabled, many of whom were blind. I'll always remember Dr. Gerhard Stalling and the trainers of the world's first guide dog school, who were the genesis for the use of guide dogs around the world.

A Light Beyond the Trenches would not have been possible without the support of many people. I'm eternally thankful to the following individuals:

I am deeply grateful to my brilliant editor, John Scognamiglio. John's advice and encouragement were tremendously helpful with the writing of this story.

Many thanks to my agent, Mark Gottlieb, for his support and guidance with my journey as an author. I feel extremely fortunate to have Mark as my agent.

My deepest appreciation to my publicist, Vida Engstrand. I am profoundly grateful for Vida's creativity and efforts to promote my stories to readers.

I'm thankful to have Kim Taylor Blakemore as my accountability partner. Our weekly word-count progress reports helped us to finish our manuscripts on time.

Thank you to Carol Hamilton, a puppy raiser for Guiding Eyes for the Blind, who gave her valuable time to provide me with knowledge on raising guide dog puppies and teaching them socialization skills.

My sincere thanks to Akron Writers' Group: Betty Woodlee, Dave Rais, John Stein, Kat McMullen, Rachel Freggiaro, Carisa Taylor, Devin Fairchild, Ken Waters, Cheri Passell, and Sharon Jurist. And a special heartfelt thanks to Betty Woodlee, who critiqued an early draft of the manuscript.

I'm grateful to my mother, an artistic woman and voracious reader, who instilled in me a passion for music and books.

This story would not have been possible without the love and support of my wife, Laurie, and our children, Catherine, Philip, Lizzy, Lauren, and Rachel. Laurie, you are—and always will be—*mi cielo*.

A Light Beyond the Trenches

ABOUT THIS GUIDE

The suggested questions are included to enhance your group's
reading of Alan Hlad's *A Light Beyond the Trenches*.

Discussion Questions

1. Before reading *A Light Beyond the Trenches*, what did you know about guide dog training and its origin? What did you know about the use of chemical weapons in World War I?

2. What are Anna's fears while serving as a German Red Cross nurse? How does her encounter with Dr. Gerhard Stalling and his shepherd influence her to join the guide dog school? Why does she believe that dogs can help restore the lives of battle-blinded soldiers?

3. Describe Max. If he had not been blinded by poison gas at the front, what do you think his life would have been like?

4. Describe Anna. What kind of woman is she? How does she convince her supervisor, Rolf Fleck, to allow her to save Nia? What does Anna do to gain Fleck's support to become a guide dog trainer? What role does she play in restoring Max's passion to be a pianist and composer?

5. Describe Bruno. What are his faults and redeeming qualities? Why didn't he tell Anna about his family's business and his role in the Disinfection Unit? How does Fritz Haber, head of the Chemistry Section in the Ministry of War, influence Bruno's behavior? Why did he have an affair with Celeste? Is there anything he could have done to save his relationship with Anna?

6. While working together, Anna and Max fall in love. What brings them together? At what point do you think Anna realized that her feelings for Bruno had faded and that she loved Max? How is the war a catalyst for their affection? What are Anna and Max's hopes and dreams?

7. Nia is a German shepherd who is saved by Anna from being euthanized. What characteristics make her unique? Describe

her relationship with Anna and Norbie. How does Nia develop an inseparable bond with Max?

8. Prior to reading the book, what did you know about the British naval blockade in World War I? Describe the conditions of the "turnip winter" of 1916 to 1917.

9. Why do many readers enjoy historical fiction, in particular novels set in World War I? To what degree do you think Hlad took creative liberties with this story?

10. How do you envision what happens after the end of the book? What do you think Anna's, Norbie's, and Nia's lives will be like?